Santa Monica Public Library
I SMP 00 2799811 1
W9-CFB-183

AN HOUR UNSPENT

Books by Roseanna M. White

LADIES OF THE MANOR

The Lost Heiress

The Reluctant Duchess

A Lady Unrivaled

SHADOWS OVER ENGLAND

A Name Unknown

A Song Unheard

An Hour Unspent

SHADOWS OVER ENGLAND • 3

AN HOUR UNSPENT

ROSEANNA M. WHITE

a division of Baker Publishing Group
Minneapolis, Minnesota

Published by Bethany House Publishers
11400 Hampshire Avenue South
Bloomington, Minnesota 55438
www.bethanyhouse.com

Bethany House Publishers is a division of
Baker Publishing Group, Grand Rapids, Michigan

Printed in the United States of America

The Library of Congress Cataloging-in-Publication Data
Names: White, Roseanna M.
Title: An hour unspent / Roseanna M. White.
Description: Minneapolis, MN : Bethany House, a division of Baker Publishing Group, [2018] | Series: Shadows over England ; 3
Identifiers: LCCN 2018018558 | ISBN 9780764219283 (trade paper) | ISBN 9780764232770 (cloth) | ISBN 9781493412440 (e-book)
Classification: LCC PS3623.H578785 H68 2014 | DDC 813/.6—dc23
LC record available at https://lccn.loc.gov/2018018558

This is a work of fiction. Names, characters, and incidents are products of the author's imagination or are used fictitiously. Any resemblance to actual events or persons, living or dead, is entirely coincidental.

Scripture quotations are from the King James Version of the Bible.

Cover design by Jennifer Parker
Cover photography by Mike Habermann Photography, LLC

Roseanna M. White is represented by The Steve Laube Agency.

18 19 20 21 22 23 24 7 6 5 4 3 2 1

In loving memory of
Maxine Snyder Higson Seward
(November 1913–May 2017)

A woman who in her 103 years created a family
with faith, love, and selflessness.

Grandma, you were more than a matriarch—
you are an example to emulate.

Let him that stole steal no more: but rather let him labour, working with his hands the thing which is good, that he may have to give to him that needeth.

Ephesians 4:28

ONE

May 11, 1915
Poplar, London, England

Barclay Pearce shouldered his way through the mob, invisible. He'd learned over the years how to blend into any crowd, and this one was no different. Stand at the back of a group of shouting men, raising a fist when they did. Even as he used the tip of his boot to nudge a few of the bricks intended as missiles out of view. His chest banded at the thought of those bricks flying through the boarded-up windows of the store.

Mr. Schmidt had long since packed up his family and fled. His used bookshop, in which Barclay had passed innumerable happy hours over the years, had been closed for months. Never mind that his family had been in England for generations—his name sounded German, which put a target on his back.

The shaking fists gave way to a forward surge of bodies.

Barclay ducked into the nearby alley, which muffled the angry shouts of the men in the streets. Most of these men had been his neighbors for the last twenty years, though only a certain sort would know it. He'd moved invisibly among them, a shadow in their streets. He'd survived. He'd built something.

And now they were tearing it down, brick by brick and piece by piece. Helping the enemy break England—though they wouldn't see it that way.

The shrill whistles of many bobbies entering the area pierced the air, but for once they didn't make Barclay's pace alter in response. For once, he wasn't the one they were after. What was a mere thief in the face of riots as widespread as these? They were running rampant all over the city, from the prosperous West End all the way down to this shadowed crevice of Poplar.

No, the police didn't care a whit about him today. He was only one insignificant thief—a thief whose hands were relatively clean right now, at that. They were after the mobs and the raging fury that swept through them.

It made no sense to him. He paused at the door he wanted, tested it. Locked. Understandable, today. But that wouldn't hinder him. Barclay glanced around to be sure no one paid him any heed and then, with the help of his favorite pick, had the door open in ten seconds flat. Yes, the *Lusitania* had been sunk. It was a tragedy. It made the war more real than ever. But why did that ocean of angry men think *this* was the answer? Did they really think that taking their fear out on anyone in London with a German-sounding name would bring that ship back to the surface of the waves? That it would teach the German High Command a lesson?

The warm, musty air in the back hallway assaulted his nose as he stepped into the creaking old building. Not old like Kensey Manor in Cornwall, with history seeping beautifully from its stones like music. Not old like the symphony halls, with their majestic columns and promise of audible glory. Just *old*. Tired. Ready to be put out of its misery.

He made his way up the familiar steps, to the flat everyone in the family thought he'd given up. But he'd kept slipping money to the landlord every month.

It was worth it, to have a place to stash things he didn't want to take with him into the good part of Town. Wouldn't do to store any stolen goods in Peter Holstein's house in Hammersmith—he wouldn't risk bringing trouble on his brother-in-law's head. Especially not now. With a last name like *Holstein*.

Plus, it provided a good drop location for Mr. V, into whose palm Barclay had pressed the second key.

He jogged up the rickety steps to the fifth floor and slid along the corridor until he came to the fourth door. A quick turn of his key, and he was in the last flat they'd called their own, Georgie, Nigel, Fergus, and him.

It was empty of all but the furniture that belonged with it—and hadn't been much fuller when the four of them had called it home. They traveled light, did their family. Because they never knew when they might have to pick up and run.

He paused for a moment, so easily able to see Georgie lounging on that lumpy, faded sofa of an evening. Grinning up at him. Trying to cover that his day's take hadn't been from where it was supposed to be. Trying to worm his way out of division duty, because he hated counting out the coins. Trying to bend every rule Barclay had ever set just to see if he could.

Blast, but Barclay missed him. Where was he now? In a trench somewhere? France, unless they'd moved the British First again. Fighting German lads no older than he was.

His throat went tight. Bad enough that Georgie was there. What if Charlie was too?

He'd never know it. Never even hear about it if his flesh-and-blood little brother died in this wretched war.

His blood went heavy and sluggish in his veins. He'd never given up looking for him, not for eighteen years. But he'd failed. Barclay had just turned twenty-eight, meaning his brother was twenty-four. But still nowhere to be found. Charlie had vanished into London's orphanage system as surely as their mother had into its prisons.

What was he like now, that brother who had been wide-eyed and full of laughter at six, when Barclay had last seen him? Like Georgie, mischievous and stubborn? Or more like Fergus, smart as a whip? Or like little Nigel, even-tempered and optimistic?

Barclay blinked, clearing his eyes of the shades of memory, real and imagined. He said a quick prayer for them all—a habit he was trying to form, even though it still felt too bold, going daily before the King and begging a favor. He'd made his livelihood based on invisibility, always reckoning it safest to stay invisible to God too. But according to his brother-in-law, Peter, that was a fool's mission. God saw him anyway, in complete clarity. So why try to hide?

And besides—it was a risk worth taking. Georgie was on the front lines, and Charlie well could be too. He—they?—needed every prayer Barclay could mutter.

The shouts outside grew louder, battering the glass in the one tiny window of the flat. He'd better hurry. The mob could turn violent at any moment, and he didn't much fancy weaving his way back through them when they did.

He'd kept this flat because it had the perfect hiding place. A few silent steps to the corner and he could pry up the splintering trim and reach into the hole it covered. His fingers closed on the large envelope Mr. V must have stashed there. They'd missed each other at Whitehall today, but there had been a simple message waiting. *You have work at home.*

Whatever this was, then, it would be what kept him busy for the next day or week or month. He could only hope it didn't involve fishing charred slips of paper from an ash bin like yesterday's assignment had. Not that the words on those slips had made a lick of sense to him, but who was he to question the man who promised him payment every week if he remained at his beck and call?

He refitted the trim into its place, slid over to take a seat on the lumpy couch, and opened the file.

Cecil Manning, clockmaker. Owns a small shop, employing three, and a team that assists him with the Great Westminster Clock when necessary.

Barclay's brows drew together. What in the world could V possibly want with a clockmaker? He read on, noting Mr. Manning's address—only a five-minute walk from Peter's house in Hammersmith—and the reason behind V's interest.

Manning yesterday had a meeting with one Mr. Anderson of the patent office. Mr. Anderson reported directly to the Admiralty, saying that Mr. Manning is developing a device that would allow aircraft to shoot through their props. This report was dismissed as unlikely to be successful and hence unimportant, but I disagree. Discover what Manning is building, if it will work, what he would need to make it viable. If there is a prototype, procure it. If plans, get them to me. I would prefer that he turn them over to the Admiralty willingly. But if he won't, take them.

Barclay hissed out a breath. A bit different, that, than slipping into an abandoned consulate and stealing paper scraps from a dead fireplace. This was more like the assignments V had given Rosemary and Willa—the kind that required gaining the confidence of a mark and then stealing from him.

The kind of job Barclay hadn't done in a year. And didn't quite know if he should do now.

He wanted to change. Was *trying* to change. But when one's government told one to slip back into one's old habits . . . was it wrong? Or justified?

He tucked the envelope into the inner pocket of his jacket as he rose and strode toward the door again. Such questions would have to wait. Just now, he had somewhere else to be.

He could hear windows breaking as he gained the street again, despite the continued shrill of the police whistles and the shouts to desist. There would be more arrests tonight—there had been hundreds already over the weekend, even in the better sections of Town. Men usually decent but who had fallen prey to that savage instinct to lash out, strike back.

They'd do better to follow Georgie's lead and enlist if they wanted to fight. And chances were they would, eventually. Those who were able. On the average day, the streets had already shifted, filled more with women and refugees than able-bodied Englishmen.

He headed the opposite way down the alley, away from the tumult. The rest of the family should just be getting to Pauly's pub.

The streets of Poplar were as familiar as his own thoughts. It took no effort to navigate through them, to nod to the familiar shopkeepers who had all barred their doors and now stood at their windows, peering out anxiously to see if the mob would surge in this direction. He slid up to a beggar hunched against one of the buildings, slipping a tuppence into her upstretched palm. "Better get inside somewhere, Mags."

Her gnarled fingers closed around the promise of dinner. "New men on our streets. From Stoke Newington. Seen 'em?"

"From Dante's crew. They won't bother you." He bent down to hook a hand under the old woman's arm and help her to her feet. "Better hurry, luv. Trouble's only a street away."

A smile appeared out of the web of wrinkles she called a face, revealing gums with only half their teeth. Poor old duck. She reached up to pat his cheek. "You're a good lad, Barclay. Your mum must be proud."

He smiled—that old wound had long since healed over. "If you hear who started this row, let me know. I don't like violence in my streets."

She cackled as she hobbled her way into the shelter of the alley. "You'd do better'n the bobbies at shutting 'em all down, you would. We ought to 'lect you to the council."

"Ha." Talk about too visible. But he'd do what he could later, after the authorities had cleared out. He watched her until he was sure she'd found a place to tuck in and then turned.

The pub was only two streets over, a steadier home than any other he'd had since he was ten. Too close to all these riots, to be sure. And knowing Pauly, he'd likely be standing at the door with that odd assortment that made him *Pauly*—a crowbar to warn looters away, and some sort of food to offer them, to remind them of why they wanted to heed the warning. His had always been a place where all were welcome, so long as they left their fights outside.

Barclay turned the corner, his gaze latching upon an unexpected sight—a nondescript grey bowler over silver-gold hair. V stood at the bus stop with a newspaper open, though the bus would have just come through two minutes ago, assuming it hadn't been drafted into use in a more affluent part of the city. Barclay frowned. Why meet him here if he'd already slipped his next assignment into the wall at the flat?

Well, it certainly wouldn't be a social call—he must have more business, perhaps some that had just come in. Barclay jogged toward him with a hint of a smile, a lifted hand, and an "Oi!" Just as he would approach any other acquaintance.

V turned toward him, his own vague smile in place, as if he were accustomed to the Cockney greeting. Maybe he was. Who could say? For all Barclay knew, the man had been born a street away. Or on Grosvenor Square. Or on the moon, for all the information he could glean from V's accent and demeanor.

"Pearce." He stretched out a hand to shake in greeting, as if they were two normal blokes.

Barclay shook. "Good to see you, V. Going home for the day?" He shot a glance at the sign for the bus. And wondered where *home* was for the man. A mansion? A box? Or did he step into a rabbit hole that swept him to a netherworld each night?

Perhaps Barclay had been reading too much of *Alice's Adventures in Wonderland* to the little ones.

V smiled a little. "Shortly. Glad I came across you. I've something for you." He tucked the newspaper under his arm and made an awkward show of opening the satchel he carried. From it he pulled a thick envelope, not unlike the one that had been stashed in the hidey-hole.

It wouldn't be another assignment, not here on the street corner. "Dare I ask?"

"Just look when you have a few minutes." He tucked the poorly folded newspaper into the satchel and closed it. "You know, I think I'd be better off catching the tube. See you at the OB in the morning?"

He phrased it as a question, but it was a command. Barclay nodded and resisted the urge to ask what they needed of him at the Admiralty's Old Building when V had already slipped him another job. But V wouldn't say, not here. He'd just have to report to the OB tomorrow and find out.

If he kept up this rate of work for them, they might as well give him a uniform.

It was such a ridiculous thought that he nearly smiled as he turned back toward the pub. He let it bloom after all when he spotted the figure rushing toward the door from the other direction, eyes alight.

Lucy no doubt had found an interesting story to regale them with at dinner, given that gleam in her eye. He lifted his brows as he neared the seventeen-year-old he'd counted as a sister since she was an orphaned babe too small to tell them her own name. He'd been the one to dub her Lucy. He suspected her parents had called her something far different.

"You look amused. What have you been up to today?"

"This and that." Her grin was infectious. "But I've been a good girl, I promise."

He chuckled and held open the pub's door for her. Of all his siblings—the ones old enough to have been involved in the family business, anyway—Lucy had seemed the least sorry to agree to give up their old ways. "I've no doubt. Any word from Georgie today?"

Her nod was eager. She must have a bit of India in her blood, to account for the almond-shaped eyes and dusky gold of her skin, but those were her only hints of who she'd once been. "A letter, yes. We didn't open it yet."

They'd have been waiting for him. Which warmed him straight to the core. Nodding his thanks, he followed her inside, where scents of roasting meat greeted them, along with a healthy dose of noise. Much of which came from their long table in the corner. Most everyone was there already, even Willa and her soon-to-be-husband, Lukas. He filled the empty seat Rosemary had left them. And when she returned from Cornwall in a couple weeks, she'd bring Peter, who would sit where Georgie used to.

Maybe someday their clan would grow outright again. If they could convince the war, through guile and prayer, not to steal any of them away forever.

Barclay took his chair in the center, where he could reach over to cuff Fergus playfully on the shoulder. The boy, getting lanky at twelve, grinned at him. "You're late."

"I was working." He fingered the new envelope V had given him, opened the flap. If he had given it to him out in the open, it must be all right to review it in public. "How was school?"

Fergus grunted. He hadn't adjusted quite as well as the younger children to the idea of going to school. And Barclay could hardly blame him—he was a bit old to be thrown into such a thing, even if he *was* as smart as a whip.

But education could change the world for him. It was worth a few growing pains. Worth the coin it cost them—using up the last of what Rosemary had earned from V the year before. If they kept working for him, they could probably, maybe, if they scrimped elsewhere, keep sending the little ones to school in the years to come.

"I still don't see why I need all this nonsense. I know my numbers. My grammar. You read history to me every night."

"I'm no professor." Perhaps he would have been, in a different world. He could imagine spending his days with books, as his father had once done, in front of a classroom of eager minds. Or *should-be* eager minds, if Fergus was any indication. But then, he also could imagine spending his days in a workshop, with gadgets and gears spread out before him. Or in business somewhere, where he could manage people all the day.

Perhaps, if he'd gone to school for more than that one blissful year before it all came apart at the seams, he could have known one of those worlds. But *this* was his world now. A family of thieves he loved as much as he did the brother he hadn't seen in nearly twenty years. A mysterious employer who gave him envelopes with . . . paper and keys? Odd. A growing faith, now that he had people to explain things to him and wrap up beautiful leather-bound Bibles to give him at Christmas.

He fingered the keys. Unfolded the papers. A few cards spilled out, snagging his attention first.

Retta, seated to his left, snatched one up, her golden brows scrunching. "'Mr. Barclay Pearce.' That much is clear enough. But where's the direction? It's—wait, this is the house across from Peter's. The one for let."

"What?" But it was. He stared at the house number under his

name on that heavy paper, then pulled forward the typewritten sheet with *V* as the only signature. His eyes went wide as he read. "V has let it for us. Says he needs us to have a reputable address, and he imagines Pete and Rosie will want their own space when they come to Town. Says we can consider it part of our retainer."

Maybe it *was* tied to the new assignment, then. Perhaps, given the clockmaker's residence in Hammersmith, V thought it would work better if they could claim a place of their own nearby.

Likely wouldn't last beyond the assignment. But still. They could enjoy it while it did.

Fergus picked up one of the keys, his face pure boyish delight. "The white one? But that's even bigger than Peter's place! I bet it has six bedrooms if it has one."

The rest of the table noted the awe on their faces and chimed in with questions and shouts of joy at the explanation. "But why, do you think?" Elinor's blond brows were drawn together, her lips pursed.

Barclay glanced behind him, making sure none of the other patrons were paying them any heed. Then leaned across the table so he could pitch his voice low. "I suspect it's because of the job he just gave me. There's a clockmaker I'm to get to know—the one who maintains the clock of Big Ben, it seems. He lives just a few streets over from Peter. V must want us to stick close."

"The Great Clock?" Lucy's brows shot up. "What's he up to? Nothing suspicious, I hope."

"No. No, some new invention V thinks could help our boys, that's all." He shifted against the niggle inside that said, *If that's all, why would you steal from him? Why repay innovation with deceit?*

"Well." On the other side of him Elinor grinned and bumped her shoulder into his. She was getting far too pretty, and it was a guarantee of headaches. It was just too much to hope that all his sisters would find blokes as good as Rosemary and Willa had.

Why did God have to send him so many sisters? Responsibility for them kept him up nights.

But Elinor's grin was oblivious to the trouble she caused just by having a dimpled smile. "That gives me a fabulous idea for my challenge to you. I challenge you to steal . . ."

He narrowed his eyes while the others all hooted and drummed their fingers on the edge of the table. "No things, El—"

"Oh, I know." Laughing, Ellie silenced the drumming with a dramatic flourish of her hand. "I challenge you to steal an hour, Barclay Pearce. From Big Ben's Great Clock."

"A . . ." He chuckled and shook his head. Their challenges had been getting more absurd lately, it was true—in part because he'd made them all swear off actual *stealing*. Aside from their increasing morality, they couldn't risk getting caught. Not now, working for V. Who paid far better than any fence ever did. "How the devil am I supposed to steal an hour?"

Elinor grinned. "You're not, I believe the saying goes. You're supposed to *fail* to steal an hour, thereby proving once and for all that you're not half the thief you think yourself."

He let a grin curve his lips, let his fingers close around one of the keys. Surveyed each of the faces of the children he'd claimed as siblings—the ones who'd let him, who'd claimed him back. The ones who had grown up with him, the ones who'd come along later, the little ones who remembered nothing but being theirs.

"The Great Westminster Clock, huh?" He flipped the key into the air like a coin, caught it, and stood to help when he noted Pauly coming their way with a tray loaded down with bowls. "Nothing to it. That hour's as good as mine."

As long as he could spend it right here.

TWO

Evelina Manning glanced again at where the sun sank below the buildings of London, stubbornly refusing to grant her the extra five minutes she'd asked of it. Five minutes, that was all. She was only five minutes late.

Which, as a clockmaker's daughter, amounted to a century. Papa would be tapping his foot along with every tick and every tock of every second on every clock. Her lips tugging up despite the minutes-past-the-hour, she made a note to write that one down when she got home. She wasn't usually one for rhymes, but Basil had a bit of the poet in him. Perhaps he'd find it diverting.

She ought to have hailed a cab—though with all the German drivers shipped off to internment camps, they were hard to come by these days. Or taken the bus—though hundreds of them had been sent to Belgium, so they were rather hard to come by just now too. Or, she granted as she heard the words in Papa's wry tone of voice, she could have just left Mrs. Knight's house *five minutes earlier*.

But she'd scarcely torn herself away as it was. Too hot had been the argument in her chest. The fire. The *need*.

It was fizzling to nothing. All their hard work of recent years. All the protests and marches and carefully planned strikes. All for naught. All because of this stupid, infernal war thought up by a bunch of power-hungry men.

It had to end soon, though, didn't it? The thing had already stretched months beyond projections. It would be over soon. And then the suffragettes would march again. The cause would live.

She would live. And in the meantime, content herself with continuing her support of women in the workplace. With all the men away, the factories employed mostly women, and the demands were high. She could at least continue to ensure the workers were treated fairly.

It was something, anyway. Something to give her days purpose.

Speeding around the last corner at a pace that would have earned her a stern scolding from Mother, Evelina ignored the ache coursing up from her heel into her calf muscle and set her sights on the familiar façade of home. Red bricks. White trim. Wrought-iron grates in perfect condition. Not a stray leaf on the steps nor a speck of dust where it didn't belong.

The Manning house ran, of course, like clockwork. Or would, if not for her.

Shadows stretched their gnarled fingers over her neighbors' rooftops, all too eager to point in accusation. *Late. You're late.*

The shadows sounded like Papa.

Evelina increased her pace, even as her leg screamed in protest. Another month, and her perpetual tardiness wouldn't matter half so much. Basil never cared if she was a few seconds behind schedule.

An arrow of pain sliced up along her Achilles tendon, making her stumble a bit. Biting back a whimper, she slowed for just a moment to ease it.

Just a moment. That was all. All it took for one of those shadows to solidify and emerge from between the houses. To slink up behind her. To clamp an arm around her waist, another around her throat. For the feel of cold metal against her esophagus to warm, to warn.

Ah, blast. It wouldn't be her first mugging, but she'd never expected such a thing *here*, in her own neighborhood. Her guard had been down. It was her own fault. And now with her leg aching and her breath already short, she'd lost a precious three seconds to react.

"Nice and easy, my pretty," a voice said, hot and sticky against her ear. "We will just—"

"What exactly do you think you're doing?" Another man appeared out of nowhere, a frown looking perfectly at home on his brows.

Evelina knew an answering one took up residence on her own. A simple mugging she could handle. But if some ridiculous man thought he had to play hero, it could quickly escalate. She eased back, into the arm that held her captive. Away from that eager blade against her neck, lest the mugger get twitchy.

The mugger got twitchy. Clamped his arms tighter around her, so that her already short breath couldn't heave up past his arm.

The newcomer didn't look shocked or wary. He looked . . . put out. Like Papa when Hans had the audacity to say that wristlet watches would overtake pocket watches someday. He wore a simple brown suit of clothes, well cut, and a matching derby, well suiting the shape of his face. And stood with complete confidence, as if he owned the very street on which he trod.

He lifted a finger and pointed first at her, then at the man holding her. "Let the young lady go, first off. Then we're going to have a chat, you and I, yeah? Because these are my streets, and you don't belong here."

Of all the insufferable . . .

Her captor retreated a step, pulling her along with him. "Stay back, mister."

Mister's eyes narrowed. "You're not English."

Evelina's ears scarcely noted such things anymore, with all the refugees in their streets. But he was right. The man's accent wasn't English. Neither, however, did it sound Flemish or French, as it would were he a Belgian.

Her captor tightened his grip still more. "I said—"

"Yeah, I don't much care what you said." Something edged into the second man's voice, too, pushing out the familiar cadence of the gentle class. Something closer to Cockney, though he certainly hadn't the look of a lower-class man. "Let the girl go this moment or every thug and thief in Poplar is going to be on your tail."

Not the police? He was threatening with *thugs*? From the worst part of the city? Evelina drew in a slow, careful breath and said a silent prayer. At the moment, she was none too sure she preferred her rescuer over her captor.

The man at her back spat out a word she didn't recognize but that rang of a curse. A second later, his arms retreated, his hands planted themselves on her back, and—oh no. She felt it coming a second before he pushed, but her screaming leg wouldn't brace itself as she told it to do, and the next thing she knew she was wheeling through the air, toward the overconfident man, while the mugger's footsteps pounded the pavement in the opposite direction.

Evelina righted herself as quickly as she could and waved an arm. "Go! Go after him!" She could have given the fellow a breath-stealing jab with her elbow, brought a knee up to disable him, delivered a blow to his nose, but chasing him down now was impossible. Her leg would betray her within five strides. "I'll dash inside and ring for the police."

But rather than listen, this man just stared over her shoulder, presumably at the retreating mugger, with narrowed blue eyes. "They're all a bit busy with the riots just now. But no need for worry. I'll find him."

"How will you *find* him? He'll vanish into the streets—"

"Exactly."

Every thug and thief. Evelina straightened and lifted her chin.

"I thank you for your assistance, sir, though it was unnecessary. And now, if you'll excuse me, my father will be anxious."

"Unnecessary?" The man snorted a laugh and turned those calculating blue eyes on her. "You could scarcely breathe and looked ready to faint."

Her own eyes went wide. "I most certainly was *not*! I had everything in hand. I am no stranger to muggers, you impudent—"

"Really. You. No stranger to muggers."

Every independent fiber of her being bristled. Evelina spun on her heel, sights set on the safety of her front door, only a few steps away. "I assure you, I have seen my fair share of violence. I am a suffragette."

Well, perhaps not in the truest sense—she hadn't ever been arrested for the cause. Hadn't therefore gone on a hunger strike. She hadn't burned or defaced any property, so the diehards among the Women's Social and Political Union probably thought her not committed. Probably thought—not altogether incorrectly—that she was more a suffrag*ist* than a suffrag*ette*. But Mrs. Knight had been so good as to take Evelina under her wing these last two years, so . . .

What kind of mugger had the gumption to accost a girl so near the front doors of so many houses, anyway? She glanced from her own door to the neighbors'. Within plain view of the windows? It wasn't right. Wasn't logical. Didn't fit.

The insufferable hero dogged her steps. "If you were going to fight him off, you would have had to act right away."

"And let me guess—a young woman of my stature and breeding would have no hope of succeeding, correct? I am but a helpless female."

"I've no idea what kind of female you are. But I know *my* sisters could have taken that bloke down in about five seconds."

She spun to face him, only a pace away from her front steps. She wasn't sure whether she was irritated with him still or a bit impressed that his sisters knew how to take care of themselves. So she let Mother's infernal lessons settle over her and kept her chin up, her gaze even on his. "You needn't see me to my door, sir. I am well, I assure you."

And he was laughing at her. Again. Though only with his eyes this time. "I can see that, miss. It's just that you're going to the same door I am. I take it you're Mr. Manning's daughter?"

Blast. No getting rid of him, then. Rather than answer, she sighed and pivoted back to her door. Even as she opened it, her apology was on her lips. "Sorry! I'm late, I know, but it isn't my fault."

But Papa wasn't there, scowling at her even while he suppressed a hopeless smile. There was only Williston, the ancient butler, creaking his way to the door. "There you are, Miss Manning. Mr. Philibert is awaiting you in the drawing room."

"Oh, good." She hadn't known Basil was back in London, but she had a few details for the wedding to run by him, anyway. Mother, even while in Devonshire with Aunt Beatrice, continued to send demands via the post, and if Evelina meant to argue, she'd do so best with her groom in agreement. And would likely still lose. She could count on one hand the number of arguments she'd won against her mother.

For now, she stepped aside, revealing her father's guest behind her to the butler. She meant to offer some introduction—though she didn't know his name, come to think of it—but paused.

Basil filled the drawing room door. And the sight of him made every cog, every gear in Evelina's workings seize. Her breath balled up in her chest. Heat burned her eyes.

He was in uniform.

The clearing of his throat sounded like a funeral knell. "We need to talk, Lina."

The last weeks he'd been gone—he'd said he was going to Shropshire to make final preparations for her at his house there. But here he was, in an officer's uniform. He must have been in training. He must have known for weeks, months what he intended to do. And he hadn't said a thing.

She stepped back, bumping into a soft-but-firm mass. "It looks as though it's a bit late for talking, doesn't it?" Her voice was perfectly calm. Low. Even. Mother would be proud.

Basil's gaze flicked over her shoulder, and his face went tight. "Who is this?"

She couldn't answer. Even if she'd had an answer to give, she couldn't have convinced her tongue to work. What was he doing? *Why?* They were to be married in twenty-six days. Twenty-six!

Maybe he wanted to move up the date. Elope.

One of the springs inside released a bit of its tension. Mother would be furious with an elopement—which made it sound like the finest idea in decades.

Behind her, a throat cleared. "Barclay Pearce. Sorry to interrupt—I am here to see Mr. Manning and happened across the young lady in the street outside."

Williston gave a perfunctory bow. "I am afraid Mr. Manning is not at home, sir. If you've a card I can take for him?"

"Of course."

Basil's gaze settled on her again. "Would you come in here, please, Lina? Please."

Her leg hurt. Felt so very stiff. She wanted to move it, she did. To follow him into the drawing room with its muted gaslights—the electric ones wouldn't be turned on this close to dark, not with the blackout. To hear whatever it was he had to say. But she couldn't. "Why would you do this? Without so much as talking to me first? I thought . . . I thought we . . . Do you not have even that much esteem for my opinion? My input?"

"It isn't that, as well you know." He shifted from right foot to left and motioned to the room behind him. His face—his face had always been as easy to read as a clock's. And now it said, *Your time is up.* "In private, my dear. I beg of you."

"You're ending things. Now, twenty-six days before the wedding? What have I done wrong?"

"No man wants a suffragette for a wife, Evelina." Mother's voice clanged in her head like a bell.

"Nor a cripple. Your daughter will be lucky to find any man at all willing to take her on, Judith." Aunt Beatrice, sniffing along.

Basil pressed his lips together. They were always rather thin, elegant. Now they all but vanished, and his eyes were clouds of regret. "You've done nothing wrong."

But he was still ending their betrothal—he hadn't contradicted that. Her calf muscle shook, and her knees may have buckled altogether had a hand not touched her elbow, steadying her.

Basil's nostrils flared as he locked his gaze on the man behind her again. "We won't detain you, sir. Given that Mr. Manning isn't in, I'm certain you've other places to be. Excuse us."

The stranger's fingers weren't exactly quick about retreating from her elbow. "My apologies. I suppose I should just let the young lady collapse rather than intrude." And the voice sounded far too close, too amused at Basil's polite dismissal. "Like I should have let her be mugged on the street outside."

"Mugged?" Alarm swept across Basil's face like a second hand, then settled into something that looked strangely like resignation. "She always does invite danger. Are you all right, Lina?"

"All right?" As if having her handbag stolen, or her jewelry, mattered a whit in light of her fiancé going off to war without so much as telling her his intentions beforehand. She wanted to rage, to slap at him, to shout and cry and scream. So, naturally, every muscle froze and every movement halted. "Of course. No harm done. Mr. . . ." What had he said his name was? "Mr. Barclay scared him off."

"In which case, we thank you sincerely for your services." Again it sounded like a dismissal. But he'd said *we*. Did that count for anything?

It didn't. That hard, cold shaft of fear that went straight

through her middle told her it didn't. She couldn't relax. Couldn't move. Not yet.

Basil turned to Williston and said something. Something about tea being sent in to ward off the fright of her close call, but Evelina paid no mind to the instructions. Tea wouldn't make this better. Nothing would. The one thing she'd ever done that pleased her mother—found a suitable husband—and she'd made a mull of it somehow. Pushed him away, into the arms of war.

Were enemy guns so much better companions than she was?

Warmth on her elbow again, and a low voice at her ear. "I'm sorry. I'd scare *this* off for you if I could."

It wasn't at all what a strange man ought to have said to her when he found himself in such an awkward situation. And yet it struck her in that moment as the most sincere sentiment she'd ever heard from anyone.

She managed to turn her head a bit as he moved toward the door, and she noted again the sandy, blond-brown hair. The bluest blue eyes. Noted them so that if ever they crossed paths again she could say something more to him than the few words that would squeak out now. "Thank you."

The corners of his lips turned up in the hint of a grin, transforming his otherwise common face into one she was sure she *would* remember. He tipped the hat he held toward her, put it on his head, and let himself out the door.

Its closing was echoed immediately by the chiming of the quarter hour from the hall clock.

Where was Papa? Was he really not at home, or had he simply made himself scarce so Basil could have a private audience? She looked to the butler for answers, but Williston had already toddled off, no doubt to give instructions on that tea she didn't want.

Basil stood just as he had been in the drawing room door, the muscle in his jaw ticking. "Good to know, I suppose, that you won't want for company when I'm gone."

Perhaps, in a different conversation, the jealousy would have been endearing. But he'd certainly never even hinted at such emotion before—what was she to make of it now? Shaking her head, she convinced her legs to obey her and strode past him, into the drawing room. "We both know this isn't about some stranger who happened across me on the street. Just tell me what I've done."

She sank to a seat in Mother's favorite chair, hoping it would give her some of Mother's indomitable courage.

Basil didn't sit. He just slouched where he'd come to a halt in front of the sofa and let loose a long sigh. "This isn't about anything you've done. It's just . . . what *I* have to do. To go, to serve."

"But . . ." She gripped the fabric of her skirt to keep from reaching toward him. They were all going, all the young men. Much as she hated it, *that* she couldn't argue. "But you've said *nothing*."

"I . . . was debating. Things."

A breath that might, on a different day, sound like laughter slipped through her lips. "*Things?* Where is your famed eloquence, Basil?"

"The eloquence you are counting on winning me a seat in Parliament, you mean?" That muscle in his jaw ticked again. "I suppose without it, without that seat, I'm not much use to you, am I? If my career takes a different track for a few years, if I fight Germans instead of other representatives—for *you*, for your precious vote—then I'm worthless."

She'd been berated enough to know the tone. To recognize the stiffening of her spine as a mechanism of defense. Even though she'd never imagined hearing such a tone from *him*. And especially with those particular words. "I don't know what you're on about, darling. Parliament was *your* goal, not my goal for you." But everyone knew he'd win a seat in the next election. He had backing from the most influential sectors, his opinion was sought and respected even by members of the House of Lords—a few, anyway. He *was* on a political fast track to a good position. Perhaps even, someday, prime minister.

But why was it suddenly an accusation against her?

He paced to the unlit fireplace and clasped his hands behind his back. "And what if I don't want to go into politics? What would then endear me to you?"

"Basil." She scooted to the edge of Mother's chair. She should go to him, perhaps. Maybe. Take his hands or . . . or put hers on his arm or . . . blast, but she never knew *what* to do in these situations. "You surely know I would be nothing but proud of you for joining up. For becoming an officer. But to keep it a secret from me—"

"I have always respected your opinion." He pivoted, that low gaslight glinting in his eyes. "And that is all you ever asked of me. Respect you. Listen to you. Champion your cause."

"I didn't even demand that, did I?" Panic clawed at her throat. Mother couldn't have been right—she couldn't have been, not about this. "You were already in favor of women's suffrage before—"

"Why did you never demand that I love you, Evelina?"

"What?" All breath evacuated her lungs. His eyes were out blazing the lamps, and she couldn't take her gaze from them.

He took one step closer but then halted, rocked, like the little toy soldier Papa had given her when she was just a girl, confined to her bed. For a moment, she had the foolish thought that she had better wind him up again so he could advance another few steps.

Then he shook his head. "Do you even *want* me to love you? Or is marriage nothing to you but an advancement of your cause? A political alliance?"

Pressure squeezed her nose. "Of course it isn't. Marriage is . . ." Many things, which her mother had enumerated for her time and again. Marriage was security and respect and solidarity.

Marriage was position and family and esteem. Marriage, if one was fortunate, carried with it some affection.

Just now, in the face of his blazing eyes, none of Mother's words sounded quite right.

Love. She forced a swallow. "I thought I was being good, not demanding words you didn't want to give. You were free to say them at any time."

Now *he* breathed a laugh, and it sounded like ice spitting against a wintery window. "So that you could look at me like *that* and thank me for my affections? I would have you return them! But you don't even know how, do you?"

Had he struck her, it couldn't have hurt any more. "You think me *incapable* of love?"

He didn't seem to have heard her. He strode forward again, past her, raking a hand through his carefully slicked hair. "Sometimes, Evelina, I swear you're naught but one of your father's automatons. His cleverest creation—you look real enough, but beneath are only gears and cogs."

She pushed herself up, willing her bad leg to hold her. "Are you quite finished insulting me?"

His eyes slid shut. "I don't mean to insult you. Just to . . ." His head tilted, as if he were listening for the perfect word to be whispered into his ear. With a sigh, he gave up and looked at her again. "I'm not what you want. What you want is a political sponsor. And a benefactor to leave you independent. But I want a *wife*. Someone who loves me. I want someone whose eyes light up when I enter a room. Who wants me to steal a kiss now and again."

"But you *are* what I want!" Her hand lifted, stretched out toward him. "I can be those things."

"Can you?" He was there before her a second later, pulling her close.

It shouldn't have shocked her, not given the conversation. The accusations. Not given the fact that they were to be married in twenty-six days. But when his mouth descended upon hers, the surprise of it made her go tense. Her hands could do nothing but land on his arms, awkward and stiff. Her back was a rod.

Still, he kissed her. More deeply than the little pecks he'd given her before. He kissed her until she finally relaxed, until her back softened, until her fingers gripped his arms. Until she *wanted* him to.

And then he stepped away, disappointment in his eyes. "I'm sorry. Perhaps if it weren't for this war . . . but I don't want a marriage like your parents have. Like *mine* had. It doesn't seem enough these days. Does it?"

He was disappointed. In her, in her kiss. Even when she'd relaxed. He'd stepped away as easily as if she were . . . an automaton. Cold settled over her.

He took another step back, his shoulders straight and unyielding. "Keep the ring. And tell your mother that she can say we merely postponed the wedding, for now, as I am being shipped out immediately. That will make it easier for her, let her protect her reputation."

Evelina dug her fingernails into her palms to keep from reaching for him again. "Please don't do this, Basil. We can work it out."

"We cannot. I'm sorry—but we both know you will have only disappointment to work through. Your heart is not broken."

If you have one.

He didn't say the words, but he might as well have. Then he simply turned to the door and, without another word, walked through it. Gone.

She waited until she heard the front door open, shut. She waited until the feeling returned, stinging, to her palms where her nails had dug in. And then, slowly enough not to alarm the servants but quickly enough to avoid them, she mounted the stairs to her room.

The wardrobe door stood slightly ajar when she went in, a wisp of white calling to her. Throat tight, she bypassed the bed and headed for the heavy wooden doors, pulled them open.

It must have been delivered that afternoon while she was out. Her wedding dress, already fitted and finished. Simple, because they were at war and anything else would have been unseemly. But beautiful and elegant, because anything else would have been unthinkable to Mother.

A mockery.

She reached in, past the white gown, until her fingers closed around the familiar cold metal. Paying no mind to the satin and lace, she pulled out one of the contraptions that had held her legs prisoner for two long years and sank to the floor with it in her hands.

"They are tools," her father had said. *"You will use them—because that is what we do with tools. You will use them until you can walk again, and you will not look at them as something that makes you weak. You will look at them as just what they are—what will make you strong. You will walk, Evelina. You will run, you will march, and you will live."*

She had believed him. She had promised him that polio would not steal her spirit, and she had worn the uncomfortable braces until she had eliminated all but a lingering limp when she was tired. She walked. She marched. She lived. Didn't she?

Or maybe she was just what Basil had accused her of being. Maybe Papa had just put a key in her back and wound her tight, and this thing she thought was living was just her spinning through the gears.

She let the brace clatter to the floor and begged the tears to come. Just to prove she could cry, like none of Papa's machines could do.

But she could not.

THREE

Barclay motioned Elinor to a halt beside him as he checked the building number against the slip of paper V had put into his palm this morning. They were in the right place. Though why this was the right place, V hadn't mentioned. The sign on the door read simply *Olson & Sons* without offering any clue as to what Olson and his sons might actually do. All he knew was that they were Swedish. And suspected of aiding the Swedes—officially neutral but mostly sympathetic to the Central Powers—in routing sensitive information to the enemy.

"Well. Shall we?" Elinor patted her carefully arranged curls, smoothed a hand over the skirt of the dress that Rosemary had stitched for her—and which she knew well made her look far too grown up—and rolled her shoulders back. Ellie made a great distraction these days.

If only she didn't enjoy it so much. It never failed to give him a headache, to see how men ogled his little sister. Sometimes he wished all the girls could have just stayed nine, when they were easy to look after.

But there was no help for it. And while Barclay was waiting for Mr. Manning to respond, V certainly wasn't just going to let him sit back and laze away a whole day. And so he was out on yet another simple assignment, a sister by his side.

He sighed. "I suppose. But do mind yourself, Ellie. Last time, I thought that bloke was going to follow us home, you had him so enamored."

Elinor, ever bent on increasing his headaches, grinned. "Let's see if I can't add another gent to my list of admirers." Without waiting for his go-ahead, she pushed open the door and sashayed into the office building.

Barclay grumbled, "You needn't be so eager," and followed her in.

"Well, given that it's the only fun you let me have anymore—"

"Can we not begin this again just now?" When he'd told the family that they were done with stealing, other than what jobs V gave them, he hadn't expected quite so much resistance from Elinor. But then, she did like giving him headaches.

"I'm not beginning anything." She pasted on a too-pretty smile and strode away from him, toward the desk at the end of the corridor, as they'd planned. Still, he had to squelch the desire to snap at her for walking away without so much as a by-your-leave.

She headed straight for the bespectacled man at the desk, perched herself on its edge, and leaned down to coo a question to him that Barclay couldn't make out.

He didn't need to make it out though—just needed to know that the bloke was paying no mind as Barclay found the door he wanted and slipped inside.

According to V, Mr. Olson himself never deigned to come in on Saturdays, though he insisted the office be manned the usual half day. So he wasn't surprised to find the lights off here in the owner's office. A few sunbeams slanted through the window though, illuminating a neat and orderly desk.

Order always made things easier. Moving silently, he stepped behind the desk and scoured its top for the envelope V had told him to look for—one with a Swedish direction on it, to a Mr. Lindgren. He checked the stack of correspondence obviously intended to be put in the post but didn't see it there.

No great surprise. If it were going through the normal post, then V wouldn't have charged him with finding it—he would have left it to Captain Hall's boys, who searched all mail leaving England. Barclay didn't envy the chaps *that* job.

Careful to keep any squeaks at bay, he eased open the top middle drawer of the desk.

And there it sat, along with a note for the private courier he had been employing to deliver his messages to Lindgren. Barclay slipped both into his pocket and moved back to the door.

He cracked it first, listening. No footsteps—but there was laughter. Ellie's, and a deeper tone that would belong to the secretary. He peeked his head out, verifying that his sister was blocking the man's view of the corridor, then slid out entirely, closing the door silently behind him.

A minute later, he was outside in the sunshine, leaning against the building as he waited for Elinor to join him. She arrived with a self-satisfied grin.

"Success?"

He nodded and then inclined his head toward home. "No trouble for you, I assume?"

"Please, Barclay. If there's anything easier than flustering a middle-aged, unattractive man in clerical work, I've yet to find it." No doubt just because she knew he hated to employ her so, she looped her arm through his elbow and smirked up at him. "And we'll be home before the morning's half over. Unless you've another job today?"

He shook his head. "That was all V gave me, aside from Manning. Let's hope he makes contact today." His brows drew together. He'd stayed awake far too long last night trying to figure out who that mugger had been, and why he'd been *there*. Hammersmith's streets weren't exactly hotbeds of crime. "I'm still uneasy about that bloke who attacked his daughter."

Ellie's release of breath sounded far too close to amusement. "This girl must have made quite the impression on you."

Barclay spared her only one sharp glance. Her mind was constantly on romance these days, it seemed—no doubt the fault of Willa and her impending wedding. And Rosie with her marital bliss. But Elinor ought to know better than to impose such things on Barclay. He shook his head and sent his gaze over the street, bustling with morning traffic. "It isn't Miss Manning who made the impression. It's that mugger. He didn't belong in Hammersmith."

A partial lie, to be sure—the bit about Evelina Manning. He couldn't quite rid his mind's eye of the image of her looking outraged as that man had put an arm over her throat. Not frightened—outraged. Exactly like any of his sisters would have—but they weren't from that neighborhood, they were used to such roughness. How had Miss Manning managed the same gumption?

And then sag so when she stood facing that Philibert chap?

Blighted idiot, that one, if he couldn't see the vulnerability behind her steel-straight spine. The fear under the courage. But then, there was no shortage of idiots in the world.

But the mugger had to be his focus right now. He knew well that V would expect him to look into and discover what he might. It *could* have been a coincidence that brought such a character to the Manning door. But Barclay was always loath to name anything such.

"You'll find him, if he's still around to be found." Ellie reclaimed her hand from his arm. Which wouldn't have bothered him, except that then she sent a little wave to some random chap who was crossing the street, along with a far-too-flirtatious grin.

Barclay didn't know whether to roll his eyes or growl. "Am I going to have to lock you in the house just to get some peace of mind?"

She apparently didn't suffer the same indecision—she rolled her eyes *and* growled. "Don't be a tyrant, Barclay. If you think I'm going to just sit at home and—and embroider or something, just because you can't handle the idea of your sisters growing up—"

"You're barely eighteen—"

"Almost *nineteen*, you mean."

"—and far too young to be thinking quite so much about blokes. Think of the example you're setting for Lucy and Jory and—"

"Oh, for heaven's sake! As if any of them looks to *me* as their example anyway!" Cheeks flushed, she focused her gaze on the street ahead of them, avoiding *his* at all costs.

As if he needed her to look at him to know what shadows would be chasing through her eyes. She'd been old enough when she'd joined their family to have suffered. More than the rest of them, in many ways. And while she'd always been sunny and bright, the insecurities, the broken pieces surfaced at the oddest moments.

But she wouldn't thank him for drawing attention to them by defending her worth, her place in the family. She never did. Instead, he opted for the easier argument—the one that would keep her angry for an hour rather than depressed for a week. "Well, I say one wedding this summer is quite enough, so no more flirting. I forbid it. When the war's over, we'll find you some good bloke like Peter or Lukas, but until then, can it."

As he'd hoped, she turned blazing eyes on him. "As if you get to dictate who I end up with, or when!"

The headache teased his temples, yes. But it should prove an entertaining walk home.

It was all *his* fault—that Mr. Barclay's. Well, not *all*. But in part.

Evelina took another sip of her tea and stared at the empty seat across the breakfast table. Sleep had barely graced her with its presence last night, but it was no excuse for wasting the day—or so she'd thought. Her brilliant plan had been to be up early, out the door at the first whiff of an acceptable hour, and to hunt down Basil.

They had to put this to rights. Now. Before Mother descended on the city again. Surely, *surely*, he would see reason after a night spent replaying their encounter. Surely.

Surely not. She set her cup on top of the note that had been awaiting her when she came down, praying, as even footfalls sounded in the hall, that it would somehow escape her father's notice.

"Good morning, Lina." Papa headed for the sideboard, his voice modulated. Absent. No doubt his mind was already busily at work on the day's problems to solve.

"Morning, Papa." She strove to ensure her tone matched his. Nothing to give away the earthquake from last night. Or the note with its few mocking words.

I know what you'll be thinking. But please don't. I've already left London. This is for the best.

Her fingers curled around her fork, though she had little desire to lift it and sample her food. Wouldn't Mother be pleased that, for once, her appetite was lacking?

Papa sat across from her with a muted smile, his plate filled with his usual: two pieces of toast, one with butter and one with marmalade, an orange—which he wouldn't eat now but would take to work with him—and a small bowl of porridge. No deviation, ever. He was dressed as always in a crisp white shirt with a brown plaid waistcoat overtop it. His sparse hair was short and tidily combed, each one in place. His spectacles gleamed upon his nose. "Did you sleep well, my dear?"

"Mmm." She never lied to her father—but there were times when she decided the truth could be ignored. "I must have been asleep by the time you got in last night. Did you tell me where you were going?"

He turned his plate a bit as he sat, so that the bowl was near his spoon and the toast at a perfect forty-five-degree angle from the edge of the table. His steaming cup of tea took up its usual spot three inches from his plate. "I met my friend from the patent office again for tea, and we ended up having dinner as well. You got along, I trust? Williston said that Basil stopped by."

"Mmm." She should tell Papa what happened. He needed to know. They needed to plan what to tell Mother. How to cancel the arrangements they'd been making for nearly a year. She should. And she would.

But her tongue couldn't find any words at that moment. Not a single one.

He was gone.

If only she hadn't been shaken already from that mugger. If only she hadn't walked in with that stranger behind her. It would have all gone differently. So many variations had played through her mind last night with each flickering shadow of an hour that ticked past. It wouldn't have happened as it had, not if Mr. Barclay hadn't been there.

Blast the man.

Papa took one bite from each of his selections, a sip of tea, and then repositioned the wire-rimmed eyeglasses better upon his nose. "Williston said another gentleman came in with you last night to call on me. Do you know what he wanted?"

Mention of him nearly made her bristle. "He didn't say, I'm afraid."

"Ah well." Another careful bite—he would take nine from each slice of toast—ten chews, a swallow. "He seems to be a neighbor, more or less—he's but a few houses down from the Fenleys.

Perhaps I'll call on him this afternoon, once I've completed the repairs on that case clock for the Lowell estate."

Evelina took another sip, letting the tea warm her blood. "I could deliver a note, if you'd like. I was planning on visiting Gloria this morning." She had to tell *someone* what had happened with Basil, and her maid of honor was a reasonable choice.

And if Mr. Barclay happened to be in when she dropped off the note, and if she happened to find the occasion to give him a piece of her mind on how a gentleman ought to behave, then all the better. To think that he had grasped her elbows before Basil—had she not been so flustered, had the very world not been shaking beneath her feet, she would have pulled away.

Maybe then Basil wouldn't have started the conversation quite where he had. And it would have gone differently. So very differently.

Papa was swallowing his next bite of porridge. "That would be kind of you, my dear. I'll jot a note off straightaway after we eat."

"Very good." She managed a few bites so as not to draw too much attention and stood when Papa did, slipping the note from Basil off the table and into her pocket. Tonight would be soon enough to talk with him about Basil. After she'd resigned herself yet again to the hopelessness of it all.

By the time she'd readied herself for a walk, the note for Mr. Barclay lay waiting on the table inside the door, and the gramophone in her father's basement workshop was four minutes into Verdi's "Grand March"—a sure sign that he was not, in fact, working on the case clock for the Lowell estate. Case clocks always demanded Beethoven. She wasn't entirely sure what called for Verdi . . . a wind-up toy, perhaps? Hadn't he been commissioned to design one for the Earl of Cayton's daughter?

She smiled at his preference and checked her hat in the hall mirror. Pulled on her gloves. Snatched up the envelope and let herself out the door. Then halted on the step as she looked at the direction.

Barclay Pearce. Oh, blast. She'd called him by his first name last night. He wasn't Mr. Barclay, he was Mr. Pearce. Yet another embarrassment.

Well, there was no winding back the clock. And really, what did it matter? Compared to the other things he'd witnessed, that little oversight was nothing. Nothing but one more cloud to shadow the day—and the sky was already grey.

When she turned the corner, a gust of wind smacked her in the face, and moisture stung her eyes. She stopped, let swell the tears that wouldn't come last night. He was gone. Really, truly gone from her life. The man she'd so happily let court her. The man she'd planned a future beside. The man to whom she'd lashed all her dreams. He was gone, because he'd decided that she wasn't what he wanted.

Evelina sucked in a long, slow breath and blinked away the brine. Did she love him? How was she to know? He was good and kind and they got along well. He had always sought her opinion. She had been happy enough imagining a life at his side, and she'd looked forward to growing closer, fonder as the years went by. Wasn't that a solid enough foundation?

Love. Wasn't it the woman who usually demanded such things, the man who was hesitant to grant it? But he'd indicated that he, perhaps, loved her. Or at least that he wanted her to love him.

Perhaps she could find where to write to him and learn how to compose a sappy love letter. Perhaps she could simply wait for him to come home again and win him back with her devotion and patience. Perhaps she could—

"Oh, excuse me." The words filtered into her consciousness even as a figure brushed against her.

Evelina sidestepped and spun. "Terribly sorry. I oughtn't stop in the middle of the sidewalk."

The young woman smiled, not looking terribly upset at the

near collision, and brushed away a strand of golden hair from her cheek. "No harm done. Good day."

Hardly. But she would get on with her errands and not stand here like a ninny all morning long, bemoaning her fate. She offered a tight-lipped smile to the woman who was already turning away and fell in behind her.

Evelina recognized many of the people who lived in the area, but this woman was unfamiliar. She wore a lovely dress, though, in a shade of pale blue, and had an enviable figure. Her face was pretty without being extraordinary, topped with brows in an absolutely perfect arch.

Someone might as well have punched Evelina in the stomach. Was *that* what this was really about? Had Basil found someone else? Someone who *could* love him as he claimed she could not?

No doubt that someone took as much care with her appearance as did this woman Evelina trailed. No doubt she had the perfect figure. No doubt she didn't walk with a limp whenever she'd been on her feet too long. No doubt she had an instinct as to when to reach out and touch his arm.

No doubt her kisses didn't leave him cold and disappointed.

The familiar railings of Gloria Fenley's house snagged Evelina's attention—and reminded her that she ought to be giving said attention to the direction upon the envelope, not to a woman who might or might not exist.

Evelina blinked away the despair and focused on the envelope. She was looking, it seemed, for Number 120. Which would be on the side of the street opposite the Fenleys'. Lifting her gaze to scan the number plates on the buildings, she sighed when she realized it was the very house where the lovely blonde was going.

It was last night all over again, except this time she was the one trailing the occupant to the house. Just the sort of awkward social encounter she despised. Perhaps she should visit Gloria first and then come back.

But no, there was a better chance of the man being gone now, in the morning, and quite suddenly she did *not* want to see him to give him a piece of her mind. She'd rather her mind have a little peace.

She sucked in a fortifying breath and positioned herself in the blonde's wake, trailing her up the steps to the front door.

The woman must have heard her coming, for she turned with lifted brows and a vague, but not unwelcoming, smile. "Can I help you?"

"Yes. I . . ." She lifted the envelope. "I've a note for Mr. B—Pearce. From my father, on whom he called last night."

The blonde's eyes lit. "Oh, you must be Miss Manning. Barclay was telling us all about the incident last night—are you quite all right?"

"Of course. Quite." Who was this woman, anyway? Mr. Pearce had mentioned sisters—but he had to be near thirty, so he was likely also married. Was this his wife? She seemed to be in her early twenties, within a few years of Evelina's own twenty-three years. Not that it mattered. Evelina lifted the envelope again, ready to just hand it over and be done with it.

But the woman—Miss or Mrs. Pearce, one way or the other—opened the door and stepped through, motioning for Evelina to follow. "Do come in. Barclay will be anxious to see how you're faring this morning. He ought to be back by now, I should think. Jory, is Barclay at home?"

With a short sigh of resignation, Evelina stepped inside.

A girl of perhaps eight or nine was seated on the main stairs, a book in her lap. She didn't so much as look up. "Not yet."

Then Evelina could still make her escape without facing him. "Well, I can just leave—"

"Retta, is that you?" The voice preceded the appearance of another young woman in the doorway to what must be a parlor or drawing room—this girl dark where the first was fair. "Oh, good. Fergus needs help with his arithmetic, and you know I'm a dunce when they start introducing letters into it. What's the point of letters in mathematics, I'd like to know."

Evelina's brows drew together. Perhaps the blonde—Retta apparently—could be Mr. Pearce's sister. They had similar coloring, at least. But this young woman looked as though she'd come from the subcontinent. She couldn't be related—at least not legitimately. But she was surely too young to be Mrs. Pearce. She looked little more than sixteen.

"That's what I tried to tell the professor." A boy appeared behind the darker girl—with ginger hair and a nose clustered with freckles. "But Barclay said it's necessary and will make sense eventually."

Retta smiled. "Then wait for Barclay and make *him* help you."

The boy—Fergus?—had turned his bright green eyes on Evelina. "Beg your pardon. Who's your guest, Retta?"

"Oh." Retta put a hand to Evelina's shoulder and nudged her forward when she'd rather have pivoted and fled. "Miss Manning. She has a note for Barclay from her father."

The exotic girl smiled. "I'm sure he'll be back directly, if you'd like to wait. I'm ready to swear off algebra and was going to make some tea—would you care for a cup?"

"Perhaps she knows how to do algebra?" The boy lifted hopeful brows.

"Oh." Evelina looked from one of them to the next. "I . . ."

"I'm Lucy, by the way." The brunette grinned and spun toward a hallway that stretched toward the rear of the house. "Who wants a cup?"

The last part she veritably shouted, and a startling chorus made reply. Evelina counted no fewer than a half-dozen voices coming from all corners of the house. Was this a private residence or a boarding school?

Fergus's gaze still drilled into her.

Evelina sighed. "I was a decent enough hand at algebra in the day. Though it's been ages."

"Well, you *have* to be better at it than Lucy." He snatched up her hand and tugged her toward a rather modestly appointed front parlor that offered nothing to sit on but one divan and a mismatched wingback chair.

"Forgive the lack of furnishings," Retta said from behind them. "We've only just moved in the other day."

That much she found believable; otherwise, Gloria would have long since been regaling her with tales of this strange collection of people.

Fergus folded himself to a seat in front of a low table on which he'd spread a collection of papers and a textbook. Seeing no real alternative, Evelina lowered herself to the floor, too, tucking her legs underneath her.

Mother would have an apoplexy if she saw her sitting so. Imagining the shade of red she'd turn made a bit of Evelina's unease shift to amusement. Just a hint of it, of course. But it was enough to inspire her to put aside her doubts and turn to the algebra. "All right, then. Where are we?"

Fergus tapped a finger to a problem scratched onto his paper.

Five minutes later, a metaphorical light had come on in the boy's eyes about that particular concept—and just in time, as the front door even then swung open.

An argument blew in on the breeze. "I am *not* being unreasonable, Elinor! I am your brother—"

"Brother, yes." The door slammed shut. "That doesn't give you the right to be a tyrant!"

"You're acting the fool."

"I'm not a fool, you're just an idiot!"

"For thinking you too good for that sort?"

Another blonde stomped into view, though at a glance she looked nothing like Retta. She was prettier, actually, with perfect curls and roses in her cheeks. “We can’t all marry rich gents, Barclay! That Rosie and Willa both managed it—”

“I don’t care about a bloke’s bank account! I care about the kind of life you’d lead at his side!” Barclay Pearce stomped into view as well.

Which seemed to propel his sister away like the wrong side of a magnet. She charged up a few steps, sidestepping the girl still reading there without so much as a glance. “You will not dictate to me who I can see—or who I can *be*.”

With that, she dashed up the stairs, nearly bowling over yet another young woman with hair a middling brown and straight as a pin.

This one looked familiar, which made Evelina frown as she watched her descend a few steps. She leaned against the railing. “What in the world is that all about?”

“*That* is about the Lord’s indomitable sense of humor in sending me so many blasted *sisters* to deal with! You’re all mad!” Mr. Pearce shoved a brown paper bag into the arms of an adolescent girl Evelina hadn’t even noticed emerge from the same hallway Lucy had gone down. “Except for you, Cressida, you’re perfectly reasonable. For now.” He tweaked the girl’s nose, earning a grin, and then stomped his way into the parlor.

He had to have spotted Evelina—*had* to have—but made no indication of it. He just fell into the wingback with a tempest of a sigh.

“Hey, what about me?” This from the girl on the stairs.

“And you. You’re still sweetness and sunshine, Marjory, and I forbid you from ever being otherwise.”

Apparently content, the little reader nodded and leaned against the wall.

The familiar one made her way down the stairs and into the room. “What has Ellie done, Barclay?”

Lucy followed a step behind, a tea tray in hand. “Is there a bloke?”

"No, not yet. But there will be someday."

"You're arguing over a man who doesn't even exist?" The woman's lips twitched.

"And it's entirely your fault, Willa—yours and Rosie's, off and marrying blokes of your own. Planting ideas in her head."

Willa. Evelina pressed her lips together, trying to stitch together the name with the familiar-ish face. Where could she have met her? At some function thrown by the Fenleys, perhaps?

Willa's grin bloomed full. "Well, there is still a month yet before my wedding. Should I call it off, for your peace of mind? I'll just go and jot a note now to Lukas—"

"My darling Lukas," Fergus said in a high-pitched voice, pretending to write upon his page of algebra, "I'm sorry, but I can't marry you because my tyrant of a brother has declared it so, and I fear I shall have to commit him to a madhouse if I don't give in. Signed, Willa Forsythe."

"Willa *Forsythe*!" That was it! But it made no sense. Evelina pushed herself rather awkwardly to her feet. "But I saw you in concert a month ago!" It had, in fact, been the last evening out she'd had with Basil. *"There's a new violinist causing quite a sensation,"* he'd said. *"Unschooled, they say, but a true prodigy—she's engaged to Lukas De Wilde, and he's been tutoring her."*

Miss Forsythe flushed and pressed a hand to her cheek. "I'll never get used to hearing that people have seen me *in concert*. Never."

"But . . ." Knowing her brow was knit in that way that would earn a scolding from Mother—wrinkles!—Evelina motioned from the musician to Mr. Pearce. "But how . . . his name is Pearce."

He looked at her for the first time today, his lips twitching. "I rather thought you'd dubbed me Mr. Barclay."

Blast the man. Heat crept up her neck to match the flush of Miss Forsythe's cheeks. "My apologies for the breach in memory, sir."

"*Sir?*" Fergus snorted.

"Fergie." This from Lucy. She slid the tray onto the same low table that housed the books, pushing several of them off in the process. And then darted back to the door to call out, "Tea's ready!"

Evelina looked from Mr. Pearce to Miss Forsythe . . . and then let her eyes go wide as the presumed owners of those half-dozen voices came from up the stairs and down the hall and, she nearly thought, from the very woodwork, until the room was all but bursting with them.

"I beg your pardon." She shouldn't ask—it was rude, and none of her concern. But how could she help it? "But who *are* you all?"

FOUR

The chatter that had been filling the air died a sudden death, and all eyes moved from Evelina to Barclay Pearce.

He didn't rise. Just grinned and pointed at the child nearest him—the reader from the stairs. "Jory, Retta, Lucy, Cressida, Willa. Fergie, of course, and Nigel there hiding behind Willa. He's a bit bashful yet, our Nigel. Elinor will no doubt not deign to join us. And . . . where's Olivia?" He pushed to his feet now and gained the doorway in two steps. "Liv? Do you need help?"

"No, I'll be right there!" It was a small voice that called down. Or, rather, a large voice that obviously belonged to a small person, given the childlike cheerfulness that filled it.

Evelina's brows may never unknit again. "*Ten* of you?"

"Twelve, before Rosie up and married in August and Georgie signed up." Mr. Pearce glanced over his shoulder at her but didn't budge from the doorway.

But they obviously weren't all siblings. To her eye, *none* of them looked particularly like siblings. Perhaps *half*-siblings, a few of them, but . . . "Forgive me. Are you all related?" Her gaze lingered a moment longer than was polite on Lucy with her dusky complexion . . . and then on little Nigel, whose skin was even darker.

That *silence* again. Mr. Pearce leaned into the frame of the door, gaze still on the stairs.

A rather familiar *thud, thud* sounded on the floorboards overhead.

"We're adopted." He said those words as easily as he'd ticked off the names, his hands hooked in his pockets as if he hadn't a care in the world.

"Oh." She pulled out a smile. "How lovely. Your parents must be . . ." What? Mad? "Bighearted."

Mr. Pearce chuckled.

Lucy clapped her hands. "Well then. Tea! Jory, give me a hand, won't you?"

Chatter bubbled up again in a variety of tones, easing the tension of that silence.

As they all moved about, finding seating wherever they could, she picked her way through them, her aim Mr. Pearce. She felt into her pocket for the letter.

A cup of tea appeared before her, in the hand of the smiling Lucy. "Here you are, Miss Manning. Guests first."

"Oh, I—"

"Do try it—I blend it myself." Her almond eyes were so hopeful that she left Evelina no choice but to accept the cup with a smile.

"Thank you." Because the girl watched her, she took a sip. And then another. "Mmm. This is delicious."

Lucy dipped her head, grinned, and spun back to the pot.

Evelina eased up beside Mr. Pearce, though she'd have to juggle the cup and saucer in order to extract the letter now. And when she drew even with him, she forgot it altogether. A small girl was making her way down the stairs on crutches, tackling the mountain of them without any hint of trepidation. With, in fact, an ease that bespoke quite a long while using them.

Just seeing those bits of wood made Evelina's underarms ache in sympathy. She still had her old set stashed away in a closet, along with the leg braces. "Did she injure her leg?"

Mr. Pearce turned blue eyes on her. "A year ago, nearly—a nasty fall into the street, where she had an unfortunate run-in with a horse. We feared for a while there that . . . Well, it didn't come to that. But the doctor says she may never walk unaided again."

"Poppycock." It slipped out before she could stop it. And she was none too sure she would have stopped it anyway. She'd had enough doctors preaching gloom and doom to last her a lifetime and more. "They said the same of me. Polio," she added at his lifted brows. "And I get on just fine."

One corner of his mouth quirked up. "There is hope for Liv, then. I suppose you achieved full mobility through sheer determination?"

"And some clever braces."

Mr. Pearce sighed. "We've looked into those. They're rather dear, though."

"My father and his friends crafted mine." She nodded to where the girl was happily taking the final few steps with nary a falter. "I was about the same age she looks to be. I daresay mine would work for her, and I know Papa would be happy to make any adjustments required."

He straightened, eyes shifting in their look, though she couldn't quite tell if they warmed or went cool. If possible, both at once. "Generous of you. But why?"

She looked back to the girl and gave her a grin. "I don't need them anymore. Someone else might as well use them."

Mr. Pearce moved aside to make room for the girl to pass. "Better hurry, Liv, before Fergie drinks it all up. And I got a few biscuits while I was out."

The little one angled a smile full of sunshine up at him. "Lemon?"

"Is there any other kind?" He reached out to ruffle her hair as she swung by. Then rested his gaze on Evelina again, not moving from the doorway. "If you're quite serious, I don't dare refuse the offer. Not if it could really help her."

"You can bring her round this afternoon, if you like. And, oh . . ." She shifted the teacup to her other hand so she could fish the note out of her pocket. "From my father. I daresay he was inviting you to call again anyway, and providing times that would work."

He plucked the envelope from her fingers and opened it. His eyes scanned back and forth across the page, then he nodded. "Three o'clock, he says."

"Perfect. I should be getting home from Gloria's then too, and I'll have the braces out for you. I can entertain your . . . sister? While you talk with Papa."

"It's very kind of you. I'm afraid I shall be in your debt."

"Nonsense. You saved me last night, after all." More or less.

"Not that you couldn't have managed on your own." He gave her that grin again, the one he'd given last night as he walked out the door. The one that transformed his face into something noteworthy.

It pulled a smile onto her lips too, without any input from her brain on the matter. She took another sip of her tea to cover it, because really, she had no business smiling today. Not given the storm that soon threatened to unleash its fury over her thanks to her utter failure—the storm known to the world as Judith Manning.

Thought of her mother brought her lips back down for sure.

She really ought to be going over to Gloria's, where she could let this new reality tick its way through her. Where she could figure out how she really felt about it all.

As soon as she finished her tea. There was something oddly soothing about sipping it while the room behind her was a buzz of happy chatter. A far cry from the silent teatime usually to be had in the Manning house. "Are you a clockmaker, Mr. Pearce?"

"Me?" He chuckled and surveyed the room full of children. "No. Though I've dabbled with it a bit. I found a book a few years ago and have been trying to repair a pocket watch. Managed one, but it was simple. This one . . . I thought perhaps your father could give me a bit of advice. I do enjoy the work."

She nodded, even though it didn't sound entirely reasonable. If he needed a watch fixed, why would he have called at their home rather than just dropping it off at Papa's shop? But perhaps he'd intimated that he'd like to learn, and the clerk had referred him to the watchmaker himself.

It must be something like that. They must have some mutual acquaintance, for him to have shown up at her door. "Lucy mentioned you'd only just moved in. Have you met the Fenleys yet? They live just three doors down, opposite side."

"Balding father, mother with the narrow face, and three stair-step children?" He lifted a brow. "Haven't met them properly, but I've seen them. We were just across the street ourselves for the last few months, until this place came up for let—my brother-in-law has that brick house there. Peter Holstein."

"Really." She knew well her surprise filled her voice. She didn't exactly *know* Peter Holstein—no one in the neighborhood really *knew* the reclusive man, though there'd been talk aplenty about him in the last year. More than one neighbor had been surprised that he hadn't been sent to an internment camp with all the other Germans. And of course, it had been the talk of the whole borough when he arrived back in Town married to a woman as chatty as he was silent. "Do you mean that your sister is Rosemary Holstein? Why, Gloria had tea with her when last they were in London."

And yet Gloria had said nothing about the woman's extensive family that was apparently staying with her. Nor had she made mention of the fact that Rosemary Holstein was apparently sister of the new violin virtuoso, Willa Forsythe.

Curious. Curious indeed.

"So your one sister is married to Mr. Holstein, friend of the king. Your other sister is Willa Forsythe, engaged to Lukas De Wilde." She turned to peek again at the unassuming brunette whose hair was slipping from its chignon. "And what of you, Mr. Pearce? If you are not a watchmaker, but unaccustomed to being called 'sir,' what do you do?"

He tipped his imaginary hat. "Errand boy to the Admiralty, more or less. When they say 'see this gets done,' I'm the one who does it."

She stared for a moment. "Don't they have sailors to do that? Or are you just not in uniform at the moment?"

He made an exaggerated wince. "No uniform for me, thank you. I get sent on the tasks that require a bit more subtlety."

He said *subtlety* in a way that shouted *mystery*. And once again she remembered his threat to the mugger from last night—*"every thug and thief."* She shook her head and took another sip of her tea. There was something about this man that didn't quite fit with Hammersmith's usual residents, to be sure. Something that put her more in mind of the types she met when she was out at the factories, checking on her friends who worked on the floors. But if he'd found employment at the Admiralty, then he surely wasn't *too* bad a character—and it explained his presence in her neighborhood. They were only a seven-minute walk from Whitehall.

But he must have less-than-savory connections, or he wouldn't have made such a threat. She could all but feel that blade pressed to her neck again, and quite suddenly she had no desire to swallow another sip of the lovely tea. Instead, she stepped back toward the low table, where Lucy was still pouring cups for the others. She slid hers onto the table with a smile. "Thank you so much, Lucy. But I'm afraid I'd better be going. My friend is expecting me."

Fergus turned big, sad eyes up at her. "I don't suppose you'd come back in a few days? You explained the algebra so much better than even Barclay."

"Oh." She snapped her head around to see what Mr. Pearce might have to say in response to that.

He laughed. "Careful, pup, or I won't help you later when you beg me." He took the same chair he'd been in before, which no one else had claimed.

Little Olivia was quick to scurry into his lap and make herself comfortable. The crutches had been leaned against the wall.

Something in Evelina's chest twisted as she watched him smooth down a curl of the girl's hair, as he reached with a smile for the cup Lucy handed him, as Fergus made some joke about her being a far prettier tutor as well.

It took her a moment to place it, this strange coiling of the spring inside her. Then it struck her—they were the sort of family she used to dream of having. Had *had* once, before polio had taken her brother's life as surely as it had her mobility. Back when her mother had actually laughed now and then, and her father had left gears strewn about the house, and she and Jacob had fought and played and shouted until the nursery rang with life.

Life. This house had it, despite its lack of furniture. The Manning house . . . It hadn't been alive, not really, in fifteen years. It had just kept ticking along, because that was what gears did when set in motion.

"Will you, Miss Manning?"

"Hmm?" She snapped back to the present, where the ginger-haired Fergus still watched her with hopeful eyes.

"Will you come back?"

She snuck a peek at Mr. Pearce, but though this was where most gentlemen would have interjected with an admonition against asking such a thing of a veritable stranger, he said nothing. Just lifted a brow, apparently content to let her answer for herself.

"Well, I . . . don't see why not." She smiled at the boy, who gave her a delighted grin in response. "Perhaps Monday or Tuesday?"

"Perfect. Barclay, can we adopt her?"

Mr. Pearce laughed again, as did a few of the girls. "We'll have to see about that, Fergie. We don't take just anyone into the family, you know."

The tease in his voice made that coiled spring inside tighten a bit more, made her lips want to pull up again in response. Made her wonder how easy or difficult it might be to fit into a family like this.

Hardly a wonder she needed to entertain right then. Figuring she had better escape before any other foolish thoughts entered her mind—or before another wide-eyed child could elicit a promise from her—she said her farewells and made for the door.

FIVE

Rain pattered down onto his open brolly, a familiar serenade that wouldn't have bothered Barclay if he weren't keenly aware of the fact that Olivia's crutches had a harder time finding purchase on wet pavement. "We can always get a cab."

For a seven-year-old, Oliva was an expert at heaving a sigh. "Barclay, I'm *fine*—and you well know we can't waste money on cabs."

A refrain he had apparently chanted too long for Olivia not to have picked it up. "I can carry you." He'd already offered twice.

Her answer was to speed up.

He bit back a demand that she slow again. She'd only see it as a challenge if he pointed out the increased likelihood of another fall. The girl had gotten rather acrobatic with the crutches.

But she hadn't balked at the idea of braces for her legs. She'd instead gone very still when he explained it. The kind of stillness that they all knew so well, that they could all fall into. The kind that waited for the *but*. Waited for the decision that they never got to make themselves. The one always made for them by how many coins were—or were *not*, as the case may be—in their pockets.

When he'd added that Miss Manning had a set and had offered

to let her use them, her eyes had gone positively brilliant. "You mean it?" she'd said. "I'll be able to walk properly again?"

He couldn't promise that—but he couldn't dash her hopes either. He could only say he didn't know how well they'd work but point out that Miss Manning certainly had no trouble getting about. And he'd seen many a victim of polio who couldn't boast the same.

They turned the corner for the Mannings' street, and Barclay sent his gaze to each and every shadow. He'd spotted that mugger last night the moment he'd made this turn, a too-dark patch in the evening's dimming light. Out of place, too still, too crouched. A stance he knew well.

His questions today hadn't turned up any helpful information about foreign thieves in this neighborhood. But then, he hadn't many contacts in Hammersmith itself. He'd go to Poplar tomorrow and ask around. Someone was sure to know something. It was just a matter of tapping into the right someone.

There were no out-of-place shadows or figures today. Nothing but the rain and a few men in trench coats hurrying through it, their hats pulled low to protect their faces, briefcases clutched in their hands. A few barristers or accountants who had stayed late on their half day, no doubt. Now on their way home, ready for a warm hearth and a steaming cup of tea.

"Which house?"

Barclay made another vain effort to keep Olivia under his umbrella, though she never consented to staying there. "Number 22." He still couldn't quite fathom how they'd come to be strolling this neighborhood with a bit of a legitimate claim. No one looked at them askance—thanks largely to the impeccable clothing that Rosemary insisted on stitching for all of them—but still.

He led the way to Number 22 and waited until Olivia was safely beside him, up the could-be-treacherous steps, before ringing the bell.

The old butler who had greeted him last night opened the door with a warm, wrinkled smile. "Mr. Pearce, good afternoon. How do you do?"

"Very well, thank you. And you?"

"Splendid. Come right in, Mr. Manning is expecting you. And Miss Manning is awaiting the young lady in the drawing room."

Olivia beamed, no doubt at being called "the young lady."

"May I take your coats? And you may put your umbrella in the stand there."

After depositing the brolly, Barclay shrugged out of his summer-weight trench coat and helped Olivia out of her jacket as well, handing them over with a smile.

They probably employed some sort of cook too. And likely a maid. Most houses in this neighborhood had a small staff, just like Peter did when he was in London. What had Miss Manning thought when Lucy made the tea today? Or when one of the girls opened the door? He would have liked to have seen the confusion overtake her face.

It would have been a far more entertaining variety of it than what he'd witnessed on her face right here last night, when her fiancé had emerged from the drawing room in an army uniform. That particular kind of shock hadn't been at all fun to behold.

Evelina emerged from the same doorway now, looking dry and warm enough to prove she'd been back from her friend's for some time. Her auburn hair was tidy and sleek, her dress the sort Rosemary called a "day gown"—decidedly less structured than the outfit she'd been wearing earlier. He rather liked that her figure filled the dress. Not that she cared about his opinion—and not that he intended to dwell overlong on her curves—but his family was all stick-thin thanks to simple lack of food, and it was . . . pleasant, he'd call it, to see a well-proportioned young lady.

She directed her smile to Olivia, bending forward slightly to lessen the difference in their heights. The eyes, blue as sapphires, that had shot sparks yesterday and spewed confusion earlier were now warm and inviting. "There you are, Miss Pearce. Have you had your tea yet? Mrs. Wright has prepared the most delicious strawberry cake, and I was hoping you could have some with me while your brother speaks with my father."

Olivia snapped her head around to Barclay, her opinion on the matter clear from the gleam in her eyes.

He chuckled. "Of course you may. Go ahead." It would take more than a few months of steady meals for the girl to forget the scarcity of the first seven years of her life. For treats like strawberries—or any cake, for that matter—to cease to be so exciting. Were they at home, he would have issued her a reminder to eat it slowly, to remember her manners.

But Liv would remember. And besides, Miss Manning had already seen them all sitting on the floor—had joined them there—so she wouldn't be shocked by a child scarfing down her cake, if Olivia did forget.

The butler returned from putting their wet coats somewhere or another and gave Barclay another smile. "If you'll follow me, sir, Mr. Manning gave instruction to show you to his workshop."

"Excellent." Perhaps his task for V would be easily accomplished—perhaps the man would simply be willing to share his innovations with the Admiralty, no need for the underhanded at all. With a peek into the drawing room to make sure Olivia was well—she even then loosed a gale of laughter—Barclay fell in behind the old man. And smothered a smile. At the butler's shuffling pace, it could well take them an hour to reach wherever this workshop lay.

But in short enough order they arrived at a door, which the servant opened but made no move to go through. The strains of some classical song or another drifted up, soft as gossamer.

Willa would know the composer. Perhaps even the name of the piece. To Barclay, it was anonymous loveliness.

"If you'll forgive me, sir, I cannot manage the stairs very well these days. Just go on down. Mr. Manning is expecting you."

"Thank you, Mr. . . . ?"

"Williston, sir." The butler bowed.

Barclay stepped onto the solid wood of the stairs and followed the music down into what was clearly a basement. But not like one of the few he'd found his way into before, with damp earthen walls and the clinging scent of mold. No, this space was all wood and light and the bright scents of metal and oil. The light, coming from a variety of lamps both gas and electric—there was only one window, high up and papered over, in accordance with the blackout restrictions—reflected gold and bronze from a fascinating variety of cogs and gears filling bins all over the space.

The light centered, of course, around the workbench. Barclay didn't hurry toward it, instead opting to take in the many gadgets lining the shelves from floor to ceiling. Clocks, of course, some ticking all in synchronicity, some standing as still as photographs. But for every clock, there were half a dozen . . . toys, he supposed. He didn't know what else to call them. Little figures of every possible shape and color, all poised as if ready to walk or dance or clap. And, given the keys protruding from their backs, they likely did just that.

Then came the other devices, many of which Barclay couldn't possibly guess at the purpose of. These took up space along the tabletops that stretched from wall to wall. A few looked similar to automobile parts he'd seen. Others like the gramophone he'd meticulously mended for Willa some years ago, so she could have music even when her violin was put away. None, however, that seemed large enough or well suited to an aircraft.

He could spend hours down here, studying each and every device. But his footsteps had apparently been noted above the record that was whispering its way to an end, as Mr. Manning looked up from whatever he was working on at the bench and stood with a smile. "Ah, good day. You must be Mr. Pearce—how do you do?"

Barclay smiled and reached out to shake his hand. "Very well, sir. And you?"

"Fine, fine. Has the rain stopped yet?"

"Not yet, no. Thank you so much for agreeing to see me. I hope I'm not interrupting your work too much." He motioned around him, rather wishing for a camera so he could take photos of each and every view and go back and study them later. For the job, he'd say.

And for his own curiosity.

"Not at all—I ought to be finishing up now anyway. Were my wife at home, she would have expected me upstairs long since." The glint in his eyes wasn't exactly of amusement. Nor of indulgence. Nor of any other warm emotion that Barclay would have expected when a man spoke of his wife—the kind Peter had when he mentioned Rosemary. Or that Lukas had when he talked of Willa. "But Lina is far more lenient with me and the hours I keep."

There was the affection, at the mention of his daughter.

Barclay's shoulders relaxed a degree. "Your workshop here is fascinating, sir. When my friend mentioned you, he failed to inform me that your work wasn't solely in clocks." He sidled to another shelf to peer at what looked like a miniature circus.

"Ah well." Mr. Manning's expression went wry, and he waved a hand. "My friends in the clockmaking world dismiss my other work as frivolous—toys, after all, nothing but toys."

A gear for an aircraft would hardly be a *toy*. But perhaps those friends didn't know about that work.

And this work was utterly fascinating. "I hardly think that deserves a 'nothing but.' Anything that can bring a smile to a child's face is beyond compare." He motioned to the key in the metal base of the circus scene. "May I?"

Mr. Manning smiled and came round the bench. "By all means, sir."

Barclay cranked the key round and round until it grew difficult. Then halted and, after a quick examination, flicked a discreet little switch.

The circus sprang to life, each animal moving—the elephant galumphing forward along its track, swaying its trunk; the bear balancing, wobbling, upon a ball; the lion tossing its head back in a teeth-baring roar as his tamer flicked a whip.

Barclay watched the actions repeat themselves, heard the tinkling of the music that went along with it, and felt six years old again. "Amazing. And you just keep this on a shelf in your basement, sir? Why is it not in some shop window with a price tag to make me blush?"

Mr. Manning chuckled. "There are a few in my shop that are similar. But some of them I keep. To give as gifts. To save for my future grandchildren. Lina loved them when she was a girl—this one especially. Her mother insisted all the toys be removed from her room at one point, but we could not simply get rid of this one." He flipped the switch off just as the big top began to open up. "I am working now on a commission for the Earl of Cayton's daughter—a unicorn that can trot up the stairs to a castle, which will open. That one will be quite a device, I assure you. I've only just begun it."

Barclay obligingly spun to look at the springs and gears strewn about on the table. "You are a true artist, Mr. Manning." He'd had no idea, when V directed him here, that he'd find all *this*.

Where, in all this whimsy, did a device linked to shooting weapons possibly fit? Perhaps V's source had been mistaken. Perhaps Mr. Manning had no such project underway.

"Lina mentioned you are a bit of a novice clockmaker yourself?"

A breath of laughter escaped Barclay's lips. "No, sir. I may have thought I was, but it's suddenly quite clear that I'm nothing but a novice tinkerer. Very far indeed from a true clockmaker. I've a bit of a hand with mechanical things, that is all."

And he could hear, as if a whisper in a long tunnel, his father's voice as he repositioned the screwdriver in Barclay's young hand. *"There is no shame in working with your hands. In crafting or fixing. We use our minds, we use our words—if God did not want us to use our hands, too, He would not have given us such capable ones."*

He wouldn't have said those words if he hadn't come from a family that *did* frown on working with one's hands . . . but for the life of him, Barclay could remember nothing about any Pearces beyond the ones that were his whole world: his parents.

Sometimes, though, he wondered. And once upon a time, had dreamed. Dreamed he'd come from a line of somebodies.

As if his long-gone relatives made any difference when he'd had to resort to stealing just to survive.

"Well, we all start somewhere, Mr. Pearce." Mr. Manning turned back to the bench, his mouth in that easy sort of smile that lived only on the corners, and only when the conversation was comfortable. "Lina mentioned you've a watch that needs fixing, but that you'd like to learn to fix it yourself?"

"It's an imposition." Clearly it was—that mountain of gears and springs and coils and screws and drivers on the table would not assemble itself into a castle, after all. Though he could only pray Manning would be too polite to dismiss him. He had to have time enough down here to find that gear the government was interested in, or to get Mr. Manning talking about it. Something to report.

Would God answer such prayers? Or was it too underhanded for the Almighty to honor? Blast, but this faith business was complicated.

Mr. Manning repositioned the wire rims of his eyeglasses. "On the contrary, sir, I find it refreshing that someone wishes to learn rather than just hire my services. It's been years since I've had any kind of apprentice. I'd be delighted to teach you."

"Really?" He heard the incredulity in his own voice but couldn't exactly call it back. So he covered it with a smile. "That's very kind of you. Are you quite certain you have the time?"

"'There is always time to teach someone eager to learn'—that is what my own mentor always says. I imagine he is repeating the same phrase even now in Switzerland. I cannot imagine Herman ever being away from his workbench." Moving back the stool he'd been stationed on before, Mr. Manning waved him over. "Have you the timepiece with you?"

"Of course." Though he'd nearly forgotten his cover story in light of the thought of Liv and leg braces. But he'd remembered to shove the watch into his pocket, and he reached for it now. Its case was beautiful—gold, with filigree. He'd found it in a gutter, where some drunken gent had probably dropped it when he stumbled into the gutter himself. If the thing actually worked, he could get a good price for it with his fence.

Not that he *needed* to fence it just now. But one never knew what the future might hold. If ever he fell from Mr. V's good graces, they'd be right back in the gutter themselves. Or back to relying on the mercy of Peter and Rosemary, anyway.

He set it on the table.

"Ah, let's see." Mr. Manning nudged his glasses again and picked up the watch, turning it over in his hands. Within a few seconds he had the case open, the works showing. "A quality piece. Certainly one you'd want to fix rather than replace."

"Yes. Only, I'm afraid it spent some time in a puddle." Barclay leaned onto the table's edge.

Mr. Manning chuckled. "I've a young friend who's convinced he can create a watch that will be unaffected by water. Until he manages it, the two will remain enemies, to be sure. But we can fix the damage."

Barclay watched as he chose a small tool and went to work, filing away each term he used, each instruction—most of it somewhat familiar from the book he had, but it was fascinating to see it all applied so deftly.

When Manning passed the tool to him, his hands weren't quite so deft. But his efforts were met with a series of exclamations such as, "Good, that's it," and "Quite right," so he kept at it. Though he suddenly knew how Fergus felt, with the unaccustomed constraints of instruction upon him.

How many years had it been since anyone had tried to teach *him* something? Usually he was the one doing the teaching. Pauly had done a fair bit of instructing over the years, but learning how to crimp the crust of a meat pie was a bit different. Still, unfamiliar as it was, it was . . . pleasant. It felt like a *thing*. One of substance.

The clocks in the room all chimed the hour in unison, making Barclay jerk upright at the cacophony.

Manning chuckled. "I beg your pardon—I should have thought to warn you. They can be a bit startling to those not used to them."

"That's all right."

"We had better stop for now anyway, so we have time to fit Lina's old braces on your sister. Though any evening you want to stop by, Mr. Pearce, to keep working on it, you are quite welcome. I'm almost always home by seven—last night was the exception and certainly not the rule. And I would welcome the company down here."

An open invitation to explore the workshop—perfect. "Thank you, sir. I'm sure I'll take you up on that." Though for now, he ought to go and check on Olivia. "And thank you, too, for the leg braces. Liv is eager to give them a try."

"I sincerely hope they can help her. You have spoken to a physician about using them, I trust?"

Barclay filled him in on the advice from one of the doctors as they meandered back through the shop. He halted at a table he hadn't seen before, half hidden as it was under the stairs.

A metal cylinder nearly filled it, looking far different from any of the other mechanisms in here. It was large and clunky and looked to be made of steel. Under it was a wide sheet of drafting paper with words on it that made his pulse kick up. *Synchronization gear*. And there was a drawing of an aircraft.

Eureka.

"Never mind that—it's nothing interesting." Manning motioned him toward the stairs.

Barclay didn't obey the gesture. Instead, he stepped nearer the table, comparing the contraption to the drawing. It was, if he weren't mistaken, barely even begun. And he hadn't spotted any parts lying about that were large enough to be put to use in it. "Synchronization—as in, with the propellers? I wasn't aware this was under consideration."

Manning sighed and turned to the table as well. "It isn't. And isn't, I'm told, even necessary. The aircraft have deflectors on their propellers, which is more than the Germans can boast. They don't need such a thing as this, they say."

An incredulous laugh slipped out. Barclay could well imagine a few of the old-fashioned gents in charge of things at Whitehall claiming just that—but they really didn't even understand the potential of fighters in the air. They were shortsighted.

V wasn't.

"Thinking like that won't win this war—we ought to be *staying* a step ahead of the Luftwaffe, to my way of thinking, and they're surely working to close that gap even now."

"Exactly." A bit of fire lit Manning's eyes behind his spectacles. Then it dimmed, died. "But a clockmaker is no doubt not the one to achieve it. It's for the gunsmiths."

"Nonsense. It's for whoever can accomplish it."

"Which, again, is not a clockmaker." Manning shook his head. "I cannot even find the parts I need."

"What if I could help you?" Perhaps he was overstepping, saying more than V would want him to . . . but no, V's instructions had said to get him to finish it and get it to Whitehall if possible, taking the designs if necessary.

An overt approach could well be his best bet here—the man obviously *wanted* to help the Royal Naval Air Service.

Manning's brows inched up. "Pardon me, sir—but it would take quite a few connections with the RNAS for you to be able to be of any assistance to me."

Barclay fixed a smile in place. "I have them." To V anyway, and through him the Admiralty. They were connections enough.

That light didn't enter Manning's eyes again—suspicion did. "An interesting coincidence, then. That the very man I should need happens to pay a visit."

For a moment, Barclay simply held his gaze, debating. He could play it like he would have done a year ago—marveled at that "coincidence" right along with him, perhaps even saying something about the Lord putting the right people together, if he wanted to borrow a few high-sounding phrases.

But the Lord was more to him these days than a happy excuse. And that strange fluttering in his chest, in the same place that bade him to change, whispered that the truth could well be his friend here.

Barclay let his shoulders relax. "Not exactly a coincidence, sir. Your friend at the patent office reported your work to the Admiralty. They sent me to see if I could help you."

"I suppose I should be encouraged by this." But the older man's gaze swept knowingly down Barclay's suit of clothes. "You are not a Navy man, though, Mr. Pearce."

"No." He couldn't keep the amusement from his voice as he said it. "I'm . . . let's call me an independent consultant."

"One with experience with aircraft, perhaps?"

"Ah, no. One with experience . . . procuring things." He motioned to the barely begun gear. "A handy skill right about now, I should think."

Manning still showed no enthusiasm. "And if I decide not to pursue this project?"

A tricky, sticky part of the truth. But that fluttering inside brushed against his heart again. Barclay sighed. "Then I'm instructed to get the design to my superiors without your leave."

"You'd steal it from me?" Manning didn't sound shocked. He didn't even sound put out. He sounded . . . hopeful. "The Admiralty is truly so eager for it?"

"My superior in particular is." He spread his hands, palms up. "Look, sir, I won't lie. I'm perfectly capable of nicking it—but I don't want to steal from you. I want to help you. Help you help our flying aces."

Manning's smile started at his eyes, bringing lines to life around them. Then moved to just the corners of his mouth. "Help would be greatly appreciated, Mr. Pearce. I intend to work on the gear in the evenings, so my invitation holds. Come any time after seven. Though for now—your sister?"

Relief blended with the music from the gramophone in Barclay's ears. He grinned. "Indeed."

SIX

The floor manager spun away, anger pulsing from him with every stride. "You, Miss Manning," he said over his shoulder, "would do well to mind your own business."

"The welfare of your workers *is* my business—it's everyone's business." Evelina charged after the stubborn old badger, motioning for Gloria and Flo to follow in her wake.

Neither of her friends had been particularly happy when she turned their pleasant stroll into a mission, but they'd come along anyway. They were good friends. Though their footsteps trailed a good ten paces back, by her estimation.

No matter. She couldn't wait for them, not if she wanted to keep up with the manager.

Young Katy, situated behind one of the looms, shot her a hopeful smile—her hands never stilling as the shuttle flew back and forth, fast enough to cause serious injury if she didn't pay close attention.

A moment's distraction—just one—and the woman could lose a finger. A hand. Her whole livelihood. Which was all the more likely to happen if the manager didn't shorten the hours required in each shift. "I'm sure you agree, Mr. Clarke, that no one wants the Great Unrest to come upon us again—especially now, when the workers' efforts are so greatly needed to sustain the war effort." This factory didn't just turn the thread into cloth for uniforms, the employees also sewed them.

The manager spun on her again with a growl that seemed to set his white whiskers to standing on end. "Are you threatening me? With more strikes?"

"I?" She widened her eyes, splayed a hand across her chest, but knew well the old man wouldn't read innocence there. Wise of him. "How could one girl like me even think of such things? No, sir, I'm simply observing that all those strikes that plagued England before war broke out could well come upon us again if the standards agreed upon *then* are not upheld *now*."

Mr. Clarke's veins bulged at his temples. "See here, you interfering chit. I've a quota to meet—men to see properly outfitted in the field. You think our boys in Gallipoli get to go home after ten hours? And take a nice break for a meal in the middle of the battlefield?"

"I think," Evelina said evenly, easing close enough to him that she could look him straight in the eye, "that your quota will be more easily met if you have the same care for your workers that *they* have for *their* men who are on those front lines. Each and every one of them is happy to play a part in keeping them safe—isn't that right, ladies?"

Their voices had been loud enough to carry over the noise from the closest machines—and she'd marched with these women before. They knew her, and knew to listen when she came.

A dozen voices called out, "That's right!"

"We only ask that *you* keep *them* safe. Limiting hours and giving them breaks results in fewer accidents, which means less time the machines have to stop, which means, ultimately, they are *more* productive. If you need the machines operational for more hours, simply run a second shift—with different workers."

Most of the employers she'd come up against recently relented at this point in the argument, the massive strikes of a few years back still fresh in their minds and the ultimate logic of the argument winning out.

Mr. Clarke, on the other hand, looked ready to strike her. And indeed, he gripped her upper arm so hard it was sure to leave a bruise and pulled her close enough that he could hiss at her between his teeth. "I don't appreciate the likes of you coming in here and trying to tell me how to run my business."

Evelina pushed down the pain and lifted her chin, holding his hateful gaze. "It isn't actually *your* business, is it? It's Mr. Dramwell's. And the last time I checked, he was quite eager to be in compliance with the new regulations. Do you think he would fancy being contacted about this? And who, do you suppose, would he blame? Them?" She motioned to the women—scads of them sitting on the stools that used to host men instead. Men now in the trenches.

Mr. Dramwell was known for his soft heart. It was why he *didn't* have anything to do with the day-to-day running of things. He hadn't the stomach for it—and had fired more than one manager in years past when someone actually worked up the courage to go to him with the workers' concerns.

If only he didn't keep hiring the same sort of chaps to replace the ones he sacked.

Clarke growled and squeezed all the harder before releasing her and stepping back. "You haven't any idea what it takes to run a place like this—you with your fancy parasol and tittering friends. You haven't any idea what it takes to *work* in one either."

Perhaps not from firsthand experience—but she'd spent hours enough wrapping injured hands and soothing the angry tears of protestors that she knew what she was fighting for. "Think what you will of me, sir. Just keep in mind that I'm *well* acquainted with the owner of this factory, and I *will* pay him a little visit if you don't obey the regulations that *he* laid down. Are we clear?"

His answer was another growl, another pivot on his heel. But he went over to the whistle against the wall and pulled the cord. "Thirty minutes for lunch!" he hollered.

Evelina granted herself a smile at the cheer from the workers and turned back to her friends.

Gloria's eyes were wide, her gaze fastened upon Evelina's arm. Flo's lips were pressed together as if she were holding back a rebuke—or ten.

Evelina sighed and shooed them toward the door. Perhaps it hadn't been such a great idea to bring her old friends along. But she'd already had an outing with them scheduled when the note from Katy Price arrived. It had seemed a reasonable plan at the time.

"Not in here," she murmured to them as she caught up. "Smile. Look victorious. They need to see we're confident, that we don't mind facing their dragons for them."

"But we *do* mind," Gloria murmured back. Quietly, at least.

"Or at least we *should*." Flo waited until they were off the factory floor and heading for the door before she shook her head. "I cannot believe your father allows you to do this. And your mother!"

Evelina grunted a laugh. "She doesn't *allow* it. She just can't stop it, not after Papa said it was all right." With one last glance over her shoulder to make sure the pesky manager wasn't following her, she urged her friends back into the warm sunshine.

Flo shuddered. "Hans would have a fit if he knew where I was! It's bad enough we've been so harassed because of his being German—but to *invite* conflict . . ."

"It's entirely different. This is conflict for the sake of others' good, not prejudice simply because you married a man with the last name of Wilsdorf." Though truly, she detested that Florence and Hans took such grief because of where he was born. He'd become a British citizen when he married Flo, but no one seemed to care about that.

"*My* father would be distressed simply at my being in Hackney!" Gloria gave an exaggerated shudder—and all but jumped into her waiting car. The driver snapped to attention and hurried to help Flo and Evelina in, though he was too late to assist Gloria.

Evelina accepted the chauffeur's help with a little sigh. And nearly echoed it again when Florence checked her wristlet watch and pressed her lips together. "I was not counting on such a long drive today. We will be lucky to get Gloria home in time for tea."

And apparently when one married a watchmaker of one's own volition, rather than simply being born to one, promptness was more important. "Mrs. Fenley won't fret if Gloria is a few minutes late." Though Evelina rather wished there were a way to keep busy during the drive home. The moment she stilled, the sight of that fabric from the factory filled her mind's eye.

Uniform fabric. The same color, the same material as what Basil had been wearing the other night. Where was he? The eastern front, the western? Taking up his new role among a group of men just as unseasoned as he was with weapons and battle strategy and a life lived in tents?

Why was that life preferable to one with her?

"Are you all right?" Gloria's words accompanied a soft touch of her fingers upon Evelina's hand.

She forced a smile. Gloria had said all the right things on Saturday. Had offered what comfort she could. But there had been something in her eyes when Evelina had shared Basil's accusation that she was an automaton—something that said, *"You're my friend, so I won't say he was right. But he was right."*

She hadn't dared share the truth behind his sudden departure with Flo. She couldn't handle another knowing, silent look from another friend.

"Well enough," she said in answer to Gloria's question. "And sorry if I've kept you out too late."

"It's no matter." Gloria patted her hand and then folded her own in her lap as the car pulled away from the curb. "You're right, my mother won't mind if I'm a bit late for tea. Why, just last week, she became so engrossed in the novel she was reading that . . ."

Evelina let her gaze go to the window as her friends continued their usual chatter—Gloria's family, Flo's excitement over her husband's new wristlet design, and exasperation over a new tax to be put on all exports. Conversation easily ignored.

Until St. James Park went by her window. Then she sat upright and even pressed a hand to the glass. "Oh! I'd heard they'd drained it, but I hadn't seen it."

"What?" Both of the women leaned forward, their gasps blending together.

The lake, once the biggest draw of the park, was nothing but a muddy expanse with a few puddles left to testify to where the water had once been.

"Oh, how sad." Florence shook her head, her brows drawn.

"A terrible waste, if you ask me. The German biplanes can't possibly reach us from the Continent. So the water couldn't possibly be a beacon for them."

If that were true, then why had the city also been put under blackout restrictions? Evelina kept her gaze on the sad expanse of the former lake. "I don't think it's the planes, is it? It's the airships—the zeppelins."

"Those lumbering things? Nonsense. They're no danger."

Flo shook her head. "It isn't the ships, Gloria—it's what they carry."

Bombs. She didn't say it, but she didn't have to. A chill worked its way down Evelina's spine without the spoken syllable.

The rest of the ride was somber. The threat would never come to anything, surely—they were safe here in London. But the constant reminders of a world at war were certainly depressing.

Then an even more depressing sight appeared when they finally pulled back onto her street. She groaned.

Aunt Beatrice's carriage was parked at the curb, already devoid of all but one trunk still strapped to the top. Which meant Mother was back. And had been back for some time already.

Suddenly the trenches didn't sound so bad after all. Would they allow a woman to enlist?

"Do you want me to come in with you?" Gloria didn't sound exactly willing.

Evelina couldn't exactly blame her. "No. We'll keep the casualties as few as possible. If I survive the bombardment, I'll speak with you tomorrow, Gloria. Florence, I'm sure Mother will invite you and Hans over for dinner soon."

Florence, even knowing nothing more than that Basil was now an officer in the army, sent her a commiserating look. "If you need us, you have only to let us know."

"Of course. Thank you." There was nothing for it but to face the enemy head on. As soon as the car rolled to a halt, Evelina climbed out.

Perhaps, given her arrival home in the Fenley automobile, Mother would assume she'd been out on an innocent promenade. She couldn't possibly know about the trip to Hackney already, so that berating may be escaped for now. She'd remembered her parasol today, so the ten seconds she'd spent in the sunshine couldn't have freckled her nose. And with her appetite flagging since Basil had left her, she may have even lost a pound, so perhaps there would be no comments about needing to tighten her corset.

As if any of that would matter once Mother realized that her prized trophy—a daughter married to a well-to-do future member of Parliament—had been snatched away.

She'd told Papa, finally, after the Pearces had left Saturday night. In a few broken whispers she'd confessed it all. The visit, the decision, the note. He, being Papa, had said nothing. He'd just taken her hand between his and held it. He'd pressed a kiss to her brow. And he'd drawn her to his side and anchored her there until a few hot tears had finally burned their way down her cheeks, as scalding as acid.

Proof that she was human, or was she just a leaking machine in the arms of her creator?

How she wished he could have fixed these broken gears as quickly as he did a clock's. And he wished it too, she knew.

The Fenleys' auto eased its way down the street, marking the time she stood there just staring at her own front door. They didn't take it out much these days. Fuel was growing scarce, thanks to the war.

Everything came down to the war these days. Everything.

Everything but Mother. She wouldn't understand why a little thing like nations trying to rip each other apart ought to have inspired Basil to break his word.

The door opened, and Williston's white head emerged. He motioned rather frantically to her, his eyes wide.

She'd been only twenty-six days away from a house of her own. So very close.

The steps felt like mountains as she climbed them, and the entryway as hot as blazes, given that the moment she stepped inside, Mother's voice screeched in her ears.

"Well, I don't care if there's a shortage, I'll not have tea without sugar, and this bowl is disastrously low. How am I to entertain with supplies like this? Do you not realize that with the wedding but three weeks away, there will be a veritable stream of guests coming for tea?"

Evelina considered, for just a moment, sneaking up the stairs to her room. But Williston closed the door behind her even then, and the soft click would not be missed by Mother, who could hear an ant marching from a mile away, if it was of interest to her.

Sure enough, she appeared in the drawing room door three seconds later, when Evelina had made it no more than a step.

Judith Manning may have looked, to an unaccustomed eye, like a demure woman. Properly petite, of average height but slight of frame—meticulously preserved by never doing more than picking at her meals and always turning down sweets. Her only indulgence was that one lump of sugar in her tea. Her hair was still a gleaming auburn—the one trait they shared—pinned in a deceptively soft-looking style. Her face was still as smooth as a woman half her age.

But she could have stared down the most battle-hardened of generals with that steely-eyed glare that she focused now upon Evelina. "*There* you are. You are nearly late for tea."

"Do you know what some people call 'nearly late,' Mother? On time." Evelina bit her tongue, but too late.

The glare narrowed. "You have yet again forgotten your manners, I see. I can't leave you alone for a second, can I? Really, Evelina, I don't know how you're going to manage to keep from embarrassing yourself and your husband when you've married. Basil will have to be always on his guard."

If she bit any harder upon her tongue, she'd begin to taste blood. And *still* it wasn't enough to keep the rebellious organ from spitting out, "Well, luckily for him, he won't have to worry with that. He's joined up, Mother. And called off the wedding."

Stupid, stupid way of telling her! She'd already planned out the best way to break the news—gently, slowly. Once Mother had been sweetened by that miserly bit of sugar. Perhaps even once she'd had a day at home to browbeat the household enough to make herself happy. Then she'd lead first with the news of his enlistment, of the necessary postponement of the wedding. And only afterward slide in the bit about the uncertainty of it taking place at all. Afterward by a week, or a month. Or perhaps a century.

Mother, of course, made no visual response. Nary a crease in her brow that could become a wrinkle, no frown that would put lines beside her mouth. She blinked, if one could count that as a reaction. "I beg your pardon?"

Evelina's throat felt as dry as the lake in St. James Park. Her shoulders sagged. "I'm sorry. I know this . . . I shouldn't have said it like that. He . . . Basil stopped by just the other evening. In uniform. He's signed up, he's already deployed. He said he doesn't want to get married." *Not to me.* "The wedding is off, Mother. He doesn't ever intend for it to happen, but he said we could say it's merely postponed, given the war."

There, a tic in Mother's cheek, below her left eye. Emotion—or what passed for it in the face of Judith Manning. "He'll change his mind, of course. If he's really a part of the war now—fool man—it won't take him long to realize the allure of home and hearth and a wife by his side."

It almost, *almost* felt like encouragement. Evelina's chin came down a notch. "I fear he won't. I'm not the wife he wants in his home or at his hearth, apparently. He says I'm . . . that I'm too cold. Unemotional."

"Oh, nonsense. If anything scared him off, Evelina, it's your infernal activism, not your control over your emotions."

"And perhaps her unattractive limp!"

Evelina flinched. "Hello, Aunt Beatrice."

"Don't shout, child," Mother said. "If you wish to greet your aunt, go into the drawing room and do it properly."

It wasn't a suggestion—just like *I didn't wish to greet her, actually,* wasn't a possible answer. Evelina shuffled toward the room, wondering for the thousandth time why her calf always seized up the moment Aunt Beatrice brought up the old limp, when she could walk perfectly well most of the time.

Rather ironic, given the mahogany cane that her aunt kept always at hand—though granted, it was more to have something to use to emphasize her points with a pound on the floor than because she actually needed the walking aid.

Her aunt was positioned daintily on the edge of the sofa cushion, looking as pinched and polished as ever. And as ready to frown.

Apparently *their* mother hadn't drilled into the elder sister the importance of keeping one's face always clear of such expressions, because she had the lines to prove she scowled more than she didn't.

"Hello, Aunt Beatrice," she said again, moving over to give the woman the expected air-kiss an inch from her cheek. "Did you have a pleasant journey?"

"Of course it wasn't pleasant, journeys are never pleasant. But I *thought* I was coming to Town for a wedding, so of course I came." Her frown lines had frown lines. "I suppose you tried to have a conversation with him about playthings. Men despise it when their wives try to address such issues."

Heat seared her cheeks. "I did not talk with Basil about such things. I had no need to do so, as he is not the sort of man to keep a mistress."

Aunt Beatrice sniffed. "All men who can *afford* to do so are the *sort* to do so. I would have thought you'd have taught your daughter of such realities, Judith."

Words that spoke only of the unhappiness of Aunt Beatrice's ten years of marriage—not of the truth. But Evelina still had to grit her teeth. Why was it she could convince factory owners to revise their stance in regard to their workers, but she could never convince her own aunt to alter her views even a degree?

Mother pinched the bridge of her nose. She wouldn't argue with her sister, she never did. She merely said, "Evelina understands how some men behave. I am sure she would never have dared discuss such indelicate matters with her betrothed."

"Her *former* betrothed." Her aunt sniffed again. "I don't fathom how your husband can bear such a smudge upon his name, sister dear."

"Cecil is resilient." Mother gestured for Evelina to sit. "And we will work this out with Basil yet, I am sure. I am not worried."

Yet her eyes glinted as hard as steel.

Evelina sank to a rest on a hard, unforgiving chair. And wished she were facing down a surly factory manager instead of her mother and aunt.

SEVEN

Barclay glanced over his shoulder and, seeing no one behind him, vaulted over the fence after the can he'd tossed a moment earlier. On the other side, he was greeted by the forlorn sight of a dozen cars parked on a derelict piece of ground near a prominent club, dust collecting on once-gleaming fenders. From what he'd been able to glean, they all belonged to men who were currently in the war. And who really ought to have had the sense to drain their petrol tanks before they left. Didn't they know that it could foul up the engines to leave it in there?

Really, he was doing them a favor. Saving their engines. And they had no need of the petrol in them just now, anyway. Whereas that friend of Captain Hall certainly did.

He didn't used to have to explain away such things to himself. Nor did he used to make a note of exactly where he liberated each item, with the silent promise that he'd return it when he could.

But things had begun to change in his mind since he spent more time reading the Bible that sat now beside his pallet on the floor. Apparently—who knew?—God didn't much care for thieves. Or rather, thought them worth saving but insisted they give it up.

Let him that stole steal no more: but rather let him labour, working with his hands the thing which is good, that he may have to give to him that needeth.

He'd read that last night in Ephesians. He'd lain awake far too long wondering exactly how one worked with his hands the thing which was good. When all one's hands knew how to do was slip coins from pockets and bracelets from wrists. He was trying to change. *Had* changed.

Still, when the director of naval intelligence looked down at one and said, *"I need petrol—find me some, now,"* one did whatever one could. And given the shortage of petrol in London at the moment . . .

He filled the can from the nearest car, using a length of hose as a syphon. And patted the poor automobile's flank as he imagined men of the generations past would have done to a favorite horse. "Sorry, old boy. But it really is best for you not to sit with petrol in you."

He wondered idly if intelligence directors from previous generations ever had their lackeys steal feed for their steeds. Probably. War came with its own rules, after all.

His can was filled before the tank was empty, so he pulled out the syphon and coiled it back up after wiping the ends with a rag he'd brought along. Then exited to the street, rather than climbing over the fence again with a filled can.

This particular street he wasn't overly familiar with, so he let his gaze roam over each sign as he walked, cataloging what was to be found here.

His feet drew to a halt as he spotted the little placard on the door across the street. *Thomas and Pearce, Accounting Office*. "Pearce." Barclay's breath hitched. Charlie had been decent with his numbers as a lad. Could he have secured education enough to become a man who made a profession of them?

Though the petrol weighed heavy in his hand, he darted across the street and peered through the window.

Two desks within, two gentlemen sitting at them. Both old enough to be his father.

He hadn't really hoped—not really. He knew well that each year that went by made it less and less likely that he'd ever find his little brother. So why that hollow pang inside at the realization that Charlie wasn't behind that glass and wood?

He shook it off and strode away before the accountants within could look up and see him hovering. If he wanted to remain on the good sides of Mr. V and Captain Hall, he had better hurry back to Whitehall.

After a brisk ten-minute walk, he turned onto Fulham Palace Road, his eyes tracking as always toward the banner billowing over the street, anchored to the side of Charing Cross Hospital. Crisp red letters on a field of white demanded *Quiet for the Wounded*.

The hush would never feel natural. Aside from the *clip-clop* of a few horses' hooves and the creak of a wagon's wheels, people made every attempt to obey. Only whispers were spoken. No shouts of greeting rang out.

Everyone knew that it wasn't just the wounded from the front in the hospital, brought there by train. Death itself hovered, and who knew but that they might draw its attention with a shout.

Barclay hurried past the five-story hospital and on to the Admiralty Building. An automobile sat silent and still in front of it—proof that no one else had returned with petrol before him. Excellent. Not waiting to be told, he set about filling the tank with his full can.

"You found some—very good." V stepped to his side, hands clasped as usual behind his back. "Dare I ask where?"

"You wouldn't ask a chap to give away his secrets, would you?" By his estimation, he could perform this same miracle another dozen or more times, if no one else thought to empty the tanks of those slumbering cars.

V gave him a hint of a smile. "No need. How is your family settling in to your new abode?"

"Quite well, thank you." He wouldn't mention that they'd yet to find beds, or a table that could fit them all. They'd done with far worse over the years. "The children love the place."

"Good. I had to imagine that Mr. and Mrs. Holstein would want a bit of privacy when they come to Town for the wedding, given her condition."

Barclay hadn't told his employer that Rosemary was expecting, but he didn't bother asking how he knew. V just *knew* things. Still, it was odd to hear him speak of such matters. Odd, really, to *think* of such matters.

Rosie, a mum. Not just to the little ones they'd taken in, but to one of her own. Funny how time slid by.

V lifted his brows. "I wanted to keep you close to Whitehall though—and to your new assignment. Have you made introductions yet?"

Barclay nodded and let the image of the gear float into his mind again. "He's rather pleased that interest has been shown in his design—though he'll likely need a bit of assistance in finding the parts he requires."

V blinked. "What exactly did you tell him?"

"The truth, much as I know it." Barclay blinked right back. "Worked well enough."

Though a wisp of breath escaped V's lips, it didn't ring of a sigh. Much. "So long as it works, your methodology isn't particularly important. He's hopeful, then, about the outcome of his design? The patent clerk seemed to think he was uncertain."

There *had* been uncertainty, to be sure. But not in the design itself, so far as Barclay could tell. "There's quite a lot of work to be done on it yet—who's to say how long it might take him? But he invited me to help, of an evening. That's when he plans to focus on it."

V's lips pressed into a line. "I'd prefer he dedicate his days to it as well—but if that is all he will spend on it now, then yes, be there. I suppose I should be grateful it leaves you free during the days to attend to other business."

Like petrol and Sweden-bound letters and whatever else Captain Hall had need of to keep his operation running. Given that it equaled steady income for the first time in his life, Barclay wasn't going to complain about the odd assignments. They kept things interesting.

"Well. Keep me up to date on Manning. And let me know of anything he needs. Report here in the morning to see what we may need you for tomorrow." With a nod, V spun back to the Old Admiralty Building.

Assuming that equaled a dismissal for the day, Barclay stowed his petrol can in a cupboard at the rear of the building and struck out.

Not toward his new home, though, nor toward the Manning residence. Not quite yet—he still had hours before the time Manning had said he was welcome. No, he had another call to make first.

It required an hour-long journey on the tube, away from the river and the neighborhoods he knew best, toward Stoke Newington. He drew a book from his pocket to entertain him on the ride and tucked it back in as soon as the right station drew near—he still enjoyed the novels of his old favorite writers, but they'd all rather lost their allure now when compared to those of Branok Hollow.

But his brother-in-law didn't have another title set to come out under his pen name for another month. So in the meantime, he'd have to make do with the stories penned by blokes *not* smart enough to get a ring on Rosie's finger.

He emerged from Manor House Underground Station and strode through the bleak neighborhood surrounding it. Yesterday's rain still puddled in the streets, and the identical rooflines of the identical buildings paraded across from him without any concern for style or grace.

No one gave him a second glance as he strode along the streets, nor when he entered the Cricketer. There were a few blokes here already, sipping at their ale and laughing, but most wouldn't arrive until their shifts at the factories had ended.

And too many were likely not here at all. Gone to the war. Or lost to the war.

But Dante was in his usual corner booth, and his teeth flashed white against his ebony skin when he spotted Barclay. "Pearce! Oi!"

Barclay conjured up a smile for one of his oldest friends and clasped his hand as soon as he was near enough. Thankfully, no one already occupied the bench seat across from Dante, so he could slide into it and shake his head when the publican approached with a pitcher of ale. "How are you, Dante?"

"Fair as can be expected. Where you been, mate?"

"Mate?" A laugh snuck out. "Are you an Aussie now?"

"No, but I've let one into the gang." There was something infectious about Dante's grin. "He's rubbed off a bit. Speaking of which—how's yours? Willa still marrying that Belgian?"

"In three weeks. Rosie and Peter ought to be back any day to help with the last-minute details. How's Clara been?"

"Beautiful as ever. I'm telling you, mate, you ought to find yourself a wife. Best thing I ever stole."

Barclay chuckled and leaned back against the hard, wooden back of the booth. "I've my fill of females, thank you very much. Why the good Lord sent me all the sisters and you all the brothers, I'll never know."

"Well now, you took little Nigel, didn't you? When he arguably would have fit better with me and mine." But there was no malice in Dante's grin, nor in his sparkling dark eyes.

"Had to do what I could to even out the gender scales in my family." And at the time, the boy had cowered in fear when Dante's lieutenant had shown up—apparently the mite had already had a run-in with the man called Rock. "Had some new chaps in Poplar last week, from your neighborhood."

Dante made a face and twirled his mug of ale around. It was half full, and would stay that way for another hour or more. The man might spend half his day in the pub, but it wasn't to drink. "Richards and Craston—I didn't realize they'd left until too late. But I trust you can keep them in line."

"They know the rules." He'd watch to see whether they'd obey them, but that really wasn't what he wanted to talk about. He leaned forward again and propped his elbows on the table. "What about newcomers altogether? Foreigners? Have you caught wind of any?"

"Belgians, you mean?"

"No. Eastern European, I think. Had a run-in with a bloke the other day in Hammersmith. Swarthy complexion, dark hair."

"Hammersmith?" Dante shook his head and fooled with the fraying hem of his jacket sleeve. "None of my boys go there, not with Whitehall so near."

"No one I know does either. Makes me wonder who this could have been."

Dante leaned into the corner of the booth, his eyes contemplative. "What kind of run-in?"

Barclay gave him the gist of the encounter. "I couldn't place the accent entirely, but definitely not Belgian. I've grown rather familiar with how they sound."

"That you have." But the grin gave way to a grunt. "I've not encountered anyone who meets that description, but I'll put my ear to the ground for you. Have you checked with Martin?"

"Not yet. Haven't had time to go to the East End."

A disbelieving puff of breath accompanied the wave of Dante's hand. "It's closer to you than I am."

"Yeah, but you're prettier than Martin."

Dante's guffaw filled the pub, brightened it. "No arguing facts. What about Claw?"

Barclay just sent him a look. "Haven't been desperate enough for answers to try *him*. Last time I tried to set foot in Hackney . . ."

"Well, I've a crew headed into his territory tomorrow. I'll have them ask about it. Say"—he leaned across the table, pitched his voice low—"I heard there was a score went down last week on the Isle of Dogs—something from the docks. That you?"

"Not me." Though he'd heard of it too, and it had made a strange little trill go through him. It had been a clever hoist. "I told you, I'm out."

"Right, man. Right."

Barclay rolled his eyes at his friend's smirk. "Believe or don't. But I'm not going to mess up the sweet deal I've got going."

It was more than that . . . but the words of admission wouldn't come. He couldn't quite bring himself to say that he'd changed. That he'd *wanted* to change. That the big leather book by his pallet on the floor made strange new truths ring in his chest.

Working with your hands the things which are good . . .

He didn't know quite yet how to explain that to someone like Dante, who had known him since his first days on the street. Longer even than Rosemary and Willa. Longer than Pauly.

But his friend knew him. His eyes went soft. "You sure you didn't find a girl? Don't know what else would make a man change his ways so fully."

"No girl." Though even as he said it, sapphire blue eyes sprang to mind.

But that was ridiculous. Evelina Manning might be pretty, but there was no use entertaining any notions there—it was one thing for a well-to-do bloke to marry a poor girl. He could support her. Quite another for a poor bloke to take an interest in a well-to-do girl, who would then have to sink to his level.

And he'd never seen the point in starting something he couldn't see ending in marriage, not given all the children that were his responsibility. But he'd never met a girl interested in sharing that responsibility, so . . .

"You ought to find one, I'm telling you." Dante lifted his mug. The ale remained at the same level it'd been at before when he lowered it again. "Clara has a sister."

Barclay chuckled and scooted out. "That wouldn't set tongues to wagging in Hammersmith at all." Not that he'd let it stop him, if he fell for a girl of Dante's race rather than his own. But it would require moving the family to a neighborhood more accepting of such things, unless he wanted to invite hardship for everyone. As it was, Lucy and Nigel always took care to use the back entrance at the houses in Hammersmith—Lucy's insistence, not his. She wasn't one to invite trouble.

"Yeah, why haven't you had us over for dinner yet, mate?" Laughing at his own joke, Dante reached to shake again. "I'll catch you at Pauly's when I've answers."

Barclay gripped his hand. "Appreciate it. Come for dinner there, at least, when you do—on me."

"You know I never turn down a meal."

"See you soon." He pivoted away, called out "Oi!" in greeting to a few other passing acquaintances on his way out, and strode back toward the tube stop.

By the time he'd regained Hammersmith, the afternoon's light was fading into evening's. The girls would have a meal on the table soon for the little ones—others in the city might complain about shortages, but what they considered short, his family considered ample. There would be chatter about that day's lessons in school, whining about algebra—Barclay grinned at the memory of finding the prim and proper Miss Manning sitting on the floor beside Fergus on Saturday, poring over his textbook—all the things that equaled home and family. He'd spend a few minutes with them.

And then venture out again to pay a visit to the clockmaker.

EIGHT

Evelina had forgotten how laborious evenings were with Mother and Aunt Beatrice both in attendance. Or perhaps she'd never really known—because never before had she managed to lose a fiancé. Now, however, she had discovered new levels of Mother's silent seething and her aunt's acidic tongue.

She rather wished Mother would simply shout, like Barclay Pearce's sister had done the other day when she stomped in. Or that Aunt Beatrice would actually deliver one of her insults *to* Evelina, instead of just *about* her, as if she were not there in the room.

They'd dined early, since her aunt insisted that meals ought to be taken at six, twelve, and six, precisely. Which meant, now that the last of the strawberry cake had been removed—*"Oh, I see there was sugar in the house, after all,"* Mother had said—there was still an interminable evening ahead of them.

Aunt Beatrice scowled at her empty plate. "I do wish your daughter had managed to learn to play an instrument better, Judith. She could have entertained us of an evening."

"Evelina has many talents." Papa winked at her, then stood from the table. "Though if you'll excuse me, ladies, I still have just a bit of work to finish this evening."

If only she could join him in his workshop—Papa never minded, but Mother always protested it hotly. And Aunt Beatrice thought it an affront against nature for a daughter to have anything to do with her father's work.

Her aunt heaved a dramatic sigh. "What a shame that you're deprived of your husband's company so frequently, Judith, because of his unfortunate need to be in a profession. Would that you had married a gentleman like Mr. Wycombe."

Mother's smile looked positively pinched. "Well, we cannot all have been as fortunate as you, Bea."

Papa froze in the dining room's door, his hand clutched into a fist. His lips were thin, tight. He wouldn't say anything—he never did—but Evelina knew it nettled him.

He pivoted back to face his sister-in-law. "If you find your sister's husband such a disappointment, and what I have earned with my *trade* so very objectionable, then you are welcome to stay in your *own* home when you are in Town instead of mine, Beatrice. We will not be offended."

Evelina's jaw dropped open. Never in her life had she heard Papa actually respond to Aunt Beatrice's prods. No one responded to Aunt Beatrice's prods.

As evidenced by the shocked gasp from the tight-laced interloper. "Well!" She stood, tossing her napkin to the table. "I'll not stay where I'm not welcome. Really, Judith, if Cecil did not want me here—"

"Of course he wants you here!" Mother's eyes were wide, her hands pressed to the edge of the table, her form caught halfway out of her chair. "I don't know what's come over him."

Aunt Beatrice narrowed her beady eyes at Evelina. "Distress over the disgrace of a broken engagement, no doubt. Your daughter will never find another match as stellar as Basil Philibert."

Evelina stood too, letting her chair's legs scrape against the floor in the process. "Or perhaps Papa does not care to be insulted in his own home. Have you considered *that* as a possible cause for his distemper?"

"Evelina!"

As if it weren't bad enough that she'd been tossed over in favor of war. Did she really have to suffer through both her mother's and her aunt's eternal commentary on it? With a shake of her head, she followed in her father's wake.

"You will not go down to that workshop, young lady!"

She gritted her teeth until they ached. "I was going to take a promenade. Exercise is good for a girl's figure, after all."

"At this time of day? Not without a chaperone, you don't."

The bell buzzed, and Evelina made a beeline for the door. She didn't much care who it was on the other side—they were going to be her escape, whether they liked it or not. Long before Williston could rouse himself from his chair, Evelina pulled open the front door.

Barclay Pearce met her appearance with lifted brows. "Miss Manning, how do you do? Is Williston all right?"

"Of course he is. Though if you value your life, you'll turn and leave right now, and take me with you." She glanced over her shoulder.

Mr. Pearce peered over it as well. "You look as though you're running from a fire-breathing dragon."

"Exactly right. And there she is now—one of a matching pair of them." It was uncharitable, but at the moment, she didn't care.

Mother emerged from the dining room with a face that their guest probably mistook for neutral, even pleasant. If he was blind to the rage boiling in her eyes. "You forget your manners, Evelina dear. How many times must I remind you to let Williston answer the door so he might announce our guests properly?" She gave Mr. Pearce her loveliest, emptiest smile. "Forgive my daughter, sir."

Evelina saw the slight flicker of her mother's eyes as she took him in from top to toe—the derby he even then swiped from his head, the impeccable suit of clothes, the unremarkable face. She'd be noting that his shirt was obviously not ready-made, that his cufflinks gleamed polished silver. And since she was completely unaware of the lack of furniture in his house and the fact that he was one of twelve adopted children, it was possible she'd deem him an acceptable escort and let Evelina escape.

"He isn't a guest." Papa's voice came from the basement stairs, where he had apparently not gotten more than halfway down. "I have issued him a standing invitation to drop by of an evening to learn a bit of my *trade*."

From the dining room came Aunt Beatrice's ever-reliable sniff.

Mr. Pearce looked perfectly at ease, even smiled as he said, "If I've come on an inconvenient evening—"

"It's a fine evening, Mr. Pearce." Papa appeared at the top of the stairs again, polishing his glasses on the bottom of his waistcoat in the way that Mother hated. "Do come in. My dear, this is Mr. Barclay Pearce, a new friend of mine and Evelina's. Mr. Pearce, my wife, Judith. And sniffing in the dining room in outrage is her sister, Mrs. Beatrice Wycombe, whose late husband was not so unfortunate as to be reduced to a trade."

To his credit, Mr. Pearce didn't miss a beat. Just bowed and said, "How do you do, ma'am?" as if such introductions were made every day.

Mother's mouth had gone tight. "How do you do? Evelina, do get out of the young man's way so he can join your father."

Evelina lifted her chin. "Papa, didn't you say you had to finish that mantel clock? It wouldn't be too much of an inconvenience if Mr. Pearce escorted me down the street and back, would it? I'm desperate for a breath of air."

Papa's lips twitched. "That would be no trouble to me at all, if our friend doesn't object."

Mother's cheek twitched at the second use of *friend* for a man who was obviously not as well off as his clothes indicated. "I really don't think Evelina—"

"I'd be delighted." Barclay Pearce—who would thereafter be known as her new best friend—clapped his hat back on his head. "It's a beautiful evening. Shame to waste it all inside."

Mother, in true form, kept on smiling. "Very well, then. Don't forget your hat, dearest."

Blast. It was upstairs, and she knew well that Mother would trail her up.

Which she did, of course. Going so far as to close Evelina's bedroom door behind her before hissing, "What are you about? Who *is* that man?"

"Barclay Pearce. He wants to learn a bit of clockmaking." Where had she tossed her blighted hat when she got home earlier? She hadn't put it away in its box, had she? That would be unlike her.

"Your room is in ruins again, I see. How you ever intend to keep a house—"

"What does it matter, Mother?" There, on her bed, where it blended in rather well with her pillows. Evelina hurried over to it and snatched it up. "Basil is gone." She spun back for the door.

Mother stood sentinel in front of it, hands planted on her hips, ready to breathe fire.

Perhaps the Admiralty could just unleash *her* on the unsuspecting Germans. The war would be over in hours.

"And *why* is Basil gone, hmm? If I learn it has anything to do with that young man downstairs . . ."

"Oh, for goodness' sake. I barely know him."

"You certainly ran to the door quickly enough when he arrived for his 'standing invitation.' Have you forgotten your betrothed so soon?"

Did she really think that of her? Her dinner turned sour in her stomach. And her anger froze. And her words went heavy and still. "Excuse me, Mother. You're in the way, and I don't want to keep him waiting."

"I'm not moving until I get a straight answer from you. What happened between you and Basil?"

Why could she not ask it in a soft voice? With eyes that begged for trust? Why could she not come closer, perhaps sit upon her bed? Maybe even reach for her hand as Papa had done?

Evelina drew in a breath. "I told you already. He wants someone who loves him. And he doesn't think I'm capable of such feelings."

"Foolish—" *Please say* man. *Take my side.* "—girl. Why did you not give him the words if he requested them?"

"Words weren't enough. Nothing was enough. I tried."

"Not hard enough, it would seem." Mother stepped aside with a shake of her head. "He'll come around while he's away. Just be sure you don't give him reason to doubt you in the meantime. Make sure that Mr. Barclay—"

"Pearce. Barclay Pearce."

She waved a dismissive hand. "As if it matters. Be sure he doesn't get the wrong idea from you, Evelina. You'll wait for Basil."

It had been her first reaction too—but coming from Mother, as a command . . . A bit of life returned to her limbs. "What if I don't want to wait for Basil?"

"I beg your pardon?"

"What if I don't want to waste the next months or even years waiting for a man who made it quite clear he doesn't want me? Why should I put my whole life on hold for him? For this blasted war?"

"Watch your tongue." Now Mother drew near, but not to offer any compassion. To shake a finger under her nose. "You'll not toss away this match we worked so hard for like so much rubbish. You'll never find a better husband, Evelina. You certainly won't settle for someone like—"

"Like Papa? Someone who has to work for what he has?" She

lifted her chin and brushed past her mother, tugged open the door. "I only wish I *could* find a man like him."

"Don't walk away from me, young lady."

Given that she was already out the door, she made no pretense of obeying that command. Just charged for the stairs, down them, and offered Barclay Pearce the brightest smile she could conjure up. "Ready!"

Something about the way his eyes flicked knowingly from her to the stairs, the way he smiled and offered his arm, made her quite certain that he knew exactly what conversation had just passed above his head. Knew it and decided to help.

"Shall we, then?"

The moment they were out of doors, that beautiful slab of wood between them and Mother, she whispered, "You are officially my best friend. I'm in your debt."

"Rubbish. We all have family woes now and then. I'm happy to help if I can." He led her down the steps and then paused. "Which direction do you fancy?"

"It hardly matters." Whichever way they went, neighbors would see and whisper. And then when word got out that Basil was on the Continent in the army, there would be assumptions. There were always assumptions.

She didn't care. Let them assume. "Is your sister speaking to you yet? Elinor?"

"Of course. Unless I dare to make a suggestion about the smallest thing—then I am instantly a tyrant again." He sighed, exaggerated and long. "Women. Begging your pardon."

"Sometimes I quite agree with you." She glanced over her shoulder toward their house, where Mother no doubt stood at a window, straining to watch them. Unless she'd deigned to descend into Papa's workshop and lambast him for his role in it all. "Though to be fair, men aren't any better."

"Perhaps we ought then to exclaim, 'People!' and leave it at that."

"Indeed." She repositioned her hand in the crook of his elbow. "Why do you not leave the reprimanding of your sister to your parents? Or are they . . . ?"

He glanced down at her, his pale blue eyes clear and serious. "My father died when I was just a boy. My mother . . . I have no idea where she is. I was ten when we were separated."

"I suppose I meant your adopted parents."

"I haven't any." He turned his gaze straight ahead, kept his posture perfect. "Not legally, if that's what you mean. There's Pauly. He took me in, as much as he dared. Gave me a meal a few times a week."

"But all those siblings—you said you were adopted."

"By each other." He looked to her again, measuring. Apparently finding whatever it was he searched for, since he continued. "We're orphans, all of us. Either through our parents' deaths or abandonment. So we banded together. Made our own way. Does that shock you?"

It should, perhaps. And maybe would have, had she learned it a week ago. But at the moment, it seemed the most natural thing in the world. The most beautiful. "Inspires me, more like. You've built a wonderful family. Absent fire-breathing dragons."

His laugh echoed off the buildings on either side of the street. "Ellie might disagree."

"Somehow I doubt it. She obviously loves you. All of them do."

The pronouncement that would have made her heart swell earned an easy, happy shrug from her companion. "I'm their brother. And they're mine, and my sisters. That's all that matters."

If only it were really so simple. She turned her face toward the setting sun, wishing it were a little hotter, a little more intense. "You can ask. About the other night. You saw enough to get the gist of what happened anyway."

Silence ticked. And then his hand brushed over where hers rested against his arm. A quick touch, then a retreat. "I don't need to ask. I know an idiot when I see one. You're better off without him."

"Am I?" No one else would say so—even Papa. What was she to do with her life if she didn't marry? She could march for the vote, but not without her sister suffragettes, and they all refused to act right now. She could talk to managers and factory owners on behalf of the workers, but that hardly filled all her days—and left her to return to a mother ready to berate her for her every venture into the unfashionable world. Not to mention that there were still those who refused to listen to her simply because she was unmarried. As though the lack of a ring on her finger made her opinions less worthy. "I'm not so sure."

"I am."

"How?" She didn't really mean to ask—he was only trying to make her feel better, he wouldn't have an actual answer anyway.

He apparently didn't realize that. He looked down at her again, their gazes tangling. "Because he mistook your strength for weakness—and your defense for offense. That's not what you need, Evelina. It's not what anyone needs."

The fact that he was right made that knot inside loosen for the first time in days. Which in turn made her decide to overlook the fact that he'd used her given name without permission. With so many siblings running about, no doubt he was more accustomed to familiarity than most of the men she knew. "You're rather wise, Barclay Pearce."

His chuckle warmed her like the noonday sun. "Mind telling Ellie that?"

"Not at all. When I come over to help Fergus with his algebra, I'll be sure to mention it."

"Hmm." He glanced behind them, toward home. "Think you still can, now that your mother's home?"

"Oh, I think it became all the more imperative that I keep my word. Can't let a lad down, you know."

"Ferg'll be glad to hear it."

Silence fell for a few easy steps, and the spring air cooled noticeably around them as the sun dipped behind the tallest of the roofs. She ought to have retrieved a wrap as well as a hat when she stormed upstairs. "And how is Olivia doing with the leg braces?"

"I think at this point she still quite prefers the crutches. But she understands the point of the things. She's not giving up."

"Good." She cast about in her mind for another topic. She could ask about the rest of his siblings, to be sure. But that was easy. And given that he'd already been witness to the most difficult of her own circumstances, she rather wanted to know something more about *him*. "So . . . your work for the Admiralty. What kinds of errands do they set you on?"

His grin flashed, but he aimed it at the street ahead of them. "Well, today I stole some petrol."

"No, you didn't."

"I did, actually. The DID—director of intelligence—had a man who needed to get to a place, and he hadn't the petrol to get him there nor the time to requisition it through the usual channels. So there you go. He says, 'Steal me petrol, Pearce,' and I say, 'How much, sir?'"

A little laugh slipped through her lips. "All right, perhaps I *do* believe you, in that case. I daresay I would steal petrol, too, if the DID commanded it. Is he your direct superior?"

"Not exactly."

"Then . . . ?"

He halted at the intersection, looked down at her again. "I work for a friend of his. I don't know his official rank or whatnot, just that he seems to know more government officials than does the king himself, and he pays well."

He looked utterly serious. And *sounded* utterly serious. And could, perhaps, *be* utterly serious. But if that were true, then

. . . "So you're not a Navy man but are some sort of agent of the Crown?"

"I don't know what I am, Evelina." That sounded utterly true as well, given the morose exhalation that accompanied it. "But the war will end at some point, and I'll have to decide, I suppose, what I'll be then. What the Lord wants me to be."

If there were a proper response to such a confession, she didn't know it. And still didn't know quite how to classify this man. What was it about him that made her think he hid secrets behind his light blue eyes, mysteries under his smile? Why did he at once reminded her of the shadows she'd skirted that morning in Hackney and the sunshine that had chased them away?

"Stop."

Perhaps it was just that he came from a different world. Perhaps *from* those shadows. Though she, more than anyone, ought to know not to judge a person by them, after all the hours she'd spent championing those who could never afford to stray far from a factory's doors.

"Evelina—*stop*. He's back." He pulled her closer to his side, his gaze locked on something behind her. And his face transformed into the one she'd first seen upon him as he'd stared down—

"He, as in the mugger?" She jerked her head around. Where was he?

Movement caught her eye more than a shape. Movement that quickly vanished.

Mr. Pearce muttered a word she'd never heard but whose general sentiments were familiar enough. His arm tightened under her hand, as if he were coiling, ready to take action. But then it unwound. "He'll be long gone by the time I get you safely home." And Mr. Pearce wouldn't, apparently, abandon her.

"What is he doing here? Casing something?" That was the word, wasn't it? Casing?

His eyes still searched the shadows. "Thieves usually avoid

this section of the city—too many uniforms about." He said it like he knew—and then shook his head and nudged her forward again. "Did he say anything to you the other night before I came up? Anything to give a hint about what he wanted?"

"Not beyond 'nice and easy.' Perhaps he would have, had we not been so rudely interrupted." And now she was joking about it—perhaps Mother was right in calling her a fool. She let him guide her a few steps along before digging in her heels. "You threatened him with thugs—dare I ask why?"

His eyes kept scanning the darkness. "I didn't exactly grow up on a good street like this one, Evelina. I know people. Who know people. But none of them know *him*." Apparently that didn't sit well, given the look on his face. "You should stay in this time of night, unless you're with me."

"Now look here—"

"Or in a large group. But he was watching us. Could just be because of Friday—or he could have had a reason for marking you to begin with."

A shiver coursed through her. "And I suppose I'm safer with you, with your thugs for friends?"

His eyes steadied again, focused on her. "My history isn't all that pretty, but I've been honest about who I am now. I suppose this is where you decide whether you can trust me, or if you'd rather take your chances with the shadows."

She pressed her lips together. Then feared it made her look like Mother so forced them to relax. He didn't speak like the men she knew—the very words were different, more than the cadence. Absent the layer of polish that so cleverly hid the heart. More . . . raw. More blunt. More . . . true. "I get the feeling there's a lot more to you than what you've told me, Mr. Pearce."

"I should hope so." That grin again, flashing and then gone. "But I do know people—that's the most important thing. I know most of the street Arabs, and this bloke—he's not a local. He's an unknown quantity. I don't like it."

He moved forward again. She didn't. Instead, she let her hand slide off his arm. She'd thought him like the factory workers—but he spoke rather of the people they feared. Which meant what? Classified him how? "What are you, Barclay Pearce? Not just an errand boy."

"No. I'm a brother." He caught her fingers in his before she could claim total freedom, pulled her along. "With a lot of friends. Come on. I'll feel better when you're inside."

"I can take care—"

"Of yourself, good. And your parents, too, I hope, and the sniveling aunt. I'll need you to do so until I can identify him." He squinted at her. "I don't suppose you can keep tabs on the rest of the street as well? Is there a neighborhood gossip you can talk to? They're always a wealth of information in this sort of business."

She moved because he tugged her. But she didn't blink. Certainly couldn't find any words.

"Too much?" He scowled. "Understandable, you're a novice. I'll send Lucy round tomorrow. She can pose as a maid applying for positions. Luce is an expert at gossip mongering. That girl could get a tree stump to talk and then keep each and every story straight for the rest of time."

"Wait." Her house was quickly approaching. With her mother. And her aunt. And Papa. "My father—why were you really seeking him out?"

His fingers tightened around hers, reminding her that she hadn't tugged them free like she ought to have done. And his smile looked warm and friendly and not at all like a shadow's should. It was sunshine rather than darkness. Honesty rather than lies. "Because I want to learn from him. And maybe help him, if I can."

She shouldn't take his word. All logic said so. And yet, she believed him.

Mother was right. She *was* a fool. She sighed her defeat.

He must have heard it. He tugged her toward her door. "Sorry to cut our walk short. We'll take another on a different day. Earlier."

What new shells would he shock her with next time? "Mr. Pearce—"

"Are we going to be friends, Evelina?"

An odd question. Perhaps she'd declared it a few minutes earlier, but that had been only a cheeky joke. "Well, I—"

"If so, then you'd better leave off the 'mister' nonsense. I'm just Barclay to pretty much everyone."

"Oh, but I couldn't call you that. Mother would . . ." She stopped at the top of the steps, before the closed door.

Behind her, Barclay chuckled. "An added bonus. Barclay. Lina."

"Blast." She caught her lip between her teeth—barely acquainted, but he could read her too well already. Knew already what made her tick. "Very well. We'll be friends . . . Barclay."

"Good. Now let's get inside. And if possible, don't leave again tomorrow until Lucy's been round. I don't suppose *you* need a maid?"

He opened the door for her, ushered her in.

She had the strangest feeling the world had just shifted under her feet. Thank the Lord she was accustomed to hobbling around even when her footing wasn't sure.

NINE

The halls of the Old Admiralty Building were rather sleepy, on the whole. There was an occasional raised voice from behind a door, but for the most part, the only people in the hallways were men too old to be in the action, but not of a high enough rank to command anything from home—men who shuffled quietly along with their mail carts and seemed genuinely happy to do so, to be doing their bit.

"Good afternoon, Wesley." Barclay tipped his hat to one of his favorite old chaps.

Wesley smiled. "Barclay. How's the weather out there? I do believe I saw a bit of sunshine again."

"You did indeed—second day in a row. I expect rain will move in by nightfall."

"I daresay." The wheels on his cart squeaked as he pushed it along. "If you're on your way to OB 40, I've a stack here for Hope."

"I'm happy to take it." He accepted the mass of envelopes and packages, tucked them under his arm, and walked beside Wesley for another few steps. "How's your rheumatism?"

"Not bad, with the sunshine. That tea you told me about seems to help too."

"Good. I hear the ginger one works just as well as the rose hip, too, if you want variety. I can bring you some next time, if you like."

A knotted hand landed on his shoulder and gave him a friendly pat. "You're a good lad, Barclay. I wouldn't object. Harder to get out to the shops than it used to be—and harder to find what I'm looking for when I do, what with all the shortages."

Shortages had always been a way of life for him—but never a reason to resign himself. Barclay smiled. "There's always a way to find things, if you know the right people."

The old gent laughed—a somewhat wheezing sound that was no less endearing for the whistle. "And I know you, so apparently I've got quite a connection now, haven't I?"

"Oh, indeed. The best connection of them all." With a wink and a grin, he turned to the left when Wesley angled to the right. "Have a good night, Wes."

"Cheerio."

Barclay jogged up the stairs, strode along the corridor, and slipped into the chambers of Room 40 without bothering to knock. He clicked the door shut again behind him and took a moment to survey the far different atmosphere here. The room was crowded with men, some at desks, some leaning against walls, some with papers, some looking upward, lips moving.

"Got it!" one of them shouted even then, dashing back to a clutter of papers in the corner under which there was presumably a piece of furniture.

This was how the war would be won. By the men with pencils in their hands rather than guns. The ones decoding every telegram the Germans sent.

"Barclay!" And one too-intelligent girl who never seemed to care that the world expected her to be more concerned with housekeeping and fashion than with mathematics.

Margot De Wilde shot out of her chair and came to his side. "For me?"

"Only if you are Commander Hope in disguise." He winked at her with all the affection he'd give his own sisters. He counted her as one—her brother would marry Willa in a few short weeks, after all. If that didn't make the girl family, he didn't know what would. "Where's your mother?"

"Running something to one of the other secretaries. Do I need to come over and help Fergus with his mathematics?"

"No, we found another tutor. Though we certainly appreciate your willingness."

Her smirk said she knew well Fergus himself hadn't much appreciated it. "Very well, then. I will see you at Pauly's tomorrow."

"Don't work too hard." He said it because he knew it would make her roll her eyes, which was the closest thing to a normal adolescent reaction she ever made.

He slid the stack of post onto the corner of Hope's desk, earning him a fleeting smile from the man who sat at it. Herbert Hope ran the day-to-day operations of the place . . . and apparently had proven himself invaluable by translating the civilians' decryptions into naval jargon that his superiors would take seriously. "Evening, Pearce."

"Hope. V said Captain Hall was here, and I was to see him."

"He was, yes. I believe he popped over to Room 53 to discuss something with Knox."

The man never seemed to stay still for long. The last time V had sent him to meet with Hall, he'd ended up chasing the man halfway across London. Today at least, he had only to go down the corridor.

He found the director just stepping out, his quick blinks taking in everything in the hallway, Barclay included. He offered a smile. "Pearce. V said you'd be by. What do you have for me?"

Barclay pulled out the letter from his pocket—which ought to have been delivered to a general on the other side of London.

"Perfect." The admiral snatched it, flipped it over. "We'll make a copy, and you can slip this one back into his post tomorrow. Come round to my office about noon."

"Yes, sir. Anything else?"

"Not tonight. Good work, Pearce. Oh—wait."

Barclay paused midpivot. "Sir?"

"V mentioned you saw plans for a synchronization gear. Have you learned anything about it yet?"

He sighed. "Manning, the clockmaker who's working on it, is having a bit of trouble. Nothing we can't work out, but it'll take some time. Still, he gave me leave to jot down what he has thus far." He reached into the inner pocket of his jacket and found the folded paper he'd slipped into it that morning.

Hall unfolded it, eyes skimming over it all. "Tell him we'll find him whatever he needs. And then let V or me know what he requires. We'll get it to him. If there's even a chance this could work, we'll get it to him. To think of the advantage this could give our aces . . ."

"I know, sir. I'll do what I can."

"I have no doubt. V only ever sends me the best."

Barclay smiled and peeled away with a rather lazy salute when he reached the stairs—Hall continued straight ahead with a chuckle.

Sunlight greeted Barclay after he'd jogged down the stairs. Sunlight and a familiar flash of grey—bowler hat, suit of clothes, and silver-gold hair.

V.

Barclay held back a moment. Then . . . well, he couldn't say exactly why the urge to follow suddenly seized him. But he'd learned over the years to obey those instincts. Had begun to wonder, even, if they were more than instincts. If perhaps they were what Peter called nudging from the Spirit. God trying to lead him and guide him.

Sometimes he thought it couldn't be that—that the Lord of the universe couldn't possibly be so concerned with Barclay Pearce, a nobody from the London streets.

But perhaps if one viewed God like a master clockmaker, then every cog, every gear, every spring was important. If one was out of line, no matter how small and insignificant, the entire device would fail. Why *shouldn't* the Lord love each member of humanity with the same level of care Cecil Manning had given that watch Barclay had found in a gutter?

And if the Master Clockmaker took such care with each cog, oughtn't said cogs have the good sense to obey Him when they felt that nudge? A spring that wouldn't coil, after all, would be replaced in a watch.

He didn't much fancy being replaced in God's world. He liked his place in it.

He slid into the alley V had gone down, careful to remain a fair distance back.

Trailing the man was a harder task than it would have been with anyone else. Whoever he was, V had the instincts of a street rat, as finely hewn as Barclay's own. Every time he got within twenty yards of him, the man seemed to feel his presence and would pause—seeming to look into a shop window or read a street sign on a building's wall but really looking about to try to spot him.

Barclay ducked over and again into the cover of another shop or down an alleyway. After fifteen minutes, he opted for a different tack and took to moving parallel. Risky—if V turned off, Barclay wouldn't know it. But more effective. He stopped pausing so often.

They seemed to be remaining in Hammersmith, but rather than aiming toward the bridge, where Barclay's new home was stationed, and the Mannings', they made their way to the other end of the borough. Perhaps V meant to take a turn through Bishop's Park. Or had business at the bishop's retreat at Fulham Palace—it was hard to say.

But the man turned neither into the park nor the church's land—he headed for a residential street, and his pace quickened as he did.

Was it possible that this was his rabbit's hole? It was strange to think that V had a home. He must, of course, but . . . here? In this pretty, perfectly normal neighborhood?

Barclay found a vantage point from a little garden across the street from where V was aimed. He could be visiting someone. More business, perhaps.

Except that he pulled keys from his pocket as he sprang rather jauntily up the steps. Inserted them, twisted, let himself in.

"Hmm." Interesting. Barclay leaned against a tree and watched a moment more through the cover of spring-green leaves.

Whatever chamber took up residence on the street side had its curtains flung wide. He could see a lamp come on within, and a shadow passed before it that looked rather like V's shape.

Another joined it—this one decidedly more petite, and rather feminine. V leaned down, embraced her.

A wife? Daughter?

Strange to think of the enigma that was his employer having a family. Someone to welcome him home. Someone who must wonder where he went when he showed up at Pauly's in Poplar of a random evening, long after darkness had fallen, or met one of Barclay's family in a random park halfway across the city.

Well. No point in lurking here all evening long. Careful to remain out of view of that window, Barclay made his way back out of Fulham, past Whitehall and Charing Cross, toward Hammersmith Bridge.

When he turned onto his own street, he spotted the Fenleys loading into their automobile, and Mrs. Markham from two doors down was fussing, as usual, with the climbing roses that grew along her bit of wrought-iron fencing. Barclay lifted a hand in greeting but didn't pause for conversation. He instead withdrew his own key and let himself into his own house and paused to glance over his shoulder to be sure no one was watching *him* from the cover of an across-the-street garden.

Satisfied, he stepped in and closed the evening out. And smiled when he heard the voice from the drawing room saying something about sines and cosines.

A peek showed him Evelina was on the couch they'd saved from a rubbish heap, Olivia looking snug and half asleep in her lap. Poor thing was no doubt wearing herself out trying to get used to the leg braces. Fergus had unearthed a scarred, rickety-looking wooden chair from somewhere and positioned it at ninety degrees to the couch. His books rested on the sofa cushion between them.

They obviously had things well in hand, so Barclay tossed his hat onto the rack—it landed perfectly on the closest hook and swung in a few tight circles before rocking to a halt—and continued down the hall toward the kitchen.

Lucy stood at the stove in what she called her shabby clothes. Evidence that she had been out supposedly searching for work as a domestic on Evelina's street, as he'd asked her to do. He could always count on Lucy. "Find a position? I hear Mrs. Manning is a delight."

She shot him a grin and kept stirring the pot of fragrant something-or-another. "Do you now? I rather heard that she's run off every lady's maid and domestic she's ever hired within a half year. And that the old butler stays on because he answers to the mister of the Mannings, who is as pleasant and easy as his wife is difficult."

He pulled out a chair at the table and made himself comfortable. "And you heard that from . . . ?"

"The cook at the house across the street, who warned me against even knocking on their door." Lucy laughed and reached for a little dish of some red powder. A pinch of it went into the pot. He couldn't have said what it was, but since they'd been able to afford some spices, Lucy'd developed quite a hand with them.

"What of our anonymous bloke? Anyone else see him?"

"A few." With a tap of her spoon against the side of the pot, Lucy set her face into an expression of bemusement. "There was a footman who had to run him off from a garden—but that was a week ago."

A couple days before the attempted mugging. "And others?"

"Just a few who had spotted him. Doesn't exactly blend in, to hear them tell it—someone was afraid he was a German informant and reported it to the authorities, but of course there was neither hide nor hair of him to be found when the bobbies arrived."

"Hmm." He wasn't German, that Barclay could tell—but that didn't mean, he supposed, that he wasn't working for them or their allies. "Anyone have any theories as to why he's haunting that particular street?"

"Scads of them. There's a chauffeur at the end of the street with a gambling problem—the housekeeper at Number 12 thinks he owes the bloke money. The maid at 17 is all but certain that he's the husband of a girl with whom her employer had been dallying. And the footman who ran him off would swear on his mother's grave, God rest her soul, that it was Prince Adalbert himself, spying for the kaiser."

Because emperors were *always* sending their sons off to spy on Englishmen in Hammersmith. "Well, that isn't farfetched at all."

"The only bit that might actually be helpful is that the chauffeur who likes the tables thinks he saw him going toward Chiswick. That at least gives you a direction."

"You're the best, Luce."

"Oh—and we had a wire from Rosie while you were out. They'll be back in Town tomorrow. And there's another letter from Georgie, just arrived. You can read it to us all after dinner."

"Excellent." He stood, moved to drop a kiss onto the top of her head, and snatched a steaming roll from the sheet of them by the stove. "You're learning to bake too?"

"I found a book."

"That's my girl." With a chuckle, he tore off a bite of the bread and tasted it. "Good as any from a bakery."

She gave him an exaggerated curtsy.

"Anything else of interest?"

"Well, as a matter of fact." She leaned close, eyes sparkling. "I also heard that Miss Manning's fiancé ran off and joined up—probably to escape having to claim a relationship to her mother—and that she's already been seen out strolling with some sandy-haired fellow."

"Any mention of how handsome this sandy-haired fellow was?"

She laughed and straightened again. "For a man who's always taken such care *not* to draw undue attention . . ."

"Some occasions call for it." He took another bite of the roll and wondered how hard it would be to get his hands on some butter these days.

No more difficult, surely, than tracking down Prince Adalbert's double.

TEN

Evelina repositioned the fob in the display case, considered for a moment, then moved it again. There, better. It would catch the afternoon sunlight now and draw the eye from the street.

"Are you finished fussing, Lina?"

She turned with a smile for Papa, who had put his topcoat and hat back on and had his satchel in hand. "No, I think I've another hour or two of fussing in me yet."

He chuckled and motioned her toward the door. "Come, my sweet. You cannot avoid your mother forever."

"I can try, can't I?" Mother seemed to get more tightly wound each and every day she was home. Her face blanker and blanker. Her posture ever more perfect. No doubt as a direct result of the ever-spreading gossip about how Basil had fled to the front rather than marry Evelina. And the fact that Barclay had dropped by four evenings out of five. "Perhaps if I could hide in your workshop with you . . ."

"I am not *hiding*. I am *working*." But the corner of his lips twitched up a bit. He opened the door, setting the bell above it to tinkling, and popped open the large umbrella they'd share on the walk back.

Sometimes she very nearly asked what had ever possessed him to marry Mother. But there were lines even she wouldn't cross. And she almost remembered a softer mother, from before polio had struck their house. Perhaps she had been different as a young woman. Perhaps they had fallen in love.

Or perhaps Mother had simply said the words when they were demanded.

Though why she would have lied, when Papa wasn't exactly the catch that Uncle Wycombe had been in the eyes of society, she didn't know.

But he was the best at what he did. He'd achieved the highest hallmarks of his chosen field. And he was *him*. Perhaps even Mother had once understood the allure of that.

"Lina . . ." Papa pulled the door of his shop firmly closed behind them so none of the rain-bejeweled wind would find its way inside. "Young Mr. Pearce mentioned that the chap who tried to mug you is still lurking about. Have you seen him again?"

Her muscles all went stiff at the mention of him. She looped her arm through her father's and shoved her free hand into the protective pocket of her jacket. "Not since last Monday, no." Which had been nearly a week ago. "Surely he's long gone by now."

"The neighbors have seen him, apparently. It makes me uneasy—he has already attacked you once. I don't understand why the authorities cannot find these people and lock them up."

"Good question."

"I would feel infinitely more at ease if you refrained from venturing out alone."

"But Papa—"

"Now, listen." His hand covered hers, tamping down that burst of frustration that bordered on panic.

He couldn't take away what morsel of independence she had. He *couldn't*. It would mean all day, every day with Mother and

Aunt Beatrice, doing nothing but embroidering linens for a home she'd never have.

"I know you value your freedom. But you cannot value it more than your life, Evelina. And if anything were to happen to you, I'd never forgive myself. Not when it's my job to protect you." He squeezed her hand. "You're the most important person in the world to me. You know that. You know how it frightened me when you took part in those marches."

"Oh, Papa." He sounded so sorrowful that an empathetic pang of it filled her chest too. "I don't *invite* harm, you know that."

"And it was a risk you took for a cause in which you firmly believe. I know that, which is why I never forbade you from doing it, nor from visiting all those factories. But, my sweet, there is someone out there who has tried once already to harm you. And so I beg you—do not go out alone."

The fact that his request was reasonable did nothing to make it settle peaceably in her chest. "I've an appointment later this week with Mr. Dramwell, though." Another note had come round from Katy. The surly Mr. Clarke had gone straight back to his previous ways after a mere three days.

"Dram will be happy enough to come to you, as well you know."

Her sigh no doubt sounded as testy to his ears as it did to her own. "To the Fenleys' at least?"

"I would prefer you didn't. But Mr. Pearce has offered to accompany you on whatever outings you desire until this fellow has been apprehended. You'll simply have to restrict them to the afternoons, when he is available."

Her lips curled up. "Mother will have a fit."

"Will she?" Papa did an admirable job of keeping his own lips perfectly in line. "She'll just have to adjust to the idea. For your safety."

Evelina chuckled. She wasn't sure why her father had taken so quickly to Barclay, but his esteem eased a few of her own concerns over the shadows in his story. Papa was an excellent judge of character.

They turned the corner, their shoes splashing through the puddle that always formed where the pavement dipped.

"I cannot decipher this fellow." Papa's voice sounded far away. And worried. "Lurking around for weeks on end, but never *doing* anything. Except that night when he apprehended you. It is alarming. Why did he target you specifically?"

A question she'd lain awake contemplating on more than one night. "Perhaps it had something to do with Basil."

"With Basil?"

"He had political enemies, didn't he? Those none too happy at the support he'd been gaining. What if someone thought to use me against him? But then after he broke things off, this chap wouldn't know whether it would still work. It would render him immobile, so to speak, but might not make him change his mind entirely about his plan."

A thoughtful hum filled Papa's throat. "It is as reasonable a theory as any I have developed."

And meant that she ought to be safe now, more or less. Soon that fellow would realize that Basil had rejected her, and obviously he didn't care enough about her to rush home for her sake.

For that matter, he'd removed himself from the world of politics, at least for the duration of the war. So whatever enemies he had in parliamentary circles ought to be appeased for now.

If they wanted to be angry with him again later, they could take it out on whatever pretty debutante he found to look at him with adoration and turn to mush in his arms.

"*You* like Mr. Pearce well enough, don't you?"

"Hmm?" Jerking herself out of her future jealousy, she angled a look up at Papa again. "Why?"

"Well, I don't want to confine you to an escort you don't like. If he doesn't suit, I could hire someone."

"Oh, there's no need for that. I like Barclay quite well." And, she had to admit, enjoyed calling him by his given name when Mother was around to overhear it. That tic in Mother's cheek never failed to make an appearance when she did.

"He's a bright young man. I never need to show him more than once how to perform a task. If he weren't already employed, I would seriously consider hiring him on as an apprentice." He moved the umbrella a bit, to better cover her right shoulder. "The other night I was telling him about the Great Clock—he never fails to ask the most insightful questions. Not to mention his interest in my . . . dabblings."

His "dabblings" had taken various forms over the years. She couldn't pretend to keep up with them all. "I'm glad he's proving a good companion, Papa."

"Mmm. Though if we want to truly test his mettle, we ought to see if he can handle your Aunt Beatrice. What say you? Shall we have him over to dine one evening soon?"

A laugh filled her throat. "That would be cruel."

"I think he might enjoy it, actually. He certainly never balks at your mother." He patted her hand again. "Let's do. If he emerges unscathed, I'll recommend him for knighthood."

She laughed again, then let the rain fill the silence as they finished the walk home. And somehow, she wasn't surprised when Williston greeted them upon their entrance with the announcement that Mr. Pearce was in the drawing room. Talk of the devil and he doth appear, as they said.

Mother occupied her usual chair, her hands folded in her lap and her smile practically painted upon her face. Evelina couldn't see Barclay from where she stood shrugging out of her damp jacket, but she had a feeling he looked far more at ease. He usually did.

She handed over her mackintosh, wiped her feet, and preceded Papa into the drawing room.

As expected, Barclay sat in the uncomfortable chair opposite Mother's as though it were the most comfortable seat in the world. No strain evident upon his face, though if Mother had been treating him to her silent stare, she didn't quite know how he'd managed it.

At least Aunt Beatrice wasn't in attendance. She probably had some charity meeting or another to attend—the only respite they ever got from her, despite Papa's shocking invitation for her to go torment her own household.

Evelina couldn't remember the last time her aunt had even opened the house in Savoy that Uncle Wycombe had loved so well. Why, when she so obviously found their house lacking?

"Ah, there he is, right on time as always." Mother stood, her spine remaining perfectly straight as she did so. "I'll leave you to entertain your . . . *friend*, Cecil. I had better check on dinner preparations. I had tea sent down to your workshop just a moment ago."

"Thank you, my dear, you are conscientious as always. Good day, Barclay." Papa's eyes gleamed as he took off his spectacles and wiped the speckles of rain from the lenses with his waistcoat.

Mother's lips thinned.

"And speaking of dinner preparations, Lina and I were just discussing how we've been remiss—you ought to dine with us one evening, young man. Isn't that right, my dear? As a thank-you—our Mr. Pearce has graciously offered to escort Evelina about town for the next little while."

"Has he?" Mother's fingers were still knotted together, fingertips pressing hard enough against her hands that they were red. "How kind."

Evelina glanced over at Barclay in time to catch his wink. Which her mother no doubt caught as well.

He grinned. "I'd be delighted."

"Saturday? And invite your sisters and their gentlemen as well. I know Mrs. Manning has been eager to make the acquaintance of the Holsteins and will no doubt crow to her friends at hosting Miss Forsythe and Mr. De Wilde."

Barclay nodded. "Certainly. I know they'll be pleased to join us."

Mother wore her panic like glass—invisible but glinting. She would indeed crow to her friends about it, but the short notice would keep her frantic in the meantime. Of course, to Barclay she said, "I didn't realize you had such esteemed family. I'll just go and check with Mrs. Wright about menu possibilities now, if you'll excuse me." She bustled from the room.

Poor Mrs. Wright would likely quit before the week was out. Which was a shame, because she could do wonders with only a pinch of sugar. Ah well.

Papa smiled just a bit. "I think I'll go and have that tea before I get back to work. Join me in the workshop at your leisure, Barclay—I've a bit of correspondence to attend to." A letter had, as a matter of fact, arrived from his mentor in Bienne before they'd left for the shop. Evelina would have ripped open the envelope then and there—Uncle Herman always told the most amusing anecdotes about the Swiss—but this was Papa. He'd not had the five minutes it would take to read it scheduled into his morning. Correspondence was reserved for afternoons.

She rather expected Barclay to follow her father toward the basement. Instead, he said, "I won't be long behind you." Once Papa had gone, Barclay moved to the window and twitched a finger her way.

Evelina joined him, a knot of dread in her stomach. Was it that man out there again? She nearly refused to look out the window—but no, that was cowardly. If the fellow was there, she wanted to know it. She wanted to know *where*.

But her brows shot up when she saw what he was pointing out. "Lucy! What's she doing out there?"

"She found a cook across the street who will buy her bread. Lets her stay tapped into the gossip."

She watched as his sister sloshed her way through the rain, toward the back entrance of the row of houses opposite. "She didn't mention that she baked."

"Well, she only just learned how a few days ago."

These people . . . Evelina sank to a seat on the arm of the chair. "And already she's selling it?"

"Luce is a whiz in the kitchen."

"And Willa on the violin and Rosemary with a needle and you with things mechanical—tell me, is there anything your family cannot accomplish, between you?"

His grin flashed at her. "Well, we haven't a suffragette among us."

She loosed a sound close enough to a snort that Mother would have been horrified. "At the moment, we're not accomplishing much anyway. I'm afraid the cause has fizzled."

"Well, the world has changed. But it's no reason for you to be disheartened, is it? I rather thought the whole point of the movement was to claim that women could make sound decisions—that they are not weak or inferior."

She leaned into the side of the chair and lifted her brows. "Of course it is."

"Now you've been given the chance to prove it, not just to say it. 'Deeds Not Words'—isn't that one of your mottos? And here's the chance for deeds." He turned from the window, faced her. "How many jobs are women filling these days that were once held by men? Who will be making all the decisions while their husbands and fathers are in the trenches?"

"That's what I've told the women in the factories." A cause the suffragettes had never really taken up—they cared only for their own fight, no one else's. But they were the same, ultimately. "This is their chance to prove themselves."

"Exactly right. Do a good enough job of it, and the voting public will have no choice but to recognize it when they get home from the war."

She certainly hoped he was as trustworthy as Papa seemed to think, because she really couldn't help but like him.

"Evelina. Come here, please."

Could Mother read her mind now? With only the smallest of frustrated huffs, she stood, exchanged a glance with Barclay, and strode into the hall, where Mother stood, scowling.

Actually *scowling*, like Aunt Beatrice. "Mother, you'll get wrinkles!"

Her scowl only deepened. "You've met his family, haven't you? When you insisted upon going to his home to tutor his brother? How many of them are there? I must decide if it would be prudent to simply invite them all."

"Oh." Blast. Mother wouldn't mean to invite the children, just those old enough to have entered society—not that any of them had. And she'd never permit Lucy to enter her house—not through the front, anyway. "You could perhaps invite Retta and Elinor as well. The others are a bit young." Or not fair enough of skin.

It made her arms tingle, there where her pulse thudded in her pale-as-cream wrist. She'd never really paused to consider the injustice of such ideals. But then, she'd never known anyone before with such a colorful family who stood to be left out.

Mother nodded and made as if to leave. Then halted so she could skewer Evelina with a narrow-eyed glare. "And don't think this alters anything, young lady. The fact that he has better connections than one might expect does not change the fact that he is a man of no prospects. You're to have nothing to do with him socially—you will wait for Basil. Understood?"

Fingers curling into her palms, Evelina spun away rather than answer. Stomped back into the drawing room, where Barclay still stood by the window.

He flicked a gaze over her head before settling it on her. Mother must still be there, watching and fuming. Waiting to see some too-warm glance or hushed exchange that she could use as a bludgeon in her next lecture. Waiting, just waiting for Evelina to do something she'd deem wrong.

Well, one was supposed to honor one's parents' wishes, right?

She went up on her toes, slid a hand to the back of Barclay's head, and, before his eyes had time to go wide, pressed her lips to his.

ELEVEN

Barclay had always prided himself on not being easily taken off guard. On anticipating what moves his companions might make next and responding before they could even finish the action. On understanding people in a glance and knowing how to counter them. It was what had helped him survive—to thrive—on the streets.

But when Evelina Manning tossed herself against his chest and pulled his mouth down to her own, he became quickly acquainted with acute, complete surprise.

It took him only a second to realize why she'd done it—to irritate her mother. But even so. That second was all it took for him to register that she smelled of flowers and rain, to note that her lips were as soft as silk. To anchor her against him with his hands on her hips.

He'd spent the majority of his life surrounded by girls—hugging them, kissing their scrapes, mopping their tears—but they were his sisters.

She was not.

"Is she gone?" she murmured against his lips.

Her fingers moved at the base of his neck, toying with his hair. Tying him in knots. Blast it all. He glanced up, past the sapphires of her eyes, to the empty hallway. "No. Still there." God would forgive him the falsehood. Probably. If he remembered to ask for forgiveness later. And convinced himself to mean it.

He angled in for another kiss.

Her fingers knotted in his hair—it needed a trim, and suddenly he was glad of it. Her other arm slid around him. And her lips—they moved under his with a kind of sweet hesitation that tasted like the honey he'd stolen when he was fifteen, when he'd wondered why people put liquid gold in their tea.

Her hand pressed against his back. Eased back to a barely there touch. "I don't see her."

They'd moved half a step, apparently, in a circle. But she hadn't pulled away except for that inch between their mouths.

He smiled. "I do. She's right there."

"Oh, is she?" Her lips turned up, too, in a smile he'd never had cause to see on a woman directed at him.

"Mmm." He moved one of his hands up to rest where her jaw met her neck, where her pulse hammered. Caught her bottom lip between his. Then her top.

Her eyes had slid shut. "I should apologize."

"Yes. Absolutely. Very rude of you." She'd retreat, if he let her. He could feel it in that quiver in the arms that rested against him. Insecurity. Regret.

"And thank you. For playing along."

He traced her cheekbone with his thumb. Who knew rain and flowers could smell so good? "You'll owe me one."

"I assure you, I don't usually . . . And I know you didn't want to . . ."

Her cheek was hot under his hand. It was distracting enough that it took him a moment to realize what she was saying. Another to take in the way she averted her gaze, the way her posture shifted just slightly.

She thought he'd found her kiss distasteful.

There was only one possible explanation for that—Basil Philibert was a blighted idiot.

"Lina." He waited until her gaze crept back upward, met his. Kept his hand there, anchoring her head. His other on her hip, holding her in place. "I usually sit on favors, wait until I really need to call them in. But I think I'll collect the one you owe me now."

Not giving her time to ask what he meant, he leaned in again, kissed her deep and long. Until her arms had gone tight around him, and then loose, and then tight again. Until he was pretty sure he'd never get that scent out of his nose.

Then he pulled away enough to meet her gaze. It was hazy. Heady. He sucked in a long breath. "Are we clear on that point?"

She nodded.

"Because I'd be happy to repeat the lesson."

A smile started in the corners of her mouth. "I may need a reminder later. But just now, I think your point has been made."

"Good." He put a few more inches between them, before he went absolutely mad. Let his hands slide back to his own sides, as she reclaimed hers. "I understand that you wanted to lash out at her. And maybe at him. You don't need to be embarrassed or regretful about that, as I've always been in favor of decisive action. And you get to decide what happens from here." Because he wasn't like Peter or Lukas. He was just Barclay Pearce, semi-reformed thief. She deserved better. "Whether it's a game you want to keep playing or not."

She pressed her lips together. Fiddled with the edge of her sleeve. But she didn't look away.

He backed up another step so he could draw in a clear breath. "But you need to know up front—I play for keeps." He had too much at stake to do otherwise. Too many hearts for which he was responsible.

She nodded and eased to the side, clearing the way between him and the door.

Her answer? Probably. And he couldn't blame her. She was reeling from a broken engagement, under fire from her mother and aunt, and there was an unknown somebody out there who'd already attacked her once. Hardly a time to get involved with someone new. Especially when "involved" would be far from simple, given their very different circumstances. Toss in the fact that they'd known each other all of a week, and she was no doubt far too reasonable to want anything more from him than proof that she was desirable.

But then, he'd built a family from people in worse circumstances, on a shorter acquaintance. They'd pledged to stay together forever, and they'd done it. Sometimes sheer grit was enough.

And sometimes it wasn't.

He dug up half a smile for her and nodded, even made it a few strides toward the door. Then couldn't help but turn back again. Slip back over to her, cup her face between his hands, and press one more soft, lingering kiss to her lips.

"That one was free." With a wink, he left the room.

And he left her smiling.

Mrs. Manning was thankfully *not* anywhere in sight, leaving him a clear path to the basement stairs. And once he was down in the workshop, the scents of oil and metal and Mr. Manning's steaming tea pushed aside those of flowers and rain.

So long as the man couldn't tell at a glance that he'd just been kissing his daughter, he might stand a chance of putting it from his mind. For a while.

Manning looked up from the sheet of paper before him with a steely glint in his eyes.

Uh-oh. Perhaps the man *was* a mind reader. Or had come back up and Barclay hadn't heard the creaking stairs. Not usually one of his failings, but he'd been rather distracted.

"Your connections at the Admiralty—exactly how far do they

extend? For my project?" He nodded toward the stairs. Toward the synchronization gear.

Daring to breathe again, Barclay lifted his brows. "My superior just assured me today that he'd get you anything you need."

"Fortuitous—given that my own acquaintances have just metaphorically patted my head and told me to stick to my toys." Manning balled up the paper and tossed it toward the brazier. "They have access to the Royal Naval Air Service?"

V and Hall would be cheering if they were here. Barclay nodded. "What do you need?"

Manning rounded the bench, strode toward the unfinished mechanism hidden in the shadows, and clasped his hands behind his back. "Well, Mr. Pearce—I'm afraid I need an airplane. Can you get me one of those?"

What an odd day this was turning out to be. Odd . . . but good. Barclay slung his hands into his pockets and let a grin take form on his mouth. He never was one to admit a challenge was beyond his reach. "Consider it got."

"You didn't."

Evelina ignored Gloria's horrified—or perhaps intrigued—whisper and hurried to keep up with Mrs. Knight. She had the Women's Social and Political Union's purple, white, and green pin on her lapel and a bounce in her step. She tugged her friend along. The streets of Westminster were crowded, largely with women, but more men in crisp suits or uniforms appeared as they neared Number 10. "Well, I can't just sit at home and wait for Barclay Pearce to show up when Mrs. Knight needs me. I had no choice but to slip out."

Gloria hissed out a breath and nearly tripped when a guard blocked their path as they turned in at the stately black building. "Well, why did you drag me along? If your mother discovers you're out when you oughtn't to be, we'll both end up in trouble."

Mrs. Knight produced a folded piece of paper, and the guard waved them on.

"Really, Gloria, you need to relax. We are grown women, not children. What could our mothers really do to us?" She craned her head back as they passed through the doorway. She'd visited Westminster Abbey once with Papa, and of course had gone up to see Big Ben and the Great Clock within him, but she'd never had cause to come to Number 10 before.

Gloria looked around as if the very carpets might nip at her heels. "She could send me to Worcestershire with Nellie and Arnold, for starters, and you know how I detest staying at Uncle Mangom's."

Evelina rolled her eyes and followed her mentor through the entrance hall and corridor. As if being sent to the countryside was the most horrible of possibilities. As if it could hold a candle to the icy rage *she* had suffered through the past two days.

They were going to have to revise the entire English language to reflect the force of nature that was Judith Manning. The phrase should no longer be "cold as ice"—they needed to change it to "cold as Judith."

She'd thought her first real respite would be when Mr. Dramwell came to call tomorrow, but when Mrs. Knight's note arrived that morning, it had been like a day of summer in the midst of a snowstorm.

The older woman hesitated for a moment at the end of the hallway and then turned to the left, into what was clearly a waiting room. She gestured for them to hurry. "I could only secure a promise for a ten-minute audience, ladies. We must be succinct and eloquent."

Gloria looked as though she might be sick. "I think I had better wait out here."

Mrs. Knight agreed with a curt nod. "Do try to stay out of anyone's way, Miss Fenley. Politics may be officially suspended, but Number 10 is no less busy for it."

Gloria sank to a seat, pale-faced, upon a stiff-looking chair.

Evelina brushed her hands over her skirt and pretended that their shaking was adrenaline and not fear. The prime minister may be more intimidating than a floor manager, but he couldn't possibly be worse than Mother.

Why in the world had Mrs. Knight wanted *her* along?

Her companion crossed the width of the room and knocked upon a door while Gloria did her best to fade into the upholstery. At the command to enter, Mrs. Knight swept in with a smile that bespoke confidence.

Evelina's stomach wobbled as she followed in her friend's wake.

A man sat at a desk and looked up with a vague smile as they entered, rising just enough to avoid impropriety. A man who was most assuredly not H. H. Asquith. Though of course he wouldn't be. The prime minister surely had scads of men past whom visitors would have to get before they stumbled into *his* domain.

"Mrs. Knight, how do you do? Lovely to see you again. Please, have a seat." He was already sitting again, leaving them the option to either do so at their leisure and prove him ungentlemanly for not waiting or hurry to sit and preserve the appearance of propriety.

They hurried.

Mrs. Knight clutched her bag and leaned forward, toward the massive desk. "Thank you so much for meeting with us, Mr. Sellers. I cannot tell you how much we value your time."

Evelina worked to keep her face free of confusion. She'd thought Mrs. Knight's note had said she'd secured a meeting with the prime minister. Perhaps she'd just said with his office?

Mr. Sellers offered another smile that was vague at best and sneaked a glance down at whatever paperwork was on his desk. "Well, I do owe Mr. Philibert a favor, so I'm happy to meet with his betrothed." His eyes, and his smile, came back up—and focused squarely on Evelina. "You must be very proud of him for serving his country, young lady."

He didn't know that Basil had called off the engagement—apparently the gossip that had been plaguing Hammersmith hadn't made its way to Westminster. But Mrs. Knight had heard—Evelina herself had told her. Why, then, had she put her in this position without so much as a warning?

Evelina fastened on a smile that she knew wouldn't look all that bright. But then, he wouldn't expect it to be. "Of course I am. He has always been a fine leader, I imagine he will inspire his men to greatness."

Mrs. Knight all but beamed. "And he was always so supportive of the cause, as I'm sure you know. He is one of our most strident backers."

With a hum as vague as his smile, Mr. Sellers glanced at his paper again. "He is, I believe, actually in favor of universal suffrage, is he not?"

"Which is an admiral final goal, of course—but we of the WSPU have always understood that changes as large as what we're requesting must be made incrementally. It's a logical first step to grant the vote to women who have some minor amount of property to their names. Universal suffrage could build upon that foundation."

Evelina fought the urge to shift in her seat. From what she'd gleaned from Mrs. Knight, the WSPU didn't intend it to be a stepping-stone at all. They wanted exactly what they said they wanted: the vote for women with property only.

It had never bothered her quite as it did now. But she was suddenly rather glad that she'd never been what they would term a true activist for them. Their activists had a tendency to end up in prison. After bombing government buildings or setting houses ablaze.

She should have simply remained a member of the National

Union of Women's Suffrage Society, who advocated equal rights for all English citizens, not just women who owned property. But Mrs. Knight had taken her under her wing, and so . . .

Apparently now she knew why.

The purple, white, and green burned through her clothing, branding her. How proudly she had claimed to be a suffragette—perhaps all along she'd been only a suffragist.

An epiphany that would have better come when she wasn't sitting in one of the offices of Number 10 Downing Street, speaking with a man who thought her still engaged to a friend of his, at the behest of a woman who had apparently only ever seen her as a means to the eloquent Basil Philibert.

She said nothing through the meeting, just let Mrs. Knight chatter and Mr. Sellers pretend that he cared when clearly all he really wanted to do was get back to his correspondence. She smiled politely when he glanced at his pocket watch, effectively declaring the meeting over, and stood. "Thank you for your time, Mr. Sellers," she said quietly.

"My pleasure, young lady. When you write to Philibert, do tell him I send my greetings."

"I'll be sure to include it in my very next letter." Which she would never write.

Not waiting for Mrs. Knight to finish gushing her gratitude for his precious ten minutes, Evelina strode for the door. To think she'd risked Mother's wrath and snuck out for *this*. A meeting that would come to nothing, that rested on a lie.

Gloria came to attention when she exited the chamber. "Well?"

She didn't want to talk about it. Certainly didn't want to admit to her friend that she'd been a fool to ever think the outspoken, daring Mrs. Knight had ever actually valued her advice or input. Why, the woman had been an intimate of the Pankhursts themselves—she'd been arrested, gone on hunger strikes, and purportedly had a hand in the infamous burning of the WSPU motto—"Deeds Not Words"—into the turf at a football stadium.

"Well, that went splendidly. Far better than I'd dared to hope." Mrs. Knight bustled up beside her, adjusting her gloves as she walked. "Mr. Sellers has the ear of Lord Asquith himself, you know. I am quite convinced that if we continue lobbying quietly for the cause during this unfortunate war, they will be ready to grant us our demands at its close."

Evelina put one foot in front of the other, moved her arms in time. Left, right, left, right, until she'd cleared the waiting room and turned left. A toy soldier, marching along a toy hallway. She didn't dare open her mouth. Not here. Not now. She'd only embarrass herself. And Basil, who'd at least had the decency to let her keep their business quiet. He wouldn't thank her for making a scene when his colleagues here still thought them attached.

Gloria bounced a bit. "I still can't believe you secured the invitation, Mrs. Knight."

"Well, we have Evelina to thank for that." The woman had the audacity to clap an arm around her shoulders and smile down at her. "I knew when you told me about Basil's going that we had better make use of what connection we could, while it still counted for something. And it did, my dear. It did. You've been a tremendous help to the cause."

Left, right, left, right. She pulled away from the arm and kept her gaze straight ahead. Down the interminable corridor with faceless men in dark suits who paid them no heed at all.

"Lina?" Gloria stepped a bit ahead and caught her gaze. "Are you feeling all right?"

"No doubt she's still in a bit of shock at the meeting. Mr. Sellers was quite taken with her though, I assure you. Your friend performed perfectly, my dear, just perfectly."

Like one of Papa's automatons, no doubt, spinning perfectly through her gears. That was what Basil would have said.

Evelina said nothing. Just kept on marching into the entrance hall and straight out the door with its uniformed guard. She was done with the WSPU. Finished. From now on, the suffragettes could pursue their cause without her. She'd focus on helping the women in the factories—women who would never own property enough to qualify for the vote the suffragettes lobbied for.

Mrs. Knight nearly ran to fall in beside her. "I do wish one could find a cab these days. Those men in there certainly hadn't thought it through when they shipped all the Germans and Austrians to camps, did they? Now we've scarcely anyone left to drive us—and the restaurants! Have you girls tried to go to a restaurant of late? There's no staff in them anymore. Simply none."

Evelina dug her fingers into her skirt. "I daresay all the poor souls in the internment camps wish they were still here to wait on you, madam."

"Oh, listen to her, Miss Fenley—so testy! I suppose I ought to have warned you that we'd be drawing on your connections, my dear, but I assumed you wouldn't mind."

"We had better take the tube, Gloria, if we want to get back in time." Evelina grasped her friend's arm and steered her toward the nearest stop.

Mrs. Knight hated the tube. She always refused to take it. "Are you in such a hurry?"

"Afraid so," she called over her shoulder. "Mother doesn't know I'm out. Good day, Mrs. Knight."

Gloria trotted beside her for a few steps before whispering, "What happened?"

"Nothing. Except that Mrs. Knight called in a favor that one of the prime minister's secretaries owed to Basil to get us a meeting that will amount to nothing." If she knew any words stronger than *blast*, she might spit out a few. As it was, she contented herself with another beat of frustrated silence.

Gloria winced. "I thought you said you'd confessed to her that the betrothal was off."

"I did."

"Oh dear. No wonder you're distressed." Because she was a friend, Gloria sent a scowl over her shoulder.

Evelina looked toward the park with its drained lake. The busy Westminster streets. Basil had spent most of his time here, when he was in Town. He kept a house just a few streets over, within sight of Big Ben. It was, in fact . . .

There. Her feet came to a halt all on their own, and she stood and stared at the brick façade barely visible through a space between two closer buildings. She'd visited him there a few times, always with one of her parents. She'd admired the neighborhood, made note of the views, the nearest shops. Looked forward to the day when she could claim it as her own. Had even, with Basil's encouragement, commissioned new decorations for the rooms that were to have been her domain.

Gloria loosed a long breath. "When we were in Number 10, I couldn't help but think of it. That he could end up there someday, living in the prime minister's residence. You should be with him, Lina. You've invested so much time into that relationship."

"I don't want it." The brick was white on that sliver of his house she could see. White, with black wrought-iron trim. She'd imagined what flowers she would pot and hang from the windows, and the garden she'd tend in the back terrace. She'd planned the meetings she could host with her suffragette—or suffragist, anyway—friends, and the marches and protests they could organize. She'd planned the schools to which she would someday send her children, and how many dinners she and Basil would likely attend each week.

Had she ever, even once, wondered what it would be like just to sit in a room with him and *be*? Had she ever imagined curling up in his arms and whispering of her hopes and dreams? Of listening to him whisper of his?

He'd been right to end it. Right to accuse her of wanting him for all the wrong reasons.

Gloria made no effort to urge her onward. "Do you miss him terribly?"

She sighed. "I didn't love him. He was right. I didn't know *how* to love him. What if I can't love *anyone*, Gloria?"

"Don't be silly. You'll find a husband, and you'll love him—you'll come to do so, even if you don't at the start. And you'll have children, and you'll love *them*, and you'll be the warm sort of mother you've always wanted to have."

She was a good friend, Gloria—Evelina let her shoulders sag and turned away from the house that would never be hers. "I kissed Barclay Pearce the other day—just to infuriate Mother."

Gloria's gasp matched her wide eyes. "And you're just telling me this now?"

"I don't know what to do. I've done a neat enough job of avoiding him since then, but . . ." But she didn't want to avoid him. She wanted to let him escort her on her errands, and she wanted to tutor his brother and laugh with his sisters, and she wanted to kiss him again.

Because her knees had gone weak. Her pulse had gone fast. Her breath had gone raspy. And her hands had known exactly where to settle, with no question of whether she was doing it right.

And there'd been no disappointment in his eyes when he pulled away. Not even a scrap.

Gloria grinned and bumped their shoulders together as they ambled toward Westminster Station. "He's not at all bad to look at—I've been paying more attention since you mentioned him last week. Why not see what happens with him?"

"Mother—"

"Oh, pooh. Who cares what she thinks? Did he kiss you back?"

"Well . . . yes." Over and again she'd let it play through her mind. The way he'd held her, come back for another. Her cheeks burned.

Gloria laughed. "Well then. Basil's ended things, you've no obligation there. I say enjoy yourself. Heaven knows the rest of the world is bleak enough just now. Why not?"

Evelina shook her head. *"I play for keeps."* He couldn't have meant that—they barely knew each other. He couldn't have any more thought than she did for what might lie in store. So why not steal a bit of fun, as Gloria suggested, while it lasted?

The turn of her lips didn't quite feel like a smile. But it at least felt human. "Why not, indeed."

TWELVE

It felt strange, ushering Mr. Dramwell into the formal parlor of her parents' house rather than marching into his office with her chin held high and her righteous purpose billowing about her shoulders like a cape. Less . . . official, somehow. Less momentous. More like she was a child playing make-believe.

It didn't help that the factory owner knew Papa and had visited before in a social capacity, a few years ago. How could he help but see the place as it had been then? See *her* as she'd been then—a wide-eyed girl who hadn't even yet become involved in any suffrage movements?

She could only pray he'd take her more seriously than Mrs. Knight apparently did. And square her shoulders, reminding herself that, no matter where they were meeting, her cause was no less just. "I so appreciate you coming here to meet with me, Mr. Dramwell. I do hope it's not too much of an inconvenience?"

"No inconvenience at all, I assure you." He looked as genuine as he sounded, his kind eyes smiling to match his lips. "I certainly understand your father's concern—and was quite alarmed to learn you'd been mugged on this very street. Horrifying."

The thought of it would no doubt cement in his mind—good-willed though it would be—that she was nothing but a damsel in need of protection. She conjured up her brightest smile and motioned him to a seat. "Oh, it was no great thing, I assure you. It would hardly have warranted mentioning to my father had the same chap not been spotted in the neighborhood again a few days later. You know how fathers worry."

His smile was as warm as sunshine as he sat across from the chair she'd chosen. "Indeed I do. Why, just the other day, my daughters . . ."

Evelina kept her smile in place as he told her about his grown daughters and their little ones, and she laughed at all the right moments. Even had they been meeting at his office, such idle chat must be indulged first, she knew.

Though she wasn't exactly sorry when he stroked his white mustache and grinned nearly sheepishly. "But I daresay you didn't ask to meet with me so we could discuss Annabelle and Lillian. Might I assume you have visited the factory again? I trust the new hours and wages you helped me implement are well received?"

Evelina sighed. This was where things always got sticky. "Well, sir, that's the thing. They *were* well received . . . while they were being observed. But I'm afraid your manager has once again demanded longer hours, without the corresponding extra wage."

"Oh dear." His brows knit, and Mr. Dramwell leaned forward, toward her. "This is . . . quite disturbing to hear. Mr. Clarke's reports have all been in proper order, demonstrating exactly what I'd requested of him. Is it, perhaps, that they would be unable to fulfill the contracts from the army if they did not work more hours?"

"It could be, but that hardly changes the danger of such long workdays, Mr. Dramwell. Nor does it negate the fact that apparently his reports have been falsified. My contacts among the workers have reported that he works them fourteen hours a day with only one fifteen-minute break. I ask you, sir, how anyone is to operate safely for so long."

The old gent sighed and rubbed at the crease between his brows. "And Mr. Clarke came so highly recommended."

"No doubt because his methods are profitable. But something I've always greatly admired about you, sir, is that you don't let the allure of profit eclipse your concern for the people in your employ."

"True. Much to the frustration of my accountants." His lips twitched back into a smile. "I do want to think that we're making a difference—providing gainful employment for women whose husbands are enlisted. Providing quality uniforms for those husbands. We are not *just* a business."

"Exactly so. *Exactly* so." If only every factory owner were of the same mind as Mr. Dramwell, the women wouldn't even *need* a champion. Though sometimes, no doubt, a liaison would still be in order. When the managers failed to rise to the same standards. "And your employees are grateful, and proud to be a part of the war effort. Pride and gratitude alone, however, do not make up for dangerous working conditions. Perhaps if you spoke with Mr. Clarke?"

"Oh, I'll speak to him, all right." His eyes went hard. "And show him to the door, as I have those before him. Though how one is to find a different sort of manager remains the question, doesn't it? He's the third one in two years that I've had to sack—and they all seem to be cut from the same cloth, despite coming so highly recommended."

"Well." She grinned and folded her hands in her lap. "Perhaps the answer, then, is to find a fellow who *isn't* highly recommended."

Amusement shifted into determination in his eyes. "You know, my dear—you may be on to something. Perhaps all I need to do is find an altogether different sort of man. One perhaps without managerial experience already, whom I can mold into the sort of leader *I* want him to be."

Who knew she'd find such a victory in her parents' formal

parlor? She may never win an argument with Mother within these walls, but it was oh-so-sweet to know she could accomplish *something*. "That, sir, sounds like just the thing."

Barclay ought to be glad to be doing something as simple as running errands with Evelina Manning on his arm, but he couldn't help but glance over his shoulder at the man who stood on the front doorstep and just stared out into nothing. "Is your father like this often?"

"Hmm?" Evelina craned around too. But she smiled. "Once in a while. When the inspiration for some particularly clever design is upon him. Odd that those times always strike—and keep him at all hours in his workshop—when Mother is in Town, isn't it?"

"Perhaps she is his muse."

Evelina snorted and shifted a little closer to his side, securing her arm a little more snuggly through his own. No doubt because she saw the curtains flicker at the front window. Still, he didn't exactly mind.

Barclay glanced one more time back at Number 22. He'd thought Manning would be rushing down to his workshop to examine the parts Barclay had dropped off. But what did he really know of the man's creative process? "You're blessed to have her, you know."

"I beg your pardon?"

He turned his gaze down, let it settle on Evelina. She still smelled of flowers and rain, even in today's spring sunshine. "Your mother. She wouldn't act as she does if she didn't love you. Want the best for you."

Her blue eyes went as cold as January. "What she wants is the best for *her*."

"The two are not always mutually exclusive, not when it comes to family."

"Well, they are in this case. She'll never be happy with me again unless I win Basil back somehow."

"And you don't want to do that?" The thought shouldn't make a little buzz of gladness twine through his chest. But it did.

She sighed, which stilled the buzz. "I don't know what I want. He's a perfectly good man, but . . ."

He shouldn't cling to that *but* . . . but he did. Even as he told himself he was a fool for it. That he really shouldn't think such things about anyone, least of all her, given all he was responsible for. He ought to just focus on getting his family through this war and figuring out how to emerge from it with some way to support themselves.

He guided her down the street, his eyes searching, as always, the empty shadows. No one lurked about who shouldn't.

Except, perhaps, for the blonde lingering on the corner. He met her gaze, lifted his brows. Elinor just gave a little jerk of her head. *Come.*

He picked up the pace a bit. "Well, you cannot blame your mother for being put out, Lina. You made quite a show of being glad to see me." It had made him grin, even knowing it was more act than truth. "And I'm hardly a catch."

Her hand tightened around his arm. "You live in the same neighborhood, have a solid position, and can claim two noteworthy men as brothers-in-law. You are an enviable catch for any middle-class girl."

Now *he* snorted. "You know very well that's not true."

"Well, *she* doesn't!"

It shouldn't have made him laugh. But it did. And why did this . . . this whatever-it-was with her seem to be defined by a series of shouldn't-haves?

Evelina seemed to notice Elinor—she stood up a bit straighter, nodded ahead. "Your sister seems to need you."

"I know." As they drew near, he noted the way his sister clasped her handbag, the tightness around her eyes that signaled tension within. Something was wrong. "Ellie, what is it?" *Not Georgie. Please not Georgie.*

His sister's gaze went from him to Evelina, back again. Apparently she decided that the other woman had become enough of a fixture that she needn't guard her words. Entirely, anyway. "Rosie sent me to find you. Pauly just rang."

Not the war office, then. Not their brother. Though Barclay's feet still came to a sudden halt. "Wait—Pauly? Used the *telephone*?"

"I know." She drew her lower lip between her teeth. "He wouldn't say much over the line, apparently. Just that you should come."

A hundred possibilities pounded his skull for why the man would ring him up—none of them good. "Right. Ellie, if you'll walk Lina back to—"

"I'm coming with you. And wouldn't need an escort the two inches back to my own front door regardless."

She'd been mugged within those "two inches" already, but he hadn't the time to point that out. What seconds he had to argue must be spent on the greater point, the one that addressed the hesitation in his sister's eyes as well as in his own gut. "Lina, you don't want to come with me there. Pauly's place is in Poplar."

Evelina just lifted her chin. "And?"

"And . . . it's no place for a girl like you." Maybe he'd recommended the pub to any number of middle-class blokes lately—since he'd met some—and even had Lukas De Wilde's mother and sister coming regularly, but that was different. Those people weren't the daughter of Judith Manning.

She'd have his head if ever she discovered that he'd taken her daughter to such a neighborhood.

Evelina must have been thinking the same thing. Which accounted for the determined smile she fixed in place and the immovable steel that straightened her spine. "It can't be any worse than the neighborhoods I go to when visiting the factories. I'm coming. This is the man you said has been a father to you—I want to meet him."

His sister nodded. "You haven't time to argue with her, Barclay. Just go."

He sighed. "Pushy, bossy women. And you call *me* a tyrant."

Given the urgent tugging in his stomach, he didn't waste any more time debating. Just started forward again, a girl on either side of him. Neither had any trouble keeping up with his long strides.

"Rosie said you should take their new car. It's parked in the carriage house at the end of the street."

Barclay nodded. That would save the time of walking to the nearest tube station and the train switches they'd have to make. Street traffic wouldn't be too bad, not with the shortage of buses and cabs in the city, and the petrol restrictions.

Peter would have saved up his allotment, though. It was his way. There'd be plenty of fuel in the auto, and likely a spare can in the boot.

Evelina hesitated just a wink. "You're taking a *car* into Poplar?"

"Well, no one will bother it." Ellie said it as if the concern were ridiculous, amusing even. Which it was, for them. "Not when it's Barclay's."

Evelina didn't ask for an explanation of that, but he could feel the curiosity—or perhaps suspicion—coming off her in waves.

Well, she'd see soon enough, he supposed. Who he was, what he came from. And if she then decided that being associated with him didn't outweigh the allure of annoying her mother, he wouldn't hold it against her. It would even be for the best. Because this whatever-it-was wasn't going to last, and his reasons for not getting involved with anyone were no less valid than they'd ever been.

Ellie left them at the carriage house shared by half the street, and Barclay led the way inside.

The attendant snapped to attention—until he saw who it was, then he grinned. "Afternoon, Mr. Pearce."

"Afternoon, Lem." He motioned to the dull gleam of Peter and Rosemary's car. "I need the car, if you please."

"Absolutely, sir. Mr. Holstein just sent a note over telling me to make certain it was ready for you. I checked it over, all's well." Lem tipped his hat to Evelina.

"I appreciate it." While the lad moved for the wide doors he'd need to open, Barclay opened the passenger door for Evelina and then went round to fish out the crank from under the seat. Soon the engine roared to life, and he had the thing easing out.

Good thing he'd insisted Peter teach him how to use his new toy when they were in Cornwall for Christmas. Though to be quite honest, it was more Rosemary's toy than Peter's. If left to his own devices, his brother-in-law probably would have kept driving the same carriage around until the wheels fell off. Then he would have put new wheels on it and driven it for another century.

Evelina didn't say much as they navigated through the familiar streets of Hammersmith. Conversation would have been a bit difficult over the clatter of the engine and the noise from the street.

And he shouldn't be surprised, anyway, that she leaned into the door opposite him, as much space between them as there could possibly be. Her mother wasn't there, after all. Still. He'd admit that his mood ticked up a few degrees when she slid a little closer after fifteen minutes.

She slid closer still as the neighborhoods they drove through began to degrade, though he knew better than to be glad of it then. It was the soot-covered buildings that inspired the nearness, the peeling paint, the crumbling bricks, where bricks were used instead of rotting wood. It was the fact that the clothing of the pedestrians went from tailor-made to ready-made to lucky-to-be-made.

She was all but pressed to his side by the time they reached

Poplar. "You grew up here?" Her voice sounded odd. Not like winter, cold and unforgiving—more like autumn, filled with heaven's tears.

Apparently it wasn't quite like the factory districts, after all.

He took in the faded cityscape and didn't quite know how to explain to her that this was home. That if it weren't for needing to report to Mr. V in Whitehall nearly every day, he'd have chosen to live here still. "It isn't as bad as it looks."

"No?"

"It's the people who make a place, Lina. And the people here—they understand pain and loss. Which makes them appreciate joy all the more." He turned down the most familiar of any street in London and pulled Peter's car to a halt at the curb outside of Pauly's. Set the parking brake and switched off the engine.

Evelina didn't wait for him to come let her out—she scooted out the driver's side, directly behind him, all but clutching his jacket like Olivia was wont to do. "Are you certain it's safe to leave the car here?"

The smirk settled on his lips before he could stop it. He turned his gaze to the street and the ever-present homeless who crouched in the nearest alleyways. Lifted a hand. "Mags!" She wasn't usually so close to Pauly's—but maybe she'd finally listened to his advice and moved her stash of belongings closer to the pub's safety.

The old woman's eyes lit, and she struggled to her feet. "Barclay, lad! Where'd you find a machine like that?"

"Borrowed it." In her ears, *borrowed* would sound like *stole*. He grinned and hurried to help her that last tricky bit to standing. "It's Rosie's, actually."

"No!" Old Maggie's eyes sparkled. "Good for her, I say. And who's this?"

Barclay turned, still supporting the wrinkled woman with one hand, to include Evelina in his gaze.

He had to give her credit. Her hands might be clutched together too tightly, but her face was absent both fear and revulsion. She even managed a smile.

Barclay's felt a bit lopsided. "This is Lina."

"Oi, she's a pretty one, she is. Good for you, lad—'bout time you listened to old Mags and found yerself a lady friend."

She didn't, he noticed, assume Lina was a new sister. Which just proved that the old woman saw plenty out of her rheumy eyes. Barclay gave her elbow a friendly squeeze. "Lina, this is Maggie. She's been watching out for me for years, haven't you, Mags?"

The old woman cackled. "Other way round, more like."

"Now, don't listen to her. Without Maggie, I wouldn't have learned half the things I know."

Maggie's face transformed into a web of happy wrinkles as she smiled.

Evelina's transformed into something soft and warm as she did too. "How do you do, Maggie? It's an honor to meet someone so important to Barclay."

"Listen to her! She sounds like a real lady, she does. You've found a good one, Barclay." She patted his arm and then eased back down. "And so've you, pretty Lina. No better man in all of London, I say."

He helped her find a comfortable spot against the pavement, pressing a few coins into her hand as he did. "Do you need a cup of tea? A meal?"

"Pauly's already seen to me. Go on in, lad. Go on in."

He nodded and turned to cup Evelina's elbow instead of Maggie's, guiding her toward the door to the pub. "And *that*," he murmured, "is how we can be certain no one will touch Peter's car."

Though she looked a bit dubious about his choice of guard dog, she didn't say anything. Just pressed close to him as he led the way into the pub.

This time of day it was largely empty save for a few creaking old blokes too bent to find employment. But Pauly was clearly at work in the kitchen, given the aromas wafting through the place. And a lad of perhaps twelve was busily scrubbing the short little stage on which Willa—and now Lukas—still played once a week.

One of these days, people would realize they could listen to London's premier musicians for free in a hole-in-the-wall in Poplar, and Pauly's would burst at the seams.

"Oi! Barclay!"

He sent a smile to the nearest of the ancient blokes. "Pence, hello. Pauly in the back?"

"Aye. Who's the twist?"

"She's called Lina." Since they'd have to go single-file behind the bar, he took her hand instead of her arm.

The other man laughed. "Barclay with a storm! Never thought to see the day!"

"Day hasn't come yet, Frankie." He flipped up the hinged counter and tugged her through, lowering it again behind them.

"I'm confused," she whispered as they moved through the swinging door, into the kitchen.

"Rhyming slang—twist and twirl is a girl. Storm and strife is wife."

"But . . . they didn't use the rhyme."

"Well, no. That would be too easy." He sent her a wink and scanned the cluttered space for Pauly.

He found him at the back counter—but not alone. Sitting on a chair pulled alongside it was a little girl probably no more than four or five, who was shoving bits of bread into her mouth like she might never see another meal.

THIRTEEN

Barclay came to a halt, not wanting to spook the child. Rather than call out, he cleared his throat.

Pauly turned, with that slow kind of care that he always used with skittish creatures, be they human or animal. He had another in his arms, this one a babe of perhaps a year. With only the soiled rags that passed as clothes for clues, Barclay couldn't be sure whether the mite was a boy or a girl.

"There he is," Pauly proclaimed in the soft, singsong voice that had first drawn Barclay out of the shadows behind his rubbish bin, into daylight. "What did I tell you, Clover? Isn't he just like I said?"

The girl shoved another bite of bread into her mouth and reached for the baby. "Give him back now."

Pauly didn't argue. He just lowered the babe into her lap, which earned a happy squeal on the little one's part. "Barclay, this is Clover and her brother, Patch."

Barclay smiled at the whimsical names and eased a step closer. "Hello, Clover. How do you do?"

Clover shoved away a strand of hair that might be red under the grime and hugged her brother close. "We ain't going to no orphanage. We ain't. They'll take him from me, and I promised Mumma I'd look after him, no matter what."

His heart fisted in his chest, and his fingers tightened around Evelina's before he let them go altogether, so he could ease forward again and crouch down before Clover's chair. "Don't worry, sweetheart. I'm not here to take you to an orphanage." He focused his gaze on the baby, careful to keep his eyes light and easy.

He was thin but not starved and seemed happy enough as he clapped his hands together and then patted his sister's face. She pinched off a piece of bread and fed it to him. But she kept her wary green eyes trained on Barclay.

"Mrs. Maloney said we'd have to go. 'Cause Da ain't coming home from the war, and the money's stopped, and then Mumma didn't come back from the bath. She got hurt somehow, Mrs. Maloney said."

He flicked his gaze to Pauly, who drew a line over his wrist with his finger. Barclay was rather glad he'd not eaten any lunch that day—it would have churned now if he had.

But he couldn't let the girl see his reaction. He smiled and held out a finger for little Patch to grasp. "Did Mrs. Maloney bring you here?"

Clover handed her brother another bite of bread. "Mags did."

"Ah." That explained her presence far better than her suddenly deciding to move. "Mags is a good friend of mine. Sweetest person I ever met." He let his words drop out of their usual cadence, adopt the ones that would be more familiar to her. "I bet yer mum asked you to watch Patch, yeah?"

Her bony little arms tightened around him. "He's my brother. I got to take care of him. It's the most important thing."

His smile felt as heavy as the past. "My mum used to tell me the same thing."

"You have a brother?"

"Charlie." He felt Evelina go still behind him. Heard the breath

Pauly sucked in. He'd never told him about Charlie. Hadn't wanted to admit that he'd failed the one who mattered most. But that heaviness in his chest whispered that it might well be the only way to win Clover's trust. "He was four years younger than me."

Her eyes went wide. "That's how much younger Patch is! I'm just five, and he's just one. Born in the same month, we were. Da said he was my present." The warm squeeze she gave the boy testified that it was a gift she'd welcomed. Then her joy faded. "I miss Da. Mumma's not the same since he left. Since Patch was born."

"I know just what you mean."

The eyes she turned on him now glistened. "Did your da go to war too?"

"No. My da caught a fever, and it ate him right up. He was a teacher—caught it from his pupils."

Behind him, Pauly pulled out a chair and sat down on it with a thud that might have been amusing if Barclay weren't so focused upon the girl.

She blinked, sniffed. "Was your mum always sad after that? Did she stop smiling?"

"Yeah, she did." Experimenting, he picked up a slice of cheese sitting on a plate on the counter and held it out to her.

She took it, nibbled.

Good. "We had to move out of our house after that. Ended up in a little flat, but even then, it was hard. Never enough to eat. Our clothes wore out."

Clover nodded. "I wish I could have stopped growing. I tried, but I couldn't help it."

Sweet thing. He offered her a grape too. "Your mum didn't want you to stop growing, though. She wanted you to get big and strong."

"I could help her more that way." Clover used her teeth to cut the grape in half, then in half again, and fed the bits to her brother. "Did you help your mum?"

He nodded. "I tried. However I could. But I was still too little to work."

"You gotta be nine." Clover sighed. "That's forever away."

"I know. And my mum couldn't work either." She could have, though. He knew that now. She *could* have—she just hadn't known how. Or wanted to. "So she started pinching things."

"Stealing?" Her mouth was a perfect *O* of horror. "That's a sin. My da said so, and he'd know. *His* da was a preacher."

Good thing God hadn't led this little one to Pauly's door a year earlier. Barclay nodded, letting the truth of it sink in deep below the walls his mother had helped him build. "I know. And I'm sorry to say that I learned how to steal too. And got quite good at it."

She fed the last quarter of grape to Patch. "Do you still?"

"No. Well . . ." A sigh leaked out. "I work for the Crown now, and sometimes they ask me to get things. To help with the war."

Her little brow puckered. "Is that different?"

"I don't know. I think so. It *feels* different." He didn't dare look at Pauly or Evelina. Pauly wouldn't judge—he never had. He'd accepted them however they were, whatever they were. He'd loved them regardless.

Lina he wasn't so sure about.

Clover pursed her lips. "What about your mum? And Charlie?"

"I don't know." That admission left him aching. And no doubt sounded like the oldest of sorrows in his voice, scabbed over and scarred. "My mum got caught when I was ten. When I came home one day, she was gone. And so was Charlie."

Tears pooled in her eyes and slipped out onto her cheeks, leaving a trail of paler flesh behind them. "You lost your brother?"

He brushed a knuckle over the baby's round cheek. "I've looked for him everywhere. Everywhere. But I've never found him."

"I'm sorry." She squeezed her brother until he squeaked in protest. "I'll never lose Patch. I won't. That's why I can't go to the orphanage, because they'd take him away from me."

They would. Which was no doubt why Mags had brought her here to Pauly's. And why Pauly had borrowed a neighbor's telephone to ring him up. "A few months after I lost my mum and Charlie, God led me here to Pauly's. And He led other kids here too—Rosemary and Willa, to start. They were orphans too. So we decided to stick together. To be a family."

She wiped her nose on her sleeve and rested her cheek against Patch's head. "That's nice, then."

"It is. We found more children like us over the years. I still don't know what happened to Charlie, but God's given me others to love. To take care of. Brothers and sisters." Now came the tricky part, the part that could send her running in a panic if he didn't phrase it just right, deliver it in just the right tone. "You could meet them, if you like. My littlest sister, Olivia, isn't much older than you. She's just seven."

Her eyes lit, but not by much. It was a cautious light. "Do you live nearby? I can't carry Patch far."

"We used to live just around the corner—but Rosie got married last year, and her husband has a nice house in Hammersmith. Have you heard of Hammersmith?"

Her brow puckered again. "The bridge?"

"There is a bridge, yes. We live pretty close to the bridge right now. We drove in Rosie's new automobile to come here today. If you'd like, you and Patch can ride back with us and meet Olivia. You could have dinner with us and maybe even spend the night with Liv. If you wanted to. We could put a crib in the room for Patch too."

Rosemary wouldn't mind if they borrowed the one she'd just bought for her coming little one. She didn't need it quite yet.

Clover looked away, thoughts racing through her teary eyes. One never knew how a child might sort through things, what conclusions they might come to. He could only let her wrestle with it and pray with all his being that she'd agree. That God would let him take two more children off the streets before the world showed them how cruel it could be.

At length, she met his gaze again. "For the night?"

"If you like. Or longer, if you want to stay with us. One of our brothers is in the war now too, you see, and another of my sisters is about to get married. The house will start to feel empty with only nine of us."

She didn't seem to see the irony in the statement. "Patch cries sometimes."

Barclay gave a solemn nod. "Little ones always do. It won't bother anyone. And there are older girls there to help you take care of him, when you need a hand. They love nothing more than a fine, handsome baby to coo over."

Pauly leaned forward, rested his meaty arms on his knees. "And if you decide you want to come back here, Barclay'll bring you right back."

What he didn't say was that she'd then be right back where she'd started when Mrs. Maloney declared her bound for the orphanage.

She nodded. "I'd like to meet your sisters. If you're sure it's all right."

"Of course it is." And it was.

Though the squeak that came from Evelina didn't sound convinced.

He was mad—absolutely mad. Sweet and amazing and so bighearted that hers positively melted in response—but mad. "Barclay." She did her level best to keep her voice light, but she knew some of her worry seeped through. "May I speak with you a moment?"

"Of course. Why don't you finish your tea, Clover, and then we can go whenever you're ready?" the madman said.

He stood, turned, all casual confidence. But his eyes hardened when he looked at her. Just daring her to question him.

She didn't *want* to question him—but someone had to, didn't they? She wasn't exactly surprised to learn that he'd done a bit of thieving as a lad, but just taking children home with him? Spotting a door that led out to a little kitchen garden, Evelina strode toward it, through it.

Living smells assaulted her as soon as she stepped outside. Chives and basil and rosemary, thyme and sage. They grew everywhere in the little garden no bigger than the water closet at her home in Hammersmith.

The space got even smaller when Barclay stepped into it and pulled the door shut behind him. "All right, get it off your chest so we can get on with it."

It was absolutely not fair that men grew to be taller than women. Perhaps Mother could shrink the distance with a single glare, but Evelina was tempted to stand on that overturned flower pot to close the six-inch gap. "I admire what you're trying to do—really. It's so very sweet. But . . . well, you cannot simply take orphans home with you—it isn't how it's done. You have to take them to an orphanage."

Barclay snorted and folded his arms over his chest. "No. I'll never send a child to an orphanage."

He said it as though she'd recommended sending them to Hades itself. Which may have made her bristle more than she meant to. Which in turn no doubt made her sound a wee bit defensive. "Why do you think they exist? Why do they receive funding? Because they know how to deal with such sad situations as these."

He just blinked at her. "And what is the goal of these orphanages, Lina? To keep the children forever?"

"Of course not." Now he was *trying* to be obtuse. "To find them families, when possible, or situate them for positions later in life."

How often had she heard Mother and Aunt Beatrice reciting such things like a motto?

"Exactly. We're just saving them a step and finding them a family now. Saving them the funds." As if that settled it, he reached for the door.

She jumped in front of it. "But that isn't how it's done! You could get in trouble—"

He snorted. "You really think anyone in the government cares if I save them the effort of housing a few orphans? Trust me. They don't."

"Well, of course they do. It's their job to care, their whole purpose."

He shook his head and leaned against the damp section of wall at his side. "Have you even *been* to an orphanage? Other than on a scheduled visit with some ladies' society, when they're sure to show you their best?"

Why would she have? She folded her arms over her chest. But the question swam. *Should* she have? "They make a difference in children's lives. Save them from the streets."

"They crowd dozens of them into a single room and always seem to be blind to the cruelties those children inflict upon each other."

"They do the best they can—"

"They'd separate them!" He stood up straight again, eyes blazing like the hottest flames. "Argue with that."

"She's just a girl. She shouldn't be responsible for the very life of a baby."

"Yes. She should. Because she's his *family.*" He shook his head, working his jaw back and forth. "You don't know. You don't know the guilt that comes with having a brother snatched from your care and taken away."

And why was he lashing out at her? *She* wasn't the one who made the system he so seemed to loathe. "I lost a brother too."

His eyes didn't so much as soften. "To polio, I know. Your father told me. Not through any fault of yours."

Papa had told him? Her arms fell away from her chest. Papa never talked about Jacob. *Never.* Neither of her parents did. Aunt Beatrice might mention him now and then, but only as a dagger meant to slice at them.

Perhaps his death had been no one's fault. But that truth did nothing to keep the family from splintering.

Would it have been worse—*could* it have been worse—if there were blame to assign?

Barclay gestured toward the kitchen and the children inside it. "They'd find him a family, maybe—he's young enough. But her? She'd end up in the workhouse. Beside drunks and lechers and . . ." He flushed to a halt, shaking his head again. "Elinor spent time in one of those. I'll not let any other child go, if I can help it."

Evelina's throat went dry. "It surely isn't that bad."

"Isn't it?" His laugh sounded far from good-humored. "You want the vote so badly, Lina—but do you even know what you'd vote *for*? Or are you so caught up in the fight that you've forgotten the reasons behind it?"

She tried to swallow, but it got stuck. "That isn't fair. You know I have causes I pursue—advocating for women in the workplace, for one. Besides which, many suffrage movements have their eye on social reform." But hers—Mrs. Knight's—didn't. Not anymore. They'd given up such pretense a decade ago, long before Evelina even knew what their cause was. All they cared about was equality, recognition. For men to admit that women weren't inferior.

But they didn't in fact want complete equality for all, did they? They were still happy to exclude the poor, the penniless.

They were happy to let children starve in orphanages or be abused in workhouses.

"Causes tend to keep a person a healthy step removed from the real problem. I admire that you do something to help those women in the factories—but it doesn't change how you live your life day by day, does it? If they go hungry, your stomach doesn't hurt with them. You go home to your nice house with your warm bed, whether you earned them a few extra pence an hour or not." He stepped closer, looked down at her. "I have the chance here to change lives, Lina. It might mean taking food out of my mouth, but it'll mean putting it in theirs. So you can either help me change things now for one little girl and her brother, or you can go on marching and arranging meetings with politicians and hoping for legislation years down the road. Your choice."

"Blast." When he phrased it like that . . . She spun around and jerked the door open, not sure if he was right or if she was just going mad along with him.

The occupants all looked up, so she took care to put on a smile and set her pace at an easy glide. Or as easy a glide as her leg would allow, anyway.

Clover—she wasn't entirely sure what kind of mother would name a little girl such a thing—smiled back. A little.

Pauly just looked past her, to Barclay, his eyes shouting doubt. Not, apparently, over the decision to take the children—that was obviously why he'd called Barclay down here to begin with. No, his doubt was apparently over his decision to bring *her* along. "Everything all right, Barclay?"

"Absolutely." His hand landed on her back, nearly making her jump. Not because she minded the touch—to be quite honest, it sent a pleasant little trill through her—but because she was surprised he still wanted to show her such affection. "I didn't introduce you, did I? Sorry about that. Pauly, Clover, this is my friend Lina. Lina, Pauly—closest thing I've had to a father since mine died."

She dipped a little curtsy. "How do you do? I've been eager to make your acquaintance, sir."

Pauly lifted bushy black brows. "Nice to meet you."

She had the sudden certainty Barclay had *not* mentioned her to his makeshift father. Which stood to reason, given the brevity of their acquaintance. And the fact that she wasn't exactly sure of her role in Barclay's life.

Still, it stung a bit. So she busied herself with approaching the children and crouching down as Barclay had done, giving the girl a smile. "Do you think Patch would let me hold him while you finish your food? I won't go even a step away, I promise you."

After debating for a moment, Clover loosened her grip on the lad. "You can try. Sometimes he gets fussy with strangers."

"Oh, I understand. I have quite a few friends with babies." She held out her arms toward the little one, who regarded her for a moment with those frank, innocent eyes that all tots seemed to have and then leaned toward her.

Savoring her victory, she held him close as she stood again, setting him on her hip. And straining her ears toward where Pauly had moved off behind her, toward Barclay.

She'd just caught a murmured, "I assure you," from Barclay when heavy footsteps sounded from somewhere above them.

A shrill voice called out, "Pauly!"

Evelina turned in time to catch him wince as he said, "Down the apples, luv!"

"Blast." Barclay covered the distance between them in two steps and smiled at Clover. "You'll have to take the rest of that with us, sweetheart. Here, I'll wrap it up for you. Quickly now." He slid the bread, cheese, and grapes into a napkin and folded it all up as the heavy tread grew louder.

Evelina's gaze found the stairs, nearly hidden from her view by a filled shelf, just as a large woman emerged with a frown on her face.

"Ought to've known. I told you no more."

Pauly's sigh sounded rather like Papa's when Aunt Beatrice and Mother were both in attendance. "Barclay's taking them, luv. Just had to wait for him to get here."

"And feed them, I s'ppose. Ye'd better pay for the food, too, Barclay Pearce."

In the two weeks she'd known him, Evelina had never seen anyone sneer at Barclay. Even Mother didn't, not to his face. But this woman—Pauly's wife, she had to assume—sneered as if he were the scum she'd just scraped off her shoe.

Evelina held Patch close with one arm and reached with the other for Clover's hand, shielding her as best she could from the woman's glare. No child ought to feel the burden of a look like that.

"Take it easy, Jill. I've bought every morsel of food we've eaten for twenty years, haven't I?" Barclay pocketed the napkin full of food—and flipped a coin onto the counter that would cover the bread and cheese.

Pauly's jaw went tight.

Jill pursed her lips and lifted a ragged shawl from a hook on the wall. "I'm going to Pris's. I'd better see neither hide nor hair of them when I get back—and I'll be doing the inventory this week, you can be sure."

Barclay rolled his eyes and scooped Clover up, positioning her on his hip without bothering to ask for permission. She didn't seem to mind, just snuggled in and even rested her head against his shoulder.

After the woman had lumbered through the door and the garden gate had snapped shut behind her, Pauly let out a long breath. "Take your money back, Barclay. You know—"

"And you know I don't mind paying for what we eat. I don't want to make things difficult for you." His voice had gone back to normal—assuming the middle-class cadence was normal and not learned—and left the Cockney hitches behind.

"But you were saving for beds."

Evelina frowned. They hadn't *beds*? Somehow she'd assumed the lack of furnishings in the rest of the house didn't extend to their bedrooms. A foolish assumption, apparently.

Barclay just chuckled. "The girls have those cots. And I'm used to the floor."

Apparently finding that satisfactory, Pauly moved his gaze to Evelina. "Begging your pardon for my wife, miss. She's . . ."

Forcing aside her muddled thoughts, Evelina smiled. "No need to apologize. She's mild compared to my mother."

Barclay chuckled again and moved toward the door that led back to the pub proper. "Did you have anything with you, sweetheart?"

Clover shook her head and peered over Barclay's shoulder, obviously making sure Evelina and Patch were following.

Evelina stuck close to his back.

Pauly brought up the rear. "Rosie sounded tired when I talked to her. She resting enough?"

"I daresay Peter's making sure of it—and what's this I hear about you actually using a telephone? Next thing I know, you'll be having one installed."

Pauly made a dismissive noise. "Dire circumstances, is all. I knew Jill'd be going out this afternoon."

"Mmm. I'll see how Rosie is when we get home, anyway. Wouldn't surprise me if she'd just stayed up late stitching Willa's wedding gown, though. They had another fitting yesterday."

Now Pauly's sigh, as they emerged from behind the bar again, sounded wistful. "She'll be pretty as a rose, I bet. Hope I don't embarrass her. Never given anyone away before."

"Wouldn't matter if you sneezed in the priest's face, Pauly. You're the only one she'd ever ask to walk her up the aisle." Barclay led the way back through the maze of tables, nodding a greeting to another chap in the back who tossed an *oi* his way—and a demand for ale that Pauly waved off.

Pauly stepped around them to get to the door first and held it open. He aimed a soft smile at Clover. "Wish I could do more."

"You've always done just enough. And taught us how to do the rest."

They stepped out into the sunshine that gleamed off the fenders of the Holstein automobile—which had attracted a bit of attention, but all of it respectful. A few lads whistled at it as they circled. "Hey, Barclay, take us for a spin?"

He laughed and approached the adolescents. Evelina paused to look back at Pauly. She never imagined herself worrying over what opinion a Cockney publican held her in, but just now, she wanted in the worst way for him to smile at her like he did at Barclay or the children or even the woman they called Mags, who was shuffling down the street at a snail's pace.

Her gaze drifted back to Barclay. He was ruffling the hair of one of the lads, his new sister as comfortable as could be on his hip. "Is he friends with absolutely everyone?" she asked Pauly.

"Except for Jill." Now there was a smile in Pauly voice—over Barclay, not her, but she was getting closer.

"And she—why does she not want to help?" How could her heart not melt, as Evelina's had, at these men's love for the children?

"It's for someone else to do, she says." He shook his head, keeping his gaze on his would-be son. "Says we pay our taxes to fund the orphanages and workhouses, and that's all anyone ought to expect of us."

With her arms full of Patch, that didn't feel like nearly enough. *Deeds Not Words*—perhaps the suffragette motto had *something* right, after all.

FOURTEEN

Afternoon's light stretched long and golden across the aerodrome, lengthening the shadows into caricatures of themselves. Barclay stood with his hands slung inside his pockets, watching the plane that circled the field. One of the pilots still in training, he'd been told. But then, the Royal Flying Corps military school had just opened a few weeks ago—he had to think that most of its pilots were still in training.

V stepped up beside him, pocket watch in hand. "The squadron commander assures me that we may take as much time as we need—anything to give his boys a greater advantage over the German aces. Mr. Manning seems quite insistent that another thirteen minutes will do, however."

Barclay chuckled and glanced behind him at where the man poked about inside a Sopwith. "I imagine he's planned it down to the second so that we'll arrive back in Hammersmith with just enough time for him to dress before dinner." He'd have to slip home for that as well—Rosemary had cornered him that morning and insisted he try on a new suit of evening clothes she'd made for him, saying it wasn't every night he dined with a young lady who wasn't already family.

As if he needed her reminding him that he ought to be nervous.

But at least she would be there, and Willa, and Peter and Lukas. Retta and Elinor had considered joining them, but the arrival of new little ones to fuss over inspired them to send their regrets.

Clover and Patch were soaking up the attention as if starved for it. Which they likely were. There'd been no talk whatsoever from the girl about leaving—and she even left Patch in a room with someone else now and then. For a minute or two.

"I am quite impressed that you convinced him to work with us outright. For some reason I expected him to be reticent, given the unenthusiastic response I know he received from some sectors."

"I'd say I'm convincing, but honestly, sir, it didn't take much. He's a good man. Just wants to do his bit."

"I didn't know many others who could actually be of assistance to him. Hence why it seemed the perfect job for you." He slid his watch back into his pocket. It was a moderately priced model, simple but precise. Barclay had helped Manning repair one of the same type just last night.

It was on the tip of his tongue to ask the man who the woman had been, in the house in Fulham. To ask if she'd be expecting him home for dinner too.

He had a feeling if he posed such a nosy question, he'd soon find himself without gainful employment. And given that he'd sworn off thievery, that would put him in quite a spot. So he'd be wise to hold his tongue.

"I hear your family has grown."

"By two." He looked to the skies again, watched the biplane circle. "Sweet little things. Clover and Patch." He wasn't quite convinced those were their real names, but the girl insisted it was all she'd ever been called, and Mrs. Maloney could provide no better information. Just a surname of Rogers.

Mr. V's lips tugged up just a bit. "Interesting names. Their parents?"

"Father dead in the war. Mother . . . slit her wrists, apparently.

I went and spoke to the landlady yesterday. She'd been down, she said, since the baby was born. Never quite bounced back. So when word came of the husband's death . . ."

A compassionate *tsk* escaped V's lips. "How are they adjusting to your home?"

"Like fish to water. Clover misses her mum and da, of course. But I think her mother hadn't been all that present recently anyway." And Patch wouldn't remember anything but the family they gave him, and the stories his sister told.

He'd make sure she told plenty in these early days, when it was all fresh, and Barclay would write it down for her. So that when her memory faded, she'd still have those bits of who she'd been before.

It mattered.

"About their settling, though." He shifted, not sure how to bring up the question. Or if it was even wise to do so. "They're all becoming rather comfortable at the house—which worries me, to be honest. You didn't mention how long you'd let it for. If it's just until Manning turns over the gear . . ."

"You think such an address will cease being handy then?" V quirked up one corner of his mouth. "Rest easy, Mr. Pearce. At least for the duration of the war and your work with the Admiralty, we want to keep you right there, where you can respond quickly when we need you. So let the children get comfortable. There's no harm."

There still was—the war wouldn't last forever. And how much harder would it be to return to Poplar or the like after a year or two or three in that house in Hammersmith? But he couldn't deny them when it was provided. That would be foolish.

"Mr. Pearce, a hand, if you please."

"Coming." Snapping himself out of thoughts of home, he pulled out the notebook and pen that Manning had asked him to bring and joined him at the Sopwith.

Manning reached for the utensils with one hand. "Could you hold this belt out of the way like so while I sketch? I'd rather not take anything apart, as I haven't the time to put it back together."

"Certainly." He positioned his fingers properly and kept them still while Manning put confident strokes upon the paper. "You're quite talented at that part too, sir. I've never been much good at drawing. My sister Retta, now—she's quite an artist."

"Oh? Shame she couldn't join us this evening." He peered into the gears behind the belt. Seeing what *could* be there, no doubt, not just what was. "I have always enjoyed the artistic aspect of my craft. A beautiful watch. A clever toy."

Yet as he said it, his tone went mocking.

"You sound as though you doubt the value of such things."

"What do such things matter, in the end?" He drew another line, frowned. Thickened it. "This is what the world is about now. Airplanes and machine guns and armored vehicles. If I want to make a difference, earn respect, then . . ."

"Is that why you're doing this?" It struck him as a rather hollow reason to turn his back on beauty, on whimsy.

"My clocks will never save lives, Barclay. My toys—they are only *toys*."

"Your *toys* are brilliant pieces of engineering."

"Which children and other clockmakers grant most readily. But the engineers, the gunsmiths think me a foolish tinkerer."

"What do they know? I don't see *them* out here solving tomorrow's problems. They think it enough to have put deflectors on the propellers."

Manning snapped his notebook shut. "And perhaps they're right. Perhaps this is unnecessary. But if I could do something lasting in this world . . ."

"Sir." Barclay let go of the belt and accepted the notebook and pen back. "You help all of London keep time."

"With the Great Clock, you mean?" Manning shook his head,

pulled out his watch, and started for the car that V had taken up position beside. "Everyone knows the clock. The man who designed it even, perhaps. No one cares who keeps it running now."

"They'd care if you *didn't*, wouldn't they?"

Manning sent him a small smile. "They'd just assign someone else the task, that's all. Wilsdorf, perhaps—he is arguably a better man for the job."

Barclay loosed a gusty breath. "Nothing against your friend, but I daresay no one with the last name of Wilsdorf would be assigned such a role just now. If the clock got off by a minute, someone would accuse him of colluding with German agents in a masterplan to throw the whole city off schedule and cause mass chaos."

It earned him a chuckle, anyway. "Sadly, you have a point. Which is a shame. Hans is the most talented clockmaker I know, in all honesty. His wife is one of Evelina's friends. Florence."

Much as he was happy to gather all the information he could on Evelina, he wasn't about to get distracted with such things just now. And they'd reach V and the Admiralty car—filled with properly requisitioned petrol today—in another thirty seconds. "Mr. Manning . . . a man has only so much time upon this earth. It seems to me that if you spend it all regretting what you haven't accomplished, you've only managed to waste what hours you have, which you ought to be spending with the people who make them count."

He paused—something Manning rarely did, Barclay had found, unless he was running early. Which they weren't. "Herman used to say something like that. He said the most precious thing in this world, and the most often wasted, was the time a man ought to be spending with his family."

Barclay smiled. "I think I'd like this Herman."

Manning started forward again. "He failed to advise me on what to do when half of my family refused to spend time with me."

"The meal was perfect, Mrs. Manning. Thank you so much for inviting us."

Evelina watched her mother smile under the charming attention of Lukas De Wilde and exchanged a knowing grin with Willa, who sat at her fiancé's side. After Mrs. Wright had stormed off in a rage midafternoon, with tonight's large dinner partly unprepared and partly on the stove, ready to burn, Evelina had known a bit of genuine fear that Mother's heart would give out then and there.

She might enjoy annoying her mother, but she'd never wish her harm—and so she'd assured her that she'd heard of a well-recommended cook seeking work in the neighborhood and run to fetch Lucy. The girl deserved a medal for saving the dinner—and Mother's sanity.

Aunt Beatrice, of course, sniffed. "I suppose it was to some people's taste. I personally prefer fewer spices in my dishes. One ought to be able to taste the meat itself, if you ask me."

Mr. De Wilde's French mutter, if she weren't mistaken, could be loosely translated as, *After you first boil the life out of it?*

Willa placed an elbow "accidentally" in his side with a too-bright apology, and De Wilde renewed his smile.

Rosemary Holstein dabbed her lips with a napkin. "Well, I certainly send *my* compliments to your cook, Mrs. Manning."

"Thank you, Mrs. Holstein. I will be sure to pass them along." Alight with the glow that only a successful social engagement could bring, Mother turned back to Willa. "I understand your wedding is to be soon?"

Willa's smile rivaled the gaslights in brilliance. "The sixth of June, yes—assuming my darling brother doesn't go mad before then with all the preparations."

The sudden stillness sounded like ringing bells in Evelina's ears. It started with her own family, of course—Mother, Papa, Aunt Beatrice. But it quickly spread to their guests, who couldn't possibly miss the way Mother's cup froze halfway to her mouth.

Willa's eyes went wide. "Don't tell me . . ."

Evelina cleared her throat. "It's no matter. *Someone* ought to put the date to use."

Aunt Beatrice was the first to recover. "June is a lovely time of year for a wedding, I always said. Though let it be noted, I suggested my niece set hers for April. Which no one can argue now would have been wise."

As if that would have kept Basil from signing up. She turned to Barclay. "I would have thought you'd enjoy all the plan making, Barclay."

"Only when he's the one in command." Rosemary grinned across the table at him, obviously adding an extra dose of cheer to her expression to compensate for the awkward moment. She placed a hand discreetly on the round of her stomach, swathed in a gorgeous blue silk. "He isn't accustomed to bowing to anyone else's wishes, though."

"One must wonder, then, how he manages in his profession. From what I understand, he is no more than an errand boy for the Admiralty." Aunt Beatrice folded her napkin and stood as if she were the hostess. "Come, ladies, let us leave the gentlemen"—she glanced at Mr. Holstein and Mr. De Wilde—"and their friends to their port."

Evelina glanced at Mother—her cheeks had gone red under her facial powder. Apparently the slight to her own position in the household, on top of the insult to half their guests, was too much even for Mother's impeccable control.

She didn't rise. And for once, Evelina was quite happy to follow her lead. Willa and Rosemary didn't even look Beatrice's way.

Barclay leaned forward. "I've been meaning to ask you, Pete, if you'd been to see King George since you've been back in London.

I saw a note from him when I fetched the post for you the other day."

Mr. Holstein hadn't said much through dinner, but his eyes were bright, sharp, and his smile knowing. "Just . . . y-yesterday. He asked . . . he asked after you all."

"My husband never runs out of stories to tell the king, thanks to my large family." Rosemary reached for his hand. "Do you, luv?"

"Pete never runs out of stories, full stop." Barclay grinned, though there was a note to it that Evelina didn't understand. Some joke between them, she would guess. She may have thought it a prod against his stammering—that's what the words would have been if coming from Aunt Beatrice's mouth, anyway—had Peter Holstein not chuckled.

Aunt Beatrice thumped her cane against the floor. "Judith!"

Before Mother could respond, a scream sliced through the house, along with what sounded like every pot in the kitchen hitting the floor.

Evelina was on her feet in half a blink, but she was still a step behind Barclay, who'd flown out the door with a speed she envied.

The scream had to be Lucy's—she was the only female in the house not already in the dining room. Despite Aunt Beatrice's shout that the entire household needn't go to check on the kitchen staff, Evelina had no doubt that their guests were all hot on her heels, as she was on Barclay's.

But when they stumbled into the kitchen, it wasn't Lucy with blood streaming from her head, but Williston. Lucy had her apron pressed to his temple, a collection of pots that must have been sitting on the counter now on the floor.

An accident? She clutched at Barclay's arm, willing her pulse to slow again. Frightening as the blood looked, Williston was alert and trying to bat Lucy away, saying, "Enough, Lucy. I must catch him."

Only then did she note the kitchen door hanging open and the cool night breeze rushing in.

Barclay lurched forward again, sidestepping pots. "Catch who—where?"

Lucy held the butler down without any great effort. "Williston was returning the pot of thyme to the garden for me and—"

"And startled a burglar, that's what." The old man made another attempt to push Lucy away. "Trying to pry open the window to the basement. I *told* you we ought to seal it up, Mr. Manning. Ought to seal the whole basement up, I say, despite that it's never flooded."

Warm hands touched Evelina's arms and moved her gently to the side. Papa followed the same path Barclay had taken, but where Barclay had hurried out into the garden, her father crouched down beside Lucy and Williston. "Are you all right, Will? Did he strike you?"

His face flamed. "Pushed me is all, sir, and I stumbled over the threshold when he did. A lot of fuss and bother and noise, but it's only a scratch on my head, from the corner of the table."

Barclay appeared back in the kitchen. "Did you get a look at him?"

Perhaps her parents—Mother had edged her way in too—assumed he spoke to the butler. But his eyes were on Lucy.

Williston shook his head. "Dark hair, I think. Or maybe a cap. I couldn't make out his height, what with him being crouched down and then leaping up."

Lucy stood, nodded to Barclay. "About your height, I think. I got a clearer view when he was pushing poor Williston. Swarthy complexion. Dark hair. And I believe I caught a glint of gold around his neck, as if he wore a necklace."

More than Evelina would have noticed in what must have been a fleeting glance. But the details didn't earn more than a nod from Barclay. The glance he sent Evelina said what his words didn't—that it matched the description of the mugger.

Many feet shuffled behind her. "You look peaked, Rosie. I think we'd better get you home."

Evelina spun around. Willa had slid an arm around her sister, and Mr. Holstein's lips were pressed together. Rosemary looked a bit pale, it was true, but not overly so. Perhaps they were looking for an excuse to leave though—she could hardly blame them for that.

Mother made the expected objection, but Willa's adamant concern for her sister's health quickly won out, and Evelina was dispatched to locate their wraps and hats. She returned a minute later with her arms full and let Barclay's family find their own pieces among the collection.

Aunt Beatrice had vanished, no doubt to devise Mother's punishment for disobeying her. Mother herself was visibly aflutter, which made Evelina nearly feel sorry for her. Papa and Barclay must still be in the kitchen with Williston.

The gentlemen were soon ushering their ladies out the door amid promises from Rosemary to return the invitation soon and assurances that she had a lovely evening.

The moment the door closed behind them, Mother all but wilted. "What a disaster."

"It's all right, Mother. The wound didn't look serious, and I'm sure Williston will be all right. And the burglar was frightened off, so he surely won't try again."

Mother drifted toward the stairs, a hand pressed to her head. "If they speak of this to their friends, we'll never be able to show our faces in polite society. As if it weren't bad enough that Basil abandoned you, now we'll be known as the family who sends their guests rushing to the kitchen with the servants."

Evelina's leg pulsed. She clenched her teeth together. And stalked back to the kitchen with the servants.

Or rather, to Papa and Barclay, Lucy and Williston, who'd been urged onto a stool.

Barclay met her in the doorway and steered her right back out the corridor. Mother, thankfully, had made it up the stairs. "Did the girls leave?"

"Yes. I'm certain Rosemary will be all right, Barclay, she didn't look *that* peaked—"

"If that bloke's still lingering in the neighborhood, we'll find him. Is my hat out here?" Not waiting for an answer, he spun about until he spotted the lone derby sitting on the entryway table.

"You're not going. Not after that man, in the dark." She grabbed at his arms.

He gripped her elbows. And grinned at her. "I have to. Rosie and Peter will cover the north and Willa and Lukas the south, but someone has to handle east-west, and Lucy won't be able to slip away without them noticing."

"But they were taking Rosemary home. She was pale."

The grin turned into a smirk. "Tell someone what they should *expect* to see, and they see it. Leaving you free to have your way—in this case, a quick exit. It's a simple mirror job."

Job. Something about the way he said it . . . She blinked. And called herself all manner of names for not seeing his sisters' motives in an instant. "How in the world did your brothers-in-law ever learn to follow you people?"

"They're good blokes." He planted the derby on his head. "Gotta run, luv. Maybe we'll catch a break and find him this time."

She grabbed him by the lapels before he could breeze out the door. Strained up to kiss him soundly. The idiot man. "Be careful."

He lingered there a moment, a whisper away from her lips. Then he said, "Carefuller than careful," and vanished out the door.

FIFTEEN

Barclay rolled his neck, listening to it creak and pop, thinking not for the first time that day that he wasn't all that fond of aging. He wasn't quite thirty, it was true, but after spending half the night chasing shadows around London, he felt downright ancient today.

Of course, that could have something to do, too, with the fitful sleep during the second half of the night while poor little Patch cried through a nasty bout of the sniffles. He'd taken his turn rocking him and mopping his face and reading to him.

Manning took a moment to stretch, too, and glanced upward. "Did I miss the opening of the door?"

Barclay rubbed at the aching muscles in his neck. He never used to be so sore after a night's chase through London's streets. Or rocking fussy babies. "No. All's been quiet." He glanced for the fifteenth time at that innocuous-looking, black-papered window high up on the wall. A thief would have to be pretty determined to try to slip through there, especially when the house was full of guests. But then, if he'd managed to get in through the basement, he could have snuck all the way up the back stairs and gone through the bedrooms without being noticed.

What was he after?

Manning sighed and glanced at one of the many clocks on the shelves. "She said they would be home by three o'clock."

Barclay fought back a yawn that he decided to blame on the low, soothing, lullaby-sounding music coming from the gramophone today. At least Mr. V had instructed him to dedicate his time the rest of the week to playing the part of Manning's assistant, now that he had schematics for the aircraft to work with. No stealing petrol or letters or anything else that required energy. "I daresay it's the fault of my sisters that she's late, sir. Rosie and Willa can go on for hours when the topic is a wedding gown, it seems."

But they would see Evelina safely home once they remembered they ought to return her. He pitied any mugger who might try to overtake them, even given Rosie's condition.

Manning's hum sounded half amused. "You have obviously not known my daughter all that long, Mr. Pearce—she was late to her own birth, as her mother said, and has been running behind ever since."

He snorted a laugh . . . and eased to a seat on the stool. It hadn't, he supposed, actually been that long since he'd met this family. Funny how they'd so quickly absorbed his time. His thoughts.

A healthy chunk of his heart.

He focused his gaze on the synchronization gear slowly taking shape on the bench. "When do you think you'll have a working prototype?"

Manning sank to a seat on his own stool. "I am not entirely sure—it being a bit different from my usual work. And having to modify so many of the parts you've found. Another week, if I can reschedule some of my prior engagements. Perhaps two." He took off his glasses and rubbed at his nose. "Once I'm certain the design is right, I'll submit it to the patent office."

"Is that necessary? Can't you just put the thing into production?"

Manning sighed. "I could, yes. Of course. But Mr. Anderson

of the patent office urged me to make sure I file all my work, especially for anything having to do with weaponry."

Barclay leaned back against the shelf. "You'll need that too, won't you? The guns they mount to the planes?"

"I have the numbers, and a sketch of the design. But an actual weapon would be quite useful, yes. I trust your friends at the Admiralty can provide one?"

"Anything you need, they said." He could fall asleep if he just closed his eyes. At least until he heard the buzz of the doorbell overhead. That brought him back to alertness. Though Evelina wouldn't ring at her own door, would she? Unless one of his sisters had reached the door first. Or if their arms were full of lace or flounces or whatever ridiculous nonsense they were on about today.

Mr. Manning checked the time again. "Only twelve minutes late. Excuse me, Mr. Pearce, I'll just run up and give her the message from her mother."

Barclay waved him on and let the next yawn have its way. Let his head loll to the side, to take in the work they'd done that day. It still just looked like bits of scrap to him. Even looking at the design Manning had sketched out, it was more mystery than machine.

He rested an elbow on the bench and pulled the sketches closer. Another sheet of paper peeked out from beneath them, covered in neat script.

Dear Herman,

My plans for the synchronization gear are going fairly well, I think. Though I'm concerned about the timing of the gears. If you were in town, I would love to mull it over with you.

Barclay put the sketches back overtop the letter, which was most assuredly none of his business.

There were no feminine voices filtering down from above. There were, in fact, masculine ones. Barclay sat up straight, trying to place the others that joined Manning's. He caught a bit of Williston's, he thought, but couldn't identify the other.

Two sets of footsteps, however, soon sounded, moving toward the basement stairs.

He stood. And wished for a strong cup of that coffee Peter and Lukas both liked, to give him a little jolt.

Manning appeared on the steps first, saying something about the pleasant weather and clear skies.

Barclay clamped his lips against the response that sprang to mind—that according to those in Whitehall, clear skies were cause for nervousness. Their intelligence said that zeppelins, or even biplanes, could begin making a run at the English coast any day.

But Manning wasn't talking to him. He was speaking to the man who came down behind him.

He looked to be near Barclay's age, within a few years anyway. He wore his dark hair pomaded and sported a mustache that curled just a bit at the ends. When he replied to Manning, his voice carried the slightest German accent.

Barclay wasn't left to wonder long who he was. The moment Manning reached the bottom of the stairs, he said, "Allow me to make introductions. Hans Wilsdorf, a young man that I like to think I mentored, though he never much needed—or heeded—my advice. And Barclay Pearce, whose recent arrival in my acquaintance has been most timely."

Barclay stepped forward, reached to shake. Wilsdorf smiled and clasped his hand. "How do you do?"

"How do you do?"

Niceties dispensed with, they both looked to Manning, who was unearthing another stool from the corner. "Hans has dropped by to show me his latest design, I suppose—no matter how many times I tell him he is wrong to pursue it."

He said it with a smile in his voice, and Wilsdorf replied with a chuckle. "I will prove you wrong yet, my friend. Wristlets are the future."

"For women, perhaps. But no man wants to look as though he's wearing a bracelet. Pocket watches will never go out of style, I say. There." He planted the third stool at an open corner of the bench. "Where do you come down on the question, Barclay?"

Barclay cleared his throat, largely to buy his tired mind a moment to process the question. "I don't believe I've ever actually seen a wristlet watch. Up close, anyway. So I daresay I am no judge."

"Allow me to demonstrate their features." With a flourish, Wilsdorf reached into his pocket, pulled out a box, and opened it. "The wristlet is a very practical addition to any man's wardrobe."

"Practical, he says!" Manning grinned like Clover had done when Jory had shared her box of chocolates with her. "The wrist is a terrible place to wear a watch—the movement of the arm is too violent, it would jostle the works and throw them off."

"Only if the works are inferior, my friend." The newcomer removed from the box a rather small watch face, attached to a leather band.

"Bah. Dust would get into such a primitive case. And perspiration and rain and—"

"Tut, tut. This one is not like the last I showed you." Wilsdorf set the watch upon the bench and flipped it first one way, then the other. "You'll notice that this one has a full case—with gaskets, to ensure such undesirables remain out of the works."

Manning shook his head. "You simply took a pocket watch and soldered a strap to it, Hans."

"No, I took a *superior* pocket watch and soldered a strap to it." He passed the device to Barclay. "One of these days you will admit that my wristlet is destined to become the watch of choice."

"One of these days you'll realize you're chasing a pipe dream. Despite your sixty employees and offices in Bienne as well as London."

Barclay looked up from his investigation of the watch, largely because of the pride evident in Manning's tone. "Sixty employees? For a watchmaker?" If one counted Barclay, and those who ran Manning's shop, he had, what . . . five? Plus a team, he'd said, to help him when it was necessary for maintenance on the Great Clock—but those he brought on only as needed.

Obviously his older friend had been in earnest when he'd declared Hans Wilsdorf at the height of their trade.

Manning turned bright eyes to Barclay. "His wristlet watch was granted the certificate of chronometric precision a few years ago—the only such device ever so honored."

Barclay lifted his brows. "Congratulations, sir. Quite an accomplishment."

"Due in large part to the innovation of my colleagues in Bienne. Which is why I have dropped by, Cecil." Hans's face lost its teasing and settled into weary lines. "This new customs duty—it will be the end of us. Thirty-three percent . . ."

"And a half." Manning nodded. "I am rather glad I do not export any of my pieces. But then, I haven't a factory producing them."

"But nearly all the wristlets I have sold have been abroad."

Barclay stroked his thumb over the fine leather of the band. It was a bit narrow, perhaps, for a masculine style. But the watch itself was as lovely as any he'd seen. He examined the back of the case, where it would rest against the wrist, and saw *W&D* inscribed there. He'd seen it before, on a watch he'd pawned some five years ago. *Wilsdorf & Davis*. At the time, it had been nothing but a funny-sounding name—and the watch hadn't fetched nearly as much as he'd hoped, even with its gold case.

"Florence and Davis and I have discussed it at length since the tax was announced. Has she said anything to Evelina yet?"

Barclay looked up. Manning had gone perfectly still. "Anything about what?"

Wilsdorf sighed. "We are relocating. For the duration of the war, at the least. To Bienne."

"No. Hans—"

"Between taking a third of our income on every watch we sell and the fact that my wife cannot go out in public without being harassed because of our last name . . ." The shake of his head was fiercer this time. "They do not care that I became a British subject. That she and her brother are as English as you. They hear only the German in my name, in my speech. I will not subject her to such treatment. Not when we can avoid it by spending more time at our house in Switzerland."

Given the look on Manning's face, the relocation of her friend would strike a hard blow to Evelina. Barclay's fingers tightened around the case of the watch. Just what she needed—another person important to her up and leaving.

Not that he could really blame the Wilsdorfs. He'd witnessed a bit of the treatment tossed Peter and Rosemary's way because of their last name, and it had made him want to bash a few heads together. If Rosie weren't the resilient, stout-blooded Cockney girl she was . . .

Manning's breath came out in a whoosh. "I am sorry to hear it. Yours is a rare talent, lad, and I will miss our repartee."

"You do not have to." Wilsdorf leaned forward, his spine still perfectly straight. Somehow proclaiming, with that one bit of movement—precise, measured—his German heritage. "Come with us."

Manning leaned back. "I beg your pardon?"

"We could use your expertise. Look at all this, Cecil." He waved a hand at the shelves, overflowing with brilliance. "The mechanisms you have pioneered—you ought to be head of an international firm yourself. Or at least a division of one. Come with us.

I know it may seem odd to work for me, but you know I hold you in the highest regard. We would make you a partner, Davis and I. He has agreed."

Manning shook his head, but it didn't look so much like refusal as bemusement. "I don't even speak French."

Wilsdorf laughed. "We will hire you an interpreter. Come, *mon ami*. Consider it, at least. Say you will."

"I will . . . not dismiss it out of hand."

"Evelina and Florence could keep each other company. And you would get to see Herman again. You could have coffee together every morning." He said it in the same singsong voice that Pauly used to convince a street rat to come out of hiding and have a bite to eat.

Manning's lips ticked up.

Barclay's heart tocked down. It was unreasonable to be upset over the prospect of saying goodbye to people he'd known so short a time, he supposed. Unreasonable to expect them to stay forever a few streets away, so he could let Evelina pretend they were involved, just to irritate her mother.

Unreasonable to already miss her.

Quite suddenly he didn't like this Wilsdorf character at all.

"I will talk it over with Judith and Evelina. When are you going?"

"Soon. The first of June, I hope."

Only a week away. If the Mannings decided to leave at the same time . . . Barclay glanced at the synchronization gear on the bench. Even if it was finished by then, the patent wouldn't have gone through. It wouldn't be ready to be handed over to the RNAS. Would Manning leave with that still undone?

Given the gleam in the man's eyes, Barclay was none too sure. Trying to suppress his sigh, he pressed on the button to release the front of the wristlet's case and looked at the white face of the watch with its bright gold numbers, just to give himself something to do.

He frowned as he read the letters under the twelve. "Rolex?"

Both sets of eyes looked his way, both seeming a bit surprised to see him still there. Wilsdorf recovered first. "My company. As easily said in any language—I labored months trying to come up with just the right word that would sound neither German nor Swiss nor English, but pronounced the same in all. And short enough to put on the face."

That was what made Barclay cock his head to the side. "I've never seen a company name on the face of a watch." And he'd fenced a lot of watches in his day. Usually that inscription on the back of the case was the only way to tell who had actually made it. The face was for the trader.

"Another of Hans's pipe dreams. That it will be the manufacturer and not the trader's name that draws customers to his product." Manning reached for the watch. "You'll never convince anyone to carry this, you know."

Barclay relinquished the wristlet.

Wilsdorf shrugged. "They have little choice, when they order a batch of them and a few have our name upon them. I am only putting it on one in six for now. But then it will be two, and then three, and someday people will buy it *only* if it says Rolex."

"Ha! That will be the day." Manning smiled again, snapped the case closed, and held the watch out to Wilsdorf.

The German stood up without taking it. "You keep it, Cecil."

"Are you quite certain?"

Wilsdorf grinned. "No shop wants to carry it anyway, with Rolex on the face." He took a step away, toward the stairs, and paused again. Sobered again. "Think over my proposal."

Manning's hand fisted around the watch. "I will."

He would. Which was exactly what Barclay was afraid of.

SIXTEEN

Evelina nearly pressed her hands over her ears. She could hum. Or sing aloud even. Just clamp her hands down and shout, "La la la la!" until they stopped arguing, as she'd done as a child.

She clicked shut the door to her bedroom, which was in fact enough to quiet the conversation. Her parents never shouted, even in the heat of battle. They just bludgeoned each other with their own sides, never listening to the other, Aunt Beatrice pounding her own nails in with a stomp of her cane.

"You have never been content with me, Judith, with what I've accomplished—this is my chance to be more. To be a partner in a company like Rolex . . ."

"Did you see that we received an invitation to the Nottinghams' fundraiser gala? I've waited twenty years for such an invitation. It will be held at the end of June, to raise money for the war effort."

"Evelina would be happy in Bienne. With Florence, away from memories of Basil."

"I do wish your husband would simply go back down to his *workshop*, Judith." *Thump, thump.* "He is ruining a perfectly pleasant morning."

It had been the same every day for nearly a week, with only

slight variations on the theme. Evelina bustled to her window and looked down to the street below, her gaze focused on the corner around which the girls or Barclay would come any minute now. Rescue. Escape.

There—Barclay *and* the girls, with Clover and Patch in tow as well. Evelina couldn't resist a smile. Once cleaned up, the girl actually looked a bit like Fergus, which would help their claims of being family.

Evelina snatched her hat and gloves from their places and put them on as she flew down the stairs.

A *thwack* from the drawing room brought her feet to a sudden halt on the last step. It wasn't the sound of Aunt Beatrice's cane. It sounded more like a magazine hitting the table with unprecedented force.

And then, the unthinkable—her mother's voice raised. "If you want to go to Switzerland so badly, Cecil, then by all means, *go*. But you'll be going alone!"

Evelina sucked in a breath and willed her feet to move again. To take her down that last step and out the door. But they didn't act fast enough, and a moment later her father stormed from the room.

But no, he didn't storm. He trudged. And he stopped when he spotted her. "Lina." He looked so tired. Not angry, not defiant, not shocked at those words that still reverberated through Evelina's head. He just looked tired. "We need to talk, my dear."

Her throat went tight. He wouldn't do it, would he? Leave? He wouldn't, not alone. But what if he meant to convince her to go with him? To leave everything she'd ever known? Gloria? Her new friends at Number 120?

"Barclay—" Her voice caught. She cleared her throat. "Barclay is on his way down the street, Papa. We can talk later, all right?"

His nostrils flared, determination edging out the exhaustion. "Tonight."

It sounded like something she expected from Mother, not from him—an ultimatum. She pasted on a smile that he wouldn't be convinced by and pulled open the door. "I'm going to Willa's performance tonight in Shoreditch, remember? Perhaps tomorrow."

Tomorrow it would be the first of June. The day the Wilsdorfs were leaving. Perhaps, once they were gone and Hans was not stopping in every other day to see if Papa had made up his mind yet, the topic would drop.

"Tonight. Before you go." Papa reached out to clasp a hand to her shoulder and then turned away. "Tell Barclay I am in the workshop, if you will."

"Of course, Papa." She stepped out onto the front step, her breath shaking as it eased out. What was she to do? Go with him? Or side with Mother? Perhaps she would try to speak with the girls about it.

She shoved it aside for now and focused on her friends. She rather liked the routine they'd established this last week—spending time with them filled in the gap that the suffragettes used to fill. Helping Rosemary prepare for her coming child, Willa for her impending nuptials.

Pretending there wasn't a wedding gown in her own armoire that she'd never wear. That there had never been a Basil. Ignoring the notes that continued to arrive from Mrs. Knight, inviting her to other private meetings with other politicians supposedly more sympathetic to their cause than ever, now that the WSPU had pledged their support of the war.

She smiled at Barclay as he jogged up the steps, whether Mother was there to see it or not. "Good morning."

"Morning, luv." He didn't do anything as inappropriate as kiss her hello, not out here on the streets of Hammersmith. But he caught her hand in his and squeezed it. And his gaze dropped to her mouth. "How are things inside today?"

"Unchanging." She forced a swallow down her dry throat. Basil had never made her heart race just by taking her hand. She wasn't sure why Barclay Pearce did. Perhaps it was just that rebellious streak Mother brought out in her, the allure of the forbidden. "Papa is in the workshop."

"As expected."

He'd yet to mention what kept him down there more hours than usual. The castle for the earl's little daughter, perhaps?

She really ought to go down soon, see if she could lend a hand with his books. But the space felt awfully close with Barclay taking up so much of it, and he'd been there most of every day. Whatever project held them so enthralled, it must be important. Time-sensitive. Otherwise Papa never would have altered his carefully fashioned schedule.

Barclay gave her fingers another gentle squeeze and then released them. "Still coming with us tonight?"

"I wouldn't miss it." It had been ages since she'd been to a concert. Since she'd been out in the evening at all, really. All the opera shows had been moved up to late afternoon, thanks to the blackout restrictions, and with only the dim gas streetlights, driving after dark was hazardous at best.

A risk she was willing to take. Especially if she could return home so late that there wouldn't be time to talk to Papa about Bienne and Hans Wilsdorf and decisions made for his career. If she could avoid choosing a side altogether. And if she didn't, if the Wilsdorfs left, surely Papa would let the matter drop. Wouldn't he?

Barclay sidled past her into the house, brushing closer to her than the wide doorway really demanded. It made her smile. And hope that she found herself left alone with him for a moment soon, so that he could find another excuse to kiss her.

When she turned down the steps, Retta and Elinor were both grinning at her, while Clover pushed Patch's pram back and forth in front of the house. She could only hope that her cheeks didn't look as flushed as they felt.

Elinor looped their arms together. "Coming with us to Pauly's again this week?"

"Oh, do!" Little Clover scrambled to Evelina's other side when Retta gently took over the pram-pushing. "We had such fun last week!"

"I would love to." Another reason to stay. She glanced over to Retta. "Olivia is not with you today?"

"Our walk yesterday left her leg rather tired. She opted to stay with Rosie. Willa and Lukas are both at Shoreditch already for a rehearsal."

"She's doing well with the braces, isn't she?" Elinor's voice was all bright hope. "*I* think she is. I know her leg tires more easily, but that's surely a good sign, right? She's working it more."

"I should think so." Evelina didn't remember exactly how long it had taken her own legs to stretch again, to strengthen. She remembered long, agonizing days. Stubbornness. Mother chastising Papa for putting her through it, Aunt Beatrice insisting that it hardly mattered—*thump, thump*—she would always be a cripple.

But she wasn't. And Olivia wouldn't be either.

They went directly to the Holstein house today, where Olivia and Clover set about hosting a tea party for their dolls—both seeming utterly amazed by the fact that Rosemary and Peter had given them such treasures for no reason at all. Retta positioned herself in front of a window with a sketchbook, Elinor brought out knitting needles, and Evelina found Rosemary in the sunny drawing room, a novel lying open on her stomach as though it were a desk.

Evelina grinned and sat beside her. "You and your husband always seem to have a book in hand."

Rosie looked up from her pages with a grin. "You ought to see the library at Kensey sometime. It was an utter ruin before I got my hands on it."

She'd already heard a brief story about how Rosemary had

gone to Cornwall as a librarian to bring order to that ruin of a room, and proceeded to capture the heart of the reclusive master of the manor. A tale befitting one of the novels they so loved, in her opinion. "I've never been to Cornwall. Is it as lovely as they say?"

"Lovelier. I know Peter will be anxious to get back, once the wedding is over." She slid a marker into the novel and set it aside. "Barclay is even more fond of novels than I am, you know."

This, too, had become a regular part of her day—one of Barclay's sisters taking it upon herself to educate Evelina on the subtleties that made up their brother. As if they really thought . . . Well, she never saw a point in correcting them.

"Yes, we've talked about novels quite a bit. His favorite author is Branok Hollow, I believe?"

"Mmm." Rosemary tapped a finger to the novel on the table, drawing Evelina's eye to the gold-embossed author's name. "I have to lock this one up when he comes over, or he'll steal it before I have a chance to finish."

Evelina frowned at the title. "I thought that one didn't release until June?"

"Peter has connections at the publisher."

"Ah." Evelina leaned back, made herself comfortable. At some point today, she meant to ask Rosemary's opinion about which of her gowns she ought to wear to the concert tonight—Rosie had impeccable fashion sense—but she was content to look just now through the open doorway connecting the drawing room to the parlor where the little girls played. Patch was toddling away from Clover, headed in their direction with a squeal.

Rosemary clapped her hands together for him. "Come to Rosie. Come on."

How did these people do what they did? Love so fully, so quickly?

Clover paused her game to watch her brother, but once he was safely on Rosemary's lap, she went back to pouring invisible tea from her little teapot.

Rosemary pressed a kiss to the boy's downy head. Then smiled at Evelina. "Puzzled us out yet?"

"Never." She sighed and leaned onto the arm of the couch. "What did you all do—before? Before your marriage and Barclay's employment at the Admiralty?" Those bits and pieces still niggled at her—his threat of thieves and thugs, his admission to Clover that he'd done some stealing in his childhood, the way he'd said *job* the other night. Obviously, he had connections to the dark underbelly of London. She was still trying to discover how *much* of a connection.

But he couldn't have really been a *thief*, other than as a child. And perhaps Rosemary and the other girls didn't even know of his past. Thieves, after all, were dirty and unsavory and untrustworthy. These people she would trust with her life. Did, she supposed, every time she ventured out with them onto the streets where that anonymous mugger no doubt still lurked.

Rosemary leaned back too, urging Patch to snuggle in. He did, though it would likely only last a minute. "Whatever we had to do. To survive."

"But what—that is, he mentioned that Elinor was in a workhouse for a while. That it was awful. But the rest of you weren't . . . ?" There were no polite ways to ask questions like this. But then, life wasn't always polite. "I suppose I'm just wondering what you *did* have to do. To survive."

Rosemary drew in a long breath and kept her gaze focused on Evelina. "If you want to know the truth of us, Lina, you ought to ask Barclay. He would tell you—he doesn't lie. All I'll say is that we did things I'm not proud of. But God has forgiven me, and Peter loves me, and somehow, though I hadn't dared hope it, things have changed for us. For the whole family. *We've* changed."

Tracing the pattern on the upholstery with a fingertip, Evelina let her gaze go unfocused. *Change.* She marched for it. Lobbied for it. But change, in her own life, had never meant more than a new address and a *Mrs.* before her name. It hadn't been something to stake her personal hope on. Or to accomplish within herself.

Change had always been a thing for others. Not a thing ever welcomed in the Manning household, where everything was expected to run like clockwork.

And the things that defied that—polio, death, crippling, broken engagements—those had never made her feel particularly closer to God. Not like Rosemary had described. Or Willa, when she'd said how the Lord had filled her heart with music to comfort her during a close scrape in Belgium.

She'd always believed the Lord was there, of course. It was just that *there* wasn't *here*. She'd always thought of Him rather like . . . well, like a clockmaker. Clever and precise in setting up the mechanism. But once He set it in motion, He seemed happy enough to let them all grind through the gears on their own.

Barclay didn't in general try to hurry along his sisters—he didn't in general *need* to. But he knew more than a little exasperation as he shouted up the stairs for the third time, "Lina is late!"

He glanced at the mantel clock just added to their furnishings two days ago, compliments of Cecil Manning—and now the nicest piece in the room by far. Evelina had been due home an hour ago, but when his sisters failed to arrive with her, he'd come searching.

Not that he didn't trust the girls to see her safely home, but he had to admit to relief when he realized she was simply still upstairs with Rosie, being fitted for a dress.

Relief, on whose heels frustration quickly followed. "Lina!"

"I'm coming, I'm coming." She was, finally, but at an amble instead of the run she should have been employing.

Barclay clenched his teeth together. Her father had tried to wave off her failure to appear with "As I've said before, Lina is perpetually late," but this went well beyond the five or ten minutes one might expect of a girl caught up in one of Rosie's stories.

He jerked open the front door of the Holstein house and swept an arm in front of him to indicate she should precede him.

She had a bag-enswathed dress over her arm and a stubborn glint in her eye that belied her easy smile as she finally reached the entryway. "Rosie is such a genius with a needle! I cannot believe her skill. Though I suppose I should, having seen how well you all dress."

Didn't she realize her father wanted to speak with her tonight? Didn't she *care*? Barclay shook his head. "If you had wanted to simply stay here and leave with us, you ought to have made such arrangements beforehand, Lina. Your father was worried."

Perhaps he sounded too much like the big brother, chastising her as he would Elinor or Cressida. But he couldn't help it.

Her chin, of course, went up. "Papa knew exactly where I was. If he was so worried, he could have come to check on me himself—but of course, he didn't have it scheduled."

Barclay paused with his hand on the latch, even though she'd finally stepped out into the dim night. Never in their acquaintance had he heard her speak of her father with that note of bitterness. He shut the door behind them, shut out what little light there'd been. The gas streetlamps were few and did little to illuminate them. "You knew he wanted to talk with you. You knew it. Why would you purposely hurt him?"

She spun, though there was little room to do so on the front step, which meant there was only a breath between them. "He's had a week to speak with me. But instead he's spent the whole time arguing with Mother, both of them just assuming that they know what's best for me. Then he demands an hour the night before the Wilsdorfs are leaving?" She shook her head. "Let him wait."

"Lina. He's your father." She had to know how blessed she was to have one, and one like Cecil Manning to boot, who clearly adored her.

He couldn't see what her eyes might hold, thanks to the brown-black of the night. But her hand landed softly on his chest and made his heart skip. "Do you want me to go to Switzerland, Barclay?"

As if his tripping pulse under her fingers weren't answer enough. "Don't—I beg you. Don't make me your excuse for disrespecting him. When we both know you wouldn't make such decisions for me."

Her hand splayed out there across his heart. "I shouldn't. But I . . . I *feel* when I'm with you. I'm not just an automaton."

"Well, of course you're not. Whoever said you were?"

Her fingers fell away.

"Ah." *Him*. This was, he supposed, why it wasn't advisable to embark on a relationship with someone who'd just had one smashed to pieces. Basil Philibert was still a specter stationed squarely between them.

He took her hand and led her down the steps. "We'd better hurry. You won't be any later than you already are on *my* account."

She made no verbal reply. But she wove their fingers together as they walked and stroked her thumb along his. Tormenting him, he supposed, for taking her father's side. Though he only took it because it was *her* side as well, she was just being too stubborn to realize it.

Her front door swooshed open before they even reached the first doorstep, Manning himself silhouetted in the golden lights of the entryway.

There were no words to capture the look upon his face. The haunted hurt in his eyes. "Evelina."

She just swept inside at a near run, with a little laugh that she had to realize no one thought was real. "Sorry, Papa! You know how time gets away from me. Rosie was fitting me for a dress for tonight, and I still need to curl my hair." She paused long enough to press a kiss to her father's cheek but then darted up the stairs. "We'll talk tomorrow!"

"Evelina!" Manning's voice was sharp, sharper than Barclay had ever heard it. He shut the door with such care that it resounded like a slam. "I asked for one hour. *One hour* of your time."

Evelina paused a few steps from the first floor. But she didn't turn around, not fully. Just granted him her profile. "I'm sorry, Papa." Then she vanished into the upper hall.

Manning's sigh lingered like poison in the air.

Barclay swallowed. "My apologies, sir. I tried to hurry her along."

"There has never been any hurrying Evelina." Shoulders sagging, Manning stepped away, toward the door to the workshop. "Thank you for trying, Barclay. Have a lovely time at your sister's concert."

If only he could.

SEVENTEEN

The music should have calmed her. The comedy act should have diverted her. The variety bit should have thrilled her. But instead, all Evelina could hear was that note in Papa's voice. The one that said she'd not only disappointed him—something she'd done so often with Mother that she ought to be immune to it—but that she'd hurt him.

Regret grated along her nerves with every move of Willa's bow as she played. Her fingers dug into her palms. She should have just granted him his hour. Never mind the anger over not being drawn into the conversation a week ago. Never mind that she didn't know her own opinion on the question. He was *Papa*. He deserved that much consideration from her.

Applause erupted around her as a befeathered actress bowed upon the stage, her plume bobbing. Evelina jerked back to the present enough to join in with nearly silent clapping.

Beside her, Barclay loosed a mighty sigh and slipped out of his chair, though he remained bent over. "Come on. Now. Outside."

Was her internal thrashing so loud it was disturbing the rest of the audience? Possibly. Even so, she likely would have resisted making a scene by exiting, had Barclay not reached for her hand and all but dragged her to her feet.

She cast a glance at the row filled with his family, ready to offer them an apologetic look, but none had even glanced their way. Frankly, *no one* seemed to notice two patrons making a brisk retreat up the side aisle. And why should they? Already the orchestra was playing a rousing little ditty while the next act wheeled out onto the stage.

Barclay pulled her through a side door, down a darkened corridor that may have made her heart thump in anxiety were it not for the warmth of his palm against hers, and out into the clear, cool night.

Moonlight glinted down on them, pale and silvery. Barclay paused a few steps outside the door, in the shelter of the alley, and turned to face her.

He was perfectly ordinary looking, when he wasn't grinning at her. Nobody the world or society would deem important. But when the silver light struck him, turning his face into angles and planes and painting him in colorless beauty, her breath caught. It made no sense that she felt this pounding in her chest over him. That her palm went hot and damp as it rested within his, that her pulse sped at the way he wove their fingers together.

It made no sense that she felt more for him than she had for Basil. That she *felt* more when with him. That she wanted to say something, do something, to wipe that mournful worry from his eyes.

The night settled in her bones, chilling her. Her shoulders sagged under his gaze. "You're disappointed in me."

"No." His fingers tightened, and his thumb stroked along hers. "I'm disappointed *for* you, Lina. Your family ought by rights to be happy—you have *everything*. But the three of you can never seem to line your gears up properly."

A breath of sad laughter slipped from her lips. "Perhaps I ought to just let you adopt me into *your* family."

His larynx bobbed behind the stylish bow tie he wore. "I don't really want you for another sister. And you can't just give up on your parents. It's not what family does."

Wasn't it? No, perhaps not. Mother had certainly never given up nagging them, even when they wished she would.

Perhaps Barclay could read her thoughts, for his brow furrowed. But then he tilted his head. "Do you hear that?"

"Hear what?" But even as she asked, she noted what must have caught his attention. A distant rumbling, like . . . "Thunder?"

"No. The skies are clear."

She lifted her face, craned her neck, and pointed to a shadow obscuring the moon. "There, see. Clouds. One of them, anyway."

He followed her finger—and pulled her back a step. "That's not a cloud."

Her hand gripped his arm, fingertips no doubt digging in. To be sure, the shadow was too solid to be a cloud, had no wispy edges. Had a form that seemed to turn even as she watched, to elongate until it was a perfect, ever-growing torpedo shape. "What is that?" Her voice came out shaky, weak.

Because she knew.

"A zeppelin." Barclay pulled her back another step, as if such a feeble retreat could get them clear of that silent, growing form. Whatever the rumbling had been, it wasn't the airship.

"Ours?"

"We don't have zeppelins. It must be German."

"No." That wasn't possible. Their very skies couldn't be invaded by the enemy on a night so fair, could they? Here, in London? Perhaps over a battlefield, but *here*?

"We should get back inside." But rather than move again, he stood rooted to the spot as surely as she did, his gaze latched on to the dirigible. As it drew nearer, meandering a bit as if following some road they couldn't see, it caught the moonlight and glinted silver. Perhaps it would have been beautiful, if it were theirs. Or if they weren't at war.

"Where do you think it's going?" And what was it *doing*?

In her mind's eye, she saw the lake in St. James Park—drained so the moonlight wouldn't glint on the water and attract airships. The windows, papered over in black or with curtains drawn after dark. All the electric lights extinguished and dim gaslights in their place. Because zeppelins carried bombs.

She couldn't swallow. Couldn't *breathe*. Could only stand there clinging to Barclay's arm while that strange silver shape grew impossibly large, until it blocked out the moon, until a soft whirring sound filled the night around them.

Until something small and dark fell from it, and fire erupted a few streets away where it struck.

She must have screamed, because it rang in her ears. Barclay's arms came around her, pulling her to his chest. "Inside," he said into her ear. "Now."

As if *inside* were any safer than outside when a monstrous machine could set a building afire from the air. She gripped his lapels and kept her face trained upward. "It's getting closer. It's still coming."

"Following the Thames, I'd bet." His voice was utterly blank, controlled. It was, she was quite sure, what abject terror sounded like in him. Because Hammersmith was on the Thames. And, farther along, so was Poplar.

He tried to corral her toward the door, but still she held her spot, gaze locked on that looming threat. More screams filled the air now, from all around, and in the distance a siren invaded the night. Flames leapt orange and red toward the sky from the building a few streets down, as if trying to reach grasping fingers upward toward its creator.

The zeppelin whirred onward. Toward them. Blocked the night sky from its stance, hunkering directly over them.

Something came whistling down.

No. She gripped Barclay's sleeve to pull him in the opposite direction from the one in which he was tugging her. *Away*. But it was no use. The bombs plunged into the roof with a terrifying sound of splintering and crashing, and new screams sliced the night. The whole world, it seemed, rumbled in protest.

But no flames shot upward with their clawing fingers. That was something, wasn't it?

Barclay dashed away from her hands, toward the door.

"Barclay!"

"I have to get my family out! Just . . . stay here."

Idiot man—who dashed *into* a soon-to-be-burning building? She shook her head and dove after him through the door, back into the dim hallway. Barclay Pearce did, that was who. And no doubt would even if it weren't his own family inside. The sort of man to bring orphans home from the street certainly wasn't the sort to abandon a whole theater full of people if there was some aid he could lend.

The panic was audible well before they emerged back into the auditorium. Crowds were pushing toward the main doors, not seeming to realize there were exits at the sides as well. A man stood on the stage, shouting for order. Barclay headed for the front rows, where his family stood, alarmed looks on their faces.

Evelina trailed him, weaving her hand around his arm to keep from becoming separated in the jostling crowd.

He glanced down at her, over his shoulder. "You could have stayed outside."

She lifted her chin. Perhaps she had never been quite the daredevil that others had been. But she wouldn't shy away from danger when there was help to be given. She *wouldn't*. "Let's just get these people to safety, shall we?"

Amid the tumult, she saw the faintest bit of a grin flutter over his lips. And it was enough to bolster her.

Barclay shouldered his way through the mob, invisible. He knew how to blend into any crowd, yes—but just now, that wouldn't help him. It wouldn't help *any* of them. He glanced toward the orchestra pit, where Willa sat on the end of her row, gaze upon him. Her eyes were wide, her face gone pale. Her lips moved in that silent question that contained her biggest fear. *"Fire?"*

He shook his head and watched her shoulders sag a bit. It could only be the hand of God that kept those incendiary bombs from burning when they hit the theater. But it meant life, and a chance to get everyone out safely, and he'd praise the Lord for it with every breath he took.

He pushed his way through the frantic crowd, toward the man shouting, uselessly, from the stage. Evelina still held on to his arm, and he knew that the rest of his family followed in their wake. Once in front of the red-faced man, he gave Evelina's hand a squeeze and then moved it from his arm so he could vault up onto the stage.

The man shot him a startled look, which Barclay met with a vaguely friendly, calming smile. He stepped close enough to be heard over the babbling mob. "Have the band play something. It'll help calm the crowds."

The man nodded—and looked upward. "I don't know how long we have to get everyone out of here."

"The bombs didn't ignite. I was outside and saw them fall. I think we can get everyone safely out." He nodded to the collection of his family. "We can help direct everyone to the exits."

"God bless you." The man leaned down to address the maestro.

As Barclay hopped down again, the orchestra was being told in no uncertain terms that they would play until every last patron was safely evacuated, assuring them they would have time to get to safety as well.

Barclay rejoined his group. "Let's try to bring some order—be sure and direct people to the side exits as well. Rosie and Peter, you take this one, and then get yourselves safely home. Girls—"

"We'll cover the opposite side and then rendezvous in Hammersmith." Retta was already nodding and heading away.

Lukas must have been visually checking on Willa. He refocused on Barclay and said, "I will help you with the main entrances. I have no intention of leaving until Willa does anyway."

Of course he wouldn't. Barclay jerked his head in agreement and grabbed Evelina's hand again. He'd prefer, of course, that they all be safely at home. But they weren't, and so the next best thing was to keep her at his side.

They started with those closest to the stage, directing them toward the side exits to help clear a path. Then slipped around through an interior corridor used by the actors and musicians to the main exit of the auditorium, where they could try to bring some order to the press of people there.

The press of people seemed rather determined not to be ordered. When Barclay tried to weave his way to a position at a door, one chap looked ready to punch him. "I say, where do you think *you* are going? Pushing through like that."

Barclay offered the man a smile that probably had no effect at all. "Just trying to help with the traffic, sir. I've already been outside—was out there when the bombs fell, as it happens—and I can assure you there is plenty of time for everyone to get out. They didn't ignite."

The man looked at him as though he were mad. "You were already out and returned *in*?"

"The better to assist you, good sir." With an imaginary doff of the hat he'd not reclaimed, Barclay sketched a bow. And noted that the line of the man's shoulders relaxed just a bit. Still tense, but no longer combative.

"Are you quite certain the theater is not on fire?" This from a lady a few bodies back, who clutched the arm of a tight-lipped man.

Barclay gave her his most reassuring smile. "Very sure, madam. And now, if you will . . ." He motioned the people nearest the door, who had been locked together in their attempts to push through first, to unknot.

Word that the building was not on fire was already being passed through the crowd—he could hear the words over and again, paired with relieved sighs and a few sobs. But it likely wouldn't take long for someone to question it, and for the question to be overheard and touted as fact. The lull wouldn't last long, not without reinforcement.

And so he pasted on a grin and called out, "Anyone who wants a glimpse of Lukas De Wilde on their way out should proceed to the door to your left, where he is assisting!"

A French exclamation came back to him over the crowd—which had the sound of annoyance but was obviously gauged to reinforce the claim, otherwise he would have made his response in English to keep from drawing attention. Lukas was a good sport.

Evelina leaned close. "What can I do?"

"Work the crowds in this area, if you would. Just move about, assuring them all that the bombs failed to ignite." He squeezed her fingers and then released her so he could reach out to steady a fellow who'd been shoved from behind. "Easy now," he said more loudly, with another grin. "Let's not let the krauts steal our good manners from us."

Perhaps it was their efforts, perhaps it was the fact that no raging inferno of a roof crashed down upon them, perhaps it was the soothing effects of the orchestra, but the crowd soon settled and was, within five or ten minutes, nearly gone. Barclay didn't dare wonder what the streets would be like, choked as they would be with the far-more-panicked people who had evacuated the buildings that *had* caught fire, but they were doing their bit, at least. Soon there was no more reason to stand sentry, and he saw his sisters slipping out their side doors with a wave.

Barclay lifted a hand in salute and then started back down the aisle. Lukas was doing the same from his position, aiming for the orchestra. Evelina took her place at Barclay's side again. "Why did you send the girls out on their own? Wouldn't it be safer to go home together?"

"In the crowds likely to be out there?" He shook his head and guided her toward Willa. "It'll be easier for one or two to slip among them without worrying about staying with the others. They know their way, they know the shortcuts, and they're more than capable of taking care of themselves. We'll all arrive quicker if we go separately than if we tried it together."

"You have such utter confidence in them." Her voice said she found it strange. And alluring. "I've never known a man who didn't view women as weaker, to be protected."

He slid an arm around her back. The urge was always there, yes—to coddle, to hold tight, to keep close. But what did that ever accomplish? His family might accuse him of being a tyrant, but when it came to this, they all knew he wasn't. Couldn't be. "The best way to protect those we love is to teach them how to protect themselves."

Her sigh was a low echo of those he'd heard from the surging crowds. "So many years I fought to be an independent woman. Then I meet all of your family, who manage it without even trying. Without the strife."

"Oh, we've had plenty of strife—just with the world more than with each other." They converged with Lukas again just as the orchestra played the final note of their song.

The maestro looked to the man still on the stage, who nodded and made a shooing motion—then wasted no more time on niceties and scurried off himself.

Willa stood, her borrowed Stradivarius in hand, and hurried toward Lukas and Barclay and Evelina. She flicked her gaze upward. "I hear sirens."

They must have been getting closer for a while—Barclay had scarcely noticed them growing louder. "The buildings down the street weren't so lucky as ours. Getting home could be interesting."

"We'll manage." She tucked her hand in Lukas's. "I need to get backstage for my case and things, then we'll leave. You go ahead and get Lina home, Barclay. If her family hears of this, they'll be worried sick."

And word would spread quickly, no doubt. Terror always did. He nodded. "The zeppelin seemed to be following the Thames. No doubt the crowds will be thickest along it."

"Noted." Willa leaned into her fiancé's arm. "And your mother and Margot are fine."

Lukas's smile may have been strained, but he offered it anyway. "I am not worried. They escaped Louvain when it burned and walked all the way to Brussels. They will scarcely blink at something so mundane as a few bombs." But the glance he sent toward the doors said he wanted to go and make sure of it, now that Willa was free to leave.

"We won't hold you up." Barclay clapped a hand to his soon-to-be-brother's shoulder and leaned in to press a kiss to Willa's brow. "See you at home."

He wouldn't let himself think about whether that horrific dirigible would make its way to Hammersmith. Or to Poplar. It would do no good to dwell on it—it would either whir its way there or head back to Germany. And whatever it did, he wouldn't know it until it was done. He couldn't beat it home, no matter what he tried.

"I want to check on the De Wildes first. I know everyone else will see to ours." Willa passed her violin to Lukas and gave Barclay a quick hug, and then Evelina.

"Good." He didn't need to say that if there was a problem, or if they just wanted more family around them, to bring them to Hammersmith. She'd know. As would Lukas. "Be careful."

"Carefuller than careful." With a ghost of her cheeky smile, Willa spun away, Lukas on her heels.

Evelina pulled him toward that same side door they'd gone out before, where Rosemary and Peter had been but occupied no longer. They'd likely be the first to make it home again. "We should hurry back. Papa will worry, you're right. And I daresay word will beat us home."

"No doubt." Especially if the zeppelin itself beat them there. He paused on the door's threshold, his insides churning too much to take another step.

"Barclay?"

"Just . . ." How many times had he worried about Georgie on the front lines? Wondered if Charlie was there, in the line of fire—assuming his little brother had survived to adulthood? How many times had he given his sisters lessons in how to take down an aggressive man or another thief? How many times had he lectured them all on how to stay safe?

But nothing he did—no amount of worry—could do a thing against a threat like this. He couldn't protect his family from bombs dropping from the sky. And those were the ones at home, not on a battlefield. For the ones away, he could do even less. Less than less. He could do *nothing*.

"Barclay?" Evelina's fingers slid up his forearm, gripped his elbow. Her voice was soft. Questioning. Worried. For *him*. No one ever worried for him. Never had. He was the one in charge of worrying for others, not the other way around.

He forced a swallow but let his eyes slide shut. "I think I need to pray. I'm still new to all this faith business, but I think . . . I think I do. Do you mind? If we take a minute?"

He felt her shift her balance beside him, heard her surprise in the intake of her breath. Then, "Of course that's all right. Let's."

He nodded, swallowed. He'd begun praying aloud with the little ones every night a couple months ago, but somehow that was different. The children didn't judge his lack of eloquence, the fact that he didn't know the right words or the proper forms. Evelina had no doubt sat in a church pew every Sunday of her life and would realize every variance he made.

But that couldn't matter. Not now, with fire raining down from the sky. It had to be just him and the Lord, no self-consciousness between them. He sucked in a breath. Breathed out his prayer. "Lord, thanks for protecting us here tonight. For keeping those bombs from catching fire. I know that was you, and I'm grateful. We could have been dead, but we're not. Now if you would please protect those we love, at home. Keep them safe. And help us to reach them safely, all of us. Rosie and Peter and the girls and Willa and Lukas."

He paused, sucked in another breath. Heard the sirens still wailing in the night. "And be with those who weren't so lucky tonight, please. Guide them to safety too. If anyone's lost, help them to find their families. If any were killed . . . then comfort those they left behind. And my brother on the front lines, Lord—please keep Georgie safe. He faces this kind of terror every day, along with all the rest of our lads fighting. Please protect them too. Georgie and Charlie, wherever he is. I have to trust you know where he is too." He swallowed again, but no other words came to him. So he said, as he'd heard Peter say, "We ask this in the name of your Son, Jesus. Amen."

Evelina's soft "amen" echoed his. When he opened his eyes, he saw hers gleaming in the dim light that reached her a step into the corridor. She blinked, and the gleam vanished.

He cleared his throat and took a step, then another. The weight on him wasn't any lighter. And yet, somehow, it wasn't quite so heavy. The burden still weighed, but it was as if another shoulder had come alongside his under it. That, he'd come to realize, was how the Lord worked. At least for him. He didn't remove the bad—He just lent him the strength to face it.

In silence, they traveled the corridor until they emerged again into the alleyway. Smoke tainted the air, flavored with the acrid odor of things burning that shouldn't be. Not just wood and coal and peat, but paper and varnish and paint and fabric.

It was a smell that dropped him back to another street, some fifteen years ago. When he'd huddled outside their burning building with Willa and Rosemary in his arms, the flat Pauly had helped them rent gone. The night they'd found Retta and Lucy, both orphaned in the fire. The night they'd sworn never to keep everything in one place again. Never to let a location determine *home*.

Perhaps he needed the reminder, with that house at Number 120 becoming so quickly familiar and comfortable. But it would pass out of their lives eventually too—everything did. Every place, every possession. They were just things, easily stolen by people or circumstances. Not at all what mattered. People were what mattered—and they could be stolen away too.

When it came down to it, all you ever had forever was what you carried inside. Memories. Faith. Love.

Evelina wove her fingers through his and coughed into her handkerchief. "What's the best way home, do you think?"

"Away from the Thames." He tightened his grip and pulled her toward the mouth of the alley.

EIGHTEEN

It seemed that morning should have dawned by the time Evelina opened the door to her house. That this nightmarish night should have ended. That at some point, they should have at least outpaced the shouting crowds.

But with each turn they made, they found someone else running toward them, declaring that yet another place along the Thames had been hit. Spitalfields, Whitechapel and Stepney, Stratford. And though the fire brigades reportedly didn't have much trouble quelling the flames, they couldn't quell the panicked rush of feet so easily. Even though they were moving away from the damaged areas as they neared Hammersmith, people were still looking up at the moonlit sky, anxiously searching the heavens for another silver-gilded monster.

Evelina could only pray that word hadn't yet infiltrated the solid walls of home. Pray it . . . but doubt it. Someone of Mother's acquaintance would have heard, and they would have telephoned. The switchboards had no doubt been wildly lit chaos tonight.

She put a hand to the latch, glanced at Barclay's grim face, and pushed open the door into the dim light of the entryway.

"Evelina!" Mother came at her like a runaway locomotive,

closing her into a hard embrace. "I heard the music hall was hit! Are you injured?"

Evelina could do nothing but stand there, stock-still with shock, while Mother fawned over her.

Mother never fawned. Least of all over her. But there she was, blubbering like a normal mother, tears in her eyes as she framed Evelina's face between shaking palms. "I thought I'd lost you."

Evelina sucked in a wavering breath. She hadn't heard that particular note in her mother's voice since they'd lost Jacob. Hadn't, honestly, thought her still capable of it—it had rather seemed that in the last twenty years, Mother had shut off the tap of her emotions.

Evelina rested her hands over her mother's fingers. "I am well. I assure you. We were hit, it's true, but there was no fire, no injuries at all. You haven't lost me."

Still, Mother stifled a sob. "I thought I had, though. And my sister would only sniff, and your father wouldn't so much as stir from his bedroom, pound as I may upon his door."

Evelina frowned, even as she pulled Mother's fingers away so she could clasp them. "That's unlike him. He retired already?" He'd never, not once, gone to bed before she was safely home.

But then, he'd never been quite so angry and disappointed in her before. She shot a look over her shoulder at Barclay, who still stood just inside the door. "Barclay can tell you all about the bombing—let me go up and assure Papa I'm well. I daresay if you told him about the zeppelin attack, he is worried, even if he wouldn't come down."

Her mother turned to Barclay with an imploring gaze. "Please do tell me what happened. When Elizabeth rang, she was so very vague and panicked. I heard only that the music hall had been struck."

"It was really more frightening than effectual," Barclay said in the same soothing tone he used with the little ones.

Evelina dashed up the stairs while he launched into how they'd stepped outside for a breath of air and saw the airship approaching, her heart thudding every bit as painfully as it had when she watched those bombs drop.

Papa had not been waiting for her. Hadn't even stirred himself from his room. Was he so upset with her that he didn't even care?

No. She knew better. She knew her father. He might be frustrated and hurt by her behavior, but that would never trump his love for her. She drew in a steadying breath as she neared the closed door of his room. Lifted her hand. Rapped upon the wood, loudly enough that it would wake him if he were asleep—Papa was always a light sleeper. "Papa? Are you awake?"

No answer came through the wood.

She knocked again, louder. "Papa?"

Only silence reached out from beyond the door. Tension banded around her chest. What if he *couldn't* answer? What if the stress of all that was going on this past week had found some weakness in his heart? She'd heard of stranger things, men just as healthy suddenly dying. "Papa?" Hearing the frantic note in her own voice, she gripped the knob. "I'm coming in!"

She waited another second for an argument but, getting none, opened the door.

Inside, his room was silent and dark and cool from the window left its usual three inches open. She turned on the low gaslight. And frowned. His bed was still neatly made, not so much as a crease upon it to show he'd sat on the counterpane that evening. The bowl on his dresser hadn't his cufflinks in it, and his pajamas were still draped on his chair, awaiting him. "Papa?" she called loudly enough that he would have heard her from the attached toilet.

Nothing.

Evelina turned off the light and tromped back down the stairs, trying unsuccessfully to unknit her brows.

Mother reached for her again the moment she stepped back onto the floor, looping their arms and patting Evelina's. "Was he relieved?"

Evelina moved her gaze from her mother to Barclay. "He wasn't up there. Hasn't been, from the looks of it. Are you certain he retired?"

"Well, I had assumed. Your aunt and I were out until ten, and he wasn't in the drawing room when we returned, nor did he answer my call down the stairs." With a sigh, she released Evelina's arm again. "Go and check his workshop. I suppose it's possible he simply ignored me."

In which case, he may not have even heard about the aerial bombings, if Mother had only told his empty bedroom. Even so. Even if he hadn't been worrying, she owed him an apology. She offered Mother a tight smile and moved toward the basement stairs.

The door was cracked open, but no music seeped out to betray his presence. Which meant only that he wasn't working, not that he wasn't there. She opened the door and took a few steps down, noting that a light burned below, but not much of one. It barely reached her on the stairs, inspiring her to reach out a hand to trail along the railing.

"Papa?" She ducked when she was halfway down, to see beyond the floor. And nearly fell the rest of the way. "Barclay!"

Flying down the remaining steps, she made it to the center of the workshop by the time Barclay's heavy tread shook the stairs. Her gaze remained latched upon the workbench. The startlingly empty, barren workbench.

Never in her life had she seen it so—*never*. No wrenches, no screwdrivers, no gears or cogs. No designs sketched upon paper, no project underway.

Barclay's sharp intake of air said it hadn't been thus the last time he was here either. And that was only this afternoon. "Where is it?" He charged toward the bench, around it, ducking down to look at the shelves beneath. Eyes wide with panic, he set his gaze over the rest of the shelves, to the table abutting the stairs, everywhere.

"What is *it*?"

"A synchronization gear he's been working on. For aircraft—so the bullets from their guns can go between the propellers, which would increase the accuracy." He huffed to a halt by her side and shoved a hand through his hair. "All his designs are gone. The device itself. All the parts we'd gathered. Where would he take them? We're still a week from testing, and that's assuming we encounter no more setbacks."

"Could he have taken it to show to someone? His friend in the patent office, perhaps?" Evelina pressed a hand to her forehead and scanned the packed shelves.

But they weren't as full as usual. Other pieces were missing too—not his favorites, not his unfinished ones, not any of the projects he would take with him if he were to do the unthinkable and follow Hans to Bienne on his own without so much as a by-your-leave. Just the bits and pieces he'd always waved off whenever she asked about them. The ones she'd never really given any thought to, as they weren't so interesting as his clocks and toys. His so-named dabblings.

Barclay's fingers brushed over her wrist and then fell away. "Perhaps, yes. His friend at the patent office. Or mine at the Admiralty—perhaps they asked to see his progress."

She nodded, holding tightly to that thought. Even though she couldn't quite imagine men from the Admiralty arriving after hours and demanding he box up his work and leave with them. But perhaps they'd had warning of the zeppelin's approach and had come here to see if Papa could help their planes defend London.

Yes, that could be it. He could even now be at the aerodrome.

Playing the part of a hero. "He usually leaves notes on the hall table. Or with Williston." Mother likely wouldn't have even checked with the butler, who would have been long since asleep. "If he's out, he would have left word."

And he *must* be out, because he wasn't at home. And so, there must be a note.

But her stomach quivered as she led the way back upstairs. Because a light had been on down here, and Papa *never* left a lamp burning while he was gone. Even were an admiral to show up and demand his help, that wouldn't overcome Papa's fastidious nature. *Nothing* overcame his fastidious nature.

Mother waited at the top of the stairs, lines of worry still dug in between her brows. "What is it? Did he injure himself down there? I don't know how many times I've said—"

"He isn't down there." A few hours ago, she would have spat it like an accusation. And even now, part of her had to wonder if Papa had obeyed Mother's shout from this afternoon and stormed off, fed up with these women in his life who never gave him the respect he deserved. Maybe he'd left them. Decided he really would just go to Switzerland, with or without them.

But if that were so, then his bedroom would have had gaping spots as well. The shaving kit would have been missing from its place, his comb, his spare set of eyeglasses, his pajamas. No, he'd not packed a bag with the intent of being away for the night. Or longer.

Barclay emerged from the basement behind her. "His work is gone as well. He must have taken it somewhere. Is there a note?"

Mother spun toward the table where it would rest, if there was one. Her hand shook as she reached out to sweep the empty expanse, as if willing paper to appear where there was none. "Nothing here."

Barclay's hand landed on Evelina's shoulder for just a moment, then retreated. "I'll check with Williston."

Mother still stared at the empty table. "It's unlike him. He never leaves without a note. And is never out this late. What if he was somewhere that was struck by the bombs? What if—"

"Mama, stop." It had been years—decades—since she'd called her mother anything but *Mother*. But then, it had been years—decades—since she'd heard such worry in her tone. Such pain. Such *feeling*. "He's well, I'm sure of it. I cannot think of any business that would have taken him to the parts of Town that were struck."

"You're right. Of course." Though she made an obvious attempt to clear her face, a faint line remained between her brows. "He's simply . . ." Apparently unable to find a way to finish the sentence, Mother sighed to a halt.

Evelina glanced to the hallway that led to the servants' quarters. "Where is Aunt Beatrice?"

"She took something to calm her nerves and retired. You know she doesn't deal well with fright."

Was she frightened for Evelina? Or just in general?

Barclay emerged again, his face far from relieved. He shook his head. "Williston says that Mr. Manning was reading in the drawing room when he retired at half past nine and made no mention of going out for any reason. Rather, he said he intended to keep reading until you both returned home."

Mother frowned. "He said that explicitly?"

"Apparently. Something about a new book that he was enjoying, and that he was glad to have an excuse to stay up reading later than usual while he waited for Evelina."

That sounded like Papa. She exchanged a glance with Mother. "We'll check the house. Failing that, you can ring up any of his friends he may have called on, and I'll check the shop. He can't have just vanished."

Barclay strode off, but Mother just sank to an unladylike seat on the stairs. "What if he . . . ?"

"He didn't leave us, Mama. He wouldn't."

"Wouldn't he? After I said what I did to him, *told* him to go alone?" Her hands shaking, Mother pressed her fingers to her cheek. "What if he simply . . . listened?"

Evelina's throat went tight. "Wouldn't he have taken a bag with him, then?" She looked to where Barclay was already returning from the kitchen, hoping he had some kind of insight.

He glanced out the windows into the dark night. "I'll check with my contacts at the Admiralty. And the shop." From his tone, he didn't much relish calling on said contacts at this hour. But Evelina wasn't about to tell him not to do so. "You ladies call whoever might know something."

If there was the slightest chance Papa was with them, then it was worth waking them up.

And if he wasn't . . . Well, if he wasn't, then she feared the gears of her life might grind to a halt, in protest that their keeper was gone.

Barclay stood before the door in Fulham, half expecting the seemingly omniscient V to open it before he could so much as ring. But all was quiet on this street—perhaps its residents were still blissfully oblivious to the clouds of terror that had descended on London this clear night. Not so much as a curtain twitched in the windows.

What if it wasn't really V's house? Or, worse, what if it *was*? Did he really want to call his employer to the door just because Cecil Manning wasn't at home when he should have been?

Yes. He did. He must. Because the moment he saw that empty bench, he'd known something had gone terribly wrong. Barclay lifted his hand and pressed a finger to the bell, listening to it chime within.

If they were to alert the authorities, he knew well what they'd say—that a man who had been arguing with his wife all week, who'd just argued with his daughter, who had an offer from a friend to join him on a trip the next day, wasn't *missing*. He was simply not at home, and obviously of his own will.

But it didn't add up.

A dim light appeared beyond the glass flanking the door, growing a bit brighter with the passing of a few seconds. An oil lamp, he'd bet—a concession to the blackout.

Lot of good *that* had done.

A moment later, he heard a bolt sliding, and a chain, and then the door swung in and a scowling V filled the space. He wore a perfectly ordinary-looking—and hence shocking—set of pajamas with a light robe overtop, and gripped that oil lamp as if he might just swing it into Barclay's head.

He edged back a step, just in case. "Forgive me for barging in, sir. But it's Manning. He's missing. And so is his work on the gear."

"*What?*" Now V stepped back and motioned with his hand. "Come in off the street."

Barclay obeyed, edging through the door with the distinct impression that it would bite him if he didn't move quickly. And sure enough, it swung closed with only a breath of clearance. "Did you hear of the zeppelin attacks, sir?"

V set the lamp on a nearby table. The soft golden glow caught the swift jerk of his head. "Blinker rang after the first of them—I only just got back to sleep, thank you very much." And was cranky when his slumber was disturbed, apparently.

Noted. "One of the bombs struck the Shoreditch Empire Music Hall." He proceeded to tell him the rest of the tale, all the way through arriving at the Manning residence and finding the clockmaker—and the synchronization gear—gone.

V muttered a curse and rubbed a hand over his face.

Barclay sighed. "It wasn't you, then. Or the RNAS. I had this vague hope . . ."

"I imagine you did. But no." V leveled a narrowed gaze upon him. "How did you know where to find me at this hour?"

"Ah . . ." Clearing his throat, Barclay slid half a step away. Just in case the man decided to heft that lamp again. Or some other handy missile. "Would you believe me if I told you I felt the Lord nudging me to follow you home one day?"

He couldn't tell if the sound V made was a laugh, snort, or sigh. "Two weeks ago, I'd bet. I *knew* I felt someone trailing me. I must be getting rusty. I didn't spot you."

"Nah—I'm just that good." Were he not so tired, Barclay probably would have thought better of the jest.

But V's lips twitched. "Hence why I hired you, I suppose. Now. Manning. You said Wilsdorf offered him a partnership in Rolex, and that he's leaving tomorrow. How can we be sure Manning isn't simply going with him?"

"He wouldn't leave without so much as packing a spare shirt." That cold spot in the pit of his stomach—the one that always warned him when a job had gone awry and the bobbies were about to descend—clenched. "I wish it were so simple. But I don't think it is."

"I don't know what resources I can give you to figure it out just now. The Admiralty is going to be scrambling to get some sort of air defense over London—every spare man and pound will be going toward that, and you can bet that the lads in Room 40 will be abuzz, trying to find some cypher they missed—or furious that their messages weren't put to use, if they *did* know of it in advance." Eyes focused on the space beyond Barclay, V pursed his lips, crossed his arms, and tapped out a rhythm.

"With all due respect, sir—I don't need the Admiralty's resources." Barclay gave him a grin. "I have my own. Another reason you hired me. I just wanted to make sure he wasn't already accounted for. And, I suppose, to have your permission to focus on finding him."

V's breath sighed out, long and low. "Of course you must, if it's possible. But we'll need you on the other tasks too—now more than ever. Perhaps you can delegate some of them to your family."

Barclay nodded. He'd been happy to give the girls a break from such work while he could, but they'd been growing bored anyway. "They'll be happy to help."

"All right, then. Report to Whitehall as usual in the morning, and we'll see what the day brings."

"V?" The voice, feminine and soft, accompanied a creaking of the floorboards overhead.

Barclay didn't glance up. Rather, he watched his employer's face, ready to see it go soft or annoyed or panicked or *something*.

It didn't. He just glanced toward the stairs. "In the front hall, luv."

Luv. He said it in the Cockney way, and it sounded at home on his tongue. Easy and comfortable. And not at all uncertain, which was a bit odd, considering that Barclay was still standing there, and the man couldn't possibly be happy about introducing him to whoever *luv* was.

A woman—presumably the one whose silhouette Barclay had seen through the window—descended the stairs without a falter, despite the lack of light. A salt-and-pepper braid hung over one shoulder, and her expression looked perfectly pleasant—all smile lines and grace—as she neared. "Who is it? I don't recognize his voice."

V shifted slightly, putting himself at ninety degrees to the bottom step. "Barclay."

That was all he said. *Barclay*. Not "Barclay Pearce" or "A chap from the Admiralty" or "A colleague" or any sort of explanation. Just his given name—something V had never once called him to his face—as if that would mean something to her.

It must have. She aimed a smile his way as she placed a hand on V's extended forearm. "Oh, how lovely. I've been hoping to meet you, Mr. Pearce." She held out her other hand toward him. "I'm Alice."

He really *had* tumbled through the rabbit's hole into Wonderland. What other proof did he need? Hoping he didn't look the utter fool, Barclay shook off his stupefaction and took her hand, kissed it. "How do you do, ma'am?"

"Better than my husband, no doubt, if you've shown up here without his leave." She smiled in a way he imagined an indulgent mother doing and leaned close. "I told him you sounded awfully clever."

Later, perhaps tomorrow after he'd slept, he'd have to go back over this conversation in his mind and examine all the oddities—like the fact that V had obviously told her about him, and that she seemed unfazed by strangers showing up at three in the morning. "Thank you."

"You sound tired. Did you offer him refreshments, darling? Let me get you a few biscuits and something to drink."

Her *darling* sounded decidedly *not* Cockney, but every bit as at home on her tongue. Barclay shook his head. "That's kind of you, ma'am, but I won't be here long enough to warrant it."

"Something to take with you, then. Give me just a moment. Don't send him out empty-handed, V."

And she, his own wife, called him simply V. Not Victor or Vernon or some surname that began with the letter. Just V. Which meant what? That it was a nickname so firmly established that it was what even those nearest the man called him?

Barclay could only smile and duck his head. "I thank you, then." He edged out of the way so she could turn from the stairs toward a dark corridor that must lead to the kitchen. She didn't reach for any light switches. Fear of more bombs falling if she turned on a light? Barclay frowned. "Do you need the lamp, ma'am?"

She chuckled and didn't so much as turn around. Just kept

walking without a falter. "It wouldn't do me a bit of good. But I do thank you for your concern."

His frown deepening, he moved his gaze to V.

A smile played at the corners of the older man's mouth as he watched his wife vanish into the darkness. "Alice is blind, Barclay."

"Oh." With that brilliant reaction echoing in his ears, Barclay shook his head. "I'm sorry."

"Don't be. In the ways that matter, she sees more than anyone I know." With a lift of his brows, V focused on him again. "Do you need anything else—other than some biscuits to see you on your way?"

It all settled on him again, as heavy as before he'd paused to pray those eternal hours ago. The danger his family had been in—was in still, as was all of London—the futility of trying to protect them all in a world gone mad, and now with the added dread over Cecil Manning. And what it would mean for Evelina and her mother if he was as gone as he seemed. "I don't know what to do for them. I want to believe he'll show up at home again tomorrow, but I have this feeling in the pit of my stomach . . ."

"I'm never one to tell a man to ignore his intuitions, especially in this case, given what Manning was working on. But I *will* say this—it can't be yours to take care of every troubled soul in London, Mr. Pearce. If Cecil Manning is gone, either by intrigue or his own design, that doesn't mean his family's care must fall to you."

To that Barclay said nothing at first. Partly because he wouldn't, *couldn't* believe that Manning had abandoned his family, even if his wife *had* told him to do just that. And partly because it just didn't ring true. Maybe he couldn't feasibly help everyone he met who needed it. But there were always those the Lord put in his path for a reason, who he *could* help. Those who his heart embraced the moment they met. He always knew, always, who he should take into his family.

And he couldn't imagine walking out of Evelina's life now.

"I've never tried to take care of every troubled soul, sir. Just the ones who need *me*, in particular. If I don't help those, who will?"

V's lips twitched up. "You are the oddest bunch of thieves I've ever met."

"Perhaps that, too, is why you hired us."

He inclined his silver-gold head. "Perhaps it is." He turned toward the corridor again just as the sounds of his wife's return reached them. "What a night it has been. Let us hope tomorrow is less exciting, shall we?"

"Cheers." His wife—it seemed wrong to call her Alice, but was "Mrs. V" correct?—held up a small bag as if toasting with it. "And here you are, Barclay dear. Some of Mrs. Haversham's famed cinnamon biscuits for the walk home."

"Thank you, ma'am." He wasn't particularly hungry, but a street rat knew never to turn down food. Especially when it was freely given. He took the brown paper sack, trusting she could hear or sense his smile. "Sorry to have awoken you both again."

Alice tucked her hand through the crook of V's elbow. He covered her fingers with his and nodded. "Think nothing of it. I'll see you in the morning."

Barclay nodded and turned to let himself back out the door.

"Barclay."

He paused with the knob in hand and turned his head.

V lifted his brows. "Try not to worry. I daresay he'll turn up in a day or two, likely with the finished gear in hand."

Barclay couldn't agree. And so he merely said, "Good night, sir. Ma'am," and set about vanishing back into the night.

NINETEEN

The confusion on Hans Wilsdorf's face was without question the most disappointing expression Evelina had ever seen. As she stood outside the Wilsdorfs' house in the morning light, her heart plummeted down into her stomach and set it to roiling. "Are you quite sure he didn't decide to join you? Or it seems possible he would at least stop by to say his farewells."

Apology colored the confusion. "I am sorry, Lina—I do not know where he might be, but he has not come by here, nor do I expect him. Not given the note he sent last evening." Hans reached into his jacket pocket and pulled out a folded sheet of paper. "Here, read it for yourself."

It probably would have been politer to refuse. But politeness wasn't her priority just now. With a bolstering look toward where Barclay stood a step away, she reached for the paper and unfolded it with shaking hands. Papa's precise script stared back at her.

Hans,

I sit down to pen this note with a conflicted spirit. I appreciate more than I can say the offer you have made me, and it is my sincere hope that I will yet be able to accept.

But my family is not ready to make such a drastic move and leave England at this juncture.

Please know that it is my intention to convince them, by whatever means necessary. However, unless something drastic changes in the next few hours, I will not be able to join you yet. I pray you understand, and I will further impose upon you to send up a prayer on our behalf as I undertake what promises to be a most difficult task.

Evelina's breath shook as much as her hand as she handed the note to Barclay and tried to lift her gaze to Hans's. Tried, but she couldn't withstand the even weight of his regard. She knew what he must be thinking—that she and her mother had done this, had stood in the way of Papa's dreams. And this was their reward. He had left. He must have done so. This must be his means of getting their attention.

Mother was right. *They'd* done this. Not just her, but Evelina too. By what she *didn't* say, refused to say, rather than what she *did*.

She cleared her throat, but it still felt tight and swollen from the emotion that wanted to burst out. "Thank you for letting me read that, Hans. And I'm sorry for . . . for . . ." For much. But Hans Wilsdorf wasn't the one she needed to say it to.

"I understand why you and your mother do not want to leave London on such short notice. I did not give your father much time to think things through." Hans accepted the refolded paper, when Barclay handed it to him and offered a small smile. "Still, I hope he convinces you all to join us. Wherever he has taken himself this morning, it is no doubt just to think things over. And I assure you, it is not with us."

She had hoped, as she'd lain awake through what remained of the night, that Papa had simply decided he would indeed go to Bienne, just as Mother had told him in her pique to do. That he'd packed up his work and spent the night in a hotel, trying to finish it before meeting Hans this morning.

But if he had made that decision, he had apparently decided not to involve Hans in it directly.

"Thank you for your time. We'll get out of your way now, so you can be off." A glance behind him showed her an automobile loaded with trunks and luggage.

Florence was even then bustling from the front door of their house, a flurry of motion and traveling paraphernalia. A smile wreathed her face when she spotted them. "Lina! Oh, tell me you've changed your minds and will be joining us."

Finding herself wrapped in the lightly perfumed embrace of her friend, Evelina's instinct to smile lost against the fresh wave of guilt and sorrow. "No, I . . . I'm afraid . . ." She pulled away, knowing well that the turning of her lips wouldn't fool her friend under normal circumstances, but praying Flo was too distracted now to notice. "I just stopped over to wish you *bon voyage*. Do let us know that you arrive safely in Bienne, won't you?"

"Of course! But we've nothing to worry about, Hans assures me. We'll be well away from the front." Florence gave an exaggerated shudder and clasped Evelina's hands between hers. "No worse than we face in London, apparently. I confess I'm a bit worried about all those I'm leaving behind—at least in Switzerland, we'll be in a neutral country."

"Neutrality didn't protect Belgium."

"But in England, we are openly at war. And apparently not beyond the reach of the German Luftwaffe." Brow creased, Florence looked to her husband. "I, for one, will be glad to be out of England. I wish we'd left weeks ago."

"Well, we shall leave today. And must do so now, if we are to make our train." Hans reached to shake Barclay's hand. "It was a true pleasure to make your acquaintance, Mr. Pearce. And Lina," he said, turning to take her hand and press it lightly, "I am sorry to have caused any distress in your family. I pray you all resolve it quickly—and in my favor." With a boyish grin, he winked and then turned to help Florence into the car.

Evelina folded her arms over her stomach, clasping her elbows, and watched them climb in with one last wave. She read cheer and even joy in her friends' eyes—excitement over what was to come. Gladness at leaving London.

Emotions she could name so easily, yet which seemed such strangers right now. She felt Barclay's fingers brush down her upper arm, but she didn't look at him. Instead, she watched the slow progress of the automobile as it eased down the street and paused at the end, waiting for a break in traffic so it could join the chaotic flow of London life.

The skies above were still clear. Blue. It should have been beautiful rather than threatening, but she wasn't sure she'd ever again look up at a clear sky without a wave of unease. Would another zeppelin whir its way over their city tonight, bring more destruction and terror?

And why, of all nights for Papa to leave them, did it have to be *last* night, when that nightmare had struck? Why did he not come back when he realized what had happened?

"Lina—"

"That's that, then, I suppose. This is Papa trying to get through to us. To get our attention."

Barclay sighed. "I cannot think so. He wouldn't do that to you."

She turned, looking up at him. "You've only known him a few weeks." Never mind that she'd known him all her life and never would have thought he'd do this to her either. But she had pushed him too far. She and Mother and Aunt Beatrice.

"I've always been good at reading people, though." He walked beside her back to his brother-in-law's vehicle, but he didn't open the door to let her in. Instead, he tipped her chin up with a touch of his finger. "Lina, it's not the only explanation. What if he didn't leave of his own will? What if it was that bloke who'd been lurking about?"

"Kidnapping?" Did he think this one of his beloved novels? Evelina shook her head. "That's ridiculous, Barclay. Why would anyone kidnap my father?"

"For his work, perhaps. He tried to break into the basement, didn't he?"

"Because he would have deemed it an easy way to get in."

Barclay's eyes glinted. "Given the size of the window? Hardly. *Easy* would have been to climb up to a first-floor window—unless what he wanted was *in* the basement. And why else would he target your family, your house? What else do you have to set you apart from any one of your neighbors?"

A headache pounded to life. Her theory about it being linked to Basil certainly didn't hold up anymore. "Aunt Beatrice's jewelry is quite valuable."

"But she wasn't in Town yet when the mugger first apprehended you."

"Perhaps that first encounter was mere happenstance—and then he continued to lurk about out of a sense of pride, especially when he realized what my aunt had with her." She shook her head and reached around him for the door. "It makes more sense than to think that anyone would go to such lengths to steal *clockworks*."

"Clockworks can quite literally make the world go round." Barclay held the door shut with a firm palm, his eyes even harder now. "And what he was working on lately—it was no clock. That gear could change the course of the war. It got the Admiralty's attention, that's why they sent me to help him with it. Who's to say it didn't get the attention of a few German agents as well?"

A fear she couldn't quite explain made her throat go tight. Not fear of Barclay. Nor of an invented German agent. But how could Papa have been working on something so serious for so long and never so much as mention it to her? "Do I even know him? I always thought I did, but . . ." She pressed her lips together and shook her head. "And what of you, Barclay Pearce? What sinister secrets of yours are going to leap out and bite me?"

Because if he was right, which she couldn't quite fathom—he'd known. He'd known that this work was dangerous. And if he was wrong, as she had to think he was, and Papa had left to escape her and Mother—it didn't change the fact that *he* was involved with admiralties and agents, did it?

But Barclay didn't flinch, didn't withdraw, didn't even blink out of turn. Rather, he gave her a warm, solemn look and sighed. "This isn't about me. But I'll find him. I promise you I will."

"I don't know that he means to be found." Just now, she didn't feel as though she knew anything. Except that Papa was gone. That the skies threatened destruction with their very blueness. And that she was so very tired. So very *heavy*.

An hour—it was all he'd asked of her, and she'd refused to give it.

"Lina." His voice contemplative, mournful, Barclay leaned over and pressed his lips to her forehead. "Hold to hope."

Evelina let her shoulders sag and, avoiding his gaze, ducked into the car when he opened the door. What did hope even mean in this situation? Should she hope he'd left them, or that he'd been stolen away? How was one any better than the other? "I don't have any hope to hold to." She mouthed it more than she said it. It was just a breath, nearly silent in the car. The last wheeze of a gear wound down . . . with no one left to wind it back up.

The tube chattered by. Someone shouted in the street below. Glass broke somewhere, and curses stained the air.

Barclay sank to a seat on the faded sofa, wincing at the spring that bit him through the lumpy cushion. He'd sat on this woebegone couch dozens of times before and never noticed the springs. He was getting soft. And that was unacceptable.

Afternoon light stretched its golden fingers through the window's grime, beckoning him back outside. And he would go. Soon. There was no reason to linger here in his old flat, having already deposited in the hidey-hole the slip of paper with the address on it that Captain Hall had requested. V would fetch it before morning, no doubt.

"And what of you, Barclay Pearce? What sinister secrets of yours are going to leap out and bite me?"

He shifted, leaned back against the creaking couch, and frowned at the question that echoed through his head. *I'm a thief.* The confession had nearly slipped from his tongue, as easily said to her as it had been to her father. But that moment wasn't the one for such revelations, not when she was so worried for Manning.

His breath eased out between dry lips. He'd always known, deep in that place his father had once nurtured, that thieving was something to be looked down on. That it wasn't what God wanted of His children. He'd known it, but the need of his belly—and those of the children in his care—had been louder.

But now he knew the Scripture to back up his father's morals. *"The thief cometh not, but for to steal, and to kill, and to destroy."*

His eyes slid shut. He'd never been that kind of thief, had he? He'd stolen. But never at the cost of a life. Never to destroy anything. That he'd known of, anyway. Did that make a difference to God?

He was none too sure. And therefore all the more grateful for the verse he knew came after that bit: *"I am come that they might have life, and that they might have it more abundantly."*

The Lord, for whatever strange reason, had seen fit to forgive them. To call them the sheep rather than the thief trying to steal away the flock.

Barclay was something new now. And yet never more aware

of all he'd been than when he'd stood there with Evelina at eight o'clock that morning outside the Wilsdorf townhouse. When he'd seen the hopelessness in her posture and known he could do so little to help her.

He could try to find Manning. But what if he couldn't? From what he'd gleaned, the family didn't have savings enough to survive all that long without the income from his shop. A couple months, and then the rent would be due, and the bills would come in, and then what? Throw themselves on the mercy of Beatrice?

Barclay lifted a hand to rub at the tension riding in his neck. For the first time in his life, he wished he were a man more like that idiot Philibert—one with a house that he owned outright, and with a bank account filled with pounds sterling. He wished he could assure her that even if the unthinkable happened and her father never returned—*God, please, no*—she would be all right. He would take care of her.

He *wanted* to take care of her. And it didn't feel the same at all as when he'd held his hand out to Clover or Elinor or Nigel. Not the same at all.

He had nothing to offer her. Nothing *secure*, anyway. Just the echoes of the life of a thief. No furnishings, no house in his own name, no *anything* that was guaranteed to be there tomorrow.

Still, he'd offer it. He would, if he thought for a moment that she would take it. Take *him*. "God, help me." His voice seeped into the room like the rain sometimes had. Through the cracks, down the beams, drip-dropping onto the floor. "I love her."

He'd realized it sometime in the too-short night, when he was worrying for her and hers instead of sleeping. When thoughts of her father wouldn't cease plaguing him. When he wondered what might happen if Manning *did* show up later today and Barclay were to ask him for permission to court her properly.

Manning would no doubt boot him right back to the gutter from whence he came.

And Evelina . . .

He opened his eyes again to stare up at the water-stained ceiling. She knew more about him than he'd told her outright, he was sure. She'd seen too much of London's underbelly not to recognize a bit of it in him. But he had a feeling she wouldn't accept a reformed thief quite so readily as she did a down-and-out factory worker. Still, if he loved her, then that meant she deserved the truth. And he'd give it to her, when it wouldn't be just another blow.

A distant church bell tolled through the window, proclaiming it time to get to Pauly's. The others would be there any minute—their last supper together at the pub before Willa's wedding.

Barclay heaved a long breath and pushed himself to his feet. He'd be glad to talk to Pauly, to assure him one more time—he'd actually rung them up at Peter and Rosemary's again—that they were all well after the bombing in Shoreditch last night.

The bombing. Not a reality he'd ever imagined facing here in London. But nothing was safe anymore. Nothing.

He glanced over at his hiding place to make sure there were no mortar crumbs or clean spots to show he'd been fussing there and then bade a silent farewell to the uncomfortable couch.

Back on the street, he sent a gaze around him that would look casual to those who didn't know him. Just a normal man looking about before stepping out. Until he sighted a familiar dark figure jogging his way.

"Oi! Barclay!"

"Dante." He hadn't seen his friend since the visit to his turf and moved to meet him, greet him with a hand outstretched for the clasping. "Joining us at Pauly's tonight?"

"Clara is already there with your sisters. One of the neighbors said he'd seen you down this way." Dante pivoted to face the way from which he'd come, stationing himself shoulder to shoulder with Barclay. "Any help from Martin on our unknown visitor?"

Barclay shook his head. "I stopped in to say hello a few days after I saw you. He didn't have any more information than we did."

"Well, I may have found something. *Maybe*." He leaned an inch closer, so that Barclay caught the scent of the soap his new missus used on his clothes. "Bloke at the Amhurst Arms said someone came in the other day matching his description. Real quiet most of the time, alone. Definitely never seen him before, but with all the refugees . . . The fellow finally spoke, though, to order a meal, and the publican said he was no Belgian. Struck him as odd, so he tried to be friendly. After his second pint, the stranger said something about being from some place that sounded like 'Stars Agora.'"

Barclay's brows pulled down. "Where the devil is that?" Stars Agora? He'd never heard of it, and he'd studied maps more than the average street thief.

Dante shrugged. "I've no idea, nor can I be sure it's the bloke you're looking for. But the publican described him well. Dark hair, swarthy complexion. And he said he wore a coin on a gold chain around his neck. That's what caught his eye and made him ask where he was from—it wasn't an English coin, nor a franc or a mark. He'd have known those, he said."

A gold chain around his neck—Lucy had mentioned the same, when she'd spotted the would-be basement burglar.

His blood galloped through his veins. "It could be him."

"Well then." Dante offered a smile—all white teeth against his dark skin. "I've earned the supper you've promised me, aye?"

Barclay laughed, even though he didn't much feel like it. Any more than he felt like eating.

No, what he felt like doing was running home, going over to Peter's study and the atlases he kept there, and poring over each and every page until he found Stars Agora. He couldn't be sure knowing where the bloke was from would lead him to the actual *bloke*. Or to Manning, though he still suspected they were connected.

But it felt like a solid lead.

"So." With a friendly elbow in his side, Dante drew him back to the here and now. "Heard Pauly asking the girls if your twist was coming tonight. I thought you said there wasn't a woman?" He cackled. "I knew there was!"

"There wasn't. Then." Not really. Of course, if one was dealing in reality, there *still* wasn't. "He means Evelina Manning—the girl this mystery bloke tried to mug."

"A Hammersmith girl?" From his tone, it was impossible to tell if Dante was impressed or dubious. He loosed a whistle from between his teeth. "She know who you are?"

Barclay sighed. "Some of it. And I daresay when she learns the rest, it'll guarantee that she's not my twist for long." But for now, she needed him. Maybe that would be enough. Maybe he could be happy just seeing her through this time and then returning to his family while she went about her life. Maybe it wouldn't leave a yawning hole inside.

"Well, all for the best, that. Two different worlds and whatnot, yeah?" Dante motioned, as they rounded the corner, toward the pub. "My Clara brought a friend of hers along. Italian. Pretty as a picture and barely speaks a word of English, so she won't know what a dog you are."

Because he had no choice, Barclay chuckled and gave his friend a shove in the arm. "Dante, I never thought I'd see the day when *you* were playing matchmaker."

"I'm full of surprises. A man of many talents."

"Mmm." He didn't much care how good he was at finding potential romances. So long as the lead on the mugger was solid. "We'll see, mate. We'll see."

TWENTY

The telegram sat on the low table, yellow and stark and mocking. Exactly where it had been put yesterday evening when a boy delivered it with a tip of his cap, not knowing that he was handing over something to destroy the last of their hope.

Evelina had entered the room without thinking of that accusatory slip of yellow. But now she couldn't advance another step, after her gaze latched on to it.

Mother nearly collided with her back. She breathed a chuckle—then it caught on a gasp. She too must have spotted the message they'd left here last night. She too must be feeling its slap anew.

Don't worry for me, I am well. Taking a trip to think things over, as I am not welcome at home. More later. CM

So short a message to signal the end of a marriage, of a family. No reasoning. No excuse. No explanation of where he'd gone or why he did so in such secrecy, without so much as packing a change of clothes.

Those words had been echoing in her head all night, all morning. Chasing away sleep again.

Mother sighed and slid to Evelina's side, her shoulders sagging in a way she couldn't remember ever seeing them do. Her fingers covered Evelina's, squeezed them. Her gaze fell to the floor and remained there. "At least we know he is safe and well. And he will surely come home soon."

Evelina angled her body closer to her mother's. Not quite leaning in to her, but almost doing so, as she vaguely recalled doing as a child, before polio changed everything. Back when she could bury her face in Mother's skirts and know a kind hand would settle on her shoulder to stroke and soothe. How she wanted to bury her face again now. "I'm sorry, Mama. This is *my* fault. Had I just granted him the hour he'd asked for . . ."

"Oh, don't be silly, Evelina." Words she had spoken so many times over the years. But they were different this time. They were gentle and warm, to match the arms that Mother closed around her. "This is not your fault. It's mine. You have always been the apple of your father's eye, and though he may have been frustrated, *you* would never make him leave. It was I who pushed him too far. I told him to go, and he took me at my word."

Evelina slid her arms around her mother's waist and held on. She said a silent prayer for words she could give to return the encouragement.

Before she could find any, the dreaded *thump, thump* of Aunt Beatrice's cane sounded, along with her horrid sniff. "I cannot fathom why the two of you are moping about as you are. Men go off on larks now and again—he will return, whether we want him to or not."

Evelina went as stiff as metal, feeling acidic words coil up on her tongue, ready to spring out at her aunt.

Mother's arms fell away, fury flashing in the eyes she raised from the floor. Fury—from Mother—aimed at her sister. Never in her life had Evelina seen such a thing.

"How dare you say such things, Bea? How *dare* you?"

Aunt Beatrice shook her head. It wasn't quite her usual

haughtiness in her stance. Almost, but something different colored her gaze. "Do resist any theatrics, Judith. Perhaps your husband has never stepped out before—that you know of—but men are all the same." Perhaps she meant the turn of her lips to be encouraging. "We shall get along just fine without him."

Evelina clenched her teeth together, but that couldn't hold back the words that pushed forward. "He is not like that—not like your husband—and we will *not* get along 'just fine' without him. *You* are the only one we would get along fine without!"

Her aunt's mouth flopped open. "Judith, will you allow your daughter to speak to me in such a manner?"

Mother's fingers clasped tightly around Evelina's. "Allow it and applaud it. For too long I've let you dictate everything to me, knowing full well how it alienated my husband and drove a wedge forever between us. But no more. I can only pray—" Her voice cracked. Shattered into a sob. She pressed her free hand to her lips and blinked. "I can only pray it isn't too late. That when Cecil comes home, he will grant me the chance to set things right."

Twin blooms of red blotched Beatrice's cheeks. "Foolish woman. Will you kowtow to his histrionics in such a way? Then you'll be giving up every inch of control you've gained over the years."

"*What* control? Yours, do you mean?" Mother's fingers tightened almost painfully around Evelina's, but she wasn't about to complain about it. "A family should not be about control. Perhaps, had I realized that before . . . had I taken pride in his accomplishments—"

"Accomplishments?" Aunt Beatrice sniffed and thumped her cane. "In his *trade*, do you mean?"

Mother lifted her chin to match the angle of her sister's, nostrils flaring. "Don't. Don't belittle him because he doesn't come from the same wealth Wycombe did—when we all know very well Cecil is a far superior man in the ways that count. He may have to work to take care of us, but he has never once betrayed our marriage vows. He has never once raised a hand to any of us or gambled away what funds we have."

Beatrice's mouth puckered. "Never betrayed your vows *before*, perhaps. Who's to say what—or who—is keeping him away now?"

Mother dropped Evelina's hand and lifted her arm, finger pointing at the door. "Get out of my house. *Now*. And don't come back until you're ready to apologize."

There might have been surprise and regret lurking somewhere in Beatrice's eyes. A bit. But if so, it quickly vanished beneath a huff of outrage as she stormed toward the door. "Well, I never. We'll see how quickly you change your tune when your meager savings run out, your husband fails to provide, and you *lose* this dismal house!"

Evelina darted ahead of her aunt so she could pull open the door for her. "If such a thing were to happen, rest assured we wouldn't impose upon *you*, Aunt Beatrice." She didn't know what they *would* do, but not that.

It wouldn't come to that, though. Papa might want to get their attention, but he was far too conscientious a man to lose his house just because of an argument with them. No, he would stay away as long as he deemed it necessary, but he would be seeing to things in the meantime. And then he'd come home, and they'd all laugh and cry together, and they'd have a new start.

It was almost, nearly, hope. Despite twenty-four-word telegrams that tried to dash every last shred of it.

"I'll order your carriage brought around for you," Mother said, "and your things sent to your house."

With a final *hmph*, Beatrice sailed out the door, head high. Evelina hadn't a clue what the woman meant to do outside in the misting rain until the carriage was ready, but she wouldn't put it past her to march down the street to the carriage house and stand there tapping her cane like a second hand until her driver had been found and put to work.

For her part, Evelina took a bit too much joy in letting the wind snag the door from her hands and shut it with a slam rather than a soft click. Though the echo of it through the house then reverberated through the hollow spots inside her chest, and she deflated with an exhale.

Silence. No strains of music coming up from the basement, though there ought to be this time of day. No ticking of the clock from the drawing room—Papa was always the one to wind it, and he hadn't been here to do so yesterday.

She met her mother's gaze. "Well. There is *something* I can take care of, at any rate." With a trembling smile, she turned into the drawing room and moved to the tall case clock. Papa had trained her years ago in how to reset it, to wind its springs, to prepare for another week of timekeeping.

Touching the weights and pendulum made her throat go tight. It was a bit like being with Papa, to be caring for the things he loved. And it made her miss him all the more.

Mother stood at her elbow, watching as she performed the careful movements. "Was I too hard on her?"

Evelina squeaked a protest at the very question. "Too hard on *her*?"

Her mother's sigh echoed through her. "I know how she sounds to you, Evelina—I do. But she has been so hurt, it is no wonder she is bitter. And she only ever began staying here because she is afraid to be on her own. She needs us."

Her fingers tightened around the pendulum. "She has a lousy way of showing it."

"I know. But . . . she has another valid point. If your father doesn't come back, if he doesn't see to the bills—we can survive only a couple months on what we have saved."

"Not to worry." Anxiety balled into a fist in her stomach. "Plenty of people get along quite well in society with more debt than income. And besides—Papa will not be gone so long. Nor will he let the payments slip while he is away. You know he wouldn't do that."

"I know." She sounded about as certain as sunshine in October. "Just part of his point, I imagine, for us to take such things into account. If he were to accept the partnership in Rolex, no doubt we'd not have to worry with such things. Hans's company is doing quite well, isn't it? Florence always seems well put together."

"Very well, yes." Not that Papa *wasn't* doing well in his business, but there was a vast difference between a one-man shop and the size of operation Hans had built. Mother was no doubt right about what it could mean to them financially to accept his offer.

But neither of them had been willing to consider that last week, had they? Not if it meant giving up what they knew. Leaving London.

What would it have meant to Papa, though? He was a man who valued his ability to provide for his family, who worked too many hours a day to guarantee that he could. And she hadn't even begun to tally what expenses they had already incurred for the wedding that was not to be—that must have added still more weight upon his shoulders.

Her fingers stilled on the clock. *Oh, Papa . . . I'm so sorry*. But only silence answered her. Dragging in a slow breath, she set the pendulum swinging and listened for his voice in the renewal of the *tick-tock*.

It wasn't there.

Mother sighed. "I had better go and ask the maid to pack up Beatrice's things."

"All right." Evelina kept her gaze on the clock that was taller than she was. It had been a fixture in this room for as long as she could remember. Familiar wood, polished metal, clear glass. When she was recovering from her illness as a girl, she had stared at it until she'd memorized each detail of the filigree work on its face, the scrolling on each number. The beauty that resided there in the functional.

That was the life Papa had always striven to give them. Functional, yes—they were not wealthy, they could not live a life of leisure. But there was beauty still. Gentility. Honor. And it was worthy of respect.

As her mother padded away, Evelina's eyes slid closed. *Please, God. Please let him know that we're sorry. That if he comes home now, today, we're ready to listen to him. Please, God. Please send Papa home.*

She continued her silent plea for a few minutes more, until Mother returned to the room and settled a gentle hand on Evelina's shoulder. "Come now, Lina. We can't just stand about all day waiting for him to return. We must show him when he comes back that we are prepared to be reasonable. That he can be proud of us. We should keep busy."

Busy. There were things to do, there always were. She had no fewer than three letters awaiting her at her small desk in her bedroom, two of which were from friends she had made in the factories, one from Mr. Dramwell. No doubt one of those would offer something with which she could fill her time.

She sighed and let her shoulders sag. "Tomorrow?"

Mother's lips turned up in a strange sort of smile—undemanding and understanding. Two things her smile hadn't been for years. "Tomorrow."

Barclay leaned onto Margot's desk, arms folded across his chest as he stared at the map she'd unfolded over the surface. "You're no help at all, Margot."

The girl didn't so much as look up from whatever she was doing in her lap—it involved a sheet of paper covered in numbers and a pen that kept adding still more of them. "Geography is not my forte. Perhaps Culbreth can help you."

"Hmm?" From a desk over, the man in question blinked and looked up. "I can do what?"

"Help me figure out where someone is from. The name of his town was given to me as Stars Agora." Barclay stared at that map of Europe, waiting for the words to leap off at him.

No such luck.

And Culbreth shook his head. "I've never heard of it."

"That would be because there *is* no Stars Agora." V's voice brought Barclay's head around in time to find his employer step up and tap a finger to the map in eastern Europe somewhere. "There is, however, a Stara Zagora in Bulgaria. Could that be what you're looking for?"

"Bulgaria." Barclay straightened, searching the area under V's finger-tap until he saw the small lettering that spelled it out. "Could be."

"But Bulgaria is allied with Germany." Margot's pen stopped its steady scratching upon the page. "Should they not be under restriction in England just as the Germans are?"

V's lips thinned. "They should be, perhaps. But they aren't. I suppose because there simply aren't as many Bulgarians in England as there were Germans or Austrians."

In which case, it would make frightening sense to send a Bulgarian—or some other nationality not as widely feared in London—here as an agent, wouldn't it? Barclay's blood chilled.

V motioned with his head and then followed his own direction, away from the codebreakers. Barclay straightened, sent Margot and Culbreth a smile he hoped convinced them not to worry, and trailed V toward Room 40's door.

The man stopped just outside it and faced Barclay with lifted brows. "I assume this isn't a casual inquiry about Stara Zagora. What man are you trying to identify? Need we be worried?"

Barclay's breath balled up, then came out in a huff. "I don't know, sir. It's the man who mugged Evelina Manning and had been lurking about the neighborhood. I still can't shake the notion that he may have had something to do with Manning's disappearance. That perhaps he was after Manning's work."

"Possible, I suppose." V clasped his hands behind his back and focused his gaze on the wall across from them, lips pursed in thought. "Did you not say they'd received a telegram from him, though?"

Barclay sighed. "Anyone could have sent that. It had nothing in it to prove it composed by Manning." Not that the Manning ladies seemed to doubt its authenticity, but it just didn't sit right. It was too vague. And he'd left no instructions for the clerk at his shop—which was utterly unlike him.

V released a thoughtful hum. "I will ask around about this Bulgarian. See if any of my contacts know who it could be, and why he is here. We may, after all, be looking at a simple street thief who has moved on to greener pastures."

"Maybe." He didn't have to say what he was thinking—that he knew street thieves. He would have been able to identify the man if he was one. Certainly if he were part of a crew . . . And even if he were an independent, the crews would know it and would have been warning him off. They were protective of their turf.

V pulled out his pocket watch, nodded. "Retta is still about the task you gave her this morning?"

A corner of Barclay's mouth turned up. His sister had been more than happy to accept the job of posing as a member of the secretary pool for the embassies so she could slip a letter to one of V's counterparts. "I imagine she'll have finished by now."

"Very good. We've put in time enough here today—Blinker has no other tasks for us just now. You go and pay a visit to the Manning ladies and see if any more news has arrived, as I know you wish to do. I'll put out those feelers."

"Thank you, sir." A bit of the weight lifted, knowing someone else was looking into it—someone as capable as V. It made him feel a bit less mad for clinging to his theory of foul play.

And a visit with Evelina would make him feel even better. He'd tell her about the Bulgarian, see if it meant anything to her. He doubted it would, but one never knew. Although first, he'd stop at home and find Lucy, see if the swarthy fellow had been spotted any more in the neighborhood in the last several days.

Outside, a protective drizzle fell, guaranteeing everyone peace of mind tonight. No zeppelins would make another foray into such weather. Barclay had never imagined being so grateful for rain, but he imagined he wasn't alone in that gratitude this week. Just as he imagined that he wasn't the only one praying for an early autumn and its guaranteed clouds.

It took him only a few minutes to gain their neighborhood, and a chance glance down one of the streets between their house and the Mannings' showed him familiar movement. Lucy, with a basket of bread on her arm that she was no doubt peddling as a means for collecting gossip. Good ol' Luce. He jogged to catch up with her just as she was slipping through a garden gate, aimed at a kitchen entrance. "Lucy."

She looked over her shoulder with a welcoming smile. "Home already? It isn't even teatime."

"On my way to call on the Mannings. Any word on our anonymous friend?"

Lucy reached under the covering of her basket and came back out with a golden-brown roll in hand, which she held out to him. "No one's seen him in a few days, and everyone's rather relieved about it."

A few days. Barclay tore off a chunk of the fragrant roll—leave it to Lucy to know he'd skipped breakfast and not yet taken time for any other meal. "Last sighting?"

"Monday evening."

The night Manning had vanished. Coincidence? He chewed his bite of bread and couldn't convince himself that it was. "Interesting."

"Gives your theory a bit of weight, doesn't it?"

"Unfortunately. It would be less worrisome if he really had just run off in a temper."

"Life seldom chooses the less worrisome route." With a commiserating sigh, Lucy turned back toward the garden path. "If I learn anything else helpful, I'll let you know."

"Thanks. And thanks." He lifted the remainder of the roll in salute and turned, leaving her to what she did so well.

He made short work of the bread and had free hands again by the time he jogged up the front steps and rang the bell at Number 22. The door swung open so quickly he backed up half a step and nearly took a tumble.

Evelina stepped out with a strained smile. "I was hoping you'd come. I've an errand to run, and I wasn't certain if I ought to go out alone or not. Mother is at an aid meeting."

"Ah. I am, of course, happy to be of service." He wanted to ask if they'd had any more word from her father, but it was a pointless question. If they had, it would have been the first thing out of her mouth. So instead of reminding her of that absence, he fastened on a smile and offered his arm. "You're looking lovely this afternoon, Lina. What errands are we running?"

She smoothed down the pale linen of her skirt, touched a hand to the rose sash. Did she know that uncertainty shouted out through those motions? Probably not. But a day or two of kindness from her mother wasn't enough to erase the years of self-doubt her every rebuke had instilled.

Perhaps someday, if she granted him a part of her life for long enough, he'd be able to convince her that she was so very beautiful, that he admired each and every curve. That it didn't matter if she wasn't in the height of fashion, or if her leg betrayed her and set her limping after she'd been on it too long.

"A visit to the garment factory in Hackney."

Barclay pushed away thoughts of her figure and accepted the brolly she handed him, though he couldn't quite erase his frown as he opened it. "I beg your pardon? A garment factory?"

Nodding, she checked her hat and joined him under the umbrella. "I had a hand in the owner firing his last manager—the ladies who work the floor come to me with their problems, as I am in good stead with Mr. Dramwell. He let me know he has hired a new man, and I thought to go introduce myself and see how the workers like him."

It shouldn't, he supposed, surprise him, given her many mentions of venturing to the factories. "Well then. Lead the way, lady fair. I'm not all that familiar with Hackney."

She sent him an arched look, eyes glimmering with the closest thing he'd seen to amusement from her in days. "Barclay Pearce, unfamiliar with a neighborhood in London? I never imagined hearing you admit to such a thing."

He chuckled as expected . . . and said a prayer that they wouldn't run into Claw while they were there. "Let's just say that it's in the turf of someone who's never much liked me. Sometimes it's wisest to steer clear of a place."

"Wait, wait. An unfamiliar section of Town *and* someone who doesn't like you?" She pressed a hand to his arm. "Unfathomable."

"You're so amusing." He turned her down the street toward the nearest tube stop. "And it's entirely Claw's fault that we don't get along, you can be sure. Pure stubbornness on his part, I tried to make amends years ago."

Evelina sidestepped a puddle and angled a dubious gaze up at him. "Do I want to know for *what* you were making amends?"

Probably not. But he had to stop sheltering her from what he'd been if he had any hope of convincing her to give them a chance at a future. That would necessitate accepting his past.

"Nothing too dastardly. When I was just a lad—ten years old—I stole something in his neighborhood. Something he'd been planning to lift himself." And the two pounds he'd gotten when he fenced the trinket hadn't been worth the years of animosity. If he had it to do over again . . . but he didn't. And there was little point in wasting energy on regrets.

He'd spend some time saying a prayer that his presence in Hackney would go unnoticed, though. He hadn't so much as set foot there in over fifteen years—better to use Dante as a go-between when necessary. But no one would be looking for him, and with the umbrella to shield his face and Evelina on his arm, it ought to be fine. He hoped.

He glanced down at Evelina to gauge her reaction to his disclosure.

Her brows were lifted . . . but so were the corners of her mouth. "You had mentioned to Clover that you were involved in such things as a lad. I imagine a gang leader running you out of his neighborhood taught you a lesson rather quickly, didn't it?"

"You could say that." It had taught him that he needed people of his own to help him, if he wanted to carve out a territory for himself. But somehow he didn't think that was the lesson she was hoping he'd learned.

Before he could dive into that ugly truth, she released a sigh so mournful that he wondered if she'd seen the fullness of his past in his eyes—but her gaze was fastened on the carriage house at the end of the street, not upon him. "Something wrong?"

She shook her head and reassigned her gaze to the vague distance. "Nothing. I was only . . . My aunt left, after she and Mother had an argument. I expected to be happy about it, and in part I am. But the house is so dreadfully *quiet* now."

"I'm sorry, I'm unfamiliar with that word *qui . . . et*? What does that mean?"

It earned him a small chuckle. Not enough, though, to chase away the storm clouds from her face.

He released a breath and let the patter of rain on the brolly speak for him. The clouds might protect them from zeppelins—but he wished he knew how to banish them from her life for good.

TWENTY-ONE

Barclay kept his head down as they left the tube platform. The rain had gone from a drizzle to an earnest shower—a welcome mask as Evelina led him through the maze of streets. Though he'd not set foot here in so long, the feel of the area was what he'd grown accustomed to over the years. Buildings stained with coal soot, dirty puddles in broken streets, and a general air of exhaustion that permeated every board and brick. Once upon a time, Hackney had been a prosperous place.

Not today.

"This way." She indicated a left at the next corner and sped around it, nearly escaping the cover of their shared umbrella.

Barclay hurried to catch up, stepped directly in a puddle, and winced at the cool water that splashed up his leg.

"Are you all right?"

"Yeah. I just . . ." When he looked up from the dark spot on his leg, to Evelina and past her, he lost all train of thought.

"What is it?" Brows knit, she stepped close to his side and followed his gaze to the unassuming brick building across from them.

"It's . . ." What was it? Just a building of flats, from the look of it, but . . . He shook his head. There was no reason for that burst of awareness. Not given how little he'd come here recently.

But before the falling-out with Claw, he'd not barricaded the neighborhood from his thoughts, had he? Perhaps he'd cased this building at some point. Perhaps he'd even stolen something from inside it. Perhaps . . .

An image flashed in his mind's eye. No, not so much an image as a sensation. A little hand tucked into his. His gaze locked on the faded dress of a woman in front of him, leading him.

"Barclay?"

"It's nothing. Old, faded memories, that's all. I suppose I'm more familiar with this part of London than I thought."

"Not good memories, from the looks of it." She squeezed his arm a bit. "Do you want to go back? It isn't as though they're expecting me today in particular. We can go home again."

"No, no reason to do that." They were here now, had already invested an hour of the day in the tube ride. Might as well see it through. "Lead on."

They walked another ten minutes before she motioned to a large building at the end of the street. "There it is. If we go in the side door there, it will lead us to the manager's office. I'll introduce myself to him and then visit my friends on the floor."

"Very good." Upon reaching the indicated door, he opened it for her and then shook the brolly, lowering it. He deposited it in the umbrella stand just inside and wiped his feet on the rug.

Evelina took a moment to smooth down the hair under her hat and then squared her shoulders. "Right. Well, let's hope *this* manager hasn't already been informed by the previous one that he'd better bar me from the building."

A low chuckle tickled his throat. "Looks as though we're both hoping for anonymity today."

"What a devious pair we are." Lips quirking up a bit, she took his arm again and indicated the corridor stretching along to their right. From directly ahead came a collection of sounds he couldn't begin to make out, but that he suspected were evidence of ample industry.

The door at the end of the corridor was open, light spilling from it along with faint music from a gramophone. He felt a hitch in Evelina's step and knew it was because she would recognize the song seeping out the door as surely as he did—one her father had always played when he was working on pocket watches.

But she shook it off with the next step. Moved into the threshold, knocking upon the frame as she did so. "I beg your pardon. Are you the new manager?"

Barclay followed her through when she moved into the room, casting a quick, encompassing glance around. It was spartan in its furnishings but cluttered with files and papers. A cabinet took up one corner, and the rest of the cramped space was occupied almost entirely by a scarred wooden desk with two chairs jammed into place in front of it. The one behind it held a man with fair brown hair, thinning on top—visible thanks to the fact that he still hadn't looked up from whatever he was doing. A plain, utilitarian cane rested against the wall behind him. The sort that proclaimed itself useful rather than for show with its very ugliness.

Barclay's eyes sought some identifier and found a small brass nameplate on the desk, half hidden beneath papers, even as the fellow said, "Yes, one moment, please."

The voice gave him pause. He couldn't possibly have heard it before, and yet . . . and yet it brought memories gushing into his mind like floodwaters. Visions of his father, bent over an essay he was marking.

That nameplate—all he could make out on it was *C-h-a-r-l*. His gaze flew to the man—younger than the thinning hair made him look from that first angle. Younger than Barclay, he'd guess, probably only in his midtwenties.

He looked nothing like the cherub-faced boy Barclay remembered protecting as a lad. But he looked exactly like his memories of their father. "Charlie." It came out a whisper, half question and half plea.

The man's brows pulled down into a frown as he looked up. "Pardon me. Have we met?" He stood, showing off a suit of coarse, ill-fitting fabric in brown. Held out a hand. "Charles Pearce—the manager, yes. And you are?"

Thank you, Lord. Thank you! So many years he'd searched, hoped, prayed—and had he been here all along, in the neighborhood Claw had forbidden Barclay from entering? Barclay's nostrils flared, and he may have forgotten to reach out and shake had Evelina's fingers not bitten questioningly into his arm.

He clasped his brother's hand, swallowed. "Barclay Pearce." It was all he could manage just then before his throat went tight.

Evelina held out her hand too. "And Evelina Manning. Forgive us for intruding, sir. I often act as a liaison between the workers and Mr. Dramwell, as I am a friend to both. Is it all right if I pay a quick visit to Katy on the floor?"

"There will be a shift change in a few minutes, if you would wait until then." Charlie's frown didn't ease. If anything, it deepened as he looked at Barclay again. "Pardon me—did you say *Barclay Pearce*?"

Would he remember him? Charlie had been only a lad of six when they were separated. He likely didn't recall their father at all. And surely he wouldn't recognize him, just to look at him. But his name? Did that mean anything to him, or did their shared surname simply jump out at him?

He cleared his throat. "That's right."

Evelina let go of his arm and offered an uncertain smile. "I'll just go on out to the floor, shall I? I'll wait for the whistle before entering, though, Mr. . . . Pearce." With a wide-eyed gaze for Barclay, she slipped out the office door.

How many times had he imagined a reunion? And yet now that it was here, he hadn't any idea what he should say. Or if he should wait for Charlie to say something first or . . . But his brother merely lowered back to his seat, his face inscrutable. So very clear of either question or recognition that it must be a mask. Any stranger would have wondered at the shared name. Such ice bespoke knowledge. "I've work to finish for the day. So if you'll excuse me, sir."

Barclay stepped nearer the cluttered desk. "Charlie. Son of Clarence and Edith Pearce. I—" Did he dare give voice to the truth? "I'm your brother."

There. He'd said it—the words he'd claimed so often concerning those who *weren't* his flesh and blood.

The words he almost wished he'd kept between his lips when Charlie's face hardened. "You must be mistaking me for someone else. I don't have a brother."

Barclay sank, uninvited, into one of the chairs in front of the desk. "I looked everywhere for you after Mum was arrested. *Everywhere*."

Papers rustled, but he had the distinct impression that his brother was shuffling them more for the point of it than because he needed to find something. "I don't know of what you're speaking. But I really must get back to work—or is that a concept with which you're unfamiliar, given a convict for a mother?"

He swallowed, but the saliva burned like acid down his throat. "Have you been angry with me all these years? Did you think I didn't *try* to find you?"

Charlie went still, and he lifted eyes the exact shade of brown that their father's had been. "If I *did* have a brother—hypothetically speaking—and our mother *had* been arrested—as a philosophical point—how hard would it have been to find a boy who'd been handed over to the local orphanage? Hmm? When at any point in the *decade* between his advent into said orphanage system and his leaving it to find work at the age of sixteen, he could have been located right *there*, two streets over from where you currently sit, sir?"

"You weren't there, though. Not right away. I don't know where they took you at first, but I went directly to the orphanage and you *weren't* there. I feared they'd taken you elsewhere in the city." And there was no shortage of overpopulated, understaffed orphanages in London, any one of which could have been assigned another small scrap of a boy. Not to mention that finding any information on one's brother was difficult when one was determined to remain out of the system oneself.

Then Claw had run him out of the neighborhood, within a month of their mother's arrest.

Charlie made a show of pulling out a paper and scanning it.

"I looked, Charlie. And I kept looking, all these years."

The whistle blew from the factory floor, cutting through his claim. Charlie stood, his face still a mask of stone and resentment. "If you'll excuse me, Mr. Pearce. My wife's shift just ended, and I don't like letting her walk home alone."

"You've a wife?" It made his throat go tighter still. So many years they'd missed. So many important moments that Barclay had no part in. He rose from his chair.

Charlie gripped the cane and leaned heavily upon it as he limped his way around the desk. "Good day, sir."

"Charlie, please." Barclay leaped to block the door, hands outstretched in a plea. "You don't have to believe me right now. You don't have to want anything to do with me. But will you at least think things over? And let me know if . . . if you decide you'd like to know more." He fished into his pocket and pulled out one of the cards V had given him.

Charlie took it, even glanced down at the words printed on the cardstock. Somehow, his face went harder still. "Hammersmith. You've obviously recovered well from a mother sent to prison and a missing brother."

Blast. He hadn't considered how that would look to the brother who'd apparently never strayed far from the last home their mother had given them. "Not really, I—it's a let house. I'm working for the Admiralty at the moment, and it's near. That's all. My employer provided it, otherwise I'd still be in my flat in Poplar."

Charlie's smile looked scoffing, cold, in a way their father's had never done, though their lips bore the same shape. "Forgive me, sir, but your clothes belie your claims."

"No. It's just that Rosie's a whiz with a needle, is all—"

"Rosie? Your wife?" But the frown returned, and he darted a glance at the door. Perhaps remembering that Evelina's name hadn't been Rosie and wondering why he'd had one young lady on his arm if he were married to another.

He certainly didn't want his brother thinking *that* of him. "No, no. My sister." *Wrong, wrong, wrong.* He realized it the moment the word slipped by rote from his tongue.

Realized it all the more when that face, already so hard, went completely blank. "Sister."

"Not by blood, of course—it's just, we stuck together as children. After I couldn't find you. I fell in with a few other orphans, and we . . ."

"And you what?" Charlie gripped his cane so tightly his knuckles went white. "How exactly did you survive all these years and eventually land a position with the Admiralty, Mr. Pearce?"

"I . . ." But he couldn't admit to the truth. He knew it in that moment, the same way he'd known as a lad which bakers to avoid at all costs and which might spare him a biscuit or two to feed the hungry mouths in his care.

But apparently he didn't have to admit the truth for Charlie to see it. He shook his head, balled up the card, and tossed it into the rubbish bin by his desk. "You're just like her, aren't you?"

Barclay winced. He supposed he *was* like their mother, at that. Taking what he could, laughing over his ill-gained successes.

While Charlie had followed instead their father's path. An honest life, even if it meant too little to give to his family.

"Not anymore. It was once a way to survive, but I've given it up."

"Right." With a laugh as cold and humorless as his smile had been, Charlie made to move around him. "A thief never changes his ways."

He moved aside, because to do otherwise seemed cruel when his brother had such difficulty with each step he took. Still, he couldn't resist one last plaintive, "Charlie."

His brother paused a step into the hallway, though he didn't turn around.

Barclay curled his fingers into his palm. "What happened to your leg?"

For a moment, he thought he'd not answer. That he'd just storm his way to the floor and find his wife and leave without ever looking back over his shoulder. But after a beat, he said, "I broke it when I was eleven. Trying to escape the workhouse they'd sent me to. It didn't heal properly."

Like Olivia, in a way. Except Peter had sent money for the doctors' bills, for the surgery, and then he'd found the Mannings and their leg braces. Little Liv would walk well enough, one of these days.

Why hadn't the Lord provided the same for his brother? Why hadn't He led Barclay to him then, when he could have helped *him*, instead of just the other orphans he'd found?

"I'm sorry." In so many ways, for so much.

But Charlie just hobbled away, his gait uneven but quick.

With a long exhale, Barclay rested his head against the doorframe and closed his eyes. So many prayers he'd said for that boy, only to be met with the hatred he'd expected to find from Claw. Not from his own brother.

After a long moment, he did the only thing he could do. He drew out another card, put it front and center on Charlie's desk, and then left the office. He'd wait for Evelina by the side door and hope she didn't ask any questions about the encounter when she rejoined him.

He'd never spoken of his brother in all these years, aside from the words he'd shared with Clover, to inspire her trust. And he'd just as soon not speak any more of him now. If he tried it, he'd end up with holes inside so gaping that he'd likely never dig his way out of them again.

Evelina cast another sideways look at Barclay. But his gaze was still locked straight ahead as the tube swayed along, not so much as a twitch in his countenance to tell her what he was thinking. She'd tried asking him subtly what had happened in the office, but he'd said only, "Nothing." She'd tried asking him outright if the Charles Pearce who now managed the clothing factory was in fact his younger brother—the Charlie he'd mentioned that day in the pub. He'd said, voice flat, "He says he has no brother."

And then he'd gone silent and still, like one of Papa's toys after it had wound down. As if he could sit just like that, not moving a muscle, forever. Or until someone wound him back to life.

They still had another ten minutes until their stop, but she'd resigned herself to sitting at his side, her hands folded over her handbag in her lap. Silent. She could have chatted about her brief visit with the workers, she supposed, but what could she really tell him? The women were pleased to have one of their own in the manager's office—husband to one of the workers, a man who had worked there himself for years. They trusted him. He was, they said, a different sort. Mr. Dramwell had heeded her advice.

But that wouldn't change anything for this man beside her.

Another minute ticked by. Barclay sat there, motionless. So motionless he must be aching. And despite the fact that she'd always been terrible at knowing how and when to reach out to people, something welled up inside that gave her no room for second-guessing. She reached over and rested her gloved fingers atop his bare ones, on his knee.

He turned his hand under hers and wove their fingers together. His nostrils flared, and he clung to her. Whispered, "Thanks."

She held tight, scooted a bit closer, and leaned into his arm. Most of the world felt so very wrong just now. So why did this, which ought to be, feel so very right?

TWENTY-TWO

It was the sixth of June. The sun was trying valiantly to break through the clouds, last night's rain had dried but for a few eternal puddles, and the world was ticking and tocking steadily onward despite the fact that it should have come to a grinding halt.

Evelina wrestled the black mood inside, behind a pleasant mask, and prayed her storm clouds wouldn't be visible to anyone else. Prayed, as she looked out of an upstairs window at Number 120, that everyone would forget that Willa wasn't the only one who'd been scheduled to be married today. Prayed *she* would forget it too. That every laugh and every bit of floating white lace wouldn't remind her of that dress shoved into the back of her wardrobe at Number 22.

Prayed that the unexpected arrival of their solicitor that morning would stop pounding its way to the forefront of her mind.

"Willa, will you sit still for five blasted minutes? I'll jab you with this hairpin, I swear I will."

Rosemary's testy voice—nearly as heavy with exasperation as with affection—brought Evelina's gaze around. Willa sat on the stool before the dressing table, fidgeting even now. Her hair had slipped out yet again to fall onto the cotton shoulders of her dressing gown. She looked about ready to growl too.

"I can't help it! I'm beginning to understand why you eloped and saved yourself all this fuss and bother."

"Want me to hold her down?" Elinor offered with a cheeky grin. "I can take one side and Retta the other."

"Or better still . . ." Retta scooped up Clover from where she'd been sitting on the floor playing dolls with Olivia and deposited her with a flurry of little-girl giggles upon Willa's lap. "There. That'll keep you from shifting too much."

Willa chuckled and planted a kiss upon the girl's cap of ginger hair. "You've been reduced to a paperweight, luv."

Clover smiled. "Your wedding dress is so pretty, Willa. Can I wear it when I grow up?"

"Of course you can, if you want. I—*ow!* Rosie, you're *this close* to being sacked—I'll have Ellie do my hair, I will."

Evelina wrapped her arms around her middle and leaned against the wall beside the window. She didn't want to be at home today, surrounded by silence and memories and should-have-beens. But she didn't feel quite as though she belonged here, either, with the happy sisters and their comfortable arguments.

Lucy filled her blurred vision, a smile on her lips but a question in her eyes. "Are you all right, Lina?"

"Is everything all right, Mrs. Manning?" the solicitor had asked her mother two hours earlier, a frown marring his features. *"Your husband has never once been so much as a day late on any of his payments in the thirty years since he set up business in London. You can imagine my surprise when his creditors paid me a visit yesterday, inquiring about his June rents. Has something happened? Is he ill?"*

Evelina's fingers dug into her side. "I'm all right, Luce. Thank you. Just somewhat of a bittersweet day."

Where was he? Surely not in London, or he would have paid

the rents. Papa was not the type to let a little thing like his family life falling apart keep him from maintaining his pristine business reputation. But even if he'd gone to the countryside or left England for Switzerland, he would have made financial arrangements, wouldn't he?

Unless he wanted Mother and her to have to deal with it. To be worried and shamed and realize how quickly their world would come tumbling down about their ears without him there to provide for them.

She'd never dreamed that such vindictiveness could reside within him.

Lucy sighed. "I can't imagine going to another wedding on the day mine should have been. Were I you, I would have holed myself up somewhere far away from all such activities and buried my woes in sweets."

A breath of laughter slipped between Evelina's lips. "Were there not a sugar shortage . . ." She shrugged. "Besides, wallowing would only leave me more miserable. Better to share the joy of my friends—and to remind myself that, all in all, I'm glad not to be marrying Basil today."

"I'm sure Barclay's a much better catch. If one ignores his finances, or lack thereof."

Had he said anything to his family about the Charles Pearce of the clothing factory? Somehow, Evelina doubted it. Not given the fact that the younger man had apparently denied any kinship—though to Evelina's eyes, they'd borne enough resemblance to each other to be brothers. Not to mention the shared surname.

How ironic that Barclay had this tribe who were adamant about calling him their brother, despite no shared blood, yet was denied by the one who ought to claim it.

To Lucy's observation, she offered a halfhearted smile. And her palm warmed at the memory of his hand in hers. After *she* had reached out. "He's certainly a very different sort of man. One who has changed my outlook on many things." Like family, and what it meant to be part of one.

How she'd failed the one she had.

Had Basil not ended things, had she been walking down the aisle today and pledging her future to his, what kind of home would they have built? He would have spent his days at Downing Street or elsewhere in Westminster, striving always to gain another notch on his political belt. She would have spent hers in the company of Mrs. Knight and her ilk, fighting for the vote for women and not caring what destruction they must threaten to achieve it. They would have had children cared for by nannies, a house full of servants capable of keeping the place running despite their never being home. They would have sat in the drawing room of an evening with their separate books, exchanged a few cool smiles and an update on their day, and then retired to their separate chambers. Just like Mother and Papa.

How empty it all looked when compared to this chaos before her now. Siblings squabbling and laughing and knowing that no matter what, they'd fight for each other. Couples looking at each other as if they could read the other's mind, as Rosemary did with her Peter, Willa with her Lukas.

Part of her craved that, even as she feared herself incapable of sustaining it.

Part of her could understand why Charles Pearce had pushed Barclay away. He had no right to have fashioned a life for himself as he'd chosen to do it, had no right to have put together a family so wonderful through sheer grit. Yet he had. Leaving one with two choices—to love and admire him for it and want to be part of said family, or to resent him for it and want to stay far, far away.

"Well, I'd better help get the little ones ready." Lucy clapped her hands and strode into the center of the room. "Jory, Liv, Cress—come with me to my room. Clover, join us when you've finished being a paperweight."

The younger girls, who had all been draped over the bed and chairs in here watching the bride's hair fail to be pinned in place, clambered after Lucy, their voices raised in demands for ribbons and curls.

A buzzing sound cut through their chatter as they exited—the doorbell. And as all the sisters were busy getting each other ready, Evelina took the excuse to push away from the wall and escape her own thoughts for a minute. "I'll answer it, if you like."

"Oh, would you? Thanks." Willa batted away Elinor, who was reaching toward her face with a rouge brush.

Evelina chuckled her way out of the room, along the upstairs corridor, and down the stairs. The men were all across the street at the Holstein residence.

The bell buzzed again as she reached the main floor, indicating a distinct impatience in the caller. For half a second, her pulse kicked up—it could be someone from her house, come to tell her that Papa was home.

Then she caught the silhouette of the figure waiting outside through the window by the door, and that hope went flat. It was decidedly female, but decidedly *not* her mother or their maid. This woman was shorter, a bit stooped. Not the carriage of anyone she knew.

Shaking herself, she stepped forward and pulled open the door with a smile that froze on her lips.

The woman on the doorstep didn't look as though she belonged in Hammersmith. Her clothing was threadbare and ill-fitting, bunching up at the wrists but straining too tight across her torso, the cloth itself cheap and dull. Her face was a web of lines that made it hard to determine her age. But her eyes were a clear, light blue. Her hair, though now a dull grey, had echoes of golden brown in a few remaining streaks.

"Good day," Evelina said, gripping the door. "Can I help you?" The woman certainly didn't look as though she were here on wedding business. But she *did* look like one of the people to whom Barclay tended to stretch out a hand.

The woman lifted a brow, shockingly haughty. "I was told this is my son's home—Barclay Pearce. And who, pray tell, are you?"

Evelina's fingers dug into the door. Barclay's *mother*? No, that couldn't be. This woman, tired and worn out and looking as though her face weren't capable of a smile, bore no resemblance to the confident young man who could juggle a whole city in his palms. Except for the eyes. The eyes *did* put Evelina in mind of Barclay's—clear and blue and able to catalog someone in a glance.

She couldn't quite manage to thaw her smile. But she summoned an answer to her tongue. "I'm a friend of the family. I'm afraid Barclay isn't at home just now—"

"I'll wait, then. I've spent my last two pence on the tube ride here, which took the best part of an hour."

"Oh. Well, I . . ." All the lessons in manners that Mother had taught her failed in the face of someone who obviously didn't care a whit about them. This woman looked earnest in her declaration to remain right where she was.

Was she really his mother? Evelina hadn't any idea—but regardless, she knew Barclay wouldn't want her to leave the woman outside. She forced a new smile. "Do come in. If you'll wait in the drawing room for a few minutes, I'll fetch Barclay for you. I'm afraid the house is in a bit of an uproar today—it's his sister's wedding, you see, and—"

"Sister?" The woman's face pinched. "Charlie mentioned some fool thing like that, but I didn't credit it. Barclay has no sister."

"Well, I realize . . ." What was the point in arguing? Evelina shook her head and motioned the woman inside. "Do come in, Mrs. Pearce. If you'll just have a seat, it won't take me long to find him." The room still had little more than a sofa, the low table, and Barclay's chair to its name, but the critical eye Mrs.

Pearce sent over it didn't seem to be noting its lacks—if Evelina weren't mistaken, it was noting its *haves*.

"Just a moment, please." She kept her pace even, steady, as she strode back into the entryway and out the door, but she nearly ran across the street to the Holstein residence, ringing the bell even as she pounded a fist upon the door.

The butler answered in seconds, his brows raised. "Miss Manning. I do hope there's no problem with Miss Forsythe? Or Mrs. Holstein?" He went pale at the thought, proving that though he'd served in the Holstein house for decades, the new mistress's family had wormed their way into his heart fully. And understandably.

Evelina shook her head. "No, no, nothing like that. I need to speak with Barclay, though, straightaway. Could you fetch him?"

"Of course." Sounding relieved at the dismissal of his fears, he motioned her inside, shut the door behind her, and set a course up the stairs.

Barclay stood in the doorway of his drawing room and couldn't quite convince his feet to move forward another step. She stood there, her back to him, in front of the fireplace, studying the trinkets the family had put in the places of honor on the mantel.

The painting Retta had done of the sun sinking behind Big Ben's tower. The vase of flowers—dried now—that a street vendor had given Ellie when she saved his purse from another thief. The set of books that Peter and Rosie had given Jory for Christmas, and which she'd deemed too pretty to hide away in her room where no one could see them. The painted enamel egg that Cressida had found broken in someone's rubbish bin and had meticulously glued back together so that, from this angle, one couldn't tell it had been broken.

They were the only decorations in the room. What would they make her think?

He had no doubt, as he studied the stooped shoulders and curved back, that this was his mother. Because Charlie was his brother, and Lina had said this woman mentioned Charlie. He'd sent her here, to the address on the calling card, though he hadn't deigned to come himself. His brother had given him back his mother.

His heart made one dull thud and then seemed to go silent. He'd been ten when she was arrested—he remembered her. But did he remember her aright? He remembered all the lessons she'd taught him in how to pick someone's pocket, to be sure. But he couldn't recall her ever smiling at him. He couldn't recall a gentle touch from her hand.

Yet surely they'd been there, in his childhood. At least before his father died. His mind must have just sorted them out in its own grief.

He cleared his throat, and she spun. He couldn't quite smile. "Mum?"

She looked so *old*. Older by far than he knew she was. But then, she'd have lived a hard life these last twenty years. When had she been released from prison? Under the lines and creases, though, he saw her. The mother he'd known for the first decade of his life. The familiar, underneath the age.

She didn't smile either. If anything, her face went more pinched. "You've done well enough, I suppose. Though apparently you didn't see fit to share your good fortune with your family. Just like your father's people."

That was it? Her greeting after nearly two decades apart? No rushing to embrace him, no exclamation of how much he'd grown or the man he'd become? No *You look like your father* or *Where have you been? I was worried.*

His throat, tight and paralyzed, refused to let him swallow. It took him a long moment to convince himself there was still air in his lungs and that he could speak. "I didn't know where you were. Or Charlie. I looked, but—when I got back from the city center that day, you were gone. And Charlie was gone. The neighbors said the bobbies had come, arrested you, and taken him off to an orphanage."

He watched her eyes—the way the ice in them flickered, the thoughts that marched through them. He didn't know her well enough anymore to say what those thoughts were, only that there were no questions in them.

Her eyes looked as they always had, in his every memory of her since his father's death. Cold, hard, and unforgiving.

She folded scrawny arms over her chest. "What's this nonsense I hear about sisters?"

Barclay finally forced his legs to carry him another step into the room. Two. He motioned toward the couch, and she sat, testing its cushions with a little bounce. Barclay chose his usual chair and sat forward in it to rest his forearms on his knees. "When I got home that day and you and Charlie were gone . . . I went to the orphanage, but he wasn't there. The landlady tossed me out, said you hadn't paid the rent through the end of the week yet. So I hunkered down in the area for a while, trying to find Charlie. Set my sights on a score—which ended up a big mistake. Apparently Claw had set his sights on the same one."

He left the name without explanation, waited a moment to see if she'd ask who Claw was.

She didn't. Just pressed her lips together, eyes never losing a bit of their calculation.

Barclay cleared his throat. "He ran me out of Hackney after that—said if ever I stepped foot on his turf again, he'd slit my throat. So I wandered about for a few months and ended up in Poplar. There's a publican there, Pauly. Have you heard of him?"

His mother sniffed. "I don't go to Poplar."

Beneath her, was it? As if Hackney was so much better. Barclay bit back that response and forced a smile. Or what he hoped looked like a smile. "Well, he saw to it that I had food enough and introduced me to a few other children in like circumstances. Rosemary and Willa. They were both a bit younger than me, didn't have any idea how to survive on the streets. So we decided to stick together. I taught them what I knew. Started calling ourselves siblings to avoid questions, and Pauly posed as our uncle to get us a flat."

She blinked at him, as if it were someone else's story. A stranger's rather than her son's.

He pushed on. "We took in others over the years, whenever we found a little one in need who wanted to stick with us. Grew up together. I always kept an eye out for Charlie, but the other day was the first I'd seen him in all these years. I suppose he must have stayed in Claw's turf—the one place in London I couldn't go."

Now something flickered in her eyes, though it wasn't an emotion he could name. And her lips twitched, though not into a smile. "You're him, then. The rival Claw's always yammering about. The one that's friendly with all the other gang leaders. The one who's supposedly stepped down."

His stomach went sick. "I'm not a gang leader."

She snorted. "If it smells like a rubbish bin, and it *looks* like a rubbish bin—"

"You're in his crew, then. Claw's." No point in arguing over the difference between a crew and a family, not with her. Not given that look in her eye.

So few people understood.

Her lips twisted up into an imitation of a smile. "I'd rather be in yours. You've done well for yourself, lad. Real well."

He leaned up again, back against the chair. "I'm afraid Claw had the right of it—I've stepped down. Got out. Gone legitimate."

His mother shook her head. "No, you haven't. No one ever does. Not for long."

"Well, I have." He paused, considered. Swallowed. "What about Charlie? Is he . . . ?"

"Straight as a pin, just like always." Mum didn't sound pleased about it. "And too good to soil himself with his old mum. Gives me a pound a month and not a pence more. As if that's enough to live on. Then condemns me for having to make the rest the only way I know how."

Laughter from upstairs echoed down through the floorboards—a stark contrast to the empty air between him and his mother.

His chest ached. "I'll help you. As much as I can. I know it looks like I've made something of myself, but most of this isn't mine—my employer provided it all." And he had a passel of children he had to provide for with his limited salary from V too. He couldn't neglect them just because Mum showed up. "Where are you living?"

She shrugged. "Here and there." Then her eyes lit, and she glanced upward, toward the laughter.

Barclay's throat ached along with his chest. "I haven't any room here, I'm sorry. There are already twelve of us." And that street-born instinct told him not to open his home to her. Not knowing so little of who she was now, what prison had made her. "And it isn't my house. But . . ." His flat flashed into his mind. Though she may resent the offering after seeing this place. "I may be able to arrange something else for you. If you're willing to venture to Poplar."

The sneer took over her whole face, line by wrinkle. "You'd shove me off into a place like that? When we've only just been reunited?"

Fingers digging into the arms of the chair, Barclay kept his face a blank, pleasant mask. He'd put it in terms she'd understand. "This is just an extended job, Mum. Not where I'll be forever. But I've a flat there. And it's my turf. I can make sure no one bothers you. Set you up a tab at Pauly's so you don't go hungry. I can provide for you, if you'll stay in my territory."

Something softened in her face. Or perhaps just lost a bit of its hardness, though he couldn't really call her expression *soft* without insulting the word. "I'll consider it."

The clock in the hall chimed the hour—he had only one left before he had to get to the church, and the footsteps overhead pounded rather frantically as the girls likely realized the same.

He didn't want them to come down here and see his mother. Another day, perhaps, but not this one. Not when Mum would see how fine their gowns were and think he was holding back, never believing that Rosie had paid for all the fabric and stitched it herself. And not when his sisters would have so many questions that would distract them from Willa's day.

No, another day. For now, he stood. "Forgive me, Mum, but I have to go. If you stop by on Monday afternoon, or tell me where to find you . . ."

She stood too, looking so different from the mother he'd known as a boy. The one his father had loved so dearly, the one who had been able to move among their old friends like a thief in the night. Quite literally, taking what was theirs to feed Barclay and Charlie. But he'd seen the start of this hunched figure, hadn't he? Those last few months, in that last barren flat.

Her smile displayed teeth grown yellow and brown. "That's a good lad. I knew you'd do right by me, Barclay. Though I haven't coin enough for the tube back—nor here again. If you could lend me that, as I wouldn't have come here were it not for you, I'd be appreciative."

Would she? He had his doubts. But he sighed and fished into his pocket for a florin. "Here."

She took the coin and then held out her arms. "It's good to see you again, Barclay. All these years, I've wondered."

That much he could believe. How could a mother *not* wonder what had happened to her firstborn? He stepped into her embrace, even though it felt strange, foreign, to be the son rather than the big brother or father figure. Even though he felt her hand slip into his pocket. Even though he felt his watch slip back out with her.

He swallowed and pulled away, careful to keep his gaze on her eyes and not her hand. "I've wondered what became of you too, Mum. I've prayed for you, and for Charlie. And I remembered all you taught me. How to get along, yes. But more, what it means to be a family. That for them, you do whatever you can. You sacrifice rather than take." It was what she'd said so many times as she fenced a necklace or bracelet she'd lifted from a former friend—*"It's for you boys. For our family. That's why we sacrifice like this. We do anything for our family, isn't that right?"*

"That's right." Her eyes remained two circles of ice as she slid his watch into her own pocket.

And he realized they looked as they always had when she'd stolen something. No regret. No affection.

He'd modeled his life, his family on those principles she'd recited over and over again. He'd repeated them. He'd believed her words.

But had she?

She nodded once and sidestepped him, headed out of the room. With his watch in her pocket, as if he were a stranger instead of a son.

For a moment, he considered letting her go without a word. But if he did that, she'd go back to Hackney and brag to Claw about her score, about how weak was Barclay Pearce.

A year ago, it would have been pride that made him object to that. Today, it was the sinking knowledge that if such rumors spread, Poplar would go downhill fast, as Claw's crew infiltrated it, trying to take the territory everyone considered his.

He squeezed his eyes shut. He'd sworn off the life—but could he ever really get away from it? *Should* he, completely, or would the Lord smile on him trying to protect the people who looked to him for protection? Was it perhaps right, good, to keep his influence intact so he could at least keep the other crews out of the place he still considered home?

"Mum. What time is it?"

He heard her stop. Felt unease snap and sizzle in the air between them. "How am I to know, lad? I've no watch. Don't you have a clock somewhere in here? I thought I heard it chime."

He turned. Slowly. Met her gaze. "What time is it, Mum?"

She lifted her chin, every line hard, chiseled. "You want to search me?"

"No." He slid his hands into his pockets. Empty now but for a few pence and a wrinkled handkerchief. "I just want you to know that I know. Take it, if that's what you came for. And take the coins in the dish by the door, if you want them. But don't take me for a fool."

She blinked. And kept looking at him as if he were a stranger. "I came to find my son."

And to see what she could get out of him. Hating how easily the cynical thought settled on his spirit, he said nothing more. Just watched her as she left.

"Are you all right, Barclay?"

He sat on the garden step at Peter's house—a towel under him so he didn't soil his wedding suit. He'd slipped back in, changed, but he couldn't quite bring himself to stay there joking with Peter and Lukas and Lukas's Belgian friends who had made the journey from Wales to share in his day.

He ought to have known that Pauly would notice his escape though, even if the bridegroom didn't. He glanced up in time to see him tugging at his tie in obvious discomfort. It made a smile tease the corners of Barclay's mouth. "I don't believe I've ever seen you looking so dapper."

"And I wish you weren't now. The things we do for our own . . ."

He chuckled. But it pierced. How was it that this man, who had no obligation to him, who'd had to fight his wife for every scrap he sent their way, considered them his own . . . yet his own mother looked at him as if he were nothing to her?

"What's the matter, lad? Something to do with why Lina fetched you?"

There was never a hope of sliding one past Pauly. He saw too much. Barclay sighed and fiddled with the sprig of mint he'd plucked from the pot by the steps. "My mother found me."

Pauly sat down beside him—hard. "Your mum? I thought . . . I don't know what I thought. That she *wasn't*, I suppose."

"Mmm. Well, she apparently *is*." He rubbed the leaf against itself until the green broke open. Until the scent wafted up. Until the oil stained his fingers.

There was a lesson in that, he supposed. Somewhere. Something about breaking and finding what was hidden within.

He didn't much like feeling like a sprig of mint.

"Not a happy reunion?"

For a long moment, Barclay didn't answer. He just listened to the tweeting of a bird perched on the edge of the roof, to the deep laughter that drifted down from the window open above him. To the painful thudding of his own heart. "She stole from me."

Pauly hissed out a breath. He knew how it would hit home. The same way it did each and every time an urchin he'd fed stole from *him*.

That wasn't how you were supposed to repay kindness. That wasn't how you treated those who helped you, or who called you their own.

Where had Barclay learned that, if not from his mother? Those lessons he'd buried deep in his heart?

Pauly shook his head and rested a meaty hand on Barclay's shoulder. "I'm sorry, son."

"I know. Me too." He'd found them, after all these years. His mother, his brother. The family he'd thought he'd lost forever. After all these years, his prayers had been answered.

And he wished the Lord had said *no* instead of *yes*. Why did He put them back together now, when it only meant bitterness between them?

Pauly's fingers squeezed. "But family isn't blood—you know that. It should be, but it isn't, not always. Family is choice. Love. Wearing a blighted tie when you'd rather be in an apron, and then walking down the aisle of a fancy church when you belong in the kitchen."

The chuckle warmed him, filled a bit of the emptiness inside. Barclay shot a grin over to Pauly. Not just a friend, not just a benefactor. He was a father. As good a one as the man he'd been born to, in the ways that mattered. "You belong exactly where you are today—with us."

"Still say Willa should have gotten married at the pub." With a final clap to his shoulder, Pauly stood. "We'd have made it look fine."

"Yeah, I don't believe Lukas's priest would have approved." He didn't stand though. Not quite yet. Another minute, that was all he needed. "How long until the car leaves?"

"Ten minutes." He gazed beyond the house, into where he couldn't possibly see. "I bet she's pretty as a rose, our Willa. Always did look like an angel in white."

Barclay snorted. "*Willa* and *angel* don't belong in the same sentence."

Pauly laughed and stepped back inside. "Well now, I don't know. She plays like one."

"Angels play harps, not violins."

"Who's to say?" Pauly's laughter rumbled as he continued a few steps. And then, muted, came, "Afternoon, Lina. Our boy's just out in the garden."

Evelina had come back? Barclay stood but paused on the

threshold, looking over his shoulder at the bits of green that had once been a mint leaf peppering the step. The fragrance still teased his nose, had no doubt saturated his fingers. It would remind him all day of his mother, of what she'd taken.

Not a watch—hope. Hope for the family he'd dreamed of rebuilding someday.

But he couldn't dwell on it. He'd focus instead on the family he *had* built. On Willa and her day, on the others determined to make it special. On Evelina, who stood in the corridor in a pretty pink dress, looking like perfection.

She met him a few steps inside and didn't say anything. Just wrapped her arms around him.

He held on, rested his head on hers, and breathed in that scent that would always make his heart thud to life—flowers and rain. For a long moment he just stood there in her arms. And then he sighed. "I'm sorry. This day shouldn't be about me. It's about happiness for Willa. And if anyone deserves to be down today, it's you."

Her hands ran up his back and then down. Soothing. "I was. But you know . . . I don't want to be. I'm glad it's not my wedding day. I'm glad to be here with you and yours."

He could think of no answer to that other than to lift his head, tilt hers up, and press his lips to hers. And he wondered, as he kissed her, if there was hope today, after all.

TWENTY-THREE

Mother took a dainty, hesitant bite of the toast, her wariness evident in every movement, despite the smile she kept on her face. Evelina held her breath. And let out a relieved sigh when her mother's eyes lit.

"It's *good*. Quite good. It tastes like bread."

Evelina laughed and let her shoulders sag. Then picked up her own toast, made from the bread she had just baked herself—rising at a rather ridiculous hour this Monday morning in order to finish it in time for breakfast. "You needn't sound quite so surprised, Mama."

"Well, you've scarcely set foot in a kitchen, other than to give the plans to the cook. How was I to know you had any more skill at such things than I have?" Mother took another bite and then reached for the dish of marmalade. "And you say the girl didn't mind teaching you? I was afraid I'd offended her when I dismissed her and hired Mrs. Adams."

Who they'd then dismissed too, after the solicitor's visit. Apparently Papa wanted them to be aware of how reliant they were upon the living he provided—point taken. They had decided together that they would avoid any undue expenditures until he came home. And unfortunately, a cook had been ranked as "undue." At least since Lucy had volunteered at the wedding to teach Evelina all she would need to know, she said, to get by in the interim. "Lucy didn't mind at all. She knew well she'd been brought in only temporarily."

And had no great desire to be a full-time domestic, Evelina was sure. Lucy seemed to much prefer the freedom to wander about the neighborhood, selling bread and collecting gossip.

"Where did you run into her? Did she come by selling bread yesterday?"

Evelina reached for the marmalade once Mother was finished with it. She might as well, she supposed, admit to the truth—*they* wouldn't try to hide it, so why should she? "She is one of Barclay's adopted sisters."

Mother put down the toast, her pleasant smiles of the last week giving way to her habitual blank anger that would have been a frown on someone less accustomed to keeping all creases from her skin. "You must be joking. She's Indian."

"She was just a baby when a fire killed her parents, and Barclay's family took her in." Evelina took another deliberate bite. Chewed. Forced a smile. "I think Papa will be quite proud of us when he comes home, don't you? He'll see that we appreciate all he provides and that we have cut all frivolity from our lives."

Mother's face didn't exactly soften. Her disapproval certainly didn't disappear from her eyes. But she cleared her throat and went back to her toast. "It feels as though he's been gone forever."

Evelina opened her mouth to respond but paused when the doorbell sang through the house. "Who do you suppose that is at this hour?"

Mother sighed, resignation in her eyes. "If I were to guess . . ."

Williston must have been close at hand—she heard the door open and an all-too-familiar voice demand, "Where is my sister?"

Mother lifted her napkin to dab at her mouth.

Evelina barely restrained a groan. It was too much to hope, she supposed, that her aunt would really have stayed away forever. She wouldn't be happy unless she had someone to command.

Beatrice filled the doorway a moment later, a glower on her face that would have sent small children screaming from the room, and a newspaper in hand that she smacked onto the table. "Have you no sense at all, Judith? Letting your daughter attend another wedding on the day that should have been her own? Reminding all of London that she is not getting married?"

Mother smiled as she picked up the paper, no doubt galling her sister with the expression. "What a good photo of you, Evelina!"

Evelina buried a grin behind her cup of tea.

"Which all of our friends have now seen, and all of whose tongues are now wagging. How could you possibly think such a public appearance was a good idea?"

"I didn't much care what anyone had to say about it," Evelina said, setting her cup back down. "Willa is a friend, and it was an honor to be invited, so I went."

"To an event dotted with publicans, papists, and a veritable rainbow of races." Aunt Beatrice huffed and slammed her cane into the floor. "If your daughter exercised a bit more prudence in her decision-making, Judith, perhaps we would not all be in this muddle."

Mother opened the paper, presumably to follow the story onto another page. "How fortunate for you then, Bea, that the muddle is not yours."

The bell rang again.

Beatrice turned three different shades of red. "Apparently it *should* be. I leave the two of you alone for a few short days, and you manage to land in the gossip columns—and not happily. Well, I see no recourse. I shall have to move back in so I can keep you in line."

She wouldn't. *Surely* Mother wouldn't stand for it. Would she?

Her mother froze, countenance empty again. "I beg your pardon, Bea. I don't recall inviting you back into my home."

"As if you would turn your sister away. We are family, Judith—and from the looks of it, I am all you have. Unless Cecil is back home again?"

A muscle under Mother's eye ticked.

Beatrice sniffed. "As I thought. Well, we do not turn our backs on family. I have my things in the carriage and will have my man bring them back in—and what's that you're eating? Why is there no porridge or sausage?"

"Well, we—"

"You've dismissed your cook again, that's what—and from what I've heard, you've not found another. How fortunate for you that I'd secured a chef. I've already informed him to pack up all our supplies and bring them over here as well. And perhaps I'll bring my new butler along too, he's far more capable than that doddering old fool your husband employed."

Williston appeared in the doorway, right on cue. Somehow *his* lack of facial expression looked regal. As if Beatrice's words weren't important enough to be hurtful. He cleared his throat. "I beg your pardon. A telegram for you, Miss Manning."

"For *me*?" Not *them*? Not from Papa, then. Curious, she reached out for the familiar yellow paper and opened it, ignoring the continued bickering of her mother and aunt.

She glanced first at the end to see by whom it was signed, frowning at the words typed there so innocuously. *Your father*.

It was from Papa? But then why send a message only to her? And why sign it so formally, when he always signed notes with the familiar name she called him? Darting a quick gaze to her mother, she pasted on a smile. "Excuse me for a moment."

Normally, Mother would have asked who had sent her a telegram. But apparently she was too busy parrying Aunt Beatrice's next verbal thrust, for she said nothing as Evelina slipped from the room.

Once in the corridor, she read the rest of the brief telegram.

Isn't safe to come home. Pearce is a thief. Your father.

That was it. Even shorter than the twenty-four words that had torn their world apart before. Only eleven words, but they were even more destructive.

Her blood ran cold. Or perhaps hot. Or maybe it stopped altogether. What was he saying? That he couldn't come home because of *Barclay*? But that made no sense. Barclay may have committed some thievery in the past—he'd admitted as much—but he wasn't trying to steal anything from Papa. He was here to help him—sent here by the Admiralty, he said.

But what if . . . ?

No. She couldn't believe he was that much of a liar. That couldn't be.

And yet wasn't the alternative to call her *father* a liar?

She looked back toward the dining room as the doorbell buzzed yet again. There was no choice but to get to the bottom of this before Mother thought to ask about the wire. She'd have to go to Number 120, that was all. Confront Barclay, if he was home, or whatever sister was there if he wasn't. While whichever of Mother's friends who was no doubt calling to gossip about Evelina's appearance in the paper came in, she'd just slip out the door and demand an explanation.

Williston shuffled back to the door, opened it. But it was an unfamiliar male voice that intruded into her thoughts, not one of the gaggle of middle-aged matrons who usually came to call of a morning. "Mr. Cavendish to see Miss Evelina Manning. It's of the utmost importance."

Safely out of sight in the hallway, Evelina's brows knit. She knew no Mr. Cavendish.

"Of course, sir," came Williston's polite reply. "If you'll but wait in the parlor a moment, I'll fetch her."

The *parlor*? The butler rarely showed anyone to the parlor. Evelina herself hadn't set foot in it since Mr. Dramwell came to visit about his factory's previous manager. Was this Cavendish perhaps an acquaintance of his?

She waited until Williston came to fetch her, a card on his salver. And only then slid a step forward. "Does his card give any indication of who he is?"

The butler held out the tray. "A barrister, I believe."

Not Papa's, though. Him they knew. Evelina picked up the card, studied it, but the man's address—at a rather impressive location, to be sure—offered no insight. "Did he say what his business was as you showed him in?"

"He did not, miss. He only offered his apologies for calling so early."

"Well." She folded the telegram around the card and slid both into her pocket. "I suppose I had better see what is so important." Answers from Barclay could wait a few more minutes.

Still, she paused for a moment outside the parlor door. Her stomach quivered. She didn't have any idea why an unknown barrister would appear at her home at nine o'clock in the morning, but it couldn't be good.

Pressing a hand to her middle to still the queasiness, she drew in a deep breath for fortification. Squared her shoulders. Pasted on a smile and marched into the room.

The man perched on the edge of the uncomfortable couch had a veritable garden of papers spread out on the low table before him, his current position—bent over the collection—showing off the shining dome of his bald head. He sprang up upon hearing her enter, of course, smoothing an impeccable waistcoat with one hand while striding forward with the other outstretched. "Miss Manning, how do you do? Delighted to finally make your acquaintance. I've heard all about you."

"How do you do?" She met him in the center of the room and put her hand in his, her smile gaining no more certainty as he lifted her hand and pressed a perfunctory kiss to her knuckles.

"I'm afraid you have me at a disadvantage, sir. I don't believe I've heard all about *you*."

"No reason you would have." He had interesting eyes. Dark brown, gleaming with intelligence, and snapping with a strange combination of sympathy and impatience. "I imagined that after receiving the news, you would be full of questions, but perhaps not certain of where to reach me, hence the early-morning visit."

The news. That queasiness in her stomach went hard and cold. "I beg your pardon. What news?"

Not Papa, please not Papa. Lord, if something has happened to him . . . But why would news come through this stranger? And what could have happened in the time since he sent that cryptic telegram?

Anything, really. Anything.

The stranger frowned. "Did you not receive a telegram from the War Office on Saturday? Or perhaps even Friday?"

"War Office?" She groped blindly for a chair and sat upon the unforgiving cushion. Not Papa. But . . . "Basil? Has something happened to Basil?"

"Did they not contact you?" Pressing thin lips together, Mr. Cavendish sat too, in a spot on the couch. "I do apologize, Miss Manning, I assumed you'd known for days already and would be anxious. He was killed in battle last week. In Gallipoli."

Basil had been in Gallipoli? All the horrific stories she'd read and heard came rushing down upon her, blurring her vision. "No."

"This must be shocking news to receive like this. I *am* sorry. Perhaps since the wedding was postponed and you were not listed officially as his wife . . . I can return at another time, if you'd prefer to deal with his estate later."

"His estate?" She blinked, pressed her hand against the hard arm of the chair, and tried to feel something. Anything. But her insides had gone hollow and full of echoes. *Gallipoli. Papa. Basil. Thief. Estate*. The words pinged back and forth, knocking against one another and leaving her head feeling as though a gong had been rung between her ears. "Forgive me, sir, but I don't see what his estate would have to do with me. We weren't, as you mentioned, married."

"Which would have affected your status in the eyes of the War Office but has little effect here." He reached for a stack of papers, clipped together, and held them out to her. "Mr. Philibert altered his will some three months ago to name you as his sole beneficiary, in anticipation of your nuptials."

"But . . ." She took the papers automatically. Glanced down at them. But only because those were the actions she was expected to perform. She saw nothing of the words upon the page, couldn't even feel the weight of the papers between her fingers. "But he ended the betrothal. Before he left for the war."

That gave the man pause. For a moment. But then he lifted his brows and cleared his throat. "Be that as it may, he did not then alter his will, so the results just now are the same. As I am certain you are aware, Mr. Philibert had no other living family aside from some very distant cousins. His estate, inherited from his parents, was without entail. He could legally leave it to whomever he chose, and he chose *you*, Miss Manning."

Impossible. She shook her head. "But that makes no sense. Not given—he was quite clear, Mr. Cavendish, when he ended things. He didn't want me to be part of his future. I cannot fathom that he didn't alter his will before he left to exclude me from it, even if he had named me as an inheritor beforehand."

And he would have thought about it. He *must* have. A man who'd given it such consideration months ago wouldn't have just neglected to make alterations when leaving for a war, when thoughts of death must by nature come into one's mind.

The barrister shuffled a few of the papers and came up with an envelope. "The only thing he changed before he left for Europe, miss, was to give me this, with instruction that if he were killed in action and I had received no other instruction, to deliver it to you along with the will and testament."

He held out the pale grey rectangle, brows raised in the expectation that she would take it.

She couldn't convince her arms to lift again. She could barely convince her throat to swallow. "And you received no other instruction?"

"No." He gave her a kind yet cool smile that made her think he was no stranger to uncomfortable conversations and leaned forward to slide the envelope onto the pile of clipped papers.

She stared at it. Did he expect her to open it now? To wait? What was the appropriate thing? She didn't know. She couldn't move. Couldn't act. Couldn't think. Barclay was a thief—it seemed he was the reason Papa had left. Basil was dead—it seemed he had left her his entire estate. The world made no sense.

Mr. Cavendish cleared his throat. "You understandably need time to absorb all this. I'll leave you with the simple facts, my information, and my sincere condolences. In short, everything Mr. Philibert possessed is now yours. The houses, both in Westminster and Shropshire, the automobile, and approximately . . ." He paused, reached for another stack of papers, flipped through them. Nodded. "Approximately eighty thousand pounds—much of which must be held for upkeep and maintenance of the properties, of course, and payment of employees. But we can review those details at a later date. For now you need only to know that his estates are running smoothly, are in good order, and are now yours."

Eighty thousand pounds. Evelina couldn't breathe. Two houses. An automobile. At least one hundred servants at the country house, she knew. She'd visited it right after he'd proposed, so she could be introduced as the future mistress and see what her duties would be.

But all that had become the past, she'd thought. A chapter edited from her life. What never would be.

So how had it become fact?

An hour ago, she'd wondered how long she and her mother would be able to afford to put food on the table if Papa didn't soon return. Five minutes ago, she'd been ready to charge from the house and demand answers from a thief. Now . . .

Mr. Cavendish shuffled the papers back into a stack and slid them toward the end of the table nearest her. "These copies are yours—review them at your convenience and please do drop into my office with any questions. I am at your disposal." With another of those sad but confident smiles, he stood. "I realize Mr. Philibert has left you with questions and sorrow—but he has also left you a wealthy woman, Miss Manning. Perhaps you can take some solace in the knowledge that he wanted to be sure you were provided for, even given your recent estrangement."

Evelina's fingers contracted, pressing wrinkles into the papers she clutched. "Thank you. I . . . I cannot quite . . ."

Mr. Cavendish nodded. "You needn't. Take some time to absorb all this shocking news. Again, my condolences. I'll show myself out."

She may have nodded. May have even muttered something that resembled a farewell. She couldn't quite be sure. She could only stare at the space where he'd been and wonder if it were all a dream. If she'd wake up and come down the stairs and find the kitchen still cool and dark and Lucy waiting outside the door to teach her how to combine flour and yeast and water into a sticky mixture that would magically rise into a loaf. If she'd wonder at Mother's smiles and sigh all over again at Aunt Beatrice's appearance. If all questions about Barclay Pearce were part of one more nightmare, easily dismissed in morning's light.

Her gaze drifted down, to the evidence of this strange reality. That stack of papers that read *Final Will and Testament* at their head. That envelope that had her name scrawled across it in Basil's familiar hand.

Her fingers shook as she set the stack upon her lap and picked up the letter. Its paper was heavy, expensive—the type Basil always used for his personal correspondence, as it would proclaim to its recipients at first touch that he was a man of worth. The first time he'd sent a letter here, Mother and Aunt Beatrice had exclaimed for five full minutes over the paper.

She traced the letters of her name. His hand was elegant but without any flourish—educated but efficient. As he had always been—or as she'd always thought him, anyway. But he'd shown a different side that night he ended things, hadn't he?

When he'd written to her during their courtship and betrothal, his letters were always exactly what a girl would hope. A bit of news, a bit of flattery, a bit of hope. A few times he'd even included a verse of poetry that he said reminded him of her.

Somehow she suspected this letter would be different. Sucking in a breath, she slipped her finger under the flap and tore it open. Pulled out the sheet of stationery that matched the envelope.

Evelina,

I hope to heaven you never read this. If you do, it's because I've been killed in the war. Ideally, I'll come home in a few months or years, have Cavendish destroy this letter, and reclaim my life. If you're reading this, then the worst has happened.

I'll be honest. Part of me still hopes that something will change while I'm gone. That you'll realize you loved me all along, and that when I come home, you'll rush into my arms and declare that life was empty without me. I hope it, and yet I can't quite believe it. As I pen this letter after telling you of my decision, I think it far more likely that you'll just file away our time together and move on. You'll find someone else, perhaps someone who can inspire feeling in you as I never could—or perhaps just someone who won't mind that they can't. And I'll eventually come home and find another girl, one who will make me forget this hollow ache inside.

I loved you. Perhaps you won't believe me. But I did. Do. There's a reason I chose you out of all the young ladies I met. Not to be rude, but we both know I could have made a match that was better in the eyes of society. Your aunt's connections were all you had to recommend you socially. I could have chosen an heiress or even a lady from a titled family. But I chose you. I chose you because I saw something in you that was unlike anything to be found in other girls. That determination that made you walk again after your illness as a child. That desire for justice that drew you to the suffragette cause and to champion the working women. That precision that you inherited from your father. Even that rebellion your mother inspires. I thought those things would equate to passion. I thought they would make us pair perfectly.

I was wrong.

If you're reading this, then you know I've left you everything. Because at this moment, I still love you. And if I can make you happy in my death as I couldn't in life, then I will be glad to do so. If you're reading this, then I've given you the one thing you ever wanted from me, Evelina: your independence. You can live where you please, make your own choices, your own decisions. Marry or not marry. You can spend my wealth to further your causes.

I pray I make it home and that we can both find happiness—together, if possible, apart if necessary. But failing that, I pray you live knowing that you're a remarkable young woman, and I'm sorry I could not be what you wanted. Sorry I could not make you love me.

Live well, Evelina. Live fully. Live as you've always wanted to do.

Yours,
Basil

Evelina tried to breathe, but the air knotted up in her chest, heaved its way up, and came out a sob. The tears she couldn't shed that night he'd ended things—the tears to prove her a girl and not a machine—scalded her eyes and burned her cheeks.

She doubled over until the cool paper soothed her forehead, until the muscles in her back and neck strained to match her heart. Until all the questions twisted into one.

Was anything she thought she'd found real, trustworthy, honest . . . or just a reaction to his leaving, inspired by a lie from the tongue of a thief?

TWENTY-FOUR

Barclay cast his gaze one last time over the flat that had once been his in Poplar. He'd let V know that he was setting his mother up in it, so they'd have to use another place as a drop. He'd paid the rent a month in advance rather than his usual week. He'd handed over every coin he'd managed to squirrel away to Pauly—save one tuppence—to cover a tab for his mother.

She'd be moving in here tomorrow.

Part of him doubted she'd show. Part of him knew she would—no street thief turned down free food and lodging.

Free. It made him shake his head. She'd look at this place, compare it to the house in Hammersmith, and think he was giving her crumbs when he had a feast set before him. But the salary V gave him only stretched so far, and with so many children to feed . . .

He didn't want to regret this decision. But he feared he would within a fortnight.

A worry for tomorrow. He latched the door behind him and strode down the hallway, the stairs, out onto the street. Walked for a minute and then paused at the familiar figure hunched in the familiar alleyway. "Afternoon, Mags."

She peeked up from her tin cup and obliged him by turning

her face into the precious web of wrinkles with one of her smiles. “There’s our lad. Word on the street is that you’re bringing your mother to the neighborhood.”

Word sure did travel fast. Barclay grinned and crouched down. “That’s right. Tomorrow. Can you keep an eye on her for me?”

That earned him a cackle. “Leave it to Old Mags. I’ll see no one bothers her.”

“I know. And see . . . if *she* bothers anyone, I hear about it quickly, will you?”

Maggie’s web collapsed into a frown. “’Course I will. But why you have to worry so ’bout your own mum?”

He just shook his head, pulled out the one tuppence he’d held in reserve for this purpose, and dropped it into Maggie’s tin cup. “Let’s hope I don’t. But . . .”

“But.” She nodded and reached to pat his cheek. “You’re a good lad, Barclay. You can count on me.”

“I know I can.” He covered her gnarled fingers with his for a moment and then let her go, standing again. The nights were warm enough now that Maggie would be sleeping right here rather than finding a more sheltered place to hunker, at least if it held off raining.

He shot a glance up at the clear sky as he turned back onto the street. No clouds would be good for those on the streets. Unless they lured another zeppelin their way.

A concern he shook off because he could do nothing about it regardless. Nothing but pray.

His prayers had felt a bit tense the last week though, ever since he’d seen his brother at the factory.

He’d prayed so earnestly, so long. For his family, for a reunion, for their care. Why was the reality of it all so much *less* than what he’d dreamed of?

He hurried to the tube stop. Hurried so he could sit on the rocking train for an hour as it wound its way back to Hammersmith, sit and worry and try to toss those worries heavenward only to feel as though they landed again at his feet.

He was a fool to put her in Poplar. He knew it, even as he knew he'd had little choice. He couldn't leave her without care, not when he had something to provide. Not when he had so many years to make up for.

Afternoon had yawned its way into evening when he debarked again in Hammersmith. It smelled different here, more hopeful.

Less honest. How long would he be able to pretend he belonged in a place like this?

"Like your father's people," Mum had said the other day. He wished he remembered more of them. Wished that the remembering would give him some claim to legitimacy. As if knowing whether his father's people were respectable would make him any more deserving of what he'd built for himself here.

No, he hadn't built it. He'd stolen it. Stolen his way into V's confidence, and that was what had gotten him this home.

He turned down his street and glanced again at the sun, where it sank below the buildings. Would he have time to call on Evelina after he grabbed a bite? Perhaps, if he hurried. He would try.

He jogged up the steps to his door, opened it, and smiled at the scents of food that greeted him. Lucy had been doing her magic again, and he'd be more than happy to taste her current creation so he could praise her for it.

"Barclay!" Jory came barreling toward him, unusual thunder marring her features. "He *took* it, and it's mine, and I told him he could read it when I was done, but I'm *not* and—"

"I *told* her I'd give it back tomorrow!" Fergus was hot on their sister's heels, his face red. "I need to read a book for school, and it's the only one we have that would be good enough. I didn't *take* it, I just *borrowed* it."

"You pinched it right from my hands!"

Barclay pressed his lips against a smile. A book. His little brother and sister were fighting over a book. For school. It was so incredibly *normal* a fight for a family that it warmed the place inside that his mother's appearance had chilled. They weren't fighting over the last scrap of food or the only blanket. Just a book.

He cleared his throat. "Jory, let Fergus borrow the book. After"—he raised a hand to ward off both their reactions—"you finish the chapter you were on. Fair?"

The irritation melted off her face. Mostly. She was a stickler for finishing her chapter, was Jory. But she never minded sharing in general. She nodded.

Fergus huffed. "She reads too slow."

"Slow*ly*." Jory paired the correction with a stuck-out tongue. "You'd think your fancy school would have taught you grammar."

"Enough, you two." Chuckling, Barclay shooed them away so he could get more than a step in the door. He took off his hat and tossed it toward the coatrack. It missed, but Fergus snagged it on his way by and righted it.

Commotion outside the front door drew his attention before he could follow his nose to the kitchen. Wailing, quick footsteps, a masculine voice. With a frown, Barclay spun back to the door and tugged it open.

Charlie and their mother were even then mounting the steps. His little brother pushed past him without so much as a hello, half carrying Mum as he hobbled with his cane. Their mother's face was lined with agony. And it was white as cream—a marked contrast to the red-stained rag encircling her hand.

Barclay closed the door behind them and shouted, "Bandages! Somebody bring bandages and whatever medicinals we have! Hurry!" He touched a hand to Charlie's shoulder. "There, to the right. The drawing room. What happened?"

Charlie, his face as hard as granite—though Barclay couldn't tell if it was from frustration or pain—uncovered their mother's hand.

The appendage was swollen, bruised, mangled, with a gash scored deep in the top of it. Mum turned her face away from the sight and choked out, "It was Claw that done it. I told him I didn't take the blighted thing, but he didn't believe me."

Claw. Barclay shook his head. "You ought to have known he'd be looking to punish you if he caught wind that I was your son."

His sisters had been charging into the room—Elinor, Retta, even Rosie was here—but all stopped short at that.

He let his eyes slide shut for a moment. He should have told them yesterday, he supposed. But they were all so tired after the wedding, it had been easier to put it off. He scrubbed a hand over his face. "Ellie, Rosie, Ret—my mum. And my little brother, Charlie. I only just found them again. And apparently I ought to have taken you to Poplar sooner, Mum. Then you'd have no reason to venture back into his turf, but to visit Charlie."

Charlie snorted. "As if she ever just visits. She only comes round when she needs money—or when she shows up like this. And I can't afford a doctor, Barclay. I just can't, but look at it. She needs one."

His sisters, well accustomed to taking things in stride, continued into the room with their medical basket.

Barclay mentally calculated the coins they had left. Barely enough for this week's groceries, given that he'd just spent all his meager savings on the flat and pub tab for her. But Rosie would lend him some. Or Willa, now that she was making an honest living. He hated to ask them, hated to realize that even now, when they slept in a real house and earned a weekly paycheck, he couldn't afford the basic care of his family. Not on his own.

But he'd do whatever it took. "I'll take care of her. But Mum, you have to stay away from Claw."

"She won't. He's the only one that lets her in his crew at all and doesn't run her off their turf." The stoic mask melting into outright pain, Charlie shook his head. "I've done what I could, all these years. Tried to get her to change. She won't listen, and I can't watch her every moment of the day. I have to work, as does my wife. And even so, she bleeds us dry. Takes what we won't give the moment our backs are turned."

Mum spat an expletive at him and tried to snatch her hand away from Rosie, who was dabbing at it with iodine tincture. Retta held her still on one side while Elinor sandwiched her in on the other.

The doorbell buzzed. Barclay looked up to see who he could dispatch to answer it—though he needn't have bothered. Lucy was already shooing the little ones back toward the kitchen, and Peter, who he hadn't realized was even here, was striding toward the door.

A moment later, an ashen Judith Manning filled the doorway, going even paler upon spotting Mum and her damaged hand.

Not exactly introductions he fancied making right now. He stepped toward Evelina's mother. "Mrs. Manning. Is something the matter?" It must be, to bring her here.

She looked as out of place as a person could, standing there in his barely furnished drawing room. Her posture was too perfect, her chin too high, her hands too still as they clutched her handbag.

Perhaps she knew she was in the presence of thieves. And former thieves. But her gaze latched on to his, and she made no indication that the continued hissing of his mother even entered her awareness. "Forgive me, Mr. Pearce. I don't mean to intrude. It's only—it's Evelina. I didn't know who else to ask for help."

"Evelina?" His empty stomach twisted. "What about her?"

Mrs. Manning shook her head and drew a breath in through her nose that made her nostrils flare. An attempt, given the quick blinks, to keep her emotions in check. "She has left. For good, she says. To be on her own."

"Left?" That hardly made sense. Where could she possibly go? Unless . . . "To join her father?"

"No. To Basil's house—*her* house now. He was killed in the war and left it all to her. His solicitor just came by this morning. He . . . he loved her still and wanted to see her cared for."

Simple words, delivered quietly, as if they weren't a deathblow.

Basil Philibert had loved her, and had proven it in a way Barclay never could. Even so, that wasn't what worried him. Not exactly. "But why would that make Lina leave?"

"It's my fault." She twisted the bag in her hands and let her gaze drop to the floor. "My sister returned this morning. After the solicitor left, Bea and I went to see what his business had been, and . . . well, you've been around them enough to know how Lina and Bea mix. My sister said something rude, and I . . . I didn't contradict her. I should have, right away, but old habits . . . My daughter, of course, didn't miss this. She accused me of choosing my sister over her and said we'd lose all the progress we had made between us. She said there was no one left she could trust and that she wouldn't share a roof with her aunt ever again. And so she simply left. I thought she'd be home by now. But when she didn't come, I went to Westminster to fetch her and . . . and she means it. She means to stay there. Alone. It isn't safe, Mr. Pearce—there are no servants in attendance just now. And she was so . . . so *empty*. So hollow. I cannot think it healthy."

One of his sisters shifted, so that she stood supporting him rather than his mother. He didn't look down and back to see which one, but given the light perfume he caught a whiff of, it must be Retta—Rosie had given her a vial of the fragrance for her birthday. Barclay forced a swallow. What must Evelina be feeling to act so? "I imagine she is in shock."

"She was so calm." Mrs. Manning fussed at one of the embroidered bits of her dress with a fingernail. "So calm as she told me that she wasn't coming home. That obviously nothing had really changed between us. She told me she'd see all the bills were paid for until her father returned, and that . . . and . . . She wasn't herself." She lifted eyes that were glassy, imploring. "I thought perhaps you could speak to her. Convince her that now is not the time to be alone. Now is the time to band together. Please, Mr. Pearce—she wouldn't hear me when I apologized. But perhaps she'll hear you."

It was the first time she'd admitted even indirectly that he was more to her daughter than a hired bodyguard there to see her safely around the city.

But he couldn't just go. Not right now. He turned back to take in his mother, who had lapsed into sniffs and whimpers as Rosie began wrapping her hand.

And Charlie, who stood there glaring at him, every accusation he'd no doubt stored up for the last twenty years shooting from his eyes. "Your girl, I take it? Well, don't let *us* stand in your way of a pretty face. Mere *family*."

"Oh, just *don't*." Elinor aimed a snarl squarely at Charlie. "Don't make him feel guilty for seeing to the woman he loves. You don't get to claim to be family and then act so."

Charlie straightened as much as he could. "Now see here—I don't know who the devil you are—"

"I'm Barclay's sister, that's who." Tossing back a golden curl, she turned to Barclay. "We can take care of things here for an hour or two while you see to Lina, and don't you dare let this blighter make you think you're failing them if you do. There's nothing you can do here that we can't do for you."

He could only blink, his throat too tight to speak.

Rosemary nodded and released Mum's hand. "Ellie's right. We'll ring the doctor and wait with your mum."

"For that matter," Retta added with a smile, "we *can* watch her every moment of every day, if that's what you want us to do. Heaven knows there are enough of us."

Charlie was shaking his head. Though it didn't look exactly like refusal. "Why would you offer such a thing? We're nothing to you."

Elinor rolled her eyes. "Oh, what a fool thing to say. You're Barclay's mum and brother? That makes you *our* mum and brother." She fastened her eyes on Barclay then. A silent, unshakeable promise. An offer of forgiveness for not telling them sooner. A message of understanding of thc tarnished joy of finding them. The exact same look Retta and Rosie offered him too.

Barclay nodded. He would thank them later, when Mrs. Manning and Charlie weren't watching with such incredulity. For now, he would simply accept it as the gift it was. "Thank you, girls. Let me go and see if Lucy will come with me. If I can't convince her home, that will at least guarantee she isn't alone." This he directed toward Judith.

Her eyes bright with unshed tears, she merely nodded her gratitude. And didn't, he noted, make any comment on Ellie's proclaiming him in love with her daughter. A kindness, that.

He turned to his mother, who refused to meet his gaze, and then to Charlie. "I won't be gone long. Sit, have a bite to eat. Get to know your new sisters." This he delivered with as much of a grin as he could manage.

Charlie didn't return it. He looked a little too mystified to do so. But he sank to a seat on the faded, lone couch. It was likely all the acceptance he'd get out of him this evening, so Barclay took it and bustled to the kitchen.

Ellie's words echoed then in his head. *"The woman he loves . . ."* He hadn't said anything to them about his newly realized depth of feeling last week. But apparently he hadn't had to. Family knew.

A few minutes later, he and Lucy—armed with a basket of food as well as a change of clothes—were seeing Mrs. Manning home and taking the tube to Westminster. With summer's long light, they had no trouble finding the right street, the right building.

No lights were on inside. It looked for all the world as though it were still shut up for the duration of the war, like quite a few of its neighbors.

Lucy let out an incredulous puff of breath as they took its measure from the sidewalk. "This is Lina's now?"

It put the houses in Hammersmith to shame—the Mannings', Peter's, theirs. He looked around at the view of London's most affluent streets, at the palace and Big Ben's tower silhouetted against the setting sun.

He stared at the giant hands that pointed out the passing of time. He'd all but forgotten Ellie's challenge to steal an hour from its face. And it hardly mattered. More important was stealing time with those he loved best. His siblings, who were so quick to accept him however he was. The mother and brother who didn't claim him so easily.

The woman waiting inside this obscenely expensive house.

Lucy nudged him toward the doorstep. "Go on, then. I'll go round back and wait until you've had a chance to talk to her."

"You don't need to wait at the back."

She snorted a laugh and cast a knowing gaze at a curtain twitching from the next door down. "I don't need to cause Lina trouble here already, Barclay. Heaven knows there will be time enough for that later."

He tried to smile, but it faded as his sister headed for the alleyway that would deliver her to the back side of the line of houses. Drawing in a deep breath, he climbed the three steps up, lifted a hand to ring. Then paused. Tested the door instead, and found it unlocked. Which brought a low rebuke to his tongue. Alone in a strange house—even in a good section of town—and she didn't think to lock the door? He let himself in and clicked it shut behind him. "Lina?"

With no lights to guide him, and no answering call, he had little choice but to poke his head into each room he came across.

The furniture was all shrouded in white cloth, making the

house feel like a funeral. Empty, silent, dead. It hadn't been shut up long enough to smell musty, but his every footfall echoed against bare floors, his every breath seemed an intruder. "Lina?"

Even with the ghostly white cloths obstructing his view everywhere he sent it, the wealth of the place was still evident in every line, every inlay in the plaster, every polished board. Basil Philibert, aside from being an idiot, had been one well-to-do bloke. The sort that, a year ago, Barclay would have targeted as a likely mark. He'd never notice a watch gone missing, or a cufflink. He wouldn't have felt the pinch if a few pounds sterling vanished from his money box.

Today he felt almost sorry for the man. All this wealth, and it had gotten him nothing. He'd died in Gallipoli alongside all the poor lads who'd signed up solely to get three squares a day. All this wealth, and it hadn't bought him Evelina's heart.

He paused on the threshold to the library. The sheets had been pulled from the furniture here, left in a heap in the corner. Shadows crept in from the corridor, clashing against evening's light from the windows, winning a little more ground with each minute.

Evelina sat in a chair by an unlit fireplace, a book open in her lap even though her face was turned toward the window.

Barclay slid into the room. "Lina?" He spoke softly, though he knew she had to have heard him coming.

She did not move. Not even a blink out of turn.

He edged a few more steps inside, noting that the library was perhaps an eighth the size of the one at Peter's Kensey Manor, with nowhere near as many books—all the shelves had intricately carved cabinets in the bottoms, and much of the wall space boasted paintings rather than bookcases. Probably all by masters.

They were Evelina's now, he supposed. An odd thought indeed. He eased toward her. Stopped in the very center of the room when her voice slid into the shadows.

"He loved poetry. I never did, not like him." She ran a finger along the edge of the tome she held. "He would quote it to me sometimes. Include it in the letters he wrote to me when he was in Shropshire. Perhaps he meant for it to turn my head." Her eyes slid shut. "Perhaps I should have let it."

Barclay's chest felt as though a giant were squeezing it. He swallowed and advanced another step. "You cannot be but who you are, Lina."

"I don't know who I am though, do I?" She didn't so much as glance up at him. Just stared at the book of poetry, surely not seeing a word. "These last few years, I've claimed the suffragette cause for my own—ignoring the parts of it I disagreed with. Pretending that I was making a difference, when I see now I didn't accomplish a thing. Not a thing."

"You helped the women in that clothing factory, didn't you?"

"I thought I'd managed something real when Basil proposed. But that was just a lie too. I couldn't make myself feel. I couldn't love him. Why couldn't I just *love* him?"

The hand squeezing his chest twisted. "Maybe you weren't meant to do so. Maybe he wasn't the man God meant for you to marry."

"God." A huff of breath escaped her lips that may have, on another day, been laughter. "God set this all in motion, didn't He? Took my brother. Took my health. Made me fight to be able to walk. Ruined my family, let my father leave us, took Basil's very life. And He just sits there in His heaven—distant as the clockmaker watching his creation wind through its gears. Not caring a whit."

"No." He moved closer, though every step hurt. "You of all people should know the clockmaker doesn't stand at a distance. He's there, always there, making sure every cog and gear is doing what it ought. Orchestrating each detail to perfection, even though the pieces in the works have no idea what He's about. We can't understand the roles we play, Lina, but we can know we're part of something. We can trust that He is using us to create something beautiful."

"Even my faith is just a pattern I follow, while you—*you*, who are a . . . a *thief* . . . lecture me on it."

His feet halted again two strides from where she sat. "I beg your pardon?"

She squeezed her eyes shut and tossed the book onto the side table with a *thwack*. "I had a wire from Papa this morning, just before I learned of Basil. Saying you are a thief, Barclay Pearce. Out to steal his work."

He sucked in a breath. And wished he had told her from the beginning, as he had her father. But Manning had known, had always known what he was. *Who* he was. He knew he had nothing to fear from Barclay.

Unless he had decided, for some reason, *not* to give his work to the RNAS. But what else would he mean to do with it? Unless . . . no, he couldn't fathom that the man would hand it over willingly to the enemy.

Barclay shook his head. "No. I was helping him, and that's all."

Her face looked impenetrable. "Apparently he didn't realize that, then. You are why he left us. *You*."

"No." He'd take the blame if it would help anything. But it wouldn't. So he slashed a hand through the air to punctuate the refusal. "Listen to me, Lina. He knew from the day we met that the Admiralty had sent me to help him finish the gear and get it to them. And he *welcomed* me, he didn't fear me."

"Then why would he say that?" Voice rising, she pushed to her feet. "Why would he accuse you of being a thief?"

Why indeed? Why send a telegram to Evelina saying such a thing? Barclay forced a swallow past his tight throat. "You want the absolute truth? I'll give it to you. I *was* a thief, and a blasted good one. Good enough that it got the attention of my current bosses in the Admiralty. But I've gone straight. The whole family has."

"The whole family?" She froze there, right in front of her chair. "Wait a minute."

Blast. He sighed. "It was what we had to do to survive. All of us, but for the littlest ones. But we've changed. We're exactly who we told you we are. A patchwork family of orphans scraping by on a government salary, unable to afford so much as a stick of furniture to fill the house that was let for us. That's us, Lina. And your father knew that. What I used to be. He didn't fear it before, and he had no reason to start. To run off with that excuse."

If anything, her expression went harder. Colder. Emptier. "You told him. And you never thought to perhaps tell *me*?"

"Lina—"

"How very fortunate, then, that you were no more than a distraction for me. A rebellion against my mother." Breathing a laugh devoid of all humor, she shook her head. "She was right. I should have just waited for Basil. Written him a sappy letter assuring him of my affections. At least that way he wouldn't have died thinking himself unloved."

But she didn't love Philibert. She couldn't. Could she? She was just saying it to jab at Barclay. "I know you're angry with me—"

"No. I'm not." And she didn't sound it. She sounded . . . empty. Just empty. "I'm simply realizing how foolish it all was. Thinking this thing between us was something real simply because you made me *feel*. So desperate to prove myself a real girl and not an automaton—but why? What does it matter?"

She stepped nearer, but not to lean into him as she'd done so often these past few weeks. Not to invite his arms to come around her. No, she planted her hands on his chest and pushed him back. "I've had enough, Barclay. Enough pretending. Enough hurting people when I can't be what they want—Basil, Papa, Mother. You. Just *go*, and forget you ever even met me."

He staggered back a step. But then he halted. "That's not the way it works, luv. If you need time, take it. But I'll be right here when you've finished mourning Philibert. Right here when you've come to grips with my past. Right here. Waiting for you to see it wasn't just a distraction. Wasn't just a rebellion." It couldn't have been. Because she'd taken up residence in his heart, and he didn't know how to let go again. He couldn't just go about his life as if she hadn't made him want more from a family than brothers and sisters.

"Look me in the eye." She stood tall, straight, still. "Look at me and believe me, Barclay. It wasn't real."

"Perhaps you didn't . . . don't love me." But he'd hoped. Of course he'd hoped. You couldn't love someone without wanting them to love you back. Praying it would grow to mean for them what it meant for you. "That doesn't mean it isn't something real."

But her eyes held nothing, no flicker of promise. "It isn't. And I don't want it to be."

She was his mother, slipping his watch from his pocket and taking it as if he weren't her son. Only Evelina was slipping his heart from his chest and crushing it as if he weren't *anything*. "That's a little harsh, don't you think? I promise you, I am a friend to your father, and he knows it. A friend to *you*, whether you want to be more or not."

"Friends?" She shook her head. "Friendships require equality, and we are not equals. We never were, and we certainly can't be now."

She glanced at the room around her. The sure proof that she had just moved into a social stratum well outside of his. Outside even of what he was capable of pretending to. Then she looked back at him, chin lifted. "I'm not angry. And I don't mean to be cruel. I like you, I respect the way you've built a family. But when it comes down to it, Barclay, you're apparently just a thief. And I suddenly find myself in possession of far too much that could be stolen."

He backed up another step, praying it would allow some of the air back into the room, into his lungs. But he still couldn't draw in a breath.

This wasn't Evelina. This haughty woman who stood with the bearing of her mother and glared at him as if he were just a street rat. As if the money she had just inherited meant more than the hours of laughter she'd shared with his family.

But what if that Evelina was gone, and this was the only one left? What if Basil's death had done to her what his father's had to his mother? What if she *had* still loved the idiot, and learning the final bit about Barclay's history was just too much for her?

He drew in a ragged breath. "You obviously want me to leave. So I will. But your mother is worried for you, Lina. Go home. Set her mind at ease."

Her face went blanker. Harder. "My mother made her choice—my aunt. Nothing has changed. Not really. Except that I no longer need to be subjected to it." She folded her arms over her chest.

"Then . . . Lucy is waiting outside, round back. It isn't safe for you to be alone."

"I don't need a bodyguard."

"I rather thought you might want a *friend*." But maybe she didn't really count Lucy as one either. Before she could say as much, he pivoted on his heel and strode from the room, hoping the momentum would carry him all the way out the front door and home again without any need for input from his mind. From his heart.

But that traitorous organ brought him to a halt just outside the library door. Made him say, "Lock the door behind me. There are thieves about, you know."

But not for long.

TWENTY-FIVE

Evelina raced up the stairs, determined to find the shelter of a bedchamber of some sort or another before Barclay could make his way round the back of the house to send Lucy in through the kitchen. She couldn't handle talking to her friend right now. She couldn't handle looking into her eyes and seeing the questions, the accusations. Just like she couldn't have handled it had Barclay not turned and left.

She'd wanted to rush into his arms, to let him soothe away the guilt and pain. Even through the anger, the betrayal burning inside, she'd wanted it. How much a fool did that make her? That the moment he admitted what he'd been, she wanted to assure him that she could see how he'd changed, how much better he'd become?

But she couldn't be so great a fool. Not because she didn't think he'd really risen above it, not because he wasn't trustworthy. But because *she* wasn't. He had changed—but she obviously had not. Couldn't. She'd been right to fear herself incapable of it. For how could a clock ever be anything but just that?

Perhaps Barclay Pearce wasn't a thief any longer, but she was just as much an automaton.

It hadn't been fair of her to drag him into a relationship meant only to be a distraction to begin with. Just like it hadn't been fair to Basil to agree to marry him for all the wrong reasons. Like it hadn't been fair to assume she could take and take from Papa without giving him the one thing he requested of her.

She didn't deserve their loyalty—none of them. And if she couldn't spare her father or Basil, she could at least spare Barclay the pain sure to come of having any affection for her.

She flew along the upstairs hallway, trying to remember which room might work for her purposes. Already she could hear the kitchen door squeaking. Another second and Lucy's "Lina?" rang through the house.

Her heart ticked like a clock wound too tight. She gripped a doorknob at random and twisted, stepped through the opening her pressure created, and clicked it silently shut behind her.

And immediately wished she hadn't. She'd chosen the master bedroom, there was no question. It was spacious, starkly masculine, had doors on each side connecting it to other rooms. Through one, she knew, was the room that would have been hers. The one that wouldn't still have a lingering scent from its years of cologne and shaving soap. The one that didn't shout *Basil* with its every decoration.

She slid her eyes shut, slid down the door at her back until the floor greeted her. Why couldn't she have gripped the knob to *her* room? The one she'd already had decorated to suit her tastes? The one that wouldn't berate her with every breath she took?

"Lina?"

Lucy obviously knew she was here, but perhaps if she couldn't find her, she would just give up the search after a few minutes and leave her in peace. Or in silence, anyway. Evelina groped at the door, found the knob and the key still in the hole under it, and turned. Then pushed herself up, to the connecting door, and locked it as well.

She should have just gone through it instead. Out of Basil's room. But a part of her wanted the punishment that the sensations brought her. Needed it.

Turning back to face the chamber, she slid over to a leather chair that welcomed her into its embrace. Basil had probably sat here hours upon hours, with a book in hand. He'd left none on the table to the right of it, but that didn't really surprise her. He'd always been the meticulous type, much like Papa. Everything in its place.

The furniture in here hadn't been draped. Perhaps an oversight on the part of the servants, or perhaps he'd had everything else already done before his final night here, had already dismissed the maids.

She spread her palms over the cool leather of the chair's arms, closed her eyes, and breathed in the rebuke.

. . . you'll just file away our time together and move on. You'll find someone else, perhaps someone who can inspire feeling in you as I never could—or perhaps just someone who won't mind that they can't.

How had he known? How, when she certainly had no history of such behavior? She'd never in her life sought a romantic engagement, not with anyone but Basil. And barely with him. So how, *how* could he have guessed that she'd find someone like Barclay?

Just to prove to herself that she could feel. To frustrate her mother. To prove a point to Basil himself. To be more than an automaton, to *live*.

But she wasn't. Couldn't.

Barclay, if he had really picked himself up so fully from such a dismal past, deserved far better. He deserved more than a woman who would use him as she'd done. Sitting in the dark below, wondering at the truth of her father's accusation, she'd convinced herself that he must be what Papa said—but looking him in the eye as he confessed . . . no. He spoke the truth. And

Papa surely would have seen far more clearly than she did that core of goodness inside him. So why, then, that telegram?

She didn't know. But Barclay would be better off far away from her family and their troubles. Free to care for his own, and to find a woman someday who could love him unabashedly, without always wondering if everything she felt was just a reaction to another loss.

Lucy's footfalls sounded on the stairs. "Lina, are you up here?"

She let her head sink into the chair behind her until her hairpins dug into her scalp.

There's a reason I chose you out of all the young ladies I met.

Squeezing her eyes shut more tightly, Evelina sucked in a long, silent breath. She didn't know why he had. Why anyone would. And the guilt of it would eat at her forever now. He'd guaranteed that when he strapped her with all of this. A constant reminder that she'd failed. Failed to be what he wanted. Failed to be the daughter her father needed. Failed to be the kind of friend Gloria and Flo wished she would be, content with promenades through the park rather than visits to factories. She'd failed at every single relationship she'd ever attempted.

A door down the hall opened, shut.

I thought those things would equate passion.

Passion. Her fingers dug into the chair. She knew from her Latin studies that *passion* meant *suffering*. Something one was willing to sacrifice for, to hurt for. It was too late to have such a thing for Basil. But she hurt now—hurt to the very core of her being for all the people she'd let down. She'd spare them what she could. Suffer alone rather than disappoint them all more.

Another door opened and shut, closer.

I've given you the one thing you ever wanted from me, Evelina: your independence.

Independence. That thing she had sought so single-mindedly all these years. That was all the right to vote had really meant to her. The only reason marriage had appealed—he had been so right about her, had seen her so clearly. All she'd really wanted was to be out from under her mother's thumb. Away from her aunt's scathing tongue. And he'd given her that in his death. He'd given her more independence than she could possibly know what to do with.

No one had ever told her that it would feel so very lonely. Make her feel so very small and undeserving.

Evelina opened her eyes, and her gaze landed on the mantel clock. Still. Silent. Time had stopped. And she was simply suspended here in this world of motionlessness.

The knob of the master chamber turned, rattled. "You do realize, I hope," said Lucy's voice from the other side of the door, sounding amused, "that locking the door is a sure sign you're in there. No other room in the house has been locked."

Evelina's gaze fell from the silent clock to the floor. Evening's shadows had crawled over the rug and clawed their way up her legs. She said nothing.

A chuckle seeped through the wood. "You know now, according to Barclay, that I come from a family of thieves. I could pick this lock in about ten seconds flat, Lina. You might as well let me in."

Blast it all. Why had she made friends with these people? They didn't follow the rules, didn't ever grant her the comfort of her preconceived notions. Even before she'd known the whole truth about them, she'd recognized that, so why had she become so attached? "Please, Lucy. I just want to be alone."

"I'm afraid alone isn't an option just now. Your mum's worried sick about you, and whatever you said to Barclay had him furious. Or upset. I couldn't really tell which because, frankly, Barclay isn't often ruffled like that." A pause, a shift outside the door. Was she getting out something with which to pick the lock? How did one even do such a thing? "Come on, then. Tell me what you said. I'm dying to know. He said only he told you of our past and that you needed some time."

Time—as if it could change anything. As if it even still existed.

She heard a scraping sound and sat upright. "Oh, do stop it! If I tell you what I said, will you *please* go away? At least to another room, if not from the house?"

"Well . . . that's not nearly as much fun as breaking in, but I suppose so."

Her shoulders sagged, her head along with them. "I simply told him the truth. That whatever was between us had been nothing but a reaction to Basil breaking things off. And that I've had enough pretending."

"Lina." How could Lucy pack such disappointment into those two syllables?

Or perhaps it was a natural part of them. Heaven knew Mother and Aunt Beatrice had always managed to say her name that way.

She'd thought that had changed, this last week. What a fool she'd been. The moment her aunt came thumping back into the house, Mother had folded. No concern or thought for Evelina's opinion.

Proof that things couldn't be but what they were. *She* couldn't be but what she was. Perhaps Barclay's family could change, but hers never could. Never would. "I wasn't trying to be cruel, Lucy. I was trying to be kind. To end things cleanly, now, before they could get unduly messy later."

A beat of silence, and then a soft, "Did it never occur to you that *not* ending things was an option?"

"No." She'd never considered the end at all. It hadn't seemed a possibility worth thinking about, even though the logical part of her must have known it was inevitable. How could a man who loved so fully, so quickly, so unhesitatingly ever have patience with someone like her?

"But why? Don't tell me it's all the typical things, you're better than that. It can't just be because of what he once was." *A thief.*

"I'm not. I'm not better than that." No better than a thief herself, taking the affections of people she should love and never giving them anything in return. And even when she tried, when she *did* love, it wasn't enough, was it? Papa had left without so much as a goodbye, and she had always loved him with all that was in her. "And it isn't about what Barclay *was*. It's about what he *is*."

"Poor, you mean? Without a family name worthy of all *this*?" Now anger colored Lucy's tone.

She'd never heard Lucy angry before. But then, they'd only known each other for, what, a month? So short a time, really.

Evelina closed her eyes again. *Poor*. It wasn't a word she'd ever once thought to attribute to Barclay Pearce. Lack of money hadn't ever stopped him, had it? It hadn't made him miserable or lonely or kept him from what he wanted to do. It hadn't stopped him from pursuing the Lord or building a family.

Barclay Pearce wasn't poor. He was quite possibly the richest man she'd ever met. *She* was the poor one. Bereft of everything that mattered. Raised to believe one must strive always for *things*, or for prestige, or for a voice.

And yet he was the one who had a voice, who could turn the tides of a whole section of the city, and he did it by taking in children, giving away bread, and treating the poorest of the poor as though they were the worthiest of his love.

It wasn't the fact that her circle would sneer at him—it was the fact that *his* circle would sneer at *her*, and deservedly so. "Will you go away now, Lucy?"

No response came. No angry shout, no reproving lecture, no huff of disbelief.

Evelina pushed herself up, figuring she deserved to see the look on her friend's face, deserved to feel the slice her soulful eyes would give. She turned the key, turned the knob, pulled the door open.

And sagged. The hallway was already empty. Still. Silent. Just like the place in her chest where her heart ought to be ticking.

Barclay crimped the edge of the last pie and set it beside its brothers on the baking sheet. Pauly's kitchen was never exactly quiet midday, not with sounds from the pub proper finding their way in. But it was as quiet just now as it ever was, and had been since he'd finished his story thirty seconds earlier.

He looked over to the burly man who had never once failed him. Never once judged him. "Any advice?"

Pauly sighed and cast a glance upward, toward his flat. "You really want to come to *me* for advice on romance, Barclay lad?"

It brought half a smile to Barclay's lips. "I haven't anyone else, have I? Peter's never been through something like this. And I'm hardly going to interrupt Willa and Lukas on their honeymoon. Georgie has spoken of a girl in his letters—should I write to *him* for advice?"

"Georgie? With a *girl*? He's only a baby."

Barclay let his lips curve up. "If you don't think I should take *his* advice, maybe you should give me some of your own."

Pauly snorted and added a liberal dash of salt to the pot of potatoes on the stove. "How about 'run while the running's good'? She may have done you a favor, ending things."

Sinking onto the stool behind him, Barclay sighed. "I thought you'd come to like her."

"I do. But I liked Jill too, at the start. Liking a twist doesn't mean she makes a good wife."

Barclay couldn't imagine Pauly—generous, big-hearted Pauly—ever liking the penny-pinching, scowling Jill to begin with. But obviously he had. Obviously there had been something to convince him to marry the woman back in the day.

He sighed and picked up a towel to wipe off his hands. "It's not in me to give up on a person, Pauly. Not when they're already a part of me."

"There's always a time to let a person go—even you know that." Pauly lifted knowing eyes to meet Barclay's gaze. "You gave up looking for Charlie eventually, didn't you? Actively, at least. You must have, for none of us to have ever known about him."

Barclay winced. "It hurt too much to talk about how I'd failed him."

"Why'd you stop looking, then?"

He dropped his gaze to the wooden countertop, worn smooth from its years of faithful service. "Claw ran me out of the neighborhood."

"You could have snuck back in, eventually. A year later, two. His anger had cooled. But instead you stayed here in Poplar."

"You're right." Barclay tossed the towel back to the counter. "I should have gone back."

Pauly breathed a laugh. "You're missing my point. You have never, never put your own wants above the children you've taken in. Never once, even when it would have meant finding your brother by blood. Because if you'd gone off looking for him, it would have meant a day of finding nothing, putting no food in their bellies. Isn't that right?"

Memories flashed—days when the hurt had been so big it had nearly overwhelmed him. When he'd seen a street that would take him back to Hackney and almost put his foot upon it. When he'd heard Willa call his name or felt Rosemary tug on his hand. When he'd realized that if he left them on their own while he searched for Charlie, they'd have nothing. They didn't know, in those early days, how to pick a pocket very well, not like he did. If they tried begging, they were run off by bigger children. And by the time they'd learned, they'd taken in Retta and baby Lucy too.

He'd stayed for them. Even though it tore his heart in two. He jerked his head in a slow nod. "I suppose that's so. Though it certainly earned me no thanks from Charlie. Nor from my mother."

"It wouldn't. But they'll see, now they're back in your life, that you'll do anything for family. Anything. Even when it hurts. Even when it means letting someone else you love walk away. Because if you chase after them, those children are the ones who would feel the lack."

He squeezed his eyes shut, trying to rid them of the image of Evelina's empty look. "You really think that's it? The last I'll ever see of her?"

"I don't know. But if she's the type to abandon you when she comes into money, then she sure as blazes wasn't one of you to begin with, and you don't need to be wasting any heartache on the likes of her."

"I suppose." Though he'd been so sure she *was* one of them. Or could be. That she understood them even without him having to lay it all out for her. Apparently he'd been wrong.

"Chin up, lad." Pauly picked up an apple, tossed it to him. Barclay snatched it from the air by rote, giving a rueful smile at the old trick to make him literally lift his chin. Pauly grinned. "You've got more family than ever, and there are twists aplenty in the world for you to fall in love with."

More family, yes—a mother who had looked completely disgusted when he'd showed her to the flat last night. And a brother who hadn't said a word to him when he got back from Westminster. Had just sat there, quiet and contemplative, and then went his separate way when Barclay insisted on taking their mother here. Who was to say if or when he'd ever come back?

Barclay had lain awake long into the night on his pallet on the floor, replaying every look from Charlie. Every word from Evelina. Over and again. What was he to do with either of them? Knock on their doors again or leave them be? He'd tried to pray, tried to read in his Bible, but that just muddled him up inside too. He'd prayed for Charlie for years already, and look how that turned out.

What if that veiled accusation Evelina made last night had

been right—that he had no right to presume to know anything about how God worked when he'd spent most of his life as a criminal? A sinner in the eyes of both God and society. Maybe that was why those prayers for his brother had backfired.

Peter promised him that he'd been forgiven when he asked, that Christ had sought out people just like him and used them to build His kingdom. But when he'd turned on his lamp last night and sought solace in that big leather-bound Bible, he'd ended up in Ephesians 4 again.

Let him that stole steal no more: but rather let him labour, working with his hands the thing which is good, that he may have to give to him that needeth.

Was he doing it? He couldn't give back the things he'd stolen, nor the money he'd gained from fencing them over the years. It had all gone to food, to rent, to cloth for Rosie and the other girls to stitch into garments. But this verse hadn't called him to make recompense directly—it had called him to *do*. To work. To make something honest so he could provide for others in need.

Did working for V fulfill that command? What if it didn't? What if God still judged him, just like society would? What if the Lord looked at him with the same blank expression he'd gotten last night from Evelina? Or from his own brother?

He put the apple down and stood, reaching for the jacket he'd draped over the back of the stool. "I'd better get going. There's work yet to be done today."

"Barclay." Pauly stepped to his side to clap a meaty hand to his shoulder. "I can't know whether she meant what she said, or if she was just lashing out. But either way, you're not alone, lad. I've always an ear and a shoulder."

Barclay summoned a smile and gave the familiar fatherly hand a pat. "I know. And thanks. Let me know if my mother doesn't come in, will you?"

"For a free meal? Oh, I'm certain we'll see her every day—and

I daresay she'll keep ordering the most expensive plate on the menu, as she did today."

He stifled a groan at the thought of how quickly that would eat through his coin and made his way back out of the pub, into the street, and toward the tube.

His feet came to an abrupt halt at the corner, though. Charlie stood there, leaning on his cane, just watching him. And his face had none of the ice nor bitterness it had before.

Barclay sucked in a breath but didn't dare speak.

His brother cleared his throat and took a step toward him. "I . . . I didn't thank you. Last night. For taking care of Mum."

His throat felt too tight to speak. But he had to respond. "You needn't. Heaven knows I owe you for all the years I wasn't around. I never meant for you to have to care for her on your own. I never meant—"

"I know." Charlie lifted his hand, held it palm up to stop him. "Your . . . sisters. They had a lot to say to me last night. Stories to tell. Sense to make of how you managed to do what you did—to patch them all together."

"That wasn't me—"

"It was." He nodded slowly, contemplatively. And when he met Barclay's gaze, their father's eyes looked at him with something he hadn't dared hope for. Respect. "It's what you always did. Why I always believed you'd come for me. And why I couldn't believe you didn't. I thought you'd died, Barclay. I couldn't think of any other reason you didn't come."

"I tried. Please believe me. I never stopped looking."

"I suppose, as an adult, I can understand that. I can see all the mountains that would have sprung up in your way. But I couldn't then. I couldn't, and that old hurt overtook me when you walked into my office." He heaved a long breath and gripped his cane. "Perhaps . . . perhaps we could start over. My wife asked me to invite you to dinner. If you'd come. It won't be anything fancy, but—"

"I'd love to." He said it too quickly, too eagerly, but his brother's lips relaxed into something nearer a smile than he'd seen from him yet.

"Tonight? At eight o'clock?"

He nodded. There was no way he could say no or even ask for another day. But even as he agreed, his heart quickened. And into his mind's eye came the image of the note that had been awaiting him on the doorstep that morning. The one he hadn't dared mention to anyone else.

He had a meeting with Claw at six.

TWENTY-SIX

Barclay stood on the street outside the building of flats, the hand in his pocket turning the key inside it over and over. It looked like every other run-down building in Hackney. But that wasn't the point. The point was that it didn't feel like a trap, while every single bit of logic told him it should be.

He kept his gaze steady on the building while his peripheral vision did its job. Noted the adolescents scurrying around the far corner. The sounds of a woman shouting from across the street, the incessant wailing of a child.

The man beside him looking none too anxious but a trifle impatient. He crossed his massive arms over his chest and braced his feet shoulder-width apart. "Problem, Pearce?"

"Just trying to sort it all." He kept his tone even. Amiable. He'd had a few conversations with Claw over the last twenty years, to be sure. He'd emerged from them alive, which was about all he could say for his own smooth talking.

Claw growled. He'd seemed a giant when Barclay was a lad—even then, when no more than a teenager, Claw had been all hard muscles and intimidation, with that ugly scar scoring his face from temple to the opposite jaw like a talon mark—hence his nickname.

Barclay wasn't afraid of scars. But he was none too fond of

the cruel heart this bloke had never tried to hide. "Can't quite determine why you're helping me, Claw."

Claw bared his teeth in what might have been meant as a smile. Perhaps. "No? Think of it as a parting gift—since you've left the life. Or is that not true? I wouldn't want to give you anything if you were still a rival, after all."

On the other side of him, Dante slid a little closer. "I told you he'd gone straight. You saying you doubt me?"

Claw narrowed his eyes, obviously measuring the situation. On the one hand, they were currently standing on a street at the edge of his territory, so the advantage there was his. But on the other hand, Dante's men were waiting just a street away. If he tried anything, they'd have a battle to rival the Marne on their hands. And no one wanted that.

At least, Barclay really hoped no one wanted that. *He* certainly didn't. This was the side of the criminal life he'd always steered well clear of.

"Look." Claw shifted, even lowered the ham hocks he called arms to his sides. "I heard you were looking for this bloke, and I thought to do you a good turn. Turning him over to you's no skin off my back. I certainly haven't no need for the likes of him. A foreigner." He spat. Just for punctuation, no doubt.

Barclay kept his shoulders relaxed and sent Dante a quick glance that said, *Easy.* To Claw, he offered a smile. "My thanks, then. Shall we?"

Not waiting to see if they followed, he jogged up the steps and through the front door. If it was a trap, he'd soon find out. But he hadn't gone that soft. That lax. He'd have noted if anything were out of place.

Inside the dim entryway, an old woman was shuffling along with an ancient broom. She looked up when he entered, and she frowned. "Don't got no more rooms. Not until the end of the month, anyway. Everyone's all paid up 'til then."

He swept the hat from his head and gave her his warmest smile. And his Cockney-est accent. "Begging yer pardon, mum. It's not a room I'm after, but a friend. Well, acquaintance, I suppose. Just met him a couple weeks back, and he gave me this direction. But he didn't mention his room number. Bulgarian chap—from Stara Zagora. D'you know who I mean?"

She leaned her broom handle against the wall and straightened with an audible crack of her back. "Grigorov, is it? 'Fraid ye're a bit late, luv. He's not been round a week or more. Though he's all paid up until the end of June, so I suppose he might come back."

A week? The same amount of time Manning had been missing. He told his racing heart to still, that it could well be a coincidence. And more, that Evelina might not even appreciate him still looking for her father.

But he'd made a promise. He meant to keep it.

He let his brows tug down. "The cheek of him—he's still got the book I lent him, he has. Don't suppose he left it in his room, did he?"

"I'm not his maid nor his housekeeper—haven't been snooping about his room."

"'Course not. Didn't mean to imply you had been." He loosed a gusty sigh. "Would I be out of place to ask you to let me up? I've only a mind to see if my book's there. You could come with me, make sure I don't take nothing."

"We both know you didn't lend him no book." She glanced toward the window that looked out over the street. Neither Claw nor Dante had followed him in—they both still stood out there, two rather intimidating silhouettes in the evening light. Her gaze eased back to him. "I don't want no trouble now, lad."

"And you won't have any from me." He let the Cockney slip away again. "Regardless of your answer. Nor from them."

She huffed. "Now there's a promise no man can make."

Wise woman. Barclay smiled. "Let me be honest with you,

ma'am. A friend of mine has gone missing—and a fellow matching Grigorov's description was seen lurking about his house. Tried to break in. I'm just trying to determine if it was Grigorov. And if so, find some clue that will lead me to my friend."

Now thunder entered the woman's eyes. "I always made it right clear that I don't harbor no criminals in this house. You mean to tell me he's been out causing a ruckus?"

"If he's the one I'm looking for . . . he tried to mug my friend's daughter. Lurked about for weeks, attempted a break-in. And now the father's vanished. My instincts say it's all related."

"Well." She rubbed at her back and turned for the rickety staircase. "Let's see if he left behind any facts to back up your instincts, yeah?"

"Thank you." He obviously should have tried honesty to begin with and not wasted time—or that prick of his conscience now irritating him—on a fabricated story. Old habits. Old habits that surely didn't endear him to the Almighty.

Maybe Lina really was right. He was the last person in the world who ought to be lecturing anyone else on what God expected of them.

He pushed away the thought and followed the landlady up the stairs, up again, and still more, until she finally led him down a dim corridor to a door that had nothing but a tin *4C* to set it apart from every other door. She pulled out a massive chatelaine with its many keys jangling together and sifted through them until she found the one to fit. A moment later, she opened the door and led the way in.

It looked about like he'd expected: empty except for the furniture that obviously came with the place. No clothing strewn about, no valise. Except . . . there, on the desk. There was still a bit of a mess on its surface. He moved toward it and sifted through the bits of rubbish, pausing when a familiar scrap caught his eye.

Unable to breathe, he reached for it—one of the posters for

the Shoreditch Empire Music Hall, advertising the variety show. With Willa's name underlined, stars drawn around it in a decidedly feminine hand.

He'd watched Evelina draw those stars the day he'd brought the poster over and asked her if she wanted to go with him. It wasn't just an advertisement for his sister's show—it was the very one that had been in the Manning house.

He spun to face the landlady, whose lips had thinned. "Take it that means something to you?"

"This was at my friend's house. The show was the night he went missing."

Her chest puffed out. "Well then. Better search the rest of this, yeah? Could be some other bit of a clue."

He found a few discarded food wrappers, a playbill, and then saw a corner of white that had slipped between the desk and the wall. Paper, and not the type used to wrap a meat pie or sausage. An envelope, with a folded sheet still inside. He fished out the envelope, extracted the page, smoothed the crease. And sighed. A letter—for all the good it did him. "I don't suppose you can read Bulgarian?"

The woman laughed and straightened from where she'd been checking the rubbish bin—empty. Apparently this Grigorov chap had thought the desk served the purpose well enough. "'Fraid not, luv."

"Nor can I." But he'd bet V or Hall knew someone who could. "Mind if I take this with me?"

"On one condition." She lifted her brows. And her lips. "Take those blokes outside with you too."

Wise woman indeed. "You have a deal, madam."

If this was what the rest of her life would be like, Evelina wasn't entirely certain it was worth living. She pulled the door shut behind her, locked it, and slipped the key into her handbag. Inside the house, time meant nothing. One hour slid into another without so much as a tick to pass it. There was nothing to be late for, no demands on her. She answered to no one, and had a staff now, ready to answer to her. Everything she'd wanted.

Useless.

She didn't waste the energy trying to smile at the lady pushing a pram down the sidewalk—Mrs. Heatherby would only sniff and look away. The snubbing didn't bother her. The fact that the community was in an uproar over Basil's death and her inheritance, given the end of the engagement, didn't bother her. All the nosy neighbors who had come to call in the last week just to ogle the house and offer empty condolences didn't bother her.

But the emptiness. The loneliness, despite the staff that the barrister had sent over when she let him know she'd taken up residence. The pounding knowledge that there was nothing better on the horizon, nothing but guilt and pain and a cold metal gear where her heart should have been . . . that was proving a bothersome companion indeed.

She'd rung up the barrister again yesterday. Told him she didn't want it all, it was too much. She'd asked for his help in selling off the estate . . . and he'd told her straight out that it was all but impossible right now. Most of London's elite were packing up and fleeing to the countryside. Who would want to invest in a townhouse in Westminster that could well be destroyed in the next zeppelin raid?

He'd promised to keep an ear out for anyone looking for such real estate. But it would take years, he'd wagered. Years.

Perhaps she'd still be able to afford a small flat somewhere, where she wouldn't feel so small and alone. But it seemed foolish. Wasteful. Like so much else in her life. She was grateful to Basil for looking after her—despite the guilt it laid on her shoulders. And she had to imagine she'd always feel this pang of sorrow when she thought of him, and of how lonely he must have felt. But this wasn't her. She didn't belong in Westminster. She was, and had always been, a Hammersmith girl.

She glanced at the Great Clock and did the math—out here where time meant something, it was nine forty-three. It would take eighteen minutes to get to Hammersmith. Her aunt's charity meeting began at ten sharp, and she was always there exactly three minutes early. That should put Evelina at her mother's house at a minute after ten, giving her a nice cushion.

She hadn't stepped foot back home yet—because her aunt hadn't stepped foot out of it. Mother had come by every day though, all smiles and gentle words. Trying to prove she had really changed. To believe her or not? Evelina didn't know, and the question had rendered her motionless.

But Mother had reminded her of her aunt's scheduled absence this morning, in case she needed to come by.

She nearly hadn't. But there were things at the house she'd like to have.

It had been the longest fortnight of her life. First the week with no Papa—and then this last one, with no one at all but the hour Mother spent with her. No father. No Basil. No Lucy or Retta or Elinor or Cressida, no Willa or Rosemary. No Clover and Olivia playing dolls in the corner, no happy squeals of greeting from Patch, no pleas for algebra help from Fergus, or Jory pressing to her side to show her the drawing in her book.

No Gloria, even—just a note that Mother brought round, saying the whole family had fled to Worcestershire, where zeppelin attacks were less likely. Far away from the shore, as her parents feared U-boats may well be staking out British waters as well.

No Barclay. Certainly no Barclay. And if she missed him, then it was a fitting punishment.

Her chauffeur—a term she'd never imagined using after Basil ended things—had the car idling in front of the house. He held open the door when she approached and offered the same smile that all of Basil's staff had been giving her this past week. Well trained. Polite. Proper.

She was so dreadfully tired of polite and proper. They never spoke a word out of turn, never hinted at any emotion in her presence. It was enough to drive a girl to madness.

She slid in, sat back. Played the role expected of her as he drove her toward Hammersmith.

There'd been no other word from Papa. No word from his barrister, coming to give Mother terms of separation. No letter from Hans saying he had shown up in Switzerland, after all. Just those two wires, impersonal and short. Why had he not written an actual letter to her? Something in his own hand? It was unlike him. And made doubts pop up at the strangest times. What if Barclay was right? What if those telegrams had been *too* short, *too* impersonal? They could have come from anyone.

When they reached the familiar Number 22, she waited to be helped out, clutching her handbag as she looked at the door that should have meant home. But it created only a hollow ache inside.

The door opened, and Williston offered a very real, not-so-proper smile. "Miss Manning! Oh, we're all so delighted you're home."

Her feet rushed her up the steps, into the entryway, and her arms shocked her by closing around the aging man. "How I've missed you!"

"There now." He chuckled—but he gave her a hearty squeeze before setting her back, and his eyes positively twinkled. "You needn't stay away, you know. This house has been like a tomb without you and your friends."

Evelina shook her head. "I can't, Will. I can't stay here with Beatrice anymore."

He sighed and shut the door. "I envy you that freedom, miss. And would ask you if you needed a butler at your new residence, were it not for my loyalty to the Manning house. When your father returns home, I'll not have him thinking I've abandoned my post."

"He would never think such a thing." Assuming he even came back. For all she knew, he'd struck off to begin a whole new life somewhere else. Unfettered by the disappointments he'd called *wife* and *daughter* for so long.

"Your mother has been a changed woman since he left, I must say." He looked up at the ceiling. Or perhaps at the chambers above it. "She said to inform you that she would be back in just a few moments, but she had to dash out for bread. Apparently Lucy hasn't been by with any for some time now, and your aunt's chef refuses to bake a good English loaf for toast. But she said she has put all your trunks in your room for you, if you wish to get started on the packing. She hesitated to begin without you, as it would have drawn her sister's attention and perhaps inspired her to remain at home this morning."

A thought to make her shudder. "Thank you, Williston."

He shuffled off with a promise to extract a cup of tea from Monsieur Le Difficult for her, leaving Evelina to tug off her gloves and slip them into her handbag, unpin her hat, and breathe in the familiar scent of home.

She ought to head directly up to her room—she hadn't all that much time to play with. An hour and a half, that was all. Ninety minutes to pack up anything she might want before next week, when Beatrice would leave again. Mother had brought her a few changes of clothes, but they'd been from her trousseau, and it had felt beyond odd to wear the elegant, costly styles.

Those weren't her. They weren't Evelina Manning. They were Mrs. Basil Philibert—and though she may be living that life, she wasn't that person. Would never be, *could* never be that person.

Instead of heading upstairs, she slid over to the door to the basement. Gripped the handle and just held it for a moment, telling herself she would regret it if she went down. She hadn't since that night they'd found him gone. The very thought had been too painful.

But she missed Papa. She needed him to smooth her hair and soothe her tears and tell her that it would be all right, even if it wouldn't be. She needed him to wrap his arms around her and call her his girl. She needed him to say he loved her. With a deep breath for fortification, she pulled open the door and switched on the light.

A few steps down, she smelled it—oil and metal and tea and pipe smoke. *Papa*. Still so strong that she almost expected to clear the floorboards and find him at his workbench, tinkering. But the gramophone stood silent in its corner, and the bench still stretched empty and forlorn. Forsaken.

She knew the feeling.

"Oh, Papa. Where are you?" Tears burned her eyes as she took the final step to the floor. It felt so wrong to be down here without him, when he wasn't just behind her on the stairs or making a quick run to the storefront. She wandered a few steps, letting her gaze run over what he'd left behind.

Everything precious. Everything she loved, that she'd thought *he* loved. The toys and gadgets and pretty baubles. The beginnings of the castle for the Earl of Cayton's daughter—had anyone at the shop let him know the piece wouldn't be done in time for her birthday?

Why had Papa left that behind, taken only his other project, the synchronization gear? It was so unlike him. Or had been, before the world had crumbled beneath their feet.

She touched a finger to a mechanical bee that, when wound, would buzz around its beautiful metal flower. Perhaps it was the war that had done it. It had made beautiful things, silly things seem irrelevant. But they weren't. They were what children remembered. They were what soldiers longed to return home for. They were what reminded people to smile.

Another step, to the princess who would dip into a curtsy, across from the prince who would bow. She remembered begging Papa to paint the princess's dress purple instead of pink. To make her hair auburn and her eyes sapphire blue.

He'd done it, even though it hadn't been what the customer had wanted. So he'd made a second one for them and given this one to her. That was her papa—always willing to indulge her, even when the indulgence meant hard work for him.

She spotted her favorite of the toys and slid to stand before it. She'd been so distraught when Mother had insisted on moving the circus out of her room and down to the workshop. She'd come down here every day for a month to wind it up and watch the elephant galumph, the bear balance on his ball, the lion tamer flick his whip as the lion roared.

Her fingers found the key and twisted it until she felt the spring go tight. Then she nudged the switch.

The music brought a smile to her lips at its first tinkling note. How long had it been since she'd watched the magic? Too long. Too long since she'd remembered to take time for the foolish. She'd been too busy visiting factories, following Mrs. Knight to marches, embroidering *Deeds Not Words* into banners, planning her wedding. Too busy to take the thirty seconds to watch the circus unfold.

She watched it now, each turn and twirl, her smile growing as she waited for the grand finale—the opening of the big top. When the music hit its zenith, it levered up, the sides peeling back to reveal . . .

She frowned. The elephant was where it had always been, but he wasn't lifting his trunk to trumpet the final ditty as he ought to have done. Couldn't, not with that watch on top of him. And why would Papa have put such a thing there?

She reached in, pulling out the metal circle fastened to leather bands on each side. Odd indeed—Papa never wore a wristlet and certainly never made one. She turned it toward the light, and opened the case. And froze.

Rolex.

He'd told her, of course, that Hans had given him a watch. But . . . but what would it have been doing in the circus tent? Why, if he was still eager to accept the partnership, wouldn't he have taken it with him? Why, if he was simply leaving to keep the gear away from Barclay, would he have taken the time to do something so odd?

It made no sense. No sense at all.

Unless . . . Unless Barclay had been right all along—unless Papa had not left his workshop willingly. Unless he was trying to leave her a message. That he wasn't going to Switzerland. That he wasn't fleeing by choice.

He'd been trying to leave her a message—that was the only reason to put something in her favorite toy. And what better to leave than the token of partnership that had caused such trouble in their family?

"Oh no. Lord, please, no. Help!" She raced up the stairs, across the entryway, out the door. She had to tell the police. She had to tell Mother.

She had to tell Barclay. He'd known, he'd known all along. Why hadn't she believed him?

"Miss?"

She ignored the call of the chauffeur and flew down the street, around the corner. Barclay first. If Papa had really been kidnapped, then he must have been right about it being over the synchronization gear, which meant that his connections at the Admiralty were more likely to be of help than Scotland Yard.

Still clutching the Rolex in her left hand, she pounded on the door to Number 120 with her right, not stopping until a frowning Retta pulled it open. "Lina! What in blazes—"

"Barclay. Is he home?" Her breath came in heaves, no doubt

from her unprecedented sprint through the neighborhood. “It’s Papa.”

Retta’s frown softened, but she shook her head. “He’s at Whitehall—the Old Admiralty Building. Or was going there this morning, at any rate, though who’s to say if he’s there still?”

He had to be. Or if not, they had to know where he was. *Had* to. She nodded and took off down the steps again.

“Lina, wait! You can’t run the whole way!”

“Watch me!” It would take no longer to run there than to walk back to her own street and find breath enough to explain to the chauffeur where she meant to go, then wait for him to meander his way through the street traffic to get her there. No, this was better. Moving, straining, *doing*.

She felt the strange looks being sent her way, but they tapered off as she went—probably because her pace slackened when she couldn’t draw in a deep enough breath. And down here, everyone hurried, and no one spoke. The semisilence struck her as eerie, until she caught sight of the banner outside Charing Cross Hospital, demanding quiet for the wounded.

Despite the perspiration trickling down her back, she shivered. How dreadful it must be to walk by such a reminder every day. Especially if one had a loved one in the war, on the front, and had to wonder if they would be on the next train into the city. Like Barclay, worrying for Georgie. He didn’t mention it much, but he must think it.

She caught sight of her goal just as her leg started cramping, tensing. Well, no matter. Even if she had to limp there, she would get there.

Though it meant gritted teeth, a few stops for a futile stretch, and several wishes that she had listened to Retta’s advice and gone back for the car. But at last she panted her way up to the door.

And promptly found a uniformed arm blocking her path. “Pardon me, miss. Your business?”

"Oh. I . . ." She still couldn't quite catch her breath. "I need Barclay. Barclay Pearce." What department did he work in? She hadn't any idea. He'd never said, not really. "I'm Evelina Manning—"

"Really!" The guard smiled. "*The* Miss Manning?"

"I . . ." He'd mentioned her? Here? Hopefully not in the last week—though if he had, this young man surely wouldn't be grinning at her. "I am. Yes."

"Well, you're in luck. I haven't seen him come back out yet today—not that that always means anything, mind you. He sometimes slips out another door. Here, Wesley!"

She followed the guard's gaze as he turned inside and saw a rather elderly fellow pushing a cart of mail. Wesley, she assumed, as he looked up.

"Could you show Miss Manning the way up? She's here to see Barclay."

"Oh, how nice." The old gent gave her a smile. "Come along, then, miss. I've a package here for Hope anyway. We'll just change the order of our deliveries, that's all."

She limped after him, grateful for his slow pace. And kept herself by force from looking over her shoulder at the friendly face of the young guard and begging him to lend her a sword or something for protection.

Because she realized quite suddenly that Barclay probably wouldn't be happy to see her. And if he wasn't, his soldier friends wouldn't be either.

TWENTY-SEVEN

Barclay paced to the window, pivoted, paced back toward the door again. Room 40 was its usual hubbub of muttering and pencil scratches and heels tapping out anxious rhythms on the floor. Usually all the nervous energy didn't bother him. Today, he wanted to tell them all to be still so Margot could concentrate.

Not that Margot De Wilde needed him to chastise her colleagues on her behalf. They certainly didn't bother *her*.

He cast a glance at the office across the corridor where Ewing sat. He was the official head of their little secret department, though Hope was the one who ran things. But his presence today meant that Barclay couldn't linger long. Ewing frowned each and every time he saw Barclay or V. Because they didn't answer to him, only to Hall. A reminder of the limits of his power.

Blast, but Barclay hated politics.

V wouldn't even set foot in the building when Ewing was here. He'd in fact instructed Barclay to meet him outside the hospital at noon for his day's assignment.

"Don't suppose you could hurry, there, Margot." He paused beside her desk and bent down to see if she'd made any progress.

When he'd turned over the letter, the intrigue had begun,

not with the missive itself, but with the envelope—which bore a postmark of Sweden. It had, in fact, been addressed to the same place as that letter he'd lifted from Olson's office a month ago, which had set V and Hall on a mission to determine exactly how involved the Swedes were with the Germans. A few of them, at least, were clearly aiding the Central Powers. The questions they must answer were how many and to what extent.

Then came the message itself. It had taken far too long for V to get a translation of the Bulgarian letter to him—not that he hadn't found someone who could do it promptly enough, but apparently the letter hadn't just been in Bulgarian. It had been encoded as well, and the translator they'd found hadn't been able to make sense of it.

He ought to be thanking Margot for agreeing to try, not berating her for taking so many blighted hours to accomplish it. He knew that. But he'd caught a glimpse of what she'd cracked thus far, and it had immediately put him on edge.

Dates. One of which had been *May 31*. The night of the zeppelin raids. The night Manning had gone missing. But it wasn't the only date on the paper, and the next one—*June 16*—was only days away.

What if there was more in the works? Another raid? Another kidnapping? What if Evelina was in danger, as her father had clearly been? It could take him days just to convince her to listen to him. To let him into her blighted fancy house.

"If you think you could do this more quickly, Barclay, you are welcome to try." Margot jotted down what looked to him like a random string of numbers and leaned over to flip through a massive, musty book. A Bulgarian-French dictionary, since she claimed she worked better still in her native tongue than in English for this sort of work.

He sighed and raked a hand through his hair. "Sorry."

She flashed him a look that grinned, though her mouth didn't.

"I am almost finished. One more sentence in Bulgarian, then the code, then into English. Ten minutes, perhaps. If you let me work."

"Right. Yes. I'll leave you to it." He strode toward the door to the hallway, sending Margot's mother a smile where she sat as one of the secretaries, and nearly collided with Wesley in the doorway. "Oh, beg pardon, Wes!" He reached out to steady the old gent. And then went utterly still when he spotted the young woman behind him. "Lina."

She looked a ruin—her hair coming loose from its pins, no hat, no gloves, her fine walking dress full of wrinkles and perspiration stains. Her cheeks were flushed crimson, her breath was ragged, and the two steps she took toward the door revealed the limp he'd so rarely seen.

He could hardly help the frown, even as his heart leapt up into his throat. "What's wrong?"

Wesley nudged him out into the hallway and then pushed his mail cart through the door, effectively keeping him from retreating back into the relative safety of the room. Not that he intended to do so anyway, but the click of the door behind him did seem to echo unduly along the corridor.

Evelina swallowed and held something out. Something leather and metal and . . . His frown deepened as he reached for it.

"Isn't this the Rolex that Wilsdorf gave your father?"

She nodded and eased back a step. "I found it in his workshop. In the circus toy. You were right, Barclay. He wouldn't have put it there randomly, it could only be some sort of message. For me—it's my favorite of his toys, he wouldn't have left it there by accident. He was trying to tell me something. That he hadn't gone because of Hans, that . . . that something is wrong. You were right. I don't think he left willingly, and now we've wasted two entire weeks, and—"

"Take it easy, now." He reached out—habit—but stopped himself before he could put a hand on her shoulder. His other hand tightened around the wristlet. "The weeks haven't been wasted. I've been searching, and I think I may have found something. As soon as Margot finishes the translation for me, we'll hopefully know more."

She blinked at him and curled her fingers into her palms. "You've still been looking? But . . . why?"

Did she really have to ask? He eased back half a step too, so his traitorous hand didn't try to reach for her again. "I promised you I'd find him. That promise isn't void just because you want nothing to do with me."

She opened her mouth, but no words came out. No noise at all. So she closed it again and looked away, toward the door Wesley had shut on them. She looked so tired, so worn out. Perhaps she was finding that life alone wasn't such a prize, even when one passed it in Westminster. But he could take no pleasure in that thought, not given the circles under her eyes. And had she lost a bit of weight? The curve of her cheek didn't look so soft as it had the last time he'd cupped it, the last time he'd touched his lips to hers.

"Who is Margot?"

"Hmm?" He blinked, clearing his mind of those memories. Letting the words sink in. "Margot, right. Lukas's little sister. Have you not met her?"

"Oh." Brows knit, she nodded. Shifted in a way that made it clear her leg pained her. "Once, at Pauly's. With what translation is she assisting you?"

How had they come to this? Polite questions, phrased with the proper inflection? From the moment they'd met, it had been different. But now . . . now she felt like a stranger. A stranger who didn't know the most important things that had happened in the last week, when she should have been the first one he'd told.

He'd tried. The next day, after finding the letter. He'd gone to her posh new house and rung the bell, and when he'd uttered his name to the high-and-mighty butler who'd answered the door, he'd been given the boot in no uncertain terms.

She was only here for her father. To help him. Because she knew Barclay's connections could achieve it. That was all, and he'd do well to remember it.

He cleared his throat and told her as succinctly as possible about the meeting with Claw, the helpful landlady, Grigorov's room. He watched her face go from red to pale when he told her about the poster, saw the light of desperation when he shared about the letter.

"Encoded?" She shook her head. "How can Margot help with that?"

He sighed to realize how little he'd been able to tell her about some things. "She . . . has a way with such things. She offered to help."

"And you think she can? Decode this letter? And translate it from Bulgarian?"

"Yeah." He couldn't help the bit of a smile that tugged at his lips. She'd obviously not had much of a chance to speak with Margot that night at Pauly's, or she wouldn't have to ask. "I think she can. She'll be out with it in just a minute, I imagine."

But Evelina's frown only deepened. "*Out*. She's *here*? Why?"

Blast. He motioned toward the door and summoned the official story to his tongue. "She and her mother work here. There's quite a need for secretaries these days." It was truth. But so vague a truth that it felt like a lie.

"Oh." At least the question eased from her face. "I imagine you helped her secure that position when they came here last autumn. That was good of you, Barclay."

He'd had nothing at all to do with it, but he could hardly say as much without explaining the whole story. And luckily, he was saved having to deflect the compliment by the door opening and Margot herself slipping out, a paper in hand.

But she didn't smile, neither at him nor Evelina. She simply handed over the translated letter with tight lips and murmured, "You had better go and find Mr. V straightaway."

He took the paper, making no objection when Evelina moved to his side to read it along with him. Not even having to tell his senses to ignore her once his eyes took in the first few words.

Time is running short. If you are certain the clockmaker can help us, then you must act quickly and get him into Central Powers–held territory. Air raids have been planned over London—perhaps you can use them as cover. You must be ready to act whenever they take place, as they will be dependent upon clear skies. Possible forays will take place on May 20, May 31, June 6. The earlier you can get him out of London, the better. Movement on the Continent will be restricted. If at all possible, you must rendezvous with my men in France on June 16; our intelligence reports that the French Tenth will be launching a campaign for Vimy Ridge on that date; the British First is already in position to aid them if necessary. I will have our mutual acquaintance waiting for you in Lens on the 16th—the troop movements ought to cover his and allow him to get in and get you out—but if the German Sixth cannot hold the ridge and he has to retreat before you find him, you will be on your own getting him to Germany.

"Blast." But even as his muscles all went tight, he could see the clockworks. The gears lining up. God's hand in it. "That's where Georgie is. With the British First, in France." He just had to get to Georgie, and then his little brother could help him get into Lens and find Manning. That was all.

He leaned over to press a kiss to Margot's head. "You're the best." Then he grabbed Evelina's hand, not much caring if she'd object to the contact. "Come on. We haven't even an hour to lose if I'm to make it to France in time—I'll drop you at home before I find V."

"You are not dropping me at home. I'm coming with you."

"No. You're not."

She tugged on his hand to slow his steps—or perhaps in an attempt to free her fingers from his. "Barclay Pearce, you know very well that a woman is no less capable than a man of—"

"This isn't about your gender, Evelina. Or even about the fact that you've tired out your leg and will therefore slow me down." A low blow, he knew. But he had to convince her to remain in the relative safety of London. He *had* to. Who knew what state he'd find Manning in? If he'd struggled . . . if his captor had responded with violence . . . No daughter ought to see her father so. "It's about the simple fact that the journey will be more easily accomplished with only one man. I know how to blend in, to slip about—"

"Not in France, you don't. You don't speak a word of French. I do. I can help."

He refused to look back at her, to see the desperation and pleading in her eyes. Refused to think of how those eyes might shift if she saw her father beaten . . . or worse. "Georgie's picked it up." He must have, at least a bit, to have that French sweetheart he'd told them about. "He'll help me if I need it."

"Once you reach him, perhaps—but how will you get to him?" She dug in her heels and pulled him to a halt, forcing him to look at her. Blast it. Her face had that determined set to it that she'd worn that first night they met. When the mugger—Grigorov—had held a blade to her throat.

When Philibert had upended her world.

When she'd put the first hook in his heart. He set his jaw. "You're slowing me down. Every minute could make the difference between finding him or not."

Her jaw matched the set of his. With a frustrated growl, she pulled her hand free and marched, limping, toward the lift she must have taken up with Wesley. "You're infuriating. Insufferable. In—"

"Invaluable. I know. No need for flattery." He jammed the button for the lift, and the door opened immediately.

The attendant offered him a lifted brow. "Since when don't you take the stairs, Barclay?"

"I'm in more of a rush than usual, John, that's all." And the stairs would exacerbate Evelina's leg. She needed to get home, rest it, and put all fool thoughts of coming with him out of her mind. He led her into the box, trying to keep his face pleasant, empty, while John closed the door, the grate, and then started their journey down.

The attendant then shot him a concerned glance. "Everything all right?"

It was on the tip of his tongue to assure him that it was. Old habit. But he had to crucify those habits, didn't he? He swallowed. Shook his head. "Not by far. If you're a praying man, I'd appreciate you saying one for me. I expect you'll not be seeing me for a while."

In this building, with all business being Navy business, and with the world being at war, no one needed to ask for clarification when statements like that were uttered. John's brow smoothed down to a knowing flat line. He nodded. "You have it. Every day until we meet again."

If they met again. Barclay sucked in a long breath as he stepped back out of the lift once John opened the doors to the ground floor. Barclay had ventured into occupied territory once before, last autumn, and his sister had nearly been killed. Lukas had been shot. He knew all too well the dangers he'd be agreeing to face.

Evelina trailed him silently across the lobby, out the front doors, and then muttered, "Blast." Followed by a curt tug on his arm. "This way. The car is waiting, though heaven knows why." Looking abnormally angry at the rather slick automobile parked at the curb, she stormed up to the liveried man standing at attention by the back door. Which he opened upon spotting her. "What are you doing here?"

The man lifted perfectly shaped brown brows. "Begging your pardon, miss. Following your orders, as told me by your friend—the young lady with blond hair. I'm afraid I didn't catch her name, as she was in quite a state, insisting I hurry to be at your disposal."

"Retta." She muttered it like an expletive and then spun to face Barclay. "Well, all for the best, I suppose. Give him the direction to where we can find this fellow you mentioned. Z, is it?"

"V." And while he wanted to order her home yet again, he couldn't deny the advantage of a car just now. And knew better than to suggest they drop her off first.

The question was, though, where could he find the man? There was still more than an hour before he was scheduled to meet him outside the hospital. Would he be somewhere else in the city, about business? En route? If so, he had no hope of finding him before noon.

But he had to try something. And so he gave the driver V's home address and muttered a prayer, as he slid in behind Evelina, that he would be there. It didn't strike him as likely, but surely it was possible.

The driver closed the door and let himself into the front, sitting so straight behind the wheel that he looked as though he had a ruler against his spine. But he nosed his way quickly into traffic, so Barclay decided to forgive him his too-perfect posture.

Evelina cleared her throat. "I shouldn't have believed those vague telegrams were really from him. Shouldn't have been so willing to believe he would leave us, when it flew against everything I knew him to be. Had I not accepted it so easily—we've lost two weeks. Two *weeks*! Who's to say where he is now? What he's suffered?"

"Lina, it wouldn't have made a difference. We had no idea who

Grigorov was until Claw finally came forward. That happened when it happened, and it wouldn't have mattered if you'd been looking before that. And it took as long as it did to decipher that letter—that's simple fact. You believed at just the right moment. Came to find me at the perfect time. You must see that—must see the Lord's hand in it all."

"The Clockmaker." She sniffed and averted her face, focusing her gaze on the smooth leather of the door. "I've been a wreck of a daughter. To Papa. To God."

"You were hurt. Reacting out of pain. But you needn't beat yourself up about it, luv. Ultimately, it doesn't matter. You came round."

"Too late." Her eyelids fluttered down, a veil over her grief.

"There's no such thing as too late. Not with God." The words came so easily to his tongue—probably a direct quotation from Peter—even as they sliced his heart. He didn't believe they were too late, not for Manning. Not given the timing of each discovery. Surely God wouldn't have led them to it only for them to find him beyond help. Would He?

But then, *too late* seemed to perfectly describe plenty of other things. He'd reached to catch Olivia when that rich bloke had kicked her into the street last year—too late to keep her from being trampled. He'd sensed a trap last autumn in Antwerp—too late to keep Willa from being captured by the Germans and a bullet from finding Lukas's shoulder.

He'd found Charlie—too late to help him navigate through the treacherous waters of growing up without a parent.

She made no response, and Barclay said no more either. Not with all those failures clanging about in his mind. Failures enough that he should no doubt question his own confidence in rushing to Cecil Manning's rescue. What made him think he could pull it off?

He wasn't sure he could, honestly. But he knew he had to try. Because though they might deny it, and though Evelina might never want him in her life again after he returned her father to her, this past month had proven a simple fact. They were family now. As surely as Clover and Patch, as Willa and Rosie, as Lukas and Peter. As any of the others.

He loved them. Both of them. All of them. Which meant he'd do whatever he could. Whatever it took.

The car pulled to a halt in front of V's terribly typical house, and Barclay said another silent prayer that he would be there. He didn't wait for the chauffeur to let him out, just reached . . . for where a handle ought to have been. But wasn't. Apparently in this car, one had no choice but to wait for the chauffeur, blast it all.

The bloke soon released him, though, and Barclay hurried out, up the walk, and rang the bell. Evelina's uneven step followed, but he ignored her. Much as he would have liked to order her back to the car, he knew she wouldn't go anyway, so why waste the breath? He just hoped that V would forgive him for introducing them.

The door swung open a moment later, and Alice filled the doorway. She was dressed this time in a simple day dress, and her eyes focused between where he and Evelina stood on the step—where a single person likely would have been, centered in the doorway. "Yes?"

"Good day, ma'am." He ought to ask her for her last name, as he still couldn't bring himself to call her by her given name aloud. But it felt presumptuous somehow to ask for what she hadn't willingly given.

"Barclay Pearce." Her unseeing gaze shifted to him, and a smile graced her lips. "What a pleasant surprise. And who do you have with you?"

How did she . . . ? Perhaps she heard her breathing, or smelled the light scent of her perfume. He cleared his throat. "Evelina Manning." He didn't know what else to call her anymore.

Apparently her name was sufficient. Knowledge lit her eyes,

and she reached out a hand. "Oh, how lovely to finally meet you, my dear. How do you do?"

"Very well, thank you." Evelina grasped her hand, which had been aimed a few inches too far to the right, and shot a questioning glance at Barclay. "And you, Missus . . . ?"

"Oh, just call me Alice, dear. And I'm quite well. Do come in, both of you. Mr. Pearce, you needn't feel any compunction over telling your lady that I'm blind. She'll realize it soon enough, I imagine."

He half laughed, half choked. He'd barely even had time to wonder how to inform Evelina of their hostess's state without being rude. "I'm so sorry to trouble you at home, ma'am. I'm looking for your husband."

"I imagined you were." The corners of her lips turning up in a smile, she ushered them into the room to the left. "I'll fetch him for you. Do make yourselves comfortable, dears."

He was here, then. Relief sagged Barclay's shoulders. And something that crossed confusion with sympathy swelled in his chest when Alice stopped in front of a stretch of wainscoting between two bookcases and knocked upon it. There was a door on the other side of the shelves to her right, which had surely been her aim. She'd seemed quite sure-footed the night he'd barged in two weeks ago, but perhaps their presence had thrown her off today. Not that it had seemed to at the door, but . . .

Then the wall swung open, and V appeared. "Yes, luv?"

Barclay's brows arched toward his hairline. "Well now. *That's* a handy thing to have."

V's gaze shot through him like an arrow. "This can't be good. And Miss Manning too." He stepped fully from whatever lay behind the false wall and pushed it closed.

Barclay watched it move back into place—the wainscoting perfectly hiding the seam. "I could do with one of those. Don't suppose you could have one installed at Number 120?"

"Barclay." Evelina widened her eyes, her message clear. *Stop wasting time.*

"Right." He looked to his employer. "It's Manning, sir. Margot cracked the code and translated the letter, and we don't have much time if we mean to recover him and his work." He pulled out the translated message from where he'd shoved it into his jacket pocket and handed it over.

V's eyes flew along the lines, his mouth tightening with each sentence he read. At its end, he sucked in a deep breath and looked up, from him to Evelina and back again. "It will be difficult to find someone who can—"

"I'll go." Barclay kept his voice measured, calm, sure. His posture exactly what it had been—because to straighten, to lift his chin, to make some other show of confidence would come across as trying to prove something. When the point was to convince him that it didn't even need proving.

Tactics that had served him well on the streets. He could only hope it would serve him well with V too.

Evelina folded her arms over her chest. "He means *we*. *We'll* go."

"I meant *I*."

V sighed. "Mr. Pearce—Barclay. You have already been behind enemy lines once. You of all people know the risks involved."

"What?" Evelina's arms slid to her sides again, as those eyes widened again. "When were you behind the front lines?"

Barclay ignored her and fastened his gaze on V, nodding. "Well, as my family always says, with the greatest risks come the greatest rewards. This is a risk I'm willing to take."

V measured him for a long moment. Then nodded, though a bit reluctantly. "Let me put some things together. It will take me a few minutes. Miss Manning, would you like to refresh yourself? You'll not have much time to do so after I've gathered what you'll need for the trip."

"Now, hold on. You can't mean to let her go." Surely he knew how cruel that could be.

But V halted Barclay's single step forward with a lifted hand. "A couple traveling into France will not attract nearly as much notice as a single man. Fools aplenty are still going to Paris for their honeymoons. Neither side will bat a lash, even if they laugh at your stupidity. But if you try to make it through alone . . ."

"Then I'll take Retta."

Evelina growled behind him. "You will *not*!"

He begged V silently. Pleaded with him. But the blasted man simply said, "You know perfectly well she'll follow you."

"I most certainly will. It's *my* father who was kidnapped."

With a long sigh, he turned to face her. "Lina. You could be killed."

She didn't flinch. Just lifted her chin. Trying to prove something. "I don't care. He left that watch for *me*, Barclay. He was asking *me* for help." With a flare of her nostrils, she turned to V. "I would appreciate the chance to tidy up. Thank you."

He could only watch as V led her from the room, watch and pray that she'd be suddenly struck by fear and back out. But she wouldn't. He knew she wouldn't. She'd come, and he'd have to keep her safe, and he'd have to believe that her father was still there to greet her, and healthy enough to do so without leaving scars on her spirit.

Too well he remembered the nightmares that had plagued Willa for months after her brief imprisonment. He would never wish that on anyone else. Especially not on *this* anyone else.

Alice came forward a few steps. "You clearly love her very much."

A breath of laughter, dry and unamused, drifted from his lips. "Is it? Clear, I mean?"

"I hear it in your voice. Undergirding the desire to protect. And colored with pain. Are things not well between you two?"

V was certainly right about his wife—she saw far more without her sight than most people did with it. He sighed and sank down onto the chair behind him. "There's nothing between us at all. Apparently."

"*Nothing* doesn't usually sound so very full of *somethings*." She eased over to the chair beside his and sat as well, smoothing her dress as she did so. "V has told me a bit about it."

"Has he?" He knew well she'd hear the shock in his voice. His employer didn't seem the type for idle gossip. Though he'd obviously shared plenty else with his wife, it was true. But Barclay's failure of a romance? Why would he even care to learn of it, much less to speak of it?

Alice's lips tipped up. "Mm-hmm. I think it reminds him a bit of our own story. A bit."

"Did you like him just to irritate your mother? And to distract yourself from another beau?" He bit his tongue, but too late. The bitterness wouldn't slide past her either.

But it didn't dim her smile. "No. But we come from two very different worlds. And it was his work for my father that introduced us—much like it's your work for V that put you in her path. Though I was only a girl at the time. And he was only a lad—one my father hired to steal for him."

Barclay sat forward. "I knew he had the instincts of a thief."

"That he does." She laughed and leaned forward too. "And I helped him perfect them, you know. Taught him how to use senses other than his eyes. He was very good at what he did—one of my father's favorite assets."

The way she said it . . . He drew in a breath. "Who did you say your father was?"

"I didn't. And I won't." But she grinned. "Suffice it to say he was in government. And that he was none too proud of having a daughter so obviously imperfect. I was kept closeted away for the first eighteen years of my life. I daresay most people thought

I'd died as a child. V was sometimes the only one, other than my governess, who ever came to visit. I couldn't help but love him. He was my whole world."

Not like Barclay and Evelina at all, then. If rather intriguing. "I can't imagine your father approved the match, though."

"He said I would no longer be his daughter if I married a common thief. That I would be forsaking all he'd given me. I pointed out that I was barely his daughter as it was, and all he'd given me was a cage." She winced, the smile lines around her mouth turning to a frown. "I don't recommend speaking so to one's father. He was furious and cut me off just as he said he would do. It was years before he agreed to meet with me again, and then only because he was dying."

"I'm sorry. That must have been difficult." All of it. Losing her family, venturing out into the world—and to a part of the world so very far from all she'd known.

Different worlds. More different even than his and Evelina's. But they'd ended up in a fair enough place, and obviously their marriage was a happy one. He'd no idea if it had always been so, of course, but now at least.

"Difficult, yes. But I never regretted my choice. Not for a moment. My husband is the most remarkable man I've ever met. And the more people I come to know, the more I realize it. The more I love him." She reached over and rested her hand on the arm of his chair. "You remind me of him, from back then. Except that you've had more of an advantage."

"I beg your pardon?"

Her smile went sad. "You at least know your name, Barclay Pearce. He never had even that."

Barclay Pearce. He'd always thought it his invisibility that made him successful. But she was right. It wasn't the invisibility at all—it was that he knew who he was under it.

TWENTY-EIGHT

Evelina stared too long into the mirror of the borrowed lavatory, trying to tell herself it didn't matter that she looked an absolute mess. After, that is, failing to convince her hair back into its chignon with a few crucial pins missing.

It didn't matter. It *didn't*. What mattered was that she would be going to find her father. And if that could only be done by traveling with Barclay to France, then so be it. She could get through a few days in his company, with her parting words to him standing guard between them. She would have to.

Not quite trusting him not to leave without her, she tried one last time to tuck in a recalcitrant strand of hair. She'd at least managed to return her face to its normal color with the aid of a cool, wet cloth. There was little she could do about her dress. But they would have to go back to their neighborhood before they proceeded to the train station anyway. He'd have to tell his family he was going. And she could then pack a change of clothes or two.

And tell Mother.

Did she dare tell Mother? Tell her the truth? But she couldn't well keep it from her. She needed to know, just as Evelina had, that Papa hadn't left them. Not willingly.

"God?" It had been too long since she'd prayed. Or at least

since she believed it mattered if she did or not. She gripped the edge of the porcelain sink. "I'm sorry for doubting you. Doubting that you cared. Just as I'm sorry for doubting him." She squeezed her eyes shut. "Please take care of my papa. Please. Keep him safe until we can get to him—and help us to get to him. I don't see how we'll find him with so little information to go on, but . . . but I'm going to trust. Trust that you have it all orchestrated." A sob tangled in her throat and came out a gasp. "Help me to trust."

She stood another moment, still and tense, until the sob passed. And in its wake came a deep breath that seemed to fill her whole being with air. They could do this. They could find him, and they could get him home. She nodded at her reflection and slipped out of the lavatory, following the voices back to the drawing room.

V had spread a variety of papers across the couch cushions. A map, train schedules, smaller things she couldn't identify right away. He glanced up at her when she entered. "Ah, good. Have you a passport, Miss Manning?"

She nodded. "I got one as soon as Basil proposed. We'd been planning . . ."

Barclay, who had also looked up when she entered, looked decidedly away at the mention of Basil.

She forced a smile. "Yes. I have one."

"Good. I'm afraid you'll have to sacrifice it so that Retta can change the name upon it, but it will make it easier if she can use the photograph from your existing one."

"Wait. Retta . . . ?"

"Is one of the best forgers I've seen in years." V sounded amused by this. Alice looked completely at ease.

Barclay smirked. "She only uses such skills these days for the good of England, mind you."

"But is far faster than official channels. I've rung up Mrs. Holstein so she could get her started on the necessary documents while you're in transit." V shuffled various papers into a stack and handed them to Barclay. "I'll wire ahead to have your tickets awaiting you at the train station. And I'll try to get word to Georgie's unit as well, letting them know that he should be given permission to assist you however possible."

Alice rose from her seat, moved to that strange portion of the wall again, and opened it with a press upon the chair rail. Evelina couldn't help but sneak a glance at Barclay, to see the way his eyes lit at the secret door. Their hostess reached in without actually moving inside and pulled out a valise.

V straightened. "That's not necessary, luv. I don't need to go anywhere."

The lady simply walked to the room's exit and set the bag down. "If you don't, you'll spend the whole time they're gone fretting, just as you did last autumn."

Evelina lifted a brow toward Barclay, but he wasn't looking at her. He wouldn't be, of course. But still. She had better get the story of last autumn's trip from him at some point, or it would drive her mad.

Barclay was sending his own lifted brow toward V. "Worried about us, were you?"

"Rightfully. Although had you told me the truth of where you were going, I could perhaps have stepped in *before* your sister fell into German hands." V strode toward his wife. "Even so, I can tend to things from here. I promised you I'd not go to the Continent again while the war is on, and I—"

Alice pressed a finger to his lips. "A request I made out of fear, not faith. Go. Do what you do."

"But—"

A second finger joined the first, though not right beside it. Spread into a V. "Darling. *Go*."

He sighed and kissed her fingers.

It broke something inside Evelina. Made her want to sink to

the floor, draw her knees to her chest, and bury her face. *Love.* That was, somehow, what those two raised fingers meant. Not *Be quiet* or *Stop arguing*. But *I love you*.

She had to turn away, to look somewhere other than at them, or at Barclay. So she cleared her throat and edged back out of the room. "I'll make sure the driver is still waiting. How long do we have before our train?"

"Two hours," Barclay said. Was his voice tighter than usual or was the fault in her hearing? "Will you be riding with us, V?"

"No. You two proceed as agreed. It's best we not be seen together entering France."

Evelina let herself out the front door before she could hear any more. She'd barely had time to ask the driver to take her back to her mother's house before Barclay came back out, a folder in hand. They made the drive from Fulham in silence, but for his insistence that he'd walk home from her house when she offered to have him let off separately.

She saw no point in arguing. All of that ought to be saved for the coming discussion with her mother. And, she quickly realized, with her aunt.

Climbing out at Number 22, she said to the driver, "I'll be only a few minutes, and then we'll go and pick up Mr. Pearce again, to go to the train station. From there, you may go home."

The chauffeur bowed, no curiosity whatsoever in his eyes, even as he asked, "And when will Miss be coming home again? I will have the car there to meet you."

"I . . . don't know. Just . . . be at my mother's disposal while I'm gone, please. I'll be in touch with her whenever possible."

Another bow.

Evelina nodded. Barclay had already slipped out behind her and was covering the distance down the street in long strides, taking him away from her. Where he'd rather be, no doubt. And for good reason.

She touched a hand to her pocket as she walked to the door. The Rolex rested there. A proof. A promise.

Her leg was still too tight. Were this a normal day, she would soak in the tub, stretch it, and be right as rain tomorrow. But then, were this a normal day, she'd not have run all the way to Whitehall to begin with.

Williston had the door open for her before she could knock, his face decidedly pale. "There you are! Praise the Lord, Miss Manning, I feared . . ."

"Oh!" She hadn't even considered what he or her mother might think about her absence. "Do forgive me. I should have found you before I left."

A dreadful thump came from the drawing room. "Apparently, Judith, even inheriting a house such as she has will not convince your daughter to keep servants in their place. As if she must answer to *them*. Although . . ." A series of thumps, followed by Aunt Beatrice's scowling appearance on the threshold. "One would think a daughter would at least have the graciousness not to worry her mother unduly. Though apparently some people cannot remember *that* these days either."

Evelina opened her mouth to retort, but Mother rushing past her sister to embrace her daughter stayed her tongue.

"I was so worried when Williston said you'd run out of the house. Retta came by just as I was getting home to say you'd gone to the Admiralty, but I couldn't think why you'd do such a thing."

Evelina drew in a long breath, returned her mother's embrace, and then pulled away enough to meet her gaze. Perhaps she *had* changed. At least enough. "It's about Papa. Look what I found—in the circus toy, downstairs." She pulled the wristlet watch from her pocket. "The one Hans gave him. If Papa had been going to join him, he would have taken it. If he had simply gone away to teach us a lesson, he wouldn't have left it in such a place. But he knew that was my favorite toy. He was leaving a message for me. And when I found Barclay, he'd discovered a letter that confirmed it—Papa was kidnapped, Mama."

Mother's face washed pale, and her hands shook as she took the watch. "I don't understand. Why? Why would anyone kidnap him?"

"The project he was working on with Barclay. It . . . it could change the course of the war in the air."

Her mother's eyes slid shut, pain battling with fear and relief. "I am glad he did not leave us. And yet I wish he had—at least then I'd know he was safe."

"We're going to find him." She squeezed her mother's hands and prayed her smile looked confident. Convincing. "Barclay and I. We're leaving straightaway. We know where he's being held, in France, and we're going to fetch him home."

"You?" Mother's face somehow paled still more. "Evelina, you mustn't. You can't go into a battle zone—leave it to the men. To Barclay, or to whomever he's—"

"I can't, Mama. He needs me. Papa, but also Barclay. I speak French, and his superiors confirm that a couple traveling together will not gain as much notice as men."

"Scandalous!" Aunt Beatrice's cane drove into the floor like a spike, her face as flushed as Mother's was pale. "No niece of mine will shame herself by traveling alone with a man!"

Her fingers went tight around Mother's and then relaxed. "Try and stop me. My reputation means nothing compared to my father's life—and as I hardly need a man at this point to support me, I don't really care what society might say anyway, if they discover it."

Aunt Beatrice's nostrils flared in outrage. "Impudent hoyden."

"Call me what you will. And while I'm being impudent . . ." She released her mother's hand, slid the watch back into her pocket, and pointed a finger at her aunt. "You'll not lord over us any longer. If you want to stay in this house because we're the only family you have, then so be it, so long as my parents allow it. But you'll remember that they don't need your money, not anymore. You are not their superior just because my father earns his own living. I've already seen to all the bills and expenses. They'll be cared for from the funds Basil left me. So do remember that you are here as a guest, and you will show my mother the respect she is owed as your hostess, not your debtor. Do you understand?"

Beatrice couldn't seem to work anything but squeaks past her lips, but the speech hadn't really been for her anyway. Evelina looked to her mother. *She* was the one who must understand. That no matter whether she found Papa, no matter whether she ever came home again, she had done what she could. Days ago, as soon as the paperwork could be drawn up. Her mother wouldn't lose this house, nor Papa his business.

It had been the only thing she could do at the time.

But no more. She offered a tight smile and a nod. "I need to hurry. The train will not wait."

Mother didn't so much as glance over her shoulder at her sister. "I'll help you. Come, then."

TWENTY-NINE

Outside Lens, France

Barclay gripped Evelina's hand and wished for the eight-hundredth time in the last twenty-four hours that she hadn't come. Bad enough to worry during the crossing of the Channel that a U-boat might be lurking. Bad enough to fear on the train across France that they'd be stopped. Bad enough to be always looking at the skies, wondering if a German bi-plane might come roaring over them like a dragon ready to breathe fire.

But now there was no wondering. They stood mere miles from the front lines. They'd had to cross old trenches. And a veritable sea of British soldiers milled about in the twilight of the French evening, every set of eyes that flicked their way looking far too interested in the arrival of a pretty girl.

She shouldn't have come, blast it all. Never mind that her ability to speak French had already proven useful. Lukas spoke it far better—he should have interrupted the honeymoon to bring his new brother along rather than let Evelina badger her way into such danger.

"How will we ever find him?" She edged a bit closer to his side as her eyes moved over the swarms of identical uniforms.

Barclay studied the unfamiliar khaki sea. He was used to crowds, to mobs, to dangerous places. But not quite like this. Here, there would be no blending in. Not with his civilian clothing, and certainly not with Evelina as a beacon by his side.

They should have found her a nurse's uniform. And him a soldier's. Had they had a few more hours . . .

"We'll start with his commanding officer. If V succeeded in his portion of the plan, he'll be expecting us." And an officer would be far easier to locate than Georgie himself.

On the horizon, the small city of Lens stood in a cluster of roofs painted gold and red in the dying sun. Was her father already there with his captor, waiting to make contact with whoever would ferry them into German territory? Or was he waiting for whatever skirmish was coming tomorrow to provide cover?

Or, worst possibility of all, had they already come, been met, and were gone? Barclay could only pray against that last option as he studied the town.

Regardless of whether it already housed Manning, it was where they'd likely find the officers. If Georgie's grumblings could be trusted, they didn't often deign to spend their time in the trenches and tents with their men.

Perhaps they could find a car somewhere. Otherwise it would take another precious hour to make the trek.

"Hello there! Are you the Pearces?"

It pierced, all right, to hear her called his wife each and every time they boarded a new vessel and she presented those false papers. Perhaps, if Retta had been given time enough to create *two* new passports, he would have insisted on a different surname for them both. As it was, he had little choice but to turn with a smile every bit as false as her name. "That's right."

The man striding their way looked pleasant enough, with a pencil-thin mustache and thin lips pulled into a smile. His uniform had a bit more decoration than most of the masses milling about, but not enough to say he was in charge. An aide of some sort, most likely. He approached Barclay with an outstretched hand.

"Lieutenant Hagley—how do you do? The captain's had me keeping an eye out. Said I'm to assist you however you need. You're George Pearce's brother, right?"

Barclay nodded. He'd been happy enough to lend Georgie his last name when he enlisted, since the lad had never known his own. But it was rather strange to hear him called by it. How long had it taken Georgie to get accustomed to answering when called Private Pearce? Or Lance Corporal now.

Hagley grinned. "A real joker, that one. Keeps all our chins up with his jests—but he's also always there when we need him."

"That's Georgie, all right." Barclay's smile went genuine. "We certainly miss him at home." And seeing him again would be one victory of this mission, no matter what the outcome of the rest. He'd be able to report to the others that he was well, that he was getting along, that he was still *him*. Assuming it was all true.

And assuming Barclay made it home to tell them.

"If you'll follow me, sir, ma'am, I'll take you to him. Unless you need the captain first?"

Barclay tucked Evelina's hand through the crook of his arm. "I believe my brother will be able to assist us, lieutenant. Thank you."

It took half of forever to wind their way through the masses of soldiers—or so it seemed, with that internal clock ticking down every second and making it less likely that they'd manage to find Cecil Manning in time. They sidestepped ruts filled with rain, skirted the latrines that punched them in the nose as they went by, and finally entered the trench system.

"Just the communication trench," Hagley said over his shoulder as he led the way into the earth. "I wouldn't take the lady into the main trenches themselves, I assure you. Here." He indicated a dug-out square off the main trench—nothing but a little shovel-made cave to protect a body from the weather. "Wait here for a moment, and I'll fetch Lance Corporal Pearce for you."

Barclay nodded his thanks, rather impressed that Evelina managed to withhold her shudder until their guide had gone. She stepped gingerly over the duckboards protecting their feet from the muck beneath them and into the dugout. "I can't imagine practically living in these things as I've heard they do."

"No worse than some of the places the family has stayed—well, if one discounts the artillery fire." He made himself comfortable on what passed for a bench in the dugout—two wooden crates with a plank between them.

Evelina stared at him. "You must be joking."

She'd want to think so, wouldn't she? Heaven forbid she have any reminders that she was here with a street rat—relying on a common thief for help. He tipped his head so that he could see the strip of sky visible between the earthen roof and the opposite wall of the trench. "Would that I were. But a London sewer really isn't any worse than a trench in France."

He caught the flare of her nostrils before she averted her face. Disgust—that was all that was left between them, apparently. At least in her mind. Disgust at what he'd been and what he'd come from. No doubt she wished she'd had some recourse other than *him* for this mission.

He rather wished she had too. Traveling with her by his side, knowing she didn't want him there, was torture.

But then, he wanted to see it through. Restore her father to her. See to her happiness in whatever way he could. It may be the last thing she ever allowed him to do for her—and so, he would do it to the best of his ability. In a way that spoke of his heart as his lips never would.

A silent five minutes dragged on between them before booted footfalls hurried their way. Barclay stood, ready to usher Evelina to the bench if it were some random soldier, removing her from view—or to greet him if it were Georgie.

His brother hurried into sight with that same grin on his face that he'd always worn, undimmed by war and the hovering shadow of death. Barclay knew relief so sharp it sliced through some of the cords of tension that had been holding him up. He grinned back and stepped out from under the dugout so he could give his little brother a fierce hug and playful cuff alongside the head. "Georgie! Look at you. You're hulking."

A slight exaggeration—but he'd come into his breadth in the year since Barclay had clapped eyes on him, his shoulders wider, his jaw squarer. He looked no less thin than ever, but more . . . well, more a man.

Georgie laughed. "Just the word everyone uses. I'm a regular giant. What are you doing here, Barclay?" His gaze darted into the dugout, where Evelina no doubt lurked in the shadows. "And who's this missus the lieutenant mentioned? You didn't say anything about a wife in your letters, and if you've gone and got married without telling me—"

"Just part of the cover, for traveling." Barclay pitched that revelation low and turned to include Evelina in their reunion. "This is Evelina Manning. One of our new neighbors in Hammersmith."

Evelina stretched out a hand as if they were on a civilized London street and said, "How do you do, Georgie? Your family has told me so much about you."

Georgie's lips twitched as he took her hand and bowed over it. "She has your manners, I see. The ones you tried so hard to drill into us."

"Tried, nothing—I *succeeded*, in everyone but you."

They shared a laugh, but Georgie's gaze had gone serious behind the mirth. "You wouldn't bring a Hammersmith girl here for anything less than a crisis. What's going on?"

There had been a day not all that long ago when Georgie would have clung to the joke as long as he could, letting someone else introduce the serious side. But apparently his shoulders hadn't been the only thing to grow.

Barclay sighed and updated him on her father's situation in as few words as possible, in as quiet a tone. He summed it up with, "From what we could discover, Grigorov means to use an attack planned for tomorrow as cover to get him into German territory. He's to meet his contact in Lens."

Georgie shot a glance in the direction of the town, though they couldn't see a bit of it from the trench. His brows were knit. "If he's in the town, we can find him. But if they're somewhere in the Artois . . . It would be next to impossible to locate him. You'd have to try to sniff out their next stop somehow and lie in wait."

Equally impossible. Georgie didn't say it, but he didn't have to. Barclay could feel his jaw go tight. "Have you any contacts in the town who could assist us?"

His brother grinned. "Of course I do. Come on—we'll go pay a visit to Minette. I want you to meet her anyway."

Minette—his girl. Barclay still couldn't fathom that Georgie had a sweetheart, but if she could help them . . . "Perfect. We're ready whenever you are."

"The captain gave me leave to lend you whatever aid you need." At that, he lifted his brows. "Do I want to know how you pulled that off?"

"V." Barclay stretched out a hand for Evelina. And was a bit surprised when she slipped her fingers so easily into his.

Georgie had signed up before he could learn all that much about their new employer—but he'd remember that job Rosemary did for him, which had been the turning point for them all. He gave one shake of his head and then motioned them to follow him back out of the trench.

Barclay kept Evelina close as they trailed his brother toward the edge of the camp. And didn't miss the fact that she clung to his hand and pressed as near to his side as walking would allow. Perhaps to the men milling about, it would look like the type of affection one would expect of a couple on an ill-advised honeymoon.

He knew very well it was trepidation, nothing more. Even if he gripped her fingers and pretended it *was* something more. For a moment. Just for a moment.

Then Georgie was ushering them to a wagon already hitched to a couple of tired-looking donkeys. He shot Barclay a grin. "Apparently V's influence doesn't extend to a lorry, more's the pity."

"I suppose even he has his limits." He helped Evelina up and, once she'd settled onto the bench, vaulted up beside her. Georgie climbed up on the other side and took the reins in hand with the ease that spoke of having done such a thing frequently.

So strange to see. In London, Georgie's experience with horses—much less donkeys—had been about as much as the rest of them could claim: he knew how to avoid their hooves when he darted across the street.

But now he clucked them to attention and had them rattling down the little road toward Lens with a casual, "Yah!" He then shot Barclay a grin past Evelina. "So, Willa's really married now too? To this violinist bloke?"

"Really and truly. You'll like Lukas. He's a good sort." He filled him in on other family news—Olivia's progress with the leg braces, Pauly using the telephone *twice* in recent months, his mother's startling reappearance—as they rattled their way over the pitted road. But the spring inside him wound a little tighter with each foot they traveled. And with each degree the sun dipped closer to the horizon.

"So, this Minette," he said as the first buildings of Lens rose around them. "You really think she'll be able to help us?"

Georgie's grin was like it had always been. And yet something altogether new. Because never before had he grinned so over a young woman, with that particular light in his eyes. "Just wait and see. Her father owns a little tavern—he reminds me of Pauly, actually. Aside from being French, I mean. She's come to know everyone in the area over the years, and if there's any news to be had, she'll have heard it."

Another minute and Georgie was pulling the wagon to a halt, hitching the donkeys to a post worn smooth from countless other horses hitched just so. He hopped down, seeming perfectly at ease as he navigated the street with its signs all cloaked in French and shadows.

Barclay followed, helped Evelina do the same, and fell in behind his brother on the narrow cobblestone streets.

Part of him wanted to look around, to soak it all in, much as he had wanted to do in Antwerp and Brussels last autumn. To see these sights he'd never imagined seeing, take in the land so foreign to him. But yet again, his purpose allowed no such leisure, so he could do no more than note the picturesque lines of the buildings and hurry after his guide.

Georgie led the way into what was clearly a pub, given the scents wafting from its doors along with laughter. This early in the evening, the crowd was far from raucous—those who come for a meal more than drink. The type of crowd Barclay knew best, and which he didn't mind leading Evelina into.

His brother paused just inside the door to look around, shouting something or another in French at a local who had called out a greeting. Barclay made an impressed face. "You've learned the language."

"Bits and pieces. And Minette speaks decent English, so we get on all right." Georgie perked up when the door to the kitchen swung open and a petite young woman rushed through with a plate of something steaming and delicious-looking in hand.

Breakfast suddenly seemed days in the past. They hadn't stopped for lunch. There hadn't been time.

And there really wasn't time now either, was there?

Except that Evelina was tugging on his arm, her eyes latched upon that tray too. "We could well be out all night, Barclay. We need to eat if we mean to keep going."

"Right, of course," Georgie answered for him. "Let's have a seat, then. Minnie!"

The girl looked their way, and her eyes lit upon spotting them.

Something inside Barclay relaxed. Would he ever stop worrying over the hearts of his siblings? Fearing that their affections wouldn't be returned? Fretting over them? Probably not. But Georgie seemed to have found someone who was just as fond of him as he was of her, so perhaps he needn't worry so much about that.

Just that they'd no doubt be separated in the war. It would probably come to naught.

Perhaps that was what the men in their patchwork family were destined for—a sad thought. Though at least Georgie'd had the good sense to fall for a girl who was at least from a similar station, if a different country. Maybe he'd find a way to work it out.

Maybe it would only be Barclay destined to spend his life with children aplenty but no wife by his side to care for them.

He settled into the old wooden booth that Georgie indicated and tried not to look over at Evelina.

Minette soon appeared at their table, leaning over to kiss Georgie on each cheek and exclaim something bright and warm in French. He replied—his accent awful even to Barclay's ears—and then motioned to them. "This is my brother, Barclay. And his girl, Evelina."

Barclay stiffened, expecting Evelina to correct him. But she wasn't really given much of a chance. Minette turned wide brown eyes on him and leaned over to kiss *his* cheeks too. "Oh, how good! Here! But why? Georgie tell me all about you and his family. Why are you not in London?"

She wasn't what one would call beautiful, this Minette. But

what her face lacked in symmetry, it made up for in that vivacious something that blinded one to any physical failings. She had dark brown hair, eyes to match, and a smile that had probably hooked Georgie's heart in about half a second.

"That's why we're here, luv." Georgie tugged Minette down to the bench beside him. "They're looking for Evelina's father. He was kidnapped, and someone's trying to get him into German hands. Their information says they would have come through here. Have you heard of any Englishmen coming through, not military?"

Minette's brow furrowed, and she tapped a ragged nail to her lip. "What is he looking like?"

Evelina scooted forward, leaned across the table. "He is around fifty-five years of age. He wears spectacles. Greying hair, which he is losing on top. I—why am I describing him? I can show you." She reached into the little handbag she'd had looped around her elbow ever since they left London and pulled out a photograph of her father.

Barclay studied it along with Georgie and Minette. In the snapshot, Cecil Manning looked much like Barclay had come to expect from him. Intelligent, serious, every hair in its proper place.

But his eyes, in this photograph, held no disillusion. No despair.

Barclay could only pray that this was the Cecil Manning they'd restore to his family.

Minette muttered something in French and then looked up again, from him to Evelina. "I have seen this man, yes. With a darker one, and an old one. They were on the road out of town, toward the German line."

"Blast." Barclay scrubbed a hand over his face. "When was this?"

"Midday. They will not have gone far, perhaps. The old one, he moved slowly. Unless they found wagon—but this is unlikely, in that direction."

"Old one." Evelina's face pinched into a question. "Who could that be? Grigorov's contact, do you think?"

"If so, the slowness could well have been put on to fool anyone watching." Barclay met his brother's gaze. "How far are we from the German line?"

"A mile, maybe. Perhaps two. If . . ." He leaned closer, pitched his voice low. "Minette's brother's in the French Tenth. The ones planning another attempt for Vimy Ridge. Whether they succeed or not, it will interfere with your rescue, Barclay. Either the Germans will be in retreat, or they'll be pushing forward. Either way, crossing the front lines is going to be risky."

Barclay straightened. "So be it. With the greatest risks—"

"This is your life though." Georgie suddenly looked older than he should, older than any of them thought him. Older than the mere passage of days could make him. "This isn't about a pretty bauble or a high-priced fence. This is you walking into enemy hands, deliberately, knowing well you might be leaving all those children behind if you die. What'll they do without you?"

Barclay's fingertips bit into the table. He'd always taken on the role of leader of the family—taken it on willingly and held it tight. He'd let himself be called a tyrant and reveled—perhaps a bit too much—in being the one who could say an ultimate *yes* or *no*. But mostly, he'd loved them. He'd loved them, and he'd fought for them, and he'd do it all again.

But that chapter was already finished, wasn't it? He shook his head. "They have Rosie and Peter, Willa and Lukas to take care of them. If something happens to me . . . They'll mourn. But they'll be fine."

They didn't need him, not like they once did. He'd done his job. He'd raised them, taught them, made them independent. "Even so." He added a grin. "Don't count me out. I'm cleverer than a bunch of soldiers, don't you think?"

Minette slid the photograph back toward Evelina. "I think I

may know a way to keep you safe. There is a train that should be coming through shortly. It will be let across the front lines. Let me fetch my papa. I bring food too, *oui*?"

"*Oui*," Evelina answered before he could. "*Merci*."

Georgie was still frowning at him. "I don't like it. This isn't London, Barclay. It isn't your turf, you don't know the area. And even if they were moving at a snail's pace, they're likely in the Artois by now. Perhaps have rendezvoused already with the German forces."

"All the more reason to hurry, then."

His brother sighed. "If there's a train coming through, it must be the Commission for Relief in Belgium. You can get into German territory with them. But getting back out's another story."

Good thing Barclay had always liked stories.

THIRTY

They moved like shadows through the night, toward the hulking beast hissing steam. By her count, they had four minutes to climb aboard that train before it was scheduled to leave the depot again. Four minutes.

She wouldn't be late—not for this. Even if exhaustion was clawing its way through each muscle and feasting upon her bad leg.

Each glance Georgie sent her was a new accusation—that she was risking his brother's life for this hopeless search. Then there had been the looks from Minette and her father. The ones they'd given as they'd pressed letters into her hands—letters meant for Minette's uncle, who lived in Givenchy, on the other side of the front lines. He'd help, they promised her. He'd help them get back into Allied territory, if she'd help them by passing along this information.

She hadn't a clue what was in the letters, or if she could get in trouble for having them. It hardly mattered, given the trouble she was already seeking. She had nodded, and she had smiled, and she had tucked the letters into her pocket.

As they neared the depot, another figure emerged from the shadows.

Georgie drew to a halt, the moonlight silhouetting him. Barclay motioned with his head. "It's all right. That's V."

The older man slunk toward them like a thief in the night, greeting Georgie with a bare nod. "I was about to seek you out when I saw you coming this way. I've already spoken with the American guarding the flour. You can hide in car Number 9. They'll search the train at the crossing, but he says they don't search very thoroughly. And as you near Givenchy, they'll slow enough for you to jump off."

They'd have to jump off a moving train? Evelina bit back her alarm. Barely. But the last thing in the world she wanted to do was show them her weakness. Prove that she wasn't as strong as Barclay's sisters, couldn't do what was necessary, shouldn't have come.

Barclay nodded as if this was but a drive through the park. "As for getting you back out . . ."

Georgie stepped forward. "Minnie's uncle will have his horses and donkeys for them to use. He's been trying to find a way to get them across the lines, before the Germans can conscript them. You'll have to take the long way round though, Barclay, through the forest. Only way to avoid the Germans. And you'll want to veer well away from Vimy Ridge."

"That's better than I could have hoped." V nodded. "I've spoken to my contacts in the French Tenth, as well as our First. From what they were willing to divulge, we have a small window indeed to get you back out and to safety. I'll remain on this side of things to coordinate your extraction."

Evelina curled her fingers into her palm. "How small a window?"

Mr. V turned to her, his expression impassable. Or perhaps it was the moonlight veiling it against any emotion. "You must keep in mind that their operations are timed down to the minute, Miss Manning. We cannot know how the Germans will respond, of course, but I do know when various waves are scheduled to attack. You must thread the needle between them or risk getting caught in the battle."

A shiver coursed up Evelina's spine.

Barclay stepped nearer. "How small a window, V?"

He pressed his lips together and handed over a folded piece of paper. "I could secure only ten minutes. Take this map, study it. You must be at the rally point I've marked between noon and ten past." He pulled out a pocket watch. "Let's synchronize our watches. I already did so with the commanders. I read three minutes past midnight."

Evelina waited for Barclay to follow suit. Instead, his larynx bobbed. "I haven't a watch to set."

"Oh, but of course you do. The one Papa helped you fix." He'd have it—he *always* had it, every time she'd seen him since those first meetings.

But Barclay just cast his gaze toward the huffing, puffing train. "I'm afraid my mother has that one. Or did have. I daresay at this point it's in the hands of whatever fence would give her a pound for it."

"What?" Evelina's hands fell to her sides. "Did you *give* it to her? Knowing she would pawn it?"

"Does it really matter?" His glance, silver in the moonlight, was all hard angles and clashing steel. "You have the Rolex, don't you?"

"Of course I have." And it shouldn't matter. It wasn't her watch, after all, that he'd let his mother sell. She fumbled for her pocket where she'd stashed the Rolex, as the band was too large for her wrist, and pulled it out. Held it out to him. Her tired hands would probably drop the pieces to the ground if she attempted to wind it.

Barclay lifted it from her fingers and opened the case. "Three after still, or four?"

"It will be four in fifteen seconds . . . Ten . . . Five . . . Now."

Barclay nodded and put the watch back together. Then looked

to her, holding up both it and his wrist. "Shall I, or back into your pocket?"

"Wear it. It will be quicker to check that way."

Had he really *given* his mother the watch? Why, if she needed money, didn't he simply give her a few pounds? Even if the watch wasn't an heirloom like the one Papa always carried, it meant *something*, didn't it? Shouldn't it?

"Would that I could give you more than twelve hours." His face hard and shadowed, Mr. V stepped deeper into the dark provided by the building. "But some things are outside my control. When the train slows, head due east. Givenchy will be within sight."

Georgie's face looked every bit as hard. "Minette's uncle's house is right on the edge of town closest to the tracks—you'll know it by the broken chimney, she says."

Every word felt like another nail driven into their coffins. How could they possibly do this?

V's gaze was still on Barclay. "You are confident you can reach the rally point?"

"He was always good with a map." Georgie clapped a hand to his brother's arm, but it didn't look as lighthearted as it was probably meant to. It looked heavy. Like goodbye. "The orienteering he taught me has certainly served me well, and I can't imagine it will serve him any poorer."

Barclay patted Georgie's hand and gave him a tight smile. "I appreciate your help with this, Georgie. It's surely the Lord who positioned you here to help, right where we needed you to be."

The younger's brows lifted. "Think so?"

"I do."

"Hmm. There's a thought." A crooked smile settled on his lips. "Not used to hearing you speak that way."

"Well. When we both come safely home, you'll get to hear a lot more of it." Barclay squared his shoulders and stepped away, toward the train. "Twelve hours—see you both then." He nodded to the men and held out a hand to Evelina.

She had no reason to take it, now that there weren't thousands of men milling around. But she did, at least long enough to let him pull her down the line of train cars, to the ninth one, and help her up into the door V slid open for them. Inside it was blacker than nightmares.

"Here," V whispered. Something dark and clunky was in the hand he reached out. "I trust you know how to fire it?"

A gun. Barclay took it, though not exactly quickly. "I know the rudiments."

"Good. Twelve hours." And then the last sliver of moonlight disappeared as the door slid shut.

Evelina fumbled in her pocket for the small electric torch Minette had passed her along with the letters. Even as she flicked it on, the train lurched into motion, sending her stumbling into Barclay. He righted her and pointed to a huge stack of cotton-sacked flour. "Behind there, I'd say."

She kept the light on long enough for them both to squeeze into place behind the flour, then turned it off again. The night devoured them. The chugging of the train filled the silence.

She swallowed. And decided it was safe enough to talk until the train stopped at the crossing. "That watch—it's what brought us together. Is that why you gave it to your mother? To get rid of it?"

He didn't so much as shift. "It had nothing to do with you, Lina."

It could have sounded simple. Encouraging, even. Instead, it rang like a slap in her ears. As if she were nothing but a vain little twit, thinking everything was about her. "Right. Of course not. I didn't mean—" She turned her face away, though he couldn't see her flush in the darkness anyway.

They were crammed together as tightly as the sacks of flour. Still, she nearly jumped when his fingers brushed hers on the floor. "It was before. She stole the watch. The day of Willa's wedding."

"What?" That, too, hurt like a twisted leg. "But you didn't tell me."

"I meant to, later. But what I needed at the time was exactly what you gave me, Lina. An embrace. Support. I imagined I'd tell you the next day, only the next time I saw you . . ."

"Right." She ought to be glad she'd provided him *something* he'd needed at the time. But it had been so little. And then she'd cut him off at the knees. For his own good as much as from her anger at being kept in the dark about his past, but he wouldn't see it that way.

"Besides." His voice lightened, brightened. Not by much. But enough. "That's not what brought us together. The watch was just an excuse to search out your father."

Of course. The real reason had been the same one that had gotten them into this. "Right. The gear."

"Primarily, yes. And then there was the Great Westminster Clock."

He might as well be speaking Bulgarian. She tried to find a more comfortable position against the grain but gave it up. "I'm sorry?"

His chuckle was soft and tired. "A game we play, the family and I. We challenge each other to steal things. Silly things, impossible things these days. When Ellie heard I'd be meeting the clockmaker in charge of it, she bet me that I couldn't steal an hour from Big Ben's clock."

A breath of laughter slipped out. Stupid. And funny. And so very *them*. "But Papa never took you to Big Ben, did he?"

"The challenge wasn't really all that important, in light of the work your father was doing."

She nodded, gritted her teeth against all the aches the hard floor inspired—body and soul—and said nothing more. Within a few minutes, the train slowed, its brakes screeching, and then it chuffed to a halt.

German shouts filled the night. Not alarmed, but still she stiffened. And when booted feet stomped their way, she curled up into as small a ball as she could manage.

Each car door slid open, then shut again. She felt Barclay stiffen beside her too, curl over her. Shrinking them both to nothingness behind that flour that would mean food to hungry Frenchmen.

The door to their car slid open, though she couldn't see any of the moonlight that would have come in. She held her breath, willed herself to disappear, and prayed as she'd never prayed before.

The soldier climbed in, whistling as he flicked his torch's beam over the mountains of flour. *Whistling*.

And then his boots hit the ground outside again, and the door slid closed once more. Evelina sagged.

The train soon moved again, though they couldn't have covered more than a few miles before once more it slowed.

"This must be us." Barclay unfolded himself, tugged her up too.

She turned on the torch long enough to allow them to get to the door and crack it open. Then switched it off and slid it back into her pocket.

Moonlight gilded the countryside. The only sound she could make out was that of the wheels on the steel tracks. Her chest banded. Even at the train's decreased pace, it seemed so very *quick*. How would they jump without hurting themselves?

Barclay didn't seem to realize this was a question. "That must be the town there. Ready?" He gripped her hand.

"No." She gripped his back. "But now or never, I suppose."

"On three, we jump together. Try to either run or roll, depending on how you land, but keep moving either way."

She pressed her lips together, not asking how he knew that. Nodded.

"One."

Please God.

"Two."

Lord, help me.

"Three!"

Choking on a muted scream, Evelina jumped as far as she could away from the train, toward the damp grass growing alongside the tracks. Her knees buckled when she hit the ground, her hand wrenched from Barclay's. *"Roll,"* he'd said. She let her momentum carry her forward and then pushed it still more, tumbling over gravel and debris and earth and grass and who knew what else until she came to a halt, heaving. But in one piece.

Barclay, the idiot, laughed as he pulled himself up and brushed himself off. "Well, that was an adventure. Are you all right?"

"Well enough." Though when she stood, she had to turn away to hide a wince. Her calf screamed at her.

"Lina."

"We'd better hurry."

He said nothing as he surveyed the distance between them and the town, but then he moved closer. Slid his arm around her waist. Not in the way he'd once done, to draw her in for a kiss. In a way that took some of the weight from her screaming leg. Just enough to help. "I hope Liv turns out like you. Able to tackle anything, no matter what."

She meant to laugh. But it sounded more like a cry. "Like *me*?"

"I daresay she'd agree. You've given her something to which she can aspire. You've given her hope."

Hope. How could she give it, when she felt so little of it herself? "You give me too much credit."

"No. I don't. But we'd better be silent now. If there are Germans in the town, there'll be a curfew. We'll have to sneak in."

She nodded and sealed her lips. A few minutes of walking, and the house with the broken chimney was before them.

Barclay led her toward the back door, upon which he knocked lightly, without any hesitation. Evelina, if on her own, would have stood there for a long moment, making sure she was disturbing the right family, second-guessing herself.

Before she even would have found the courage to knock, the door was cracking open, a man's face filling the space.

"*Bonjour*. Or *bonsoir*. Or . . . whatever time of day it is." Barclay offered a tight smile. "Minette? She . . . *elle* . . ."

"Oh, for goodness' sake, Barclay." Evelina shook off her fatigue and elbowed him aside, summoning a tight smile of her own. In French, she said, "Please forgive us for intruding, *monsieur*. Your niece, Minette, and her father sent us to you. We have letters from them." She pulled away from Barclay and fished the contraband letters from her pocket.

Their would-be host didn't open the door any wider, but he took the envelopes, opened the one on top, and tilted it into the moonlight. She had her doubts it would prove enough to read by, but apparently she was mistaken, given the change in his expression. He looked up, around, and opened the door wide. "*Dépêchez-vous.*" *Hurry.*

She'd never been so happy to step into a dark kitchen. "*Merci. Parlez-vous anglais?*"

"A bit." He moved to the window and pulled the curtains wide, letting in a stream of moonlight. "I do not dare light lamp. This all light. Jacques say you brother of Georgie's? Looking for wife's father."

"That's right." Barclay kept his voice low. "A Bulgarian man took him. Minette said she'd seen them, and an old man, coming this way."

Their host nodded, sending a heavy dark curl over his forehead. "Three men arrive at dusk. Dark man. Man with . . . eh . . ." He motioned to his eyes and drew the outline of spectacles.

Evelina nodded. "Eyeglasses, yes. That's my father!"

"And old man. They try find room, but all filled with Germans." He spat out a word in French that Evelina didn't know but whose gist she understood quite well. "Friend Remy open doors. Old man, he say, no sleep outside. Offer wine cellar, but the dark one, he . . ." He mimed shaking a fist, moved a hand from his mouth as if loud words were exploding from it. "Demand bed. For *him*. Say others prisoner. Lock them in cellar."

"Both of them?" She looked to Barclay, though the shadows didn't reveal what expression might be on his face. "Surely if the old man is Grigorov's contact—"

"Perhaps he wanted one of them to stay with your father and keep him from escaping." Barclay stepped closer to the Frenchman, hands outstretched. "Please, can you help us find your friend's house? This wine cellar?"

But the man shook his head. "Streets not safe. Germans. No one out at night, or . . ." He pointed a finger at his head and made a muted imitation of a gunshot.

She shivered. And prayed he was exaggerating. "But we must find him, *monsieur*. We cannot wait until morning—they will leave again, and . . ." And the two armies encamped nearby would no doubt begin their artillery bombardments.

"Jacques say you take my horses to him, *oui*? This good. I hide them from Germans too long already—they already take donkeys. You take my horses—*trois*, three I have—and sneak across to Jacques. But not in dark. Dawn come soon enough—Remy laugh that dark one drink much wine. He sleep late in stolen bed, *oui*?"

"But—"

"Lina." Barclay slid to her side again and slipped that arm around her waist. "We can hardly find him without help. Let's just rest for a bit. Then we'll be better for what's to come, yeah?"

Her shoulders slumped. Her heart screamed that each moment they wasted was one in which her father's life hung in the balance. Her head insisted that she'd not be able to rest, not knowing he was so close.

But her leg betrayed her, buckling when she tried to take a step toward their host, to beg him again.

Barclay pulled her back to his side. "We rest. Dawn is soon enough."

It wasn't. But she couldn't argue. Couldn't even speak. If she opened her mouth, she knew well that nothing but hysteria would spill out.

And so she let the man lead them to a little room attached to the kitchen, where a narrow cot was jammed up against the wall. She let Barclay ease her onto it. Just for a moment, though. Until she'd battled back the emotion clogging her throat and taken a moment to rub at her traitorous leg. Then she whispered, "You can take the bed. I'll not sleep anyway."

"Yes, you will. And I'm used to the floor." To prove it, he stretched out upon the dusty wood, so that the scant square of moonlight struck him right in the chest.

What was the point in arguing? She lay back too, and turned onto her side. That square of moonlight looked like a door on his chest—like one of the little compartments Papa made into his toy people, so he could access their works. A door straight into his heart.

She closed her eyes and wished she were brave enough to open it.

THIRTY-ONE

The first blush of dawn was kissing the horizon, washing rose-gold light over the Artois, when Barclay slid his picks into the lock of Remy's wine cellar door. Remy himself stood, sleepy-eyed, behind them, exchanging hushed French whispers with Minette's uncle, who had whispered this morning that his name was Hugo.

Evelina leaned against the door at his side, looking anxiously from his picks to their hosts. And looking nearly as exhausted as she had when she'd lain down on that cot four hours earlier. Shadows stained her eyes, and her cheeks were as pale as the moonlight that had lit their way. "He surely has another key somewhere. Even if Grigorov took the original—"

"You want him to wake the whole house looking for it? Relax, Lina. This will only take a few seconds."

The lift of her brow cast doubt on his claim, but he just rolled his eyes and set to work. Even now, she didn't want to think about the tools his trade had given him—even now, when it would save her father.

Please Lord, let it save her father.

He set to work, smiling as he felt the tumblers move aside. It wasn't that complicated a lock. Within a few seconds, a beautiful *click* bespoke his success. "There, see?"

Evelina didn't look all that comforted, despite that he'd just gotten them one step closer to their goal. "It's really that easy? You mean to tell me that anyone can simply—"

"It was a simple lock—it's a wine cellar, not a vault. And yes. I mean to tell you that a skilled lock-pick can gain entrance rather easily. Hence the wisdom of a bar or chain as well." But as this was hardly the time for a security lecture, he straightened again, glanced back at the Frenchmen for their nods of permission, and then pushed open the heavy door.

All was dark and quiet in the cellar, and it smelled of earth and must. He fished out Evelina's small electric torch from his pocket and switched it on, letting its yellow beam search the place before he stepped inside.

He didn't exactly expect a company of Germans to leap out and arrest him. But he didn't exactly *not* expect it either.

The only figures he saw, however, were two forms lying on a few blankets.

"Papa!" Evelina kept her exclamation quiet, at least, as she darted past Barclay down the few steps and into the dark space. She was still limping this morning, though not as badly as last night. Not that she seemed to notice as she flew over the rough gravel floor.

A moan came from the figures, and shifting. Barclay followed her down in time to recognize Cecil Manning's profile as he turned. The second form, more rotund than Manning, didn't stir. Barclay could make out nothing about him but white hair that caught the light and hands so wrinkled that he immediately doubted his own claim that this second bloke was a guard.

Manning shot up to a sitting position with a wince when he spotted his daughter. "Lina! What are you doing here?"

"Shh." She fell to her knees beside him and threw her arms

around him. "Oh, Papa. I'm sorry. I'm so sorry I doubted you. I thought you'd left us. I should have known better. And I—I'm sorry for the way I behaved before you were taken, for ignoring you, for—"

It was her father's turn to hush her, to hold her close and smooth back her hair. "Lina. My sweet Lina. You oughtn't to have come. Why did you come? I left the watch so you would know, but I never meant for you to follow. I didn't think you *could*." He looked over her head, met Barclay's gaze. Accusation rested within his. "Why did you bring her here? Don't you realize there is a war set to rage nearby?"

Barclay left the door open to provide what light it could and sidled toward them. "I do, in fact. We must hurry."

Evelina pulled away abruptly. "Is that . . . ? Is that Uncle Herman?"

Manning heaved a sigh, nodded.

Barclay lurched forward another step. "Your mentor?"

Another nod. Manning pushed himself to his feet. "It is my fault. I'd written to him, you see, getting his advice on a problem I was having with the gear. I'd just received a letter back that day. I had it on my bench when Grigorov . . . I tried to tell him the gear wouldn't work, that its problems were too great, but he found the letter. Instead of being convinced to leave me and the gear, he instead was convinced that I needed Herman's help in completing it." He shook his head, sorrow in every line of his bearing. "Another agent kidnapped him, apparently. We just met up with them two days ago. Poor Herman. He's too old for such nonsense."

"*Pardonnez-moi*."

Barclay spun back toward the door, where Remy had poked his head in. The Frenchman motioned with his hand. "*Dépêchez-vous*."

A command Barclay had heard countless times from Hugo in their brief acquaintance. *Hurry*. He nodded. "Come, sir. We have to move quickly. The bombardment could begin any moment, and I for one don't mean to be caught in it." He strode over the remaining distance and reached down to the prone man.

Herman was just blinking awake—with a rather understandable moan. Barclay had spent many a night on hard ground, but not hard *graveled* ground. He crouched down and lent the old chap a hand in sitting up. "There we are. We're getting you out of here."

"Yes, do hurry. We've only three horses, but we'll make do, I'm sure." Evelina's tone was alarm covered in a thin veneer of calm.

Barclay's breath leaked out. Putting two of them on one horse would slow them down. But not so much as going it on foot would do. "We've a fair bit of distance to cover by noon. For now, we need to get out of here before Grigorov wakes up."

Manning had been trying to bring a bit of order to his appearance but halted with his hands on his collar. "You haven't secured him in any way? Grigorov? You expect us to waltz away under his very nose?"

"Remy assures us he was much in his cups. He should be incoherent for a while yet."

Herman was grunting his way to his feet. "Lina! I can hardly believe it." As if they were in a park rather than a prison, he held out his arms and gave her an indulgent smile. "Look at you. All grown up and pretty as a picture."

As the old man embraced Evelina and kissed her cheeks in the European fashion, Manning stepped closer to Barclay. "He will find us. This is a fool's errand, you must know that. There is no way we can move quickly enough to evade him. If he realizes we are on horses, he will simply find a car."

"We'll manage." He'd pray, and he'd trust, and he'd follow whatever path the Lord opened.

God had led them this far. Set up every piece, every cog, every gear. He wouldn't abandon them now.

"And if we're caught," Evelina said, turning back to her father, "then Grigorov will simply have to take one more captive. I'm not leaving you again. If it comes to it, then we'll go together to Germany. And we'll work so cleverly to undermine them that they'll *wish* they'd let us waltz away under their very noses."

Barclay's free hand curled as he watched her reach for her father's hand. And hold tight to it.

Love swelled up so fast within him that it nearly cut off his air. This was the Evelina he'd so quickly come to admire—the one who wouldn't sway from the right path once she recognized it. The one who refused to turn away from danger when it stood between her and her goal. The one who stared down dragons without flinching, whether they be the monsters of politics or customs or the most terrifying of all—one's own demons.

This was his Evelina. The woman he'd come to love for her every determination.

Even though that determination had taken her from him once already . . . and could take her again now.

If he let it.

"Well, we certainly don't want it to come to that, do we?" Papa said with a decisive nod.

Evelina looped her arm around her father's, not liking the wincing way he moved. But then, she was moving much the same way. They would push through it, and they would recuperate once they were safely back in England.

They made it to the cellar steps, hobbled up them, out into the pink-hued dawn. Barclay pulled the door shut behind them and fished around in his pocket. He pulled out a small piece of metal and slid it into the lock.

Remy edged forward, dark brows creased. "What are you doing?" he asked in French.

Evelina translated for Barclay, who smiled. "Jamming the lock.

Neither picks nor key will work with that in there, which should buy us some time while Grigorov rants and rails about it. Tell Remy it will only take a magnet to pull it out again—he can brilliantly think of it before our Bulgarian friend insists on an axe."

She relayed the message as best she could—though she'd never had cause to learn the French for *lock-pick*—and watched their conspirator's face shift into a devious smile. He nodded.

Evelina's smile faded as she watched Herman amble toward the road at a pace he probably thought to be full-speed. New worry sprang to life. Three horses for the four of them—she would obviously have to ride either with her father or Barclay, perhaps changing between them for the sake of the horses. She could only hope Herman would be all right riding for a few hours.

He had to be in his eighties by now, and his health hadn't been exactly sound for years. How many times over the years had Papa shared with them his concern for his mentor? If one added in how he had likely suffered already on his unwilling trip from Switzerland . . .

"Grigorov was already quite impatient with him," Papa whispered, his gaze on Herman's back as well. "I think he is convinced they made a mistake in taking him. He has threatened multiple times to simply shoot him and be done with it—and I rather believe he would."

A shiver overtook her that had nothing to do with the cool morning air. "We'll get him safely home again. I promise you—"

A loud *boom* interrupted her. Not exactly near, but loud enough to make her jump. Her heart race. Her head go light.

Barclay muttered something and lurched into action. "It's started. Quickly, we must—"

"*Venez par ici*." Minette's uncle motioned them between the houses, his gestures frantic. "Come. My horses—they are at forest's edge."

"Hurry." Evelina tugged her father forward.

More artillery fire rent the quiet air, sending a flock of birds in the field into screeching flight. Her heartbeat felt every bit as loud. It would surely rouse Grigorov. Not to mention make their task of regaining the Allied lines more difficult.

But she would see it as Barclay had said—one more wheel in the clock, turning just as it should under the Almighty's hand.

They would get out of this. She didn't know how, but they would.

Not until they were mounted on the frightened horses and setting out through the Artois did any of them speak again. And then Papa's voice came softly from in front of her, strained by more than just the echoes of artillery.

"I can only imagine what your mother thinks of me. What she *will* think when she learns that my work has already been sent to Germany."

"Oh, Papa, no." She held him tight, praying silently with every fiber of her being—for safety, for provision, and for healing of the heart of this man she loved so dearly. "She misses you. So much. The zeppelin raids awoke her from a long sleep, and then your disappearance . . . I had forgotten what she could be like without those walls around her heart. But she is a changed woman." She knew it as she said it. Knew she'd turned too quickly from her mother in the face of Aunt Beatrice. "I think she desires nothing more than the chance to start afresh with you."

"Even knowing I have aided the enemy, however unwillingly?" He sighed, shaking his head.

Evelina squeezed him. "I cannot quite believe I am saying this, but give her a bit of credit, Papa. She will not hold this against you."

"Do you really believe that?" He turned around as much as he could manage, showing her the spark of hope in his creased face.

She drew in a breath of the sweet country air, even as another *boom* sounded in the distance. "I do."

That hope sparked brighter. "I cannot tell you how long I've prayed that she would remember who she used to be. If this has actually accomplished it when nothing else did . . . Well, the Lord uses even our broken pieces in the most remarkable ways, doesn't He?"

Her gaze flicked to the horse in the lead, where Barclay led the way. Broken by the world, a part most of society would cast aside. But here he was, risking the family he'd built for *hers*. She nodded. "He does. He does, at that."

THIRTY-TWO

Barclay didn't imagine he handled the workhorse he rode with the same effortlessness that Georgie had the donkeys, but he tried to seem confident as he guided the creature along the path through the woods.

They were headed in the right direction for their rendezvous, but the trip would take them considerably longer than it had by rail. And since they couldn't push the horses, given the double load one was being asked to carry, they'd be cutting it closer than he'd have liked.

In the distance, the incessant sound of artillery fire pierced the air, guaranteeing his nerves remained on edge.

Even more terrifying were the sounds coming from over the ridge. His gut had been tight and insistent ever since he'd heard the first engine sound, and it hadn't eased any in the intervening mile. They were getting closer to whatever it was. And he didn't dare assume it would be allies—he was all but sure they hadn't made it out of Central Powers territory quite yet.

Barclay checked the watch on his wrist. Consulted the map he'd folded to a convenient shape and rested against the saddle. And pulled on the reins until the old mare came to a halt. If he was reading the map right, they'd intersect with those noises soon. They'd be found, they'd be at best detained, and at worst . . .

Something had to be done. And the certainty of *what* settled on him with that same solid weight he knew so well. The one that had always said, *Give the little one your food* and *You don't need a coat, not like he does*. That certainty he was only now beginning to realize was God, showing him the way to love those put in his care.

"Shall we relieve this horse?" Manning pulled his mount to a halt as well, seeming oblivious to the commotion beyond the ridge.

"Yeah." Barclay dismounted, praying he didn't look totally inept as he did so, and moved round to help Evelina down from behind her father.

He did a fine job of avoiding her gaze on that part. It was when he motioned for her to mount his horse that he couldn't keep it up.

"Shouldn't you get on first?"

He looked then. At the worry burning in her eyes—he suddenly suspected she had heard those terrifying noises too—and at the lines of exhaustion and pain around them.

If all went according to plan, he'd see her again at the rendezvous in an hour and a half. If it didn't . . . then he'd be happy enough with this image of her, to take with him wherever he went. "No. You can ride alone for now. I'll walk for a spell."

"Barclay, no." Evelina reached out a hand and, when Barclay strode a few steps away, followed. "We haven't time for your heroics. Get on the horse with me, and we'll keep going. We can't be that far from the rendezvous."

"We're not." And that was frankly what worried him. They couldn't lead a whole band of German soldiers toward V and whoever he might have enlisted to help them. They *couldn't*. It would put everyone at far too much risk and all but guarantee a fire fight. No, he had to get them out of here and cover their tracks. Otherwise they'd all end up dead. "I can catch back up to you without any trouble after I've covered your tracks." The ground was soft, but there were leaves enough from last autumn that he could disguise the way they went at that fork in the path just ahead.

"We're not separating!"

They had to—if they *all* stopped while he was covering the tracks, it increased the likelihood of being seen. Not to mention that if running became necessary, those tired horses couldn't possibly outpace the threat, not with two of them on one. He turned back to the horses. Herman was closest, his gaze keen. Barclay held out a hand. "Glad I got to meet you, sir. Manning said wonderful things about you."

Herman shook, his nod grave and knowing. "Perhaps we'll have a chance to become better acquainted, lad. I daresay I'll spend some time in London after this rather than hurrying back to Switzerland. I'll need the rest."

"Perhaps." It was all the promise he could make, and the old bloke knew it.

Barclay turned to Manning. "You have a watch?"

Manning wore a frown that looked as though it might never fade again. "Of course. But why—"

"Synchronize it to mine, if you will, which is synchronized to V's and the army's. Timing is crucial. You must be at the rally point between noon and ten after." Barclay straightened his arm with a jerk to free his wrist from his sleeve. "You know, when next you see Wilsdorf, tell him I rather like this design. Quick and easy to access—I bet the army would agree."

"Barclay." Evelina had followed him, of course, and tugged on his arm. She sounded none too pleased, but he didn't look at her to see if her face matched her tone. Not yet.

He cleared his throat. "I have ten twenty-eight and thirty seconds."

Manning's hand trembled a bit as he pulled out the stem and turned the knob. "Setting to ten twenty-nine on your mark."

Evelina tugged again. "Barclay Pearce, you will not ignore me. And you will *not* go off on your own! We'll meet Mr. V together, and we'll all go home together. Do you understand me?"

He lifted a finger. "Fifteen . . . ten . . . five . . . and mark."

She grabbed his finger and used it to yank him away half a step.

"Barclay." Manning slid his watch back into his pocket. "Lina's right. Stay with us, we'll be stronger together. And I'm none too sure I can find this rally point on my own."

"Yes, you can." He pointed to the forked path, indicating the branch to the right. "Just follow that path another mile. It'll lead you straight to the road where V is set to meet us. Remember—don't come out of the cover of the woods until noon." He hesitated another moment and then pulled out the pistol V had given him. "Here. Just in case."

Manning took it, though his lips were a thin line.

Evelina shook her head wildly. "Get back on the horse, Barclay. It's only a mile, you say—we can push the beast that far without injuring it."

"Lina—why are you arguing with me? You have to know you'll be faster without me—and I'm the most capable of running that mile to catch back up, you can't argue with that. It's no different than that night at the music hall. We separate, we do what needs done, and we meet up again, safe and sound." No different from half the jobs they'd done over the years—escape was always the most crucial part. And seldom did it involve keeping their hands tucked safely in each other's. No, all too often it meant separating. Each tackling their own risk.

Evelina didn't seem to like that analogy. "That's supposed to make me feel better?"

He sighed. "Just go and take care of your family."

Perhaps seeing the fury in her eyes shouldn't have set his heart at ease. But it did. Because she wouldn't be so furious if she didn't feel *something* for him. "And what of *your* family, Barclay

Pearce, hmm? What am I to tell *them* when you get yourself shot or killed or taken prisoner?"

She'd meant to shake him. But Barclay just smiled and wove their fingers together. How quickly he'd grown accustomed to the feel of her hand in his—and how hard it had been *not* to feel it there, once the habit had been formed. "Tell them I love them."

Her eyes blazed all the brighter. "That will hardly appease them when I return without you, with no explanation as to why you were imbecile enough to go off on your own!"

"Then tell them . . ." He paused, waited to see how the words sat on his tongue. In his spirit. They lingered there for a moment, sweet and sure. And so he said them. "Tell them I love *you*. And I couldn't put you at risk. Not when it was within my power to improve your chances. They'll understand that."

Her eyes swam with tears that glinted like glass in the sun. "That's not fair."

"Life isn't. You can't get around that." He reached up to cup her cheek, savoring the feel of her face under his fingers. "I'd do it all again, Lina. Every bit of it. Even if it can't be for keeps, I don't care. I love you like I've never loved anyone. Like I never will again."

"No." She gripped his hand tighter and blinked away that shimmering glass. "If you loved me, you'd stay with us. Make sure we get there safely. Make sure Grigorov doesn't come—"

"He won't follow you back across the line." He hoped it was true. Prayed it. But even then, another rumble echoed over the ridge. They had no time to waste. "I will cover your tracks. You've got to help your father and Herman get to safety. They need you."

"They need *you*. Not me. I'm just—"

"Don't." He rested his forehead against hers, even though that meant he couldn't look her in the eyes so well. "You're every bit as capable of doing what needs to be done right now." He pressed a kiss to her lips, because he couldn't help himself.

It might be goodbye. Forever. And if so, he needed that one last brush of tomorrow. To savor the scent of flowers and rain.

Then he stepped away. "Go and save your family, Lina."

Her eyes were still glassy. Her jaw was clenched tight. And he wasn't quite sure if she meant to punch him or kiss him again when she followed the step he'd retreated.

She did neither. She simply tilted her face toward his and said, "Promise me. Promise me you'll make it to the rendezvous."

"Lina."

"You never break your promises, right? So swear it. Here and now, or I won't let you go."

He made it a point not to promise things he couldn't deliver. And he was none too sure he could deliver on that. Still, if intent mattered for anything . . . "I promise. I'll meet you at the rally point at noon. Sooner, if I can."

Her nod matched the arms she folded over her middle—stiff and taut. Without another word, she stepped past him and back to the borrowed horse, mounting without even waiting for a hand up.

Barclay watched while the trio nudged their mounts into motion, onto that wider right-hand path. He could almost understand, just now, why Philibert had left rather than face her anymore, knowing she didn't love him as he loved her.

Almost. But not quite. Because even if it was unrequited, love didn't run. It stayed and fought. It did whatever needed doing.

And just now, what needed doing was covering their tracks.

He was no country boy, to have a hand at this sort of thing, but he'd covered plenty of city tracks before. And with a bit of luck, whatever soldiers lurked nearby were no more accustomed to the woods than he was. He stomped out the most noticeable prints, grabbed a branch and set about obliterating the shoe marks he left behind, the shallower hoofprints, then scattered last year's leaves over them for a goodly ways. He wished he had something to stamp false tracks on the left-hand path, but he made do with using a stick to fake a few—thankfully, that path got rocky and wouldn't take prints easily anyway.

Another check of his wristwatch told him he had just a few more minutes to play with. He spent them climbing a bit farther along the left-hand path, following its snaking up the ridge. Perhaps he could get a glimpse of whatever was over it. Perhaps whatever he saw would ease that tension inside instead of making it worse.

Then a different sort of sensation fluttered over his neck. One he knew all too well. He stopped, held his breath, and took account.

No birds tweeted. The wind made no gust through the trees. But there, to his left, was the snapping of a twig.

He turned. And hadn't time to utter so much as a prayer before Grigorov stepped out from behind a wide oak, a cruel-looking pistol leveled at his chest. "*You*." The man spat it like an expletive. "Where are the others?"

Had he been lying in wait here, thinking this the more likely path his escaped prisoners would take? He must have been. The left-hand path, from what he could tell from the map, led to a larger road than the one V had designated. It would have made more sense if they were simply trying to get out of German territory as quickly as possible.

He was glad V never chose the obvious way. Lifting his arms to show himself unarmed, Barclay shook his head. "Not here. I don't know where. We were separated and—"

Grigorov pulled the trigger, sending a bullet into the tree by Barclay's side, his face not flinching a muscle as he did so. Then he aimed again at Barclay himself. "No lies. I ask you again—where are they?"

"And I say again—I don't know." Or rather, he *did* know that providing an answer wouldn't spare his life if this man meant to kill him.

He was keenly aware of his disadvantages—he didn't know this land, didn't know what cover he could find other than the trees. He had no weapon on him aside from his lock-picks.

The Bulgarian's lip curled. "You are wasting your efforts, you know. Even if you say nothing, I will find them. And I will kill them all, other than the clockmaker himself. The rest are more trouble than they are worth." He shifted his aim from chest to head. "See what you have accomplished with your interference, thief? I will kill you. I will kill your girl. I will kill her father's feeble old friend."

Let him that stole steal no more: but rather let him labour, working with his hands the thing which is good, that he may have to give to him that needeth.

The verse from Ephesians filtered into his mind as it had done so often since he'd first read it. He flexed his fingers, remembering the feel of those too-thin pages, of the supple leather of the cover.

Had he done the thing that was good, this half year? Had he labored enough to provide for those who were in need?

When he stood before the Father, would He call him *thief*, as this man did—or *son*?

The wind stirred, cooling the trickle of sweat down his back. Whispering peace into his spirit. He'd changed his life. He'd been forgiven. If he died today, it would be with the knowledge that Christ had paid his debt and made him clean before the Father. That he'd done what he could to be the person God called him to be.

And there was hope—if Grigorov meant to recapture Manning rather than kill him, there was hope for the rest of them too. It meant he would pursue, but not with guns blazing.

Barclay let half his mouth pull up into a smile. "You're too late. They've already rendezvoused with our army."

"*Ne*." Grigorov advanced a step.

More noise coming from the north. Wind? Birds in the trees?

No, heavier. Earthbound. He hoped with all that was in him that it was but a pack of deer, startled out of their hiding by the commotion beyond the ridge.

But it didn't matter. Barclay lifted his brows. "Afraid so, old boy. Go after them and you'll find yourself in the crosshairs of the British First."

"Ne!"

Barclay saw the twitch of his finger and dove just as it tightened on the trigger, as the shot filled the air, and then it was all leaves and dirt and tree roots trying to grab him. He rolled with the motion of his dive, every turn a prayer.

Another bullet bit the dirt where he'd just been, another the tree he'd stopped behind. Barclay scrambled to his feet, forcing his breath to still, his pulse to quiet so he could listen. All but hugging the tree, he listened for the footsteps that would tell him from which direction Grigorov would come at him. Though it was hard to discern above the thrashing.

"Come out, thief. You cannot hide behind a tree forever."

From the right, for sure. He slid a hand into his trouser pocket and pulled out those feeble weapons—the slender lock-picks. "Don't be so sure."

Footsteps—the thrashing was definitely human footsteps, many of them. Coming over that ridge. Blast. Escape didn't seem likely, but he could buy them more time. Time enough to get to where Grigorov couldn't reach them before V did.

What he wouldn't do for a nice London alleyway right now instead of a forest—one with windows and doors and fire escapes, and friends always waiting to come and help him. But having only trees to offer him help, he slid around his current one to the left, away from the footsteps, and darted a glance over his shoulder.

He made a run for the next tree, heard another *crack* from the gun, felt a sting on his arm—a graze, nothing more. No worse than a thousand other scratches he'd gotten over the years, which he reminded himself of as the pain bit. He gained the tree's cover, scouted out the next one.

How many bullets did Grigorov's gun hold? He'd already used, what, five? If it was six, then he had a chance.

If it was more. . . .

The thrashing steps were drawing closer, and he could now hear voices too, calling out in what was clearly German. No doubt investigating the gunshots.

Maybe they'd just take him prisoner. Maybe someday he'd see them again—Evelina and her father. Rosie and Peter, Willa and Lukas. Ellie and Lucy, Retta and Cressida. Georgie, Fergus, Nigel. Jory, with a book in hand. Liv, walking strong and tall. Clover and Patch. Pauly.

He squeezed his eyes shut for a second, dragged in a breath. Charlie and Mum—they had the others now, at least. At least he'd managed to give Charlie that, others to help him with Mum.

A throaty yell came at his tree, and he spun to meet it. A crouch and a dive, the kind he'd learned on the streets, aimed at his opponent's knees. Another bullet went wild as Barclay plowed into Grigorov's legs.

They both crashed to the ground, Slavic curses scorching the air. Barclay had never sought brawls, but a few had found him over the years, and he knew enough to hold his own. He dodged the gun aimed at his head like a club. Jabbed the pointed end of the pick into the closest thing at hand—Grigorov's thigh. While the man howled, Barclay wrenched the gun free of his grip.

The thrashing was all but upon them now, the shouts echoing through the trees.

Barclay levered up to his knees and aimed the gun at Grigorov's head.

It was war, and this man was an enemy—an enemy out to kill those he loved. But still he couldn't do it. It wasn't who he was.

He built families, he didn't tear them apart, and this man was surely somebody's son. Brother. Husband.

He flipped the gun in his hand so he was holding the barrel instead and knocked the bloke upside the head. Grigorov went slack.

Barclay didn't have time to make sure it wasn't a trick. He leapt to his feet and took off at a run, gun still in hand. With a bit of luck, he could be out of sight before the Germans found the form he'd left behind. Maybe they'd assume Grigorov the enemy, not him. Maybe they wouldn't even pursue him. Maybe . . .

"Halt!"

The single syllable, recognizable even in its German pronunciation, wouldn't have stopped him. But before he could have obeyed even had he meant to, another *crack* split the air. And then there was dirt in his mouth, under his hands, in his eyes.

It didn't hurt. It just wept—his spirit, his soul. And he prayed as the boots closed in. Prayed that he'd covered their tracks well enough. Far enough. That he'd bought them enough time to get to V. Prayed that God would either take him quickly or give him the strength to keep from telling the enemy anything to compromise those he loved.

Prayed that Evelina would forgive him for breaking his promise.

THIRTY-THREE

Evelina gripped her elbows and stood perfectly still, her eyes trained on the only possible approach to the rendezvous. There was only one road in, open fields on either side. He couldn't possibly sneak up from another direction. This way, this was the way from which he'd appear.

So why hadn't he?

Mr. V paced by her, his pocket watch resting in his palm as it had been for the last seven minutes. And twenty seconds. Not that she was counting each tick. In the lorry parked behind them, Herman quietly snored. The horses were tied to the back of it, ready to be led to Jacques and Minette.

Papa rubbed a hand down her back. "He'll be here. He'll make it. Barclay is a clever young man."

"Of course he will." She said the words, but they sounded tinny and false. Like a recording piped through an automaton. "He still has two minutes and a half."

He'd make it. Never mind that if he were to do so, he ought to be in view by now on the road. Surely if he were in sight, that would be good enough. Wouldn't it?

"Lina." Papa stepped in front of her, blocking her view. Dipped his head a bit to better meet her gaze. "Is there anything you'd like to tell me? About you and Barclay? A question he'll be asking me soon, perhaps?"

He gave her a soft smile, as if now were a perfectly reasonable time to discuss such things. And as if such things were even possible. She tried to swallow, but her throat was as tight as that corset her mother had made her wear during the last Season. "There's nothing to tell you, Papa. Whatever may have been between us . . . I ended it. After I heard about Basil." She'd already filled her father in on all that had happened at home in his absence.

Her father's smile faded into its opposite. "Why? You two seemed to get on so well. I rather thought . . . and it wasn't just my thought. I heard what he said to you. He loves you."

And blast him, but it made her eyes burn again, and she had to look away. "You know what he is. What he was. He was a thief. Up until recently, before V hired him."

V, pacing past them again, snorted. "Had he not been a thief, my dear—the most excellent sort of one—I never *would* have hired him."

Papa's expression didn't shift a whit, nor did his steady gaze. "And this is why you ended things? Because you discovered this fact?"

"Yes. No. I don't know, exactly. He said you knew, but then . . . I suppose that telegram wasn't really from you. Where you accused him of being a thief, and that was why you couldn't come home."

He breathed a laugh. "No, that would have been Grigorov's frustration with him constantly foiling his plans, I should think. Barclay did indeed tell me from the start what he'd been. And what he was. Should I hold his family's beginnings against a man who would risk his own life to help others?"

She ran a finger over the frayed seam of her borrowed sleeve. "Even if you didn't, the rest of the world would."

"Given how wealthy a woman Basil has left you, I believe you now have the right to thumb your nose at whatever the world may say." He touched a finger to her chin. A silent command to look at him again. "Is that really your objection to him? That you are too far above him in station?"

"No." She shifted so she could see past him, to the empty road. Where *was* he? "It's just . . . I was unfair to him, Papa. It was a reaction to the broken engagement. A need to *feel* something, to prove that I could. But it can't be real. It can't have been *love*."

"No?" He turned to watch the road too, standing close enough that their arms touched. "So if he fails to come round that bend in the next thirty seconds?"

Something made her chest heave—a sob, a gasp, she wasn't sure what to call it. But she had to splay a hand over her chest to try to still it, and words were well beyond her. She could only shake her head at that suggestion.

He would come. He *must* come. He . . .

"Time is up." V didn't just sound serious as he snapped the cover of his pocket watch closed. He sounded grave. As solemn as death. "I'm sorry, Miss Manning. But we cannot wait any longer."

"Just another minute. He's coming, I know he is." He had to be. He'd promised, and Barclay Pearce was nothing if not true to his word. When he promised a child a family, that child would never be lonely again. When he said he would take care of someone, that someone could never doubt the care.

When he said he played for keeps, one might as well turn over her heart.

She shook her head, her breath coming in short, uneven bursts. "Perhaps his watch slowed. He was wearing the wristlet—those aren't as accurate, are they? It could have lost time."

"No. Not Hans's." Papa clasped her by the shoulders, his face as full of death as V's. "I'm sorry, Lina. I shouldn't have pushed you to realize your feelings. Not before we knew."

"We don't *know* anything!" She pulled away, spun to face both of them—those men so ready to abandon him just because he was a few seconds late. "He's coming. He's on his way, I know he is. If we leave him now—"

"If we don't, we could *all* be killed, caught in the crossfire." V reached for her arm. "I'm sorry, Miss Manning, you know I am. You know how highly I regard him. But—"

"*No.*" She wouldn't just stand here and listen to them consign him to death. She certainly wouldn't be pushed into the lorry like some kind of . . . of helpless female whose hand they should pat.

She took a large step back, out of their reach. And then spun on her heel and took off as fast as her leg would allow. Faster. Because pain didn't matter. All that mattered was finding him. They surely wouldn't leave without *both* of them.

She'd made it only halfway to the bend in the road when she heard the roar of the lorry's engine. She didn't slow, but she did look back—not surprised to see V pointing the vehicle toward her rather than away, toward safety.

She pumped her legs faster, despite her gait going so uneven with her limp. There would be no outrunning the lorry, but if she could just make it to that bend, see past it—he would be there, within sight. She *knew* he would, and then V would simply fetch him and her both. And she could chide him for being late. Slap at him for making her worry. Throw her arms around him and—

Another roar of an engine from around the bend ahead of her brought her to a halt in the middle of the road. Chest heaving, she glanced back, to where the grim-faced V drove his lorry toward her. A second lorry came into view from the opposite direction.

It wouldn't be Barclay—he had no business having an automobile. But then, he *was* a thief. Why not borrow transportation if he was running out of time? In the face of life or death, she had a feeling he would deem that perfectly acceptable. And frankly, she agreed.

She ran another few steps toward the unfamiliar vehicle, until it drew close enough that she could see that there were four men within. And when she saw their faces, her feet stumbled to a halt.

Barclay, yes. Barclay slumped against the rear seat with his eyes terrifyingly closed. But one who must be Grigorov too—and two men in German uniforms.

"Barclay!" He must be alive—they wouldn't have him with them if he were dead, would they?

She should wait for V to stop his lorry, to give some instruction. She should, but she couldn't. When the German auto slowed, she made a dash for it, shouting his name with every step, willing him to open his eyes. The lorry halted, helter-skelter in the road, and she managed to tug the handle of the rear door open before arms clamped around her waist and pulled her away.

"Nice and easy, my pretty," her captor said, his voice hot and sticky against her ear. Grigorov. "I had thought to use the thief as a bargaining chip with his superior, but you are even better."

"Let her go." Though his voice was gravelly and he looked pale as the moon, Barclay pushed off the seat, nostrils flaring and eyes wide. "I swear to you, Grigorov, if you so much as pinch her—"

"You will do what, thief? You will be silent, the clockmaker will come with me, and then I will let my compatriots decide whether the rest of you live or die. Make a move from that truck without my leave, and you will be riddled with holes in two seconds."

Guns. The Germans had guns—the fierce-looking kind that one had to hold with two hands. And under their smooth cheeks and neatly trimmed hair, they looked far too eager to pull the triggers.

Evelina went utterly still in Grigorov's hold. *Please, Father, deliver us. Somehow, deliver us, I beg you. So that he can go home to his family—they need him, even if he says they don't. And so that Papa can go home to Mama, and they can have a fresh start. Please, God. Please.*

Barclay's eyes, though hazed with pain, didn't waver from her face. He slid a few inches closer to the door—he halted again when one of those nasty gun's barrels poked at him, but she could see him fully in the doorway now. See the way his finger tapped his thigh.

Her brows knit. Was that some sort of signal?

"Let the girl go, Grigorov." V's lorry must have come to a halt too. His voice, raised to be heard above the dueling clatter of the engines, came from a few feet away, just behind them. "It's her father you want, not her. Release her and we'll negotiate."

Negotiate? That wasn't right. V wouldn't bargain her father away, not after coming all this way to find him. And for that matter, she would have thought it would be her father out in the road, demanding this overdone bully release her.

If it wasn't, then it meant they had a plan.

Barclay widened his eyes. Darted them behind her, then back to her. Tapped his thigh again.

If she were one of his sisters, she'd know what he meant her to do.

Grigorov pulled her back a step—but not evenly. There was something halting in his movement, something awkward. Something she recognized from long familiarity—pain.

He was injured. "There is nothing to negotiate," he said. "We have the guns. Tell the clockmaker to get out now or his daughter dies before his eyes."

She took the opportunity to wince, so that he wouldn't notice her hand moving down to her side. Eyes locked on Barclay's, she positioned her hand as near as she could guess to the part of his leg that Barclay had indicated. He twitched his finger upward just a bit, so she raised her hand another inch.

He nodded but looked beyond her. Taking it all in, she knew. Waiting to give her the signal.

"Well now." V sounded, strangely, amused. "I wouldn't say you have *all* the guns."

One more second, two. Then Barclay said, "Now!" and all chaos broke loose.

She dug her nails into Grigorov's thigh, twisting and turning until his scream filled her ears and his grip loosened. Then she dove away from him, even as Barclay was lunging out of the lorry.

Bullets were flying, though she couldn't have said from where. From *everywhere* it seemed, in quantities that seemed far too high. Shouts blistered the air, in German and Bulgarian and English.

Too many in English. More voices than just V's and Papa's and Herman's, and they continued after the foreign ones stopped.

At some point, Barclay's familiar arms had closed over her, and they stayed there, blocking her view, after the shouts and bullets ceased.

Boots crunched over to them and stopped a foot away. "Sorry I'm late, big brother. Didn't have a watch."

"Georgie." With a laugh that was more relief than amusement to her ears, Barclay eased off her. "I'll give you mine. Though I suppose it's Mr. Manning's, really."

"Give it to him." Papa's voice sounded close and yet far, underscored as it was by those running engines. "Give him *all* my watches! God bless you, young man, and all your chums!"

Evelina peeled herself off the ground, each limb shaking. The Germans were sprawled in their lorry, Grigorov lay unmoving behind her. But a solid dozen Englishmen scurried over the scene, among them the lieutenant who had shown them to the trench the day before.

And Barclay's brother stood there with a grin far too boyish for the circumstances, a hand held out to her. "Give you a hand, luv?"

"Thank you." She slid her quaking fingers into his so he could help her to her feet, then stood there as he did the same for Barclay. Aware of her father talking still, of V, of others she couldn't name. Their voices were just part of the din.

She kept her gaze on the only *him* that mattered, and the

moment his brother had gotten him to his feet, she threw her arms around his neck, nearly toppling him again.

"Easy, luv." They stumbled back a step, his chuckle sweet and deep in her ear. "I told you I'd get here, didn't I?"

"You fool of a man." She tightened her arms, buried her face in his neck. Whispered into his ear, "I love you. Again and always and a thousand times, I love you."

"Lina." His hands were on her neck, his fingers toying with the hair that had slipped loose in the melee. "I think I'm going to need you to say that each of those thousand times."

"And so I shall." She held him as tightly as she possibly could, until he pulled back enough to press his lips to her ear, her cheek and, when she turned her face up, her mouth.

Those feelings surged—the ones she had chased, the ones she had doubted. The ones that were lovely and warm but so much less than this solid something that had taken up residence inside her. Not a feeling at all. A *knowing*. A certainty that no matter what, this would still be.

Love. The thing worth fighting for. Worth dying for. But more—worth living for.

Georgie cleared his throat. "Don't mean to interrupt, but we're still in a tight spot here, Barclay. Better clear you out before the French move in. They're losing ground on the ridge."

"Blast." Barclay pulled away, though he kept an arm around her. "Right. Are you chaps going to reinforce them?"

"Not that we've heard. Just lending a hand to a couple of our own." Georgie clapped a hand to Barclay's arm. "Give my love to everyone at home."

"Of course. And here." Still not moving his arm from Evelina's shoulders, he reached with his other hand to unhook the wristlet. Held it out with a grin. "To improve your timing."

Georgie took it with a laugh and strapped it on, looking impressed. "Well now, this'll be convenient. Won't have to go digging around in our pockets to see the time. Hey, chaps, look at this!"

It didn't seem like much of a farewell for the brothers. And yet, somehow, seemed perfect. Not so much a goodbye as a silent promise to meet again. Evelina slid her arm around Barclay's waist.

They moved a step toward their lorry, but on the next, Barclay hissed out a breath and nearly stumbled. She caught him, looked down, and hissed out a breath of her own. "Your leg! What happened?" The lower half of his trouser leg was a mess of blood and dirt.

He straightened again and stepped more gingerly. "Just a little bullet wound. I'd forgotten about it there for a bit."

He wouldn't again, she'd bet. She'd keep her arm right there around his waist. Shaking her head, she smiled up at him and limped along with him. "We'll be a matching pair."

He gave her that grin—the one that had made her think, the evening they met, that she'd never forget his face. "I'll hold you to that, Miss Manning."

She lifted her chin. "According to my passport, it's Mrs. Pearce. A promise I intend to hold *you* to, sir."

He cocked a brow and reached for the door of V's lorry. "You want to marry a thief? That sounds awfully risky."

"I believe your family has a saying about risks." She climbed in, smiling at Herman, who didn't appear to have budged from his seat.

Barclay climbed in behind her with a chuckle. "You know, we do, at that. And I do believe I've just found the sweetest reward of them all."

EPILOGUE

One Year Later
Westminster, London, England

Barclay handed a penny to Manning, a bit bemused at the request for one. "Are you quite serious?"

His father-in-law slid the coin onto the giant pendulum of the Great Westminster Clock. "It is a precise instrument, Barclay lad. The smallest adjustment is all that's required." He straightened and looked over his shoulder, to the team of workers who all appeared to be finishing up their maintenance of Big Ben's clock. They'd come down from the various iron catwalks and stairs and gathered by the half wall of brick. "Ready, chaps?"

"All finished, sir. Ready to start him back up on your mark."

Manning nodded and pulled back his sleeve so he could see the Rolex on his wrist—a recently arrived birthday gift from Hans, after they'd regaled him last Christmas with their tales of how the soldiers had loved the wristlet they'd left with Georgie. "We've two minutes yet."

Barclay slung his hands into his pockets and craned his head back so he could see the moonglow through the face of the clock. Silver through white, outlined in deepest night. It was a beautiful thing—one he'd never honestly expected to see. "I can't quite believe we're doing it—stealing an hour from Big Ben's clock."

Manning chuckled and turned to take in the view too. "Hardly *stealing*, son, when it's in accordance with the Summer Time Act."

"Semantics. An hour is going missing, and I had a hand in taking it." He grinned, just because he knew it would make his father-in-law smile too.

It didn't take much, these days, to earn a smile from Cecil Manning. Not given the wife who awaited him eagerly at home, the sister-in-law who had learned to occasionally hold her tongue—*occasionally*—and a slew of children he'd given leave to call him Grandpapa. Too much here in London, he had said, to want to leave it all. Bienne could get along without him.

Barclay glanced at his own wristlet. Needlessly, but he couldn't help it. Happy as he had been to lend a hand with the resetting of the clock for the new so-dubbed Daylight Saving Time—all part of the war effort, to cut back on the amount of fuel needed for lights after dark—his stomach was reminding him that he'd skipped lunch again, and Pauly would have a plate ready for him.

Not to mention that Lina and the rest of his family would be gathered round one of the tables. V had said even he and Alice would make it tonight.

Soon enough Manning was counting down the seconds, and the team did whatever magic made the Great Clock run again. But the hammer didn't strike Big Ben. Not anymore. Not until the war was over. The only indication of the new hour was the minute hand moving up to the twelve.

"Rather sad, isn't it?"

Manning nodded and adjusted his cuff back over his watch. "But necessary, if it can help keep London safe."

They stood there a moment more, looking through the clock's face into the dark of the night. The city was cloaked in shadows, but for the moon. With the air defense in place, zeppelins hadn't done much more damage in London itself—but one never knew when the German Luftwaffe would launch some new foray over England's shores, and no one wanted to tempt them nearer.

The Germans had done it first—installed synchronization gears on their planes to allow them to shoot between the propeller blades. Perhaps their engineers had utilized the designs Grigorov had sent, perhaps not. They'd never know that. But he and Manning had reworked the plans and turned them over to their own air force. The skies were equal again, more or less. And clear tonight. Barclay tilted his head back to better center the slant of silver light through the clock. Seeing the moon and stars didn't ignite fear as it had a year ago, it was true. But he didn't think he'd ever forget seeing that hulking silver shadow block out the moon.

"There he is! See, darling, I told you."

Barclay lowered his head again and raised his brows at the new footsteps on the limestone stairs. Two sets, to match the two feminine heads that appeared. "I thought not just anyone was allowed up here, Cecil."

The roll of his wife's eyes wasn't lost in the darkness as her father chuckled. She shifted the little one on her hip and smoothed down a tuft of his hair as Lucy emerged from behind her, Rosie and Peter's little Will in her arms. "Someone was missing his papa," Lina said. "He wouldn't go to bed for anyone else."

So she'd hefted him up the three hundred thirty-four stairs to come and see him? Barclay breathed a laugh. There was never any convincing her to do the easy thing when she'd gotten a notion into her head. "So you decided to take a little stroll, I see."

Patch lunged for him with wild arms. "Dada! Read me story."

Barclay took him with a grin and leaned over to press a kiss to Evelina's cheek. "Not even Clover and Liv could settle him?"

"Well, they couldn't be lured home from Mama's so they are sleeping there tonight."

"Oh, good." Manning pressed a kiss to his daughter's cheek, one to Lucy's, and tousled Patch's hair. "I finished the ballerina toy—I'll be able to show it to them first thing in the morning."

"And it was such a nice night, we decided to take the little ones for a bit of a walk. Though granted, when I agreed I didn't realize we'd be climbing all the way up here." Lucy drew in a long breath and looked up at the face of the clock. "Well, look at that. You finally did it, Barclay—you stole an hour from the Great Clock. It's about time."

"Hush, you." Barclay gave his sister a playful scowl, then stepped closer to his wife as they turned for the stairs. "Feeling any better?"

Even in the moonlight, he could see the flush of her cheeks. She pressed a hand to her stomach as they started down. "For now. Rosemary assures me the sickness will pass soon. But then Willa points out that she's *still* sick, and she's six months along, so I can only hope."

"You all are going to need to purchase an entire neighborhood, if you keep growing at this rate." Her father held out his arms toward Patch. Usually Grandpapa was one of his favorite people in the world, but just now the little one whined something in the negative and buried his head in Barclay's shoulder.

Suited him fine. "Nah, we fit well enough in the houses we have. We like things cozy. Right, Lina?"

"I wouldn't have it any other way." She shot a glance toward a window. A few streets over, Basil's house sat. Or what *had* been his. Had been, so briefly, hers. Was someone else's now—she'd managed to sell it, much to the surprise of Philibert's solicitor. Not exactly at a price it could have commanded before the war, but she'd wanted to be free from it, she'd said. And with the funds, she'd purchased the house across from Peter's in Hammersmith for the family. And put aside the remainder for their work in the poor sections of the city.

Working with their hands the thing that was good.

They walked home with their usual banter. Patch was tucked into bed without so much as a peep, and Lucy settled in downstairs with their nephew and a book—it was her night to stay home with the little ones. Within a few minutes of arriving, he and Evelina were out the door again, on their way to join the others in Poplar.

She didn't so much as flinch anymore when they stepped off the tube platform and into the shadows. But then, every thief and ruffian who was out greeted her by name with a tip of his cap. It always made Barclay suppress a grin. Who'd have thought a Hammersmith girl would be so popular in Poplar?

"I was thinking of names," she said as they set their sights on the glow coming from Pauly's.

Barclay gave an exaggerated groan. And tucked her close to his side. "Not this again. As I told your aunt, we are *not* naming our child Cuthbert. I don't care what great-uncle-twice-removed bore the name."

She laughed, as he'd known she would, and slid her arm around his waist. "I was going to suggest Clarence, if it's a boy. For your father. Though if you don't want to entertain my suggestions . . ."

"That would be . . . perfect."

"You think your mother will like it?"

He sighed and looked toward the street where she may or may not be right now. Depending on if she were in the mood to behave herself, or if she'd snuck back out to Hackney. "Who's to say? But Charlie will."

"I know."

He was there already, at the table in the far corner of the pub, when Barclay led Evelina inside. Charlie and his wife, both smiling and looking right at home with the others. Laughing, joking, passing round a basket of bread. Charlie looked up when they neared, and he smiled anew. At Barclay.

Maybe someday he'd get used to it. Maybe someday it would be old hat, old news, something to be taken for granted. But not yet. A year wasn't nearly enough time to get used to having his brother back in his life, willingly, after so many years apart.

"Oi! Barclay! Saved you a seat." Charlie shoved out a chair in demonstration.

Maybe someday he'd be able to look at this collection of people and not be filled with awe that they were his and he theirs. He sat with a grin. "Think Pauly has any more champagne hiding in the back, or have we celebrated too much in recent years?"

Rosemary lifted her brows from her seat halfway down the table. "What's the occasion?"

"Your brother's official legitimacy, perhaps?" From his place at the opposite end of the table, V grinned. "One more week, Mr. Pearce, and you'll be in the Navy."

According to V, all of Hall's employees would soon be given commissions in the reserves—a defense against the brigade of women out to brand civil servants as cowards—but he had no intention of wearing his uniform whenever he could avoid it.

Hard to blend into a crowd as a naval officer.

He gave an exaggerated shudder. "That is most assuredly *not* what we'll be celebrating. No, Rosie-Posy, we need to toast my ultimate supremacy. Elinor, I've finally done it. I've stolen an hour right from Big Ben's clock."

His little sister laughed, her dimples flashing. "Along with every other clock in England!"

"Because I'm just that good. And I believe that settles it once and for all. I am, without question, the best thief in London. Perhaps in the whole world." Because he wasn't a thief, not anymore. He was perhaps an agent of the Crown. Soon to be a Naval officer. A brother, a father. For the last six months, a husband. Manning and V both called him *son* half the time . . . even if his own mother didn't seem to know the meaning of the word.

But most important, his Father called him *son* too. Heir to something he never could have stolen, even if sometimes it felt like he had. He didn't deserve the grace he'd been offered. But then, no one did.

His family hooted, argued, bantered. And Barclay just sat back with a grin and exchanged a smile with Evelina. *Best* might not be the right word to describe himself, after all.

But he was, without question, the most blessed.

A Note from the Author

I've been looking forward to writing Barclay's story since the SHADOWS OVER ENGLAND series began—and I hope you've enjoyed getting to know the big brother of my family of thieves. As always, I mix fact and fiction in this book, and I wanted to take a moment to clarify which was which.

First of all, I had so much fun giving a small role to Hans Wilsdorf, the founder of Rolex. He was a remarkable man who created a remarkable company, revolutionizing the watchmaking world. Today, wristwatches are the standard—thanks largely to Wilsdorf's determination to make them so. The Rolex I describe in *An Hour Unspent* is based on the models put out by Rolex in that era, and the conversation about slipping the brand onto the faces of one watch in six was indeed the strategy employed, as shared in Wilsdorf's journals. What's more, it was in large part the Great War that aided in the wristwatch's popularity—those few soldiers who had them loved the ease they provided in telling time, which was often very critical for operations. During World War II, many soldiers invested in a Rolex, because they were the most dependable. When Wilsdorf learned that the watches were stripped from Allied prisoners, he swore he would replace any Rolex confiscated by the Nazi army—and did.

Another invention obviously of great importance to the story is the synchronization gear, which allowed pilots to shoot their guns through their propellers. The English had armored their props with deflectors, which put them at the advantage; the German military commissioned Dutch designer Anthony Fokker to copy them. Instead, he created the synchronization gear. There is certainly no evidence that he needed the help of stolen plans from a British clockmaker to achieve this—that was purely my imagination, inspired by how the intricacies of clockmaking could be put to use in weaponry as well as toys.

Zeppelins were a very real part of the war, and though by today's standards they caused little damage, they brought terror upon the people of England and made clear nights something to fear. There were only a few successful zeppelin raids over London, one of which was the night of May 31, 1915. An incendiary bomb was indeed dropped upon the Shoreditch Music Hall—but didn't ignite. Naturally, when I learned of that bit of history, I had to include it!

A quick note on the involvement of a few Swedes in the war—though officially neutral, the Swedish government was in fact sympathetic to the Central Powers, and for the duration of the war, they aided the Germans in getting messages from Germany to their various ambassadors around the world (all of which had to pass through England) by sending them in a convoluted path routed through Sweden. This came to be known in Room 40 as the Swedish Roundabout. They discovered it in 1916 and, rather than shut it down, used it to gather intelligence. Though the Roundabout itself wasn't discovered yet during the time this book is set, I thought it would be fun to hint at it with Barclay lifting some implicating letters, and thereby alerting Hall to those sympathies.

And finally, a bit about the English suffrage movement. Before the war, the cause was quite often violent, as strident supporters lashed out against the public and then went on hunger strikes when they were arrested. But as Barclay points out to Evelina in the story, the war in fact gave the women of England a chance to prove their mettle. They kept the country running while the men were off at war, and proved through their deeds in England's hour of need what their words had never achieved. The vote was granted soon after the end of the war.

I hope you've enjoyed your journey through England alongside my unique family of thieves, and I pray you learned this truth alongside our clockmaker: the most precious thing in this world, and the most often wasted, is the time we ought to be spending with those we love.

Roseanna M. White is a bestselling, Christy Award–nominated author who has long claimed that words are the air she breathes. When not writing fiction, she's homeschooling her two kids, designing book covers, editing, and pretending her house will clean itself. Roseanna is the author of a slew of historical novels that span several continents and thousands of years. Spies and war and mayhem always seem to find their way into her books . . . to offset her real life, which is blessedly ordinary. You can learn more about her and her stories at www.RoseannaMWhite.com.

Sign Up for Roseanna's Newsletter!

Keep up to date with Roseanna's news on book releases and events by signing up for her email list at roseannawhite.com.

More in the SHADOWS OVER ENGLAND Series

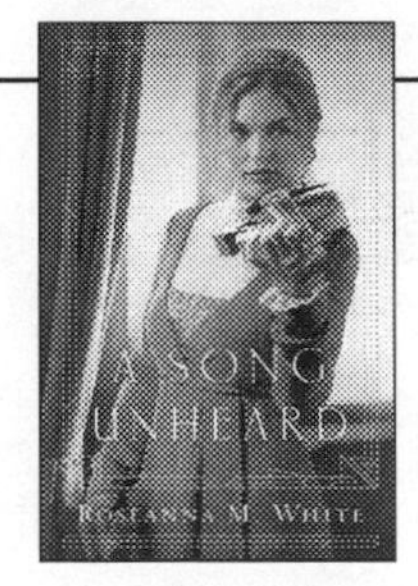

At the outset of WWI, high-end thief Willa Forsythe is hired to steal a cypher from famous violinist Lukas De Wilde. Given the value of his father's work as a cryptologist, Lukas fears for his family and doesn't know who to trust. He likes Willa—and the feeling is mutual. But if Willa doesn't betray him as ordered, her own family will pay the price.

A Song Unheard, SHADOWS OVER ENGLAND #2

You May Also Like . . .

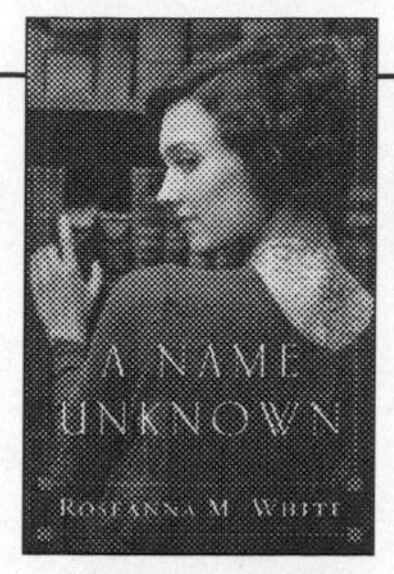

Growing up on the streets of London, Rosemary and her friends have had to steal to survive. But as a rule, they only take from the wealthy, and they've all learned how to blend into high society for jobs. When, on the eve of WWI, a client contracts Rosemary to determine whether a friend of the king is loyal to Britain or to Germany, she's in for the challenge of a lifetime.

A Name Unknown
Shadows Over England #1

When Brook Eden's friend Justin, a future duke, discovers she may be an English heiress, she travels to meet her alleged father. Once she arrives in Yorkshire, Brook undergoes a trial of the heart—and faces the same danger that led to her mother's mysterious death.

The Lost Heiress
Ladies of the Manor

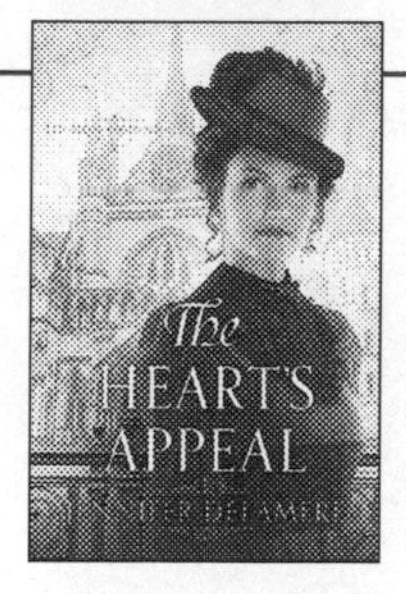

Julia Bernay has come to London to become a doctor—a glorious new opportunity for women during the reign of Victoria. When she witnesses a serious accident, her quick actions save the life of barrister Michael Stephenson. He rose above his family's stigma, but can he rise to the challenge of the fiercely independent woman who has swept into his life?

The Heart's Appeal by Jennifer Delamere
London Beginnings #2
jenniferdelamere.com

You May Also Like . . .

Gentlewoman Rachel Ashford has moved into Ivy Cottage with the two Misses Groves, where she discovers mysteries hidden among her books. Together with her one-time love Sir Timothy, she searches for answers—and is forced to face her true feelings. Meanwhile, her friends Mercy and Jane face their own trials in life and love.

The Ladies of Ivy Cottage by Julie Klassen
TALES FROM IVY HILL #2
julieklassen.com

Forced to run for her life, Kit FitzGilbert finds herself in the very place she swore never to return to—a London ballroom. There she encounters Lord Graham Wharton, who believes Kit holds the key to a mystery he's trying to solve. As much as she wishes that she could tell him everything, she can't reveal the truth without endangering those she loves.

A Defense of Honor by Kristi Ann Hunter
HAVEN MANOR #1
kristiannhunter.com

Stable hand Nolan Price's life is upended when he learns that he is the heir of the Earl of Stainsby. Caught between two worlds, Nolan is soon torn between his love for kitchen maid Hannah Burnham and the expectations and chances that come with his rise in station. He longs to marry Hannah, but will his intentions survive the upstairs-downstairs divide?

A Most Noble Heir by Susan Anne Mason
susanannemason.com